Reviews for Hell on $5 A Day:

"A galloping, worlds-spanning adventure that Dante himself might have enjoyed... The story is a two-fisted odyssey full of bone-crushing blows and skull-spitting hammerlocks. Bulmash lavishly choreographs each explosive obstacle in painstaking detail and unabashed gusto... readers should be forewarned that the author also has a penchant for the grisly and isn't afraid of going for the throat and tearing out a larynx or two."

- *Kirkus Reviews*

I0627846

"The locales of hell, purgatory and heaven are brought to life (afterlife?) with detailed and evocative descriptions, with the Divine Comedy providing helpful signposts along the way. After this debut, I'm looking forward to the next books in this series."

– *Steven R. Nelson (Amazon Customer)*

"I've read 97 books in the last year (don't judge...it's how I stay somewhat sane in this crazy world). This just made the top three."

– *Matt (Amazon Customer)*

"I was a little worried going in when it came to a novel with vampires, but I was happy to see the author skip through the trite cliches and move on to a very original work that was highly entertaining."

– *PJ Hagerty (Amazon Customer)*

"Highly recommended. This isn't your typical vampire story. A must for anyone who enjoys vampire novels."

– *Jane (Amazon Customer)*

Books in The New Heroes of Old™ Series:

(future titles are in italics and subject to change – dates are estimated)

The Alain Beaudreaux Arc
- Hell on $5 A Day
- *Sodom All Over Again (2026)*
- *New York, by Midnight (2027)*

The Danny Levine Arc
- *The Bow of Gilgamesh (2028)*
- *Flutes, Fairies, And FOMO (2029)*
- *A Wild Shiksa Appears (2030)*

The Kevin Twice Arc
- *If The Tower Will Not Come to Kevin (2031)*
- *It's 166 Miles to Chicago (2032)*
- *Those Whom the Gods Would Destroy (2033)*

The Kurt Gray Arc
- *Multiversal Health Care (2034)*
- *The Luckiest Guy Ever (2035)*
- *The Daughter of Fate (2036)*

HELL ON $5 A DAY

By Greg Bulmash

Book One of *The New Heroes of Old*™

Disclaimers

THIS IS A REVISED EDITION

What does that mean? It means that some phrases that didn't read right for the audiobook got smoothed out, a few words got changed for accuracy, chapter titles were added, and some errors were corrected. There are no plot changes or retconning.

PERSONS LIVING OR DEAD

Please remember that this is a work of fantasy and fiction. Any appearance by persons living or dead is simply an accident or for pop-culture reference. They're imaginings, figments of the author's imagination. Do not believe anything they say or do (or is said about them) in this story.

TRIGGER WARNINGS

Characters in this book fight, swear, smoke tobacco, and drink alcohol. There are also vivid depictions of murder, body horror, sex, rape, and torture. With vampires and humans traveling through Hell, there's going to be some weird stuff, especially in the gift shop. While *Kirkus Reviews* liked the book, the term "horrifically ghastly" was used to describe a violent scene.

THIS BOOK MAY UPSET YOU

Heaven, Hell, and Purgatory are locations in this book. Demons, angels, vampires, and even God show up as characters. And they might not be portrayed in ways that match your beliefs.

It wasn't written to challenge your beliefs or lead believers astray. It's *fiction*, make believe, a modern fairy tale. If you fear you might be offended, you're probably right and should put this down now.

Chapter 1: The Blood of a Virtuous Man

Undisclosed Location, Spring of 1942

Every guy in the room was giving their best-practiced cold stare. That was the extent of the hard body language because they were all in hospital gowns that tied in the back. Tough-pose options are limited when you're trying to keep a thin layer of cotton between your bare ass and a steel chair. Even more so when not putting your balls on display matters. But the cold stares were on display, maybe even intensified as compensation.

They were all tall, except Sampson. Alain found that ironic. Sampson was the fidget in the bunch, a street hustler. He'd been running a Three Card Monty game ever since he was tall enough to peer over the box. He was also the only black guy in the group.

Vinnie was Bronx-born. You could hear it in his voice. He sounded like every two-bit street hood Alain had seen in a gangster movie. He was smart too, but you'd never know it unless you caught him at it. Despite posing as a wisecracking tough guy, he was a few IQ points below genius level, based on the chart Alain had "accidentally" seen. Still, that only ranked him third in the group of five.

Coming in a distant fifth was Granger. Granger was a Georgia farm boy. He gave Sampson and Vinnie the hairy eyeball pretty regularly; didn't like being grouped in with non-whites. Alain didn't know all the facts, but from what he'd heard, three cars of local cops had arrived at a barn dance after a disturbance call. They found 20 men lying on the floor and Granger the only one standing, holding a half-full jug of moonshine. He put a couple of cops down too, and he didn't spill a drop until one of them tapped him on the back of the head with a billy club.

The last of the group was Reese, number one on the IQ chart. Alain had no idea where he was from or what his story was. He was the quietest of the bunch and the tallest; not skinny, but wiry. When he spoke, it was slow and measured, not any kind of laconic drawl, but more a kind of precision to make sure you heard every word because he wasn't going to repeat any.

They were all in the Army for one reason. It was wartime and each had come before a judge who gave them a choice between the Army or jail: fight Hitler and Hirohito for freedom and democracy or fight your bunkmate for the last roll of toilet paper. You decide.

Alain got it when he tried to stop a couple of thugs from hassling a black kid. The kid, maybe 12, was coming out of one of the few stores in Alain's Louisiana town that allowed blacks inside. Even if the shopkeeper didn't mind the boy coming in, the two thugs did. He didn't hold any particular love for black folk, didn't hate them either. Most of the time he didn't give them much thought. But two full-grown men picking a fight with a child was just wrong.

By the time the cops were cuffing Alain, the child was gone and the two thugs were both unconscious. No one else saw or was willing to testify to what happened. As for the kid, Alain didn't blame him for not wanting to go to the cops and tell the story. He and his family probably would have been hurt pretty bad if they stood up for Alain.

2

The prosecutor portrayed him as a loner, a quiet, big-boned, bookworm weirdo, who had inexplicably attacked two upstanding citizens without provocation. It took the jury all of 30 minutes to come back with a conviction.

So, there he was, sitting in a surgical gown in an Army medical facility, four hardcases for company, going through a weeklong battery of physical exams and bunking down in an empty infirmary ward.

They'd been told they would find out today why they'd been yanked from their units and brought here to be poked and prodded. But everyone was too tough, too hard to gossip and speculate. They all sat silently, trying their best to look mean in their gowns.

"Gentlemen," a voice said through a speaker in the ceiling, "please proceed through the door to your left."

Being closest to the door, Alain led the group into a darkened room. The room seemed to have no windows and only the one door was visible. When it shut behind them, they were left in pitch black. None of them had been through any physical exertion recently, but Alain could hear a ragged breathing, almost a panting.

The light clicked on. The source of the breathing was a bedraggled man, his skin gray, his hair greasy and clumped, his features gaunt. He had been placed in a cage and he sat cross-legged, his back hunched and his head tilted up just enough to give them a hooded, baleful glare. He had perfected the look all of them had been trying to achieve just moments ago.

His clothing looked like it had been borrowed a long time ago from a movie studio, something off of Ronald Colman in A Tale of Two Cities, or better yet, Leslie Howard in The Scarlet Pimpernel. Velvet coat, lace cuffs, pants that ended at the calf... It might have been fine once, but now it was frayed and threadbare, as if the man had put it on in the 19th century and hadn't taken it off since.

The voice came from the speaker in the ceiling. "Gentlemen, this is a vampire."

The group snickered, muttering jokes and comments of disbelief under their breaths, even Alain. Vampires were Bela Lugosi. *I vant to suck your blood*, he thought.

"He's real," the voice chided.

"So why are you showing him to us?" Vinnie shouted at the speaker.

"We're not," said the voice. "We're showing you to him."

"Huh?"

The lights went out and the sound of metal scraping against metal could be heard, as if the cage were opening. Sampson screamed.

The others started shouting. Alain remained quiet and moved slowly backwards, one hand groping behind him, one out in front of him to ward off any incoming bodies. When he finally reached a wall, he began sliding along it, trying to find the door. He found the door frame, but the inside of the door was smooth, knobless, and the space between it and the frame... maybe if he had a crowbar.

He moved a few feet away from the door, backing himself into a corner. It wasn't the best position, but it was the one that left the smallest part of him exposed and limited any vectors of attack. The shouting and screaming went on all around him. Granger was begging to be let out, Vinnie was shouting challenging obscenities, Reese was shouting for everyone to "shut the Hell up," and Sampson's screaming stopped. Granger's screaming began.

Vinnie's voice became more desperate; the challenging obscenities gave way to rapid repetitions of "holy Christ!" Granger kept screaming and Reese stopped calling for quiet. Vinnie, like Alain, seemed to have picked a single spot, and Alain didn't know where Reese was

4

until Granger's screaming stopped. Alain heard the thud of two bodies colliding and assumed Reese had tackled the vampire. This was quickly backed up by Reese's voice shouting "you goddamn cocksucker!"

Vinnie got back some of his bravado, cheering Reese on. "Get that goddamn vamp, Reese!" There was the sound of feet moving, but it seemed like just one pair, as if Reese was up and dancing around the vampire. Alain could hear the sound of flesh hitting flesh. Alain didn't much like Reese, but he had to give him credit for trying to box a vampire in the dark.

The vampire muttered "I tire of this" and it went quiet except for some feral-sounding grunting and slurping. Vinnie was now mumbling in a whimpering voice, "Hail Mary, full of grace..."

The grunting stopped. Vinnie continued praying and Alain listened with all his might to hear a footstep, a rustle of dilapidated velvet. Then Vinnie's whimpers gave way to a short-lived scream which cut off with a gurgle in his throat. There was more grunting and slurping for a couple of minutes, then it stopped.

Alain pressed back harder against the wall. There was no point in praying. If God was interested in helping him, God wouldn't have put him in this room in the first place. Even after minutes in the darkness, Alain's eyes hadn't adjusted. It was just too black. All he could do was listen. He slowly stretched one arm out in front of him, moving it side to side like a blind man's cane, his other arm pulled back and cocked to let a fist fly if the searching arm made contact with anything.

The searching arm was grabbed from the side, yanked to pull him away from the wall, then twisted up behind his back in a submission hold. Alain could feel the vampire's breath on his neck. "Do you know the best part about being a vampire?" a voice whispered in his ear.

Alain didn't reply. "Not a fucking thing," the vampire said. "The other four were pathetic. But you smell of... character. It's been a long time since I tasted the blood of a virtuous man." The vampire trailed off in reverie, but his voice was quickly back in Alain's ear. "I am sorry for what will happen to you. I truly am."

The teeth sank into Alain's neck, a scream escaped his throat, and consciousness fled.

Chapter 2: Soul Surgery

Regaining consciousness in hard-fought steps, Alain came to realize that he could not move. He didn't open his eyes. He just lay there and breathed. The smell of the air was acrid, like he was downwind from a couple of factories with all smokestacks at full.

Wiggling his fingers, tensing his muscles, he found he wasn't paralyzed. He was restrained, strapped to whatever bed he was in. He opened his eyes by degrees, letting them adjust to the light without necessarily letting anyone who might be in the room know he was awake yet. He listened for the sound of someone else breathing, but there was nothing.

He was in a hospital room, but different than the infirmary rooms he and the hardcases had been in before... before... His head pounded as he tried to recall what had happened. He let go of that and inspected the room as best he could, considering his limitations.

At first glance, the windowless walls seemed to be cream colored, but the unevenness of it made Alain think it might be whitewash that had yellowed in more places than not. Above his bed hung a single bulb without a shade. Its meager glow gave the impression it was waging a valiant struggle to hold on.

There wasn't much else in the room and Alain wasn't sure what there should be. Aside from the infirmary accommodations over the last week, he'd never been in a hospital room and wasn't a big fan of the types of movies that gave you good looks at them. Best he could tell, the room's contents consisted of him, the bed, the light bulb, a sink, and those infernal straps.

What had happened after the lights went out? There was the metallic sound and the... was it a vampire? It ate the others. It apologized. And then...

To his right he heard the door open and the clunks of plodding footsteps approach. A woman's face hovered over his, a suppurating wound where her left eye should have been, a layer of dried pus around the empty socket. The smell was revolting and when a fly landed on the crust to take a walking tour around the socket, Alain nearly vomited. "Shettle down," she barked, her speech slurred, coming from a mouth that was missing half of its teeth and part of a lip. As her hand moved up, he saw a large syringe, the needle rusted and dull. "Jusht shtay shtill," she said, bringing it down toward his throat.

Alain tried to thrash, pinch his leg, avoid the approaching needle while he woke himself from this nightmare. The slow approach of the needle turned into a quick jab, darting down out of his field of vision. It caught him in the neck, just under his jaw, and he could feel the needle sink into his flesh, expelling its contents. He thrashed his head, jerking the needle out of the nurse's hand, and it waved from the point where it lodged in his neck, thrown side to side as he tried to fling it away.

A coldness moved out from his neck, a deep chill hitting each muscle in its path, taking control away from Alain. He raised his hips, throwing the weight of his body against the restraints, his shoulders and head shaking limply, already caught in the grip of the paralysis. The cold worked its way into his stomach and down his legs, each muscle losing its tension and going flaccid as it chilled. Alain couldn't work his jaw to shout for help and eventually his toes gave up the fight, the coldness suffusing his entire body.

The nurse pulled the syringe from his neck, rolling his head to the side, his eyes staring at her midsection. At least from that viewpoint, she looked like a normal nurse - if you could ignore the blood spatters on her apron. "Don't worry," she said, "we'll be done with you shoon and then we'll shend you home."

Done with me?! Send me home now, his mind screamed as a dire sense of claustrophobia settled in. He was trapped in his body, unable to fight, unable to resist. All he could do was lay there and shout silently for release as the nurse walked to the door, opened it, and made a gesture to someone standing outside. She was followed in by two orderlies, pushing a gurney. The orderlies looked normal. There were no open wounds, major sores or rashes, but it was no comfort to Alain.

The fact that they released his restraints was of no comfort to him either. They did it because they didn't need them. He was helpless. No, he protested as they lifted him, limp as a boiled carrot and seeming to weigh as much as one, dumped him on the gurney, and wheeled him into the hallway. Let me go! Let me go! Let me go! He paused for a mental breath and pleaded as loud as he could think. Please!

The gurney was jarred momentarily as he passed through a set of swinging doors. And then it came to a halt. Two pairs of hands grabbed him again, hoisting him from the gurney onto another table, and a bright light was pulled into place over him. "Patient's name," he heard a male voice ask.

"Beaudreaux," the nurse replied. Alain could feel his soul shivering, as if the cold from the shot had not only worked its way through his muscles, but through every part of him. He had never wanted anything worse in his life than to be out of there, to be somewhere safe.

"Yes," the male voice said. "Vampire. Five in a day. Well, let's get cracking. I have to get back to torturing the wife." Two other voices laughed in response.

Alain concentrated all his effort on moving. He had to get up, get out of there. And as he felt the cold metallic touch of a knife against the skin of his upper abdomen, his panic kicked into overdrive. He could almost feel his brain hurt as he desperately tried to get some message from it to his muscles.

The knife bit into his flesh. Starting just at the very bottom of his rib cage, the knife dug deep and Alain felt it all, the intense pain leaving no doubt in his mind that this was absolutely real and there would be no waking up from it. Though he showed no outward sign, he redoubled the struggling within his mind, frantic to stop this.

Sawing through muscle, skin, and whatever else got in its way, the knife cut slowly downward. Alain couldn't scream, couldn't even grit his teeth as he looked up into the light. But through the haze of pain and fear, something screamed for his attention. What the doctor was sawing through had to contain some veins, some arteries. But, oddly enough, though Alain felt the pain, he didn't feel the blood. It should have pooled out onto his skin, run down the sides of his stomach, pooled under his back. But there was no dampness, just pain.

When the incision had been cut to about five inches long, the knife was withdrawn and metallic clamps were attached to the sides of the incision, stretching it open. Prayer was no use, he couldn't scream, he couldn't even cry in frustration. He could just lie there and be hurt.

The light dimmed for a moment and Alain felt a surge of relief. If he couldn't escape, the least his brain could do for him now was make him pass out. Sadly, the surgery continued, the pain continued, and the light came back.

Then it dimmed again. The dimming had come from a blink. His muscles were frozen, but Alain realized he was still breathing, he still unconsciously blinked. That meant some signals were getting through from his brain. Concentrating, he tried to take control of those muscles.

A hand entered the hole in his stomach, going in at an angle up under his ribcage, near the diaphragm. Alain tried to tune out the pain and slow his breathing, exerting all his effort in taking a deep breath. Slowly he inhaled and when his body wanted to exhale, he applied his mind to making the lungs take in more air. His breathing paused and then a small gasp of air was added before his lungs pushed the air out.

His concentration was disrupted by the hand inside him. It had found what it was groping around for. The pain was intense as the hand gripped it and started pulling. It felt like Alain was being turned inside out. He wanted to grit his teeth against the pain, but he couldn't. All he could do was concentrate on taking in another slow, deep breath, trying to blink his eyes while he did. He achieved both.

Yeah, he shouted in his mind. It wasn't much, breathing and blinking when he wanted to, but it was a start.

Whatever the hand had gripped was slowly being pulled out of Alain, being forcibly uncoiled from within him and dragged into the open air. The progress was slow, a man's voice grunting slightly. Whatever it was inside him that they were trying to remove didn't want to come out.

Breathing deeply again, Alain could feel his muscles warming. Tentatively, he tried to move a finger. The finger jerked, then slowly curled up under his palm. He brought up two at once next, then made a fist, rotating it ever so slightly at the wrist.

The doctor lost his grip on whatever he'd been pulling and a length of it shot back inside Alain, making a shlorp noise. "Son of a bitch," the doctor cursed, catching it with a grunt.

Now that Alain had gained some control of his body, the pain was more intense, but he wasn't frightened and he was breathing deeply. That made all the difference, the cold in his muscles dissipating. He gradually gained control, concentrating on each major muscle, gently clenching and unclenching it a couple times before moving onto the next. He left his mouth open, resisting the impulse to grit his teeth.

With a final grunt, the doctor yanked on whatever they had been pulling out of him. "Cut it," he said.

The strand was snipped near the incision and the remainder of it retracted into Alain's body like a rubber band that had been snapped. With all the energy and control Alain could muster, he brought his legs back quickly and kicked out against the operating table, sending himself sliding off backwards.

He didn't have as much control as he thought and an attempt to swing himself so he could land on his feet ended up with him rolling off and falling onto the floor with a body-quaking thud, but Alain was back on his feet quickly.

The operating room was staffed by a doctor, the nurse, and one of the two orderlies. On a gurney at the foot of the table lay what they'd taken out of him: a pink mass, almost like intestines, but it was melting and flowing, not off the gurney, but upward and outward, squirming and undulating as it began to take on a shape.

"What the hell is that?" Alain shouted.

The nurse went running out of the operating room as the orderly started advancing on Alain. The doctor, on the other hand, stood by the undulating pinkness. He had that sort of unflappable self-confidence, most often displayed by politicians and other fools who think that they are too important for someone to take a swing at them. "It's your soul, of course," the doctor said. "Or at least part of it."

As they circled, Alain saw two things: First, the pink mass was stretching and flowing into a vaguely humanoid shape, though it was still very blurry and child-size. Second, he was approaching the instrument tray.

"SOP," the doctor blathered on, oblivious to the explosive nature of the developing situation. "You think you'd get all that power without a little collateral?"

Closer to him than to the orderly lay a bone-handled knife he assumed had been used as a scalpel. Alain decided there was no time like the present to see how coordinated he could be. He leapt forward, grabbed it, and leapt back, holding it in front of him defensively. "Get back," he said to the orderly, taking up a fighting stance, holding the knife ready to strike.

The orderly stopped, but didn't back away. He looked at Alain, then at the knife, and chuckled. Meanwhile, the mass on the gurney was getting more distinct. Rather than sprout arms, the pink material flowed off of what could be a torso, defining the arms, slowly splitting them away. As they separated from the mass, they curled up over its chest and it rolled up into a fetal position, issuing a high-pitched moan from its forming mouth.

Noticing Alain's distraction, the orderly moved closer. "Get BACK", Alain yelled, taking a swipe at the orderly. But rather than jump back, the orderly stepped into the blade's arc, letting it draw a path across his stomach, tearing through his shirt and cutting a shallow wound in the flesh. He stopped and cringed, obviously feeling it, but he didn't bleed. Alain stepped back, panicked by what he'd just seen.

To Alain's right, another orderly burst into the room and approached from the other side. Amidst all this, the doctor hadn't left his spot, watching the proceedings with a detached amusement.

"If you two can hold him..." the doctor trailed off as he prepared a syringe. The two orderlies continued their advance.

Better than being caught between two of them, Alain knew he had to rush one. He chose the one to the right, between him and the door. Stutter-stepping forward, he stopped, pivoted on his right foot, and moved forward at a forty-five-degree angle to the path leading directly toward the orderly, avoiding the orderly's grab for him. Raising his arm as he twirled, he put his weight behind the knife, slashing it across the orderly's throat, and came out of the twirl heading backward into the swinging doors. Dropping the knife, he grabbed the cart with the pink, moaning mass on it and dragged it with him as he burst through the doors into the hallway.

His hold on the cart kept him from falling over as he backpedaled through the doors, but the cost of that came quickly, the cart adding its weight to his as he slammed into the wall on the other side of the hall. Alain pushed off quickly and charged off to his right, the cart careening ahead of him.

As he ran down the hall, searching for an exit, he realized what kind of sight he must be. A naked man, running through a hospital, pushing a cart with what was now looking to be a moaning, naked boy on it. He knew if he didn't get out of there quickly, he could expect police at every exit, and if he didn't get some clothes, he couldn't expect to get very far even if he did get out.

Turning a corner, he slammed open the door of the first room he saw. It was empty. He turned and ran further down the hall. He would have expected to be challenged by this point, at least seen some other nurse or patients in the halls. Reaching another room, he threw the door open, but the room was empty. It seemed almost as if he was the only patient on the floor.

At the end of the hall, he found a stairwell entrance, but there was no way the cart was going down the stairs.

He looked at the figure on it. The pulsing and undulating had finished and a small boy lay there, maybe five or six years old given the size of him. He remained curled in the fetal position and was the reddish pink color of a newborn, but the moaning had subsided into a mild whimper. A closer look at the boy's face made Alain's legs go wobbly.

It was the face he saw every time his mother took out the photo album. It was the face in all the pictures his dad had taken with the Kodak Brownie when Alain was a boy. Now it was on this thing on the table, and somehow Alain had given birth to it... by cesarian section.

The thought of cesarian section made his legs go even more wobbly. They'd just cut a big hole under his ribcage, reached in, and tore something out of him, yet here he was on a dead run through the hallway with a cart careening ahead of him. He felt his abdomen, expecting to find a big bloody wound, but it was smooth and dry, no sign he'd ever been opened up.

His head felt like a rocket about to blast off from his body, and without its support, he was going to topple. He shook it hard and slapped himself twice to bring the world back into focus. He was losing sight of his goal... get the Hell out of this place.

Alain looked at the stairwell and then at the child. Whatever it was, whoever it was, he couldn't leave it. He picked it up and the child wrapped its arms around his neck. Its legs around his torso.

Alain tore down the stairs, taking flights at a canter, one hand on the safety rail, one holding the boy. As he progressed downward, the numbers beside the doors counted down... 7, 6, 5, 4, 3, 2... and Alain stopped.

The first floor and presumably the exit were just one floor down, but the problem of clothes hadn't been forgotten. He listened at the 2nd floor door, then opened it a crack and peeked out, getting views up and down the hallway. It was empty. Slowly, Alain crept out.

Three steps out the door, before he could even take in his surroundings, he was hit from the left by a flying tackle. He went down and the boy bounced out of his arms, skidding across the floor while Alain struggled with his attacker. But the struggle was in vain. A second orderly joined in, and within moments, Alain was laying on his stomach, a knee on his back, feet on both hands.

Straining to look to the far periphery of his vision, he could see the boy on the floor. Alain would have expected the boy to curl back up into a ball and begin moaning again, but the boy scrambled to his feet and launched himself at the men pressing Alain to the floor.

Another orderly grabbed the boy and pulled him off, the boy snarling and screaming unintelligibly. As the orderly carried the boy away, he reached out. "Alain," he screamed with the fear and rage of a child being torn from a parent. "Alain!!"

Boy and orderly passed through a set of swinging doors which muffled the sound of the boy when they closed. The screams grew distant until Alain could not hear them at all.

All Alain could hear now was the cursing of the orderlies, the quiet hum of some nearby machinery, and the clop of a pair of sensible shoes approaching from directly ahead of him. The shoes moved around to his side and stopped by his head. "This ought to take care of things," a female voice said.

He felt the pain of a dull needle in the side of his neck and everything went dark.

Chapter 3: The First Raid

Alain tugged the pull-tab of the zipper, opening the extra-large duffel bag, and got out carefully, mindful he was 30 feet up and in a makeshift treehouse barely broader than he was. Classic vampires slept in coffins, but vampires in the modern army slept in duffel bags with double sided zippers. The thick green cloth of the outer bag was tough and durable, blocking out most sunlight. A thick interior lining of dark folded silk contributed a second layer of solar protection with the added benefit of being less like sandpaper than the interior of your average duffel.

Alain and his unit often hid themselves in branches of trees as they slept during the days, camouflaged from the ground by the dark foliage and their dark duffels. Alain could hear a symphony of zippers as his squad-mates awoke.

They had no official unit designation. Officially, they didn't exist. Officially, they were dead. Officially, Uncle Sam had regretted to inform their families and they'd all been given military funerals with honors.

Having their families told they were dead had rankled all of them but Reese. It turned out his "Army or prison" moment had come after he broke both his father's arms. He claimed it was self-defense, but the prosecution brought a doctor to the stand who testified that the nature of the breaks were consistent with taking a baseball bat to someone's arms... repeatedly.

The four of them disengaged their duffels and dropped to the ground, quickly folding them and stowing them on their packs. Alain took their bearings with a sextant and compass while Sampson broke out four bottles of blood.

Vinnie sipped at his gingerly. "If I gotta drink deer blood one more night, I'm gonna eat a civilian," he complained.

They'd all been fed bottled blood, "borrowed" from a Red Cross blood drive, and that was the best the Army was willing to do for them. The DI for their vampire training spelled it out: "You can eat all the nip, kraut, and wop soldiers you want once you complete your training and get shipped out. But you will NOT feed on Americans, and you will NOT feed on civilians."

Granger fed on Americans the night he rose, 2 soldiers to be precise, and was officially "decommissioned." He was staked, beheaded, wrapped in silver wire, and then cremated. They all had to watch... every step. When you wake up to find out you're a vampire, then watch a practical demonstration of how the Army can still kill you, if need be, that kind of thing stays with you.

Now they were in the Ardennes forest, near where it covered part of France's border with Germany, heading toward a remote base. They were about 15 miles away and it was late summer, giving them around 10 hours of usable night. If they double-timed it, they could hit the base and be safely away before dawn.

It wasn't that they had to be holed up at sunrise. That was a recent misconception, a lesser-known myth from German folklore that got a big shot in the arm from a German named F.W. Murnau. His film *Nosferatu, a Symphony of Horror,* showed the demon-like vampire fearing the sun and it entered popular culture as a characteristic of vampires.

Alain and the rest of his unit knew that it wasn't. Sunlight didn't kill them, though it rendered them near powerless. They could not heal wounds as easily, their heightened senses dimmed to human levels, the sunlight caused mild discomfort in their eyes and on any exposed skin, and they got no benefit from drinking blood during the day. Daytime drinking neither satiated their hunger nor gave them the euphoric sense of power and well-being that nighttime drinking provided. Sleeping during the day merely allowed them to awake at the height of their powers, refreshed and ready to go. It wasn't a necessity, just a convenience.

If an operation ran into daytime, their packs would get heavy. Getting up into the trees and "duffeling up" would become difficult, if not impossible. If they encountered enemy soldiers, they'd have little or no advantage in speed or strength. And while they still couldn't be killed with bullets, they could be knocked out of commission, leaving them more vulnerable to a true killing blow.

* * * *

As a vampire, he didn't need a magnifying scope, which suited Vinnie just fine. The Army's version of a sniper rifle, a refitted Springfield M1903, was crap. The sights fogged up regularly and they blocked the magazine, so you had to load one cartridge at a time. The plain old Springfield with iron sights did the job as he tracked Reese, Sampson, and Beaudreaux, watching them prepare the base for attack.

The base backed up against the hill to cut off attacks from that direction. That didn't mean the Germans ignored the hillside, but they gave it less attention than the other camp borders, figuring the bare hillside was too exposed and no one could abseil down fast enough to avoid the periodic searchlight sweeps. No one expected that assailants coming from that direction would drop like stones.

Two large tanks of processed fuel sat near the back fence, which abutted the hillside. These and the motor pool were the primary targets. Alain and Sampson each stood in the shadow of a different tank, holding large rods of metal that resembled railroad spikes. Reese had slipped into the barracks where the day crew slept. The signal to begin was when the screaming started.

At the first scream, Alain and Sampson drove their spikes into the fuel tanks, like stakes into the hearts of giant metal beasts, and ripped holes in the sides, sending fuel pouring onto the ground. Each dropped his spike and ran for a guard tower on the opposite end of the compound, scaling them in three leaps and taking out the lights. On that signal, with Alain and Sampson safely away, Vinnie fired.

His rifle was loaded with phosphorous incendiary rounds, similar to the ones used in fighter planes. They couldn't puncture the tanks, particularly not from a distance. But at that distance, even from a high angle, he could easily light the fuel coming out of the tanks, and that flame would ride the streams back up into the tanks... The blooms of flame that rose up along the hillside made Vinnie skitter back from the heat and blink purple spots from his vision.

There was no leaping down the hill now. Vinnie slung his rifle and ran down the back side, careening through the woods. Reese had started a panic, but now that Alain and Sampson had accomplished their primary objectives, eliminating the guards and the fuel, one would help him herd the nervous personnel and soldiers into the base mess while the other tore off pieces of the vehicles and used them to bust up the rest. If Vinnie took too long to get there, he'd have last pick.

Their instructions were clear. Leave no one alive or able to come back from the dead. They would each pick a victim, feed quickly, behead the bodies, then burn the mess hall to the ground. Anyone they didn't have the time or hunger to feed on got a bullet. The tactic was tried and true. It worked for them.

As Vinnie leapt the 12-foot gate, the only sound came from the roaring fires. He headed straight for the mess where he found the selection process in progress. Sampson was walking around the twelve prisoners who were still alive, sniffing the air as he passed, while Reese seethed. Vinnie wasn't too happy about it either.

Alain had been promoted to sergeant before they left the States, giving him command of the unit. That meant he decided who got first pick of prisoners. As sergeant, he could have taken it for himself, but he always went last, and he tried to be even-handed with the three of them, making them take turns at going first. Fair as it was, Vinnie and Reese still had issues when Sampson got to go first. They both believed that honor should be for whites only.

It generally didn't matter who went first, though. They all had different tastes in victims. Sampson liked his Germans fat. He said the fat ones ate lots of sausage and it made their blood thicker. He'd sniff around to find the plumpest one who smelled most of pork.

Reese liked older ones who drank. Vinnie made a lot of jokes, but not about this. Reese had a hair-trigger temper and it had only taken a couple of beatdowns after a needling joke to convince Vinnie this topic was off limits.

Alain would let them pick one for him. It wasn't that he was too hoity toity to pick his own, he just couldn't. In the beginning, he'd stare at one, then another, precious time slipping away, until one of his unit would just grab one and throw it at Alain. And while the others would feed with vigor, enjoying the pleas and screams of their victims, Alain would usually knock his unconscious with a blow to the headfirst.

Reese had picked his, meaning Vinnie went third and had the responsibility of picking Alain's. Vinnie preferred females, when possible, pretty-boys in a pinch. For Alain, he picked the oldest, scrawniest soldier he could find.

As Vinnie walked back with his picks, Sampson opened fire on the remaining prisoners with a German machine gun he'd picked up outside. Once he was assured all of them were either dead or dying, he gave a nod.

Reese flung Sampson's prisoner at him, then grabbed his own. Screams filled the air as Reese, Vinnie, and Sampson bit down on their prisoner's necks. Alain's prisoner shouted at the sight before he was turned to face Alain. "Entschúldigung," Alain said before he clouted the guy on the head, knocking the soldier out before he fed.

Chapter 4: Vampire Lessons

Back when they'd first been turned, after the "incident" with Granger, they'd been taken to a classroom within the infirmary facility where an Army scientist conducted an orientation. They sipped blood out of bottles through straws that first time. Alain had to balance two strong and conflicting urges as the scientist spoke. The first was the urge to keep his cool and not flip his lid in front of Reese, Sampson, and Vinnie. The other was the urge to start screaming and never stop. But he sat there, sipped at his bottle, and tried to pretend everything was normal as he reflected on the calming effect of peer pressure.

Maybe it was the shock of seeing Granger "decommissioned," maybe it was the news that they were now undead fiends, but the cold stares were gone. Reese was trying to maintain it, but it was like watching a sleepy kid nodding off in class. If he didn't know anyone was looking at him, the anger would gradually fade as Reese's expression turned to worry, then return with a twitch as Reese seemed to remember he was trying to look tough.

Alain was physically the biggest in the group now that Granger was gone. An inch shorter than Reese's six-foot-two, he outmassed

Reese's wiry frame by at least 20 pounds or more, with a physique resembling a young Jack Dempsey. He came by it honestly from hard work at the docks and then practicing Savate with his dad. Savate was a form of French kickboxing and sparring with Alain was his father's way of staying fit and limber. Alain had liked it because, well, how many teenage boys got to kick their father in the head? And get complimented for it?

After a 30-minute lecture on their new status and new powers, the scientist opened the floor up to questions. All four hands shot up. "Beaudreaux," the scientist said, pointing his pencil at Alain.

"Who was that child they cut out of me?"

The scientist's eyebrows rose. "You saw that?"

Alain nodded. "I'd like to interview you later, Beaudreaux," the scientist said, nodding at an associate at the back of the room to ensure a note was made of it. "Best we can tell is that the child was your innocence. It's a part of your soul and it's kept in Hell to anchor you there."

Now Alain's eyebrows rose. "So that was real and I was in Hell?"

"Your soul was. Next question... Rinaldi."

"How often do we have to drink blood," Vinnie asked.

"Every three to four days."

"What happens if we don't?"

"We'll have a practical demonstration of that soon."

* * * *

Over the next few days, they learned more about their relationship with blood. Human blood was not only best, but vital. Drinking animal blood or eating meat could stave off the need for it for two or three days at most. Pork was best. The Army scientists suspected it was because pigs were omnivores. There was something about their blood that made it more like human blood than the blood of a carnivore or herbivore. After omnivore blood, herbivore blood was best. And you could find pigs and cows all over the world.

Still, animal blood was, to the best of the Army's knowledge, merely a stopgap measure.

Alain wondered how the Army had any knowledge. Were there other Army vampires before his group? If so, what happened to them? Who was that vampire that turned them and what happened to him? When he asked, he'd get the same response. They'd pass that up through channels and get him an answer as soon as they could.

For the practical demonstration of how long they could go without blood, the four vampires were placed in a locked ward, reinforced to keep them from escaping. The first couple of nights, they felt fine. It was boring. They played cards, listened to the radio, read books and magazines, and got on each other's nerves. On the third night they were mildly nauseated and lethargic. The fourth night, the ache started.

It began in the upper arms and the chest, the kind of muscle ache you might have with a mild flu. It got into your joints too. Their shoulders and elbows hurt, the ache gradually moving into their hands. But it hurt as much to lay still as it did to move. The ache was there, regardless.

Added to that was the craving. It wasn't a mere hunger like an empty stomach triggers. It was in their heads, their chests, their arms, their legs. It was like every part of their bodies had been hollowed out and they could feel the emptiness yearning to be filled. From elbow to wrist and shoulder to elbow, the aching joints felt as if they capped the emptiness on both ends like water-tight doors on a submarine.

Alain got the idea to submerge himself in a bath. They had previously inspected the ward they were in, mainly out of boredom, and found there was a therapy room with a large, round, sunken pool, heated by a pump so it could stay hot for hours. He snuck away and turned it on at its top setting, then stretched, moved, and rubbed his joints, trying to ward away the pain while he waited for it to heat. When the temperature gauge redlined at 105 degrees Fahrenheit (on its way to a maximum of 115), he stepped in and sat down on the ridge that ringed the pool, slouching down in his seat to submerge himself to his chin.

Alain's sighs brought the others running. There was room for them all in the tub and they all stripped off, nearly jumping in. "It pains me to say this," Reese sighed among a chorus of sighs, "but you're a goddamn genius, Beaudreaux."

"And it pains me to thank you, Reese," Alain said.

"Hey," Vinnie piped up. "One of you touched me with your toe. Don't none of you faggots get any ideas. Next toe that touches me, I'm gonna break off and eat." Almost as one, Alain, Reese, and Sampson stretched out their legs and touched Vinnie with their toes.

Later in the evening, Vinnie briefly had the idea of breaking up the furniture and burning it under the heating unit to get the water even hotter. He dropped it when Alain reminded him they had no matches, all the furniture was metal so they couldn't stake each other, and even if Vinnie could do it, that meant he'd have to get out of the tub.

The fifth night the ache had spread. It was in their knees and backs, in the heels and balls of their feet. When their clothes rubbed their skin, it set off a cascade of pins and needles. It was like having your whole body fall asleep. And their stomachs ached like they were having their innocence ripped out all over again.

The vampires alternated between soaking in the tub and moaning, clawing at the door and demonstrating their creativity at cursing, and getting in shoving matches with each other when one complained about the other's moaning or cursing. After sunrise, the pain dissipated and they slept again.

On the sixth night, they felt better when they rose. Strong, pain free, it was like the last couple of days never happened. Then Vinnie had to say something and ruin it. "Those guys were full of shit," he said, doing some toe touches, his back to the wall. On the next toe touch, he froze and toppled forward in an almost slapstick somersault, ending up laid out flat on his back, twitching and blinking, a pained squeak escaping his mouth.

Sampson pointed and laughed just before following his finger forward to lay on his stomach, his laughing grin now a rictus with drool running out, twitching, blinking and squeaking just like Vinnie.

Reese and Alain both rushed for their beds. Reese pitched forward, his chin hitting the bedframe with a clunk before he fell down on his back next to the foot of the bed. Alain leapt for his bed, twisting in the air, hoping to land on his back and at least freeze like that. He froze just before he landed, too consumed with a fiery pain to care that he'd overestimated, bounced off the bed, hit the floor and rolled under the next bed in the row.

The ache was but a pleasant memory in comparison to the cramps they were suffering. They couldn't curl up, couldn't moan, couldn't muster the control to drag themselves to the tubs. They just lay where they fell, barely able to move, twitching and squeaking. If the catatonia broke, it was merely so a wave of convulsive cramps could wash over them. If they got a break between the catatonic cramps and the convulsive cramps, every muscle would feel so fatigued they were sure they couldn't move it. Each one of them thought they were going to die and they were all hoping that death would get there fast.

A half hour later, blood came through a slot in the bottom of the door in four tin cups on a tray. The tin cups had been warmed enough that the scent of blood bloomed up from them and filled the infirmary room. The smell alone relieved the cramps and fatigue enough to let them roll onto their stomachs and crawl toward it. Each took a cup and curled around it, taking their first sip of warm blood.

Everyone's reached the point where they had to pee so bad, they thought they would wet their pants if they didn't reach a bathroom in five minutes. Fifteen minutes later, with a few escaped drops wetting their underwear, they finally got to a toilet, and the feeling of relief was one of the best things they had ever felt in the history of feeling things.

Add to that a hot shower, your first cup of coffee in the morning following a rough night, and the first gasp of breath right after an uncontrollable belly laugh. That was how the blood felt. They didn't have to wait for it to course down into their stomachs and then be distributed out through their veins. The first touch on their tongues was all they needed for their muscles to relax, their joints to unstiffen, their empty voids to begin filling. And as they drank, it just got better.

They weren't so much blood suckers as blood junkies, and that bothered Alain... a lot.

Chapter 5: Ambush at Dusk

It took a few months of nighttime raids before the Germans figured out what they were dealing with and began active countermeasures: a squad of soldier-priests led by a German vampire who helped them track the Americans.

Sampson was out hunting four-legged food for the squad and had picked off a wild boar. They were plentiful, they were pigs, and the unit didn't have to hurt some farmer's livelihood by stealing a domesticated pig. It was a younger one, maybe 100 pounds, and he'd hung it by its feet from a tree, bleeding it into a rubber collector sheet that funneled the liquid into a canteen.

The German vampire came from downwind, trying to catch Sampson by surprise, but he wasn't quite as stealthy as he thought. As the German lunged for him, Sampson moved out of the way and the German got a face full of boar, twisted, clipped the tree with his shoulder, then bounced off into a barrel-roll before regaining his feet.

The German was probably Alain's size, maybe a tad smaller. He definitely outclassed Sampson in weight and reach. Sampson tried to fake him out, and get around him, but the German was both fast and nimble, cutting him off at every attempt, but never actually trying to engage him. Sampson heard the approaching soldier-priests and realized the German vampire was trying to distract him and hold him while they snuck up. Why fight when his approaching buddies could do it for him?

Since going forward or backward wasn't an option, Sampson went up, scaling the trunk of the closest tree. The German climbed up after him. When Sampson was 20 or so feet up, he waited for the German's hand to get within inches of his boot, then leapt. If Sampson couldn't get through or around, he'd go over. By the time the German realized what was happening, Sampson already had a lead, but Sampson kept it narrow. If the German wanted to introduce Sampson to his friends, Sampson had a few friends to introduce too.

Once he got within earshot of where the unit had been breaking camp, Sampson stopped and made a stand, waiting for the vampire to get closer. The German vampire approached slowly, sniffing the air and listening intently. "Come on, you German vampire," Sampson shouted, emphasizing the last two words. "How many buddies you got out in the woods?" The vampire merely answered by emitting a high-pitched screech, presumably intended to help his squad-mates locate him.

Back at the camp, Vinnie and Reese quickly secured their gear, tying their duffels onto their packs, getting ready to move out. "Stow that gear," Alain whispered.

"Are you nuts," Vinnie asked.

"That's an order, Rinaldi," Alain barked in a harsh whisper. "Reese, get around their flank and find out what's approaching."

Reese continued securing his pack. Vinnie, seeing him, did the same.

"What the Hell are you doing, Reese," Alain growled.

Reese looked him in the eye, speaking calmly and quietly. "Deserting."

It took all of Alain's self-control not to stand up and yell at Reese. "We've got a man out there, putting his life on the line for us."

"So, let's hump it and make sure his sacrifice isn't in vain," Reese replied, smiling a sardonic grin.

Alain lost his cool. "We are not leaving a man behind!"

Reese put a finger to his lips and shushed Alain. "If you think I'm risking my neck for that n***er," he said quietly, "you can go fuck yourself." He said it almost cheerfully and smiled at Alain afterward.

Reese stood up, shouldered his pack, gave a flippant salute, and ran off. Vinnie looked after him, looked at Alain, shrugged, and took off after Reese. Alain was tempted to follow just so he could beat the ever lovin' stuffin' out of them, but that would have to wait. He wasn't going to leave Sampson hanging.

The German anti-vampire unit may have been trained in fighting vampires, but they weren't trained in stealth. They crunched around in the woods like priests in boots. The fact that they actually were priests in boots wasn't an excuse. Sending ill-trained men like this on a vampire hunt was like sending a marching band after a murderer. The only difference was the priests had the right weapons for the job, unlike the poor shnook in the marching band who'd have to bludgeon the murderer to death with a tuba.

Alain circled around behind them and scouted the party, counting five soldier-priests coming up behind the German vampire. The German wouldn't risk engaging Sampson one-on-one, and Sampson seemed to think that was a very good idea. The two of them stood there, waiting as the German's unit came up from behind him and Alain came up behind them.

The Germans had spread out to cast a wide net behind their pet vampire. Alain planned to take them out one at a time, sneaking up, covering their mouths, and snapping their necks. But there was a complication. Each priest wore a hooded chain mail shirt made of silver.

Alain changed his plan on the fly, speeding up as he approached, throwing an elbow at the German priest's head as hard as he could. Between his vampire strength and vampire speed, the elbow hit like a war hammer, crushing the back of the priest's skull and driving bone fragments into his brain. The priest dropped like a marionette with the strings cut. *Sleeves one, silver zero*, Alain thought to himself.

Alain took out the other four priests in a similar manner, then circled back around so he could come up behind Sampson. When he entered the German vampire's sightline, Sampson and the German were leaning against trees, about 30 feet apart, each smoking a cigarette while the German vampire hummed a bouncy polka tune.

"Your friends are dead," Alain said, walking up confidently beside Sampson, which was more difficult than it looked. The disadvantage of stronger senses was that you could smell cigarette smoke more intensely from farther distances. Standing next to Sampson was like standing in a room full of smokers with the windows closed. Alain didn't need to cough, but the urge to wrinkle his nose and blink his eyes was hard to resist.

The German vampire looked to be barely older than 19 or 20, the sort of fresh-scrubbed blond Teuton that Hitler favored as his master race. If it hadn't been for the black uniform of a junior officer in the SS and that German sneer, the kid could have played Flash Gordon's younger brother. Slowly straightening up, the German casually stubbed out his cigarette on the tree behind him and dropped the butt in a tobacco pouch, demonstrating that he believed he was going to be around later to smoke it.

Placing the pouch back in his coat, he smiled and waved at Alain before emitting another of his high-pitched screeches. The screech covered the twang of a crossbow firing and a split-second later Sampson was falling to the ground with a thick wooden bolt piercing his heart.

Alain guessed where the bolt had been fired from and scanned the trees as he crouched down and picked up a pebble. About 30 feet behind the German vamp and 20 feet over, he saw a soldier-priest he must have missed, most of his body blocked by a fallen tree, sighting down a crossbow at Alain.

Alain shook his head. The vamp must have started smoking first, luring Sampson into lighting up. The smell of the smoke would have covered the scent of the approaching soldiers while the vampire's humming would have covered the sound of the sniper creeping up and getting in position. The soldiers farther back in the forest were merely the sweepers. The sniper followed more closely, getting in place first and waiting for Sampson's back-up to show so he could get multiple kills.

Alain threw the pebble as hard as he could, sidearm, catching the soldier priest between the eyebrows, just under the ridge of his silver hood. The pebble bored through the man's skull like a bullet and he slumped, a finger twitch sending the bolt with Alain's name on it firing harmlessly into the ground 10 feet away.

The German vampire's nonchalance vanished. He looked frightened for a moment, but replaced it quickly with anger. Alain ran toward him, goading him to come forward. The German took the bait, rushing toward Alain. Just as they were about to collide, Alain swerved so they ran past one another.

Alain ran to where the crossbow bolt pierced the ground and grabbed it, turning and running back toward the German, who had recovered from the near miss and was heading toward Alain at breakneck speed. The two of them slammed together so hard Alain's eyeballs rattled, but he wrapped his left arm around the German's midsection to keep them from bouncing apart.

When they hit, Alain had the bolt in his right hand, his fist at the base, the bolt pointing upward, and his fist held low near his belt. Perhaps the German had been expecting an overhand strike or thought that overhand was the only way a fatal blow could be delivered. Whichever it was, he didn't defend against Alain's right hand, opting instead to try to wrap Alain up and throw him to the ground, expecting to wrestle. But Alain took advantage of the embrace to jam the tip of the bolt through the German's upper abdomen, in under the rib cage, and speared his heart from beneath.

The German's embrace went slack and Alain let him drop to the ground.

He thought momentarily about burying Sampson, but didn't see the point. It would serve no religious purpose and even bugs had better sense than to nibble at a vampire carcass. When the sun came up, Sampson and the German would start dissolving. In a few days there'd be nothing left of them but their clothes.

Alain ran back to the campsite, secured his pack, and took off in the direction Vinnie and Reese had gone.

Chapter 6: The Burning Barn

Alain found the lamb bleating next to its dead mother. A casual inspection would have looked like a wolf got to it, but he could smell Vinnie and Reese on it. The carcass was still lukewarm in the cool night air, meaning they'd fed recently. Alain scanned the tree line ahead of him, but he neither saw nor heard any sign of the two.

He'd only been a few minutes behind them at the outset, but they'd all been trained in evasion. Even knowing the same tricks, Alain had lost their scent a couple of times over the past four days, expanding their lead to most of a night or more, then gradually closing it again.

Alain looked back at the lamb. He needed to feed or he was going to start feeling it soon. As guilty as he felt about feeding on such a young creature, probably not even weaned from its mother's milk, it was going to die anyway without its mother. And without its blood, he might lose Vinnie and Reese.

The lamb struggled as he picked it up. Alain had mostly given up on prayer, figuring God had forsaken him, but he couldn't shake his grandmother's Catholic upbringing completely. "Forgive me," he prayed silently before quelling the bleating with a bite to the throat.

His tongue tingled. A sense of well-being washed over him, so strong, so powerful, it was like that tin cup of warm blood on the sixth night of the "practical demonstration" the Army had so kindly provided.

He and his unit had fed on sheep before. As the Army said, they were inferior to pigs, but superior to carnivores. Experience bore that out. But pigs paled in comparison to this. This was every bit as good as human blood. He resisted the urge to drink all its blood in one go, taking just enough to quell the aching and quiet his cravings, then tried to drain some of its blood into his canteen, adding a few drops from a small bottle containing an anticoagulant solution. Still, he felt more satiated and stronger from those few mouthfuls of lamb's blood than he'd ever felt after gorging on a pig.

The irony wasn't lost on Alain. The substitute for the blood of man was the blood of the lamb. There was probably no scientific basis for why that would be, but the symbolic significance couldn't be denied.

He wondered why vampire lore hadn't mentioned this fact. Then he realized how ridiculous that sounded. Where was the big book of vampire lore? At some vampire university in Transylvania? He barely knew enough about his own condition to write a "Welcome to Vampirism" pamphlet, and half of what he knew he learned from the Army. He needed to stop being shocked at how little he knew.

Maybe most vampires knew about lamb's blood, but they never told the Army. It wouldn't be the first time the Army didn't know something. Maybe there were huge communities of vampires in Australia and New Zealand, living solely off lamb's blood and leaving their human neighbors alone. Not every vampire had to be some bedraggled French dandy or creepy Transylvanian count. Maybe half the guys on the night shift at the meat packing plants in Chicago were vampires, bringing home lamb's blood as a fringe benefit.

Alain snapped himself out of his reverie and picked up Reese's scent again, taking off after it. He hoped they'd either get hungry enough to eat a lamb or run into some Nazi soldiers soon, because if they didn't, civilians could end up in danger.

* * * *

Alain reached the barnyard gate and prayed that Vinnie and Reese were stopping here to feed on the farm animals, not the farmer. He looked around for something he could use as a weapon and saw a pitchfork leaned up against the fence. He thought about breaking the handle to use as a stake when a woman's scream came from the barn. He shrugged off his pack, grabbed the pitchfork, and went running toward the barn.

Alain burst through the closed barn doors, seeing Vinnie at the far end of the barn, standing over a girl in her late teens or early twenties. She didn't appear to have been bitten, just frightened. The scream was bait.

Instinctively, Alain dropped to the right, throwing himself at Reese's legs as Reese came from the side and swung a stake at the spot Alain's chest had previously occupied. Reese jumped to avoid Alain and danced to regain his footing as Alain rolled back onto his feet. Reese and Alain briefly circled each other, Alain pulling back to get more distance between him and Reese, but allowing Reese to position him so Vinnie was at his back.

Turning, Alain got himself perpendicular to the plane created by Vinnie and Reese so he had one on each side. Ten feet behind Reese, in the corner of the barn lay a slumped human body, an older man, probably the girl's father. Alain could smell the fresh blood. Reese had just fed.

Alain could imagine the conversation where Reese talked Vinnie into waiting to feed on the girl while he fed on the old man. They could lure Alain in and Reese would be freshly fed, while Alain would probably be aching and distracted, his reaction times slow, making him easy prey for Reese.

Alain threw the pitchfork like a spear. The imagined conversation had been right about the slow reaction times, just the wrong vampire. The pitchfork took Vinnie in the neck and drove him back toward the barn wall, embedding its tines in the wood. If Vinnie had been freshly fed, he'd have dodged it easily.

Alain turned back to face Reese, who caught him around the waist with a low tackle, his shoulder driving into Alain's stomach and lifting him off his feet. He pushed Alain backward into a low wall of hay bales that collapsed on the two of them.

Reese rose first. Standing over Alain, Reese grabbed a bale and started bashing him with it. With his arms up to guard against the thudding blows of the bale, Alain noticed that Reese was straddling his left leg. Alain lifted his legs, brought them together and threw his weight into a sideways roll, bringing Reese down. Alain untangled his legs from Reese's and scrambled to a standing position.

Vinnie was struggling to pull the pitchfork out of the barn wall and his neck. Meanwhile, the girl he'd had on the floor was now up and holding an oil lamp. Actually, Alain realized, she wasn't so much holding it as swinging it and lofting it right towards him. "Die, you son of a bitch," she yelled in French.

It was Reese's vampire speed that saved Alain. He popped up, facing Alain, and took the lamp between the shoulder blades. The oil splashed out on his clothes and began to burn. Alain hadn't seen anyone of any gender remove their clothes that fast. Reese had his shirt and pants off in a jiffy, dropping them to the floor and stomping them out. And that jiffy was all the time Alain needed to find a weapon.

With the last stamp on his clothes, Reese looked up, trying to find Alain. Alain, behind him, dropped a loop of bailing wire around his neck and tightened the makeshift garrote with all the strength being a vampire gave him. Reese panicked as it bit into the flesh of his neck and he scrabbled at the wire with his fingers, but Alain put a knee in his back and pulled harder. The wire cut most of the way through Reese's neck, wrapping around the spinal cord. With a yank, Alain cracked the bone and pulled the wire through. Reese's head fell to the floor. His body stood there and jerked for a moment before toppling down beside it.

In the tunnel vision of his attack on Reese, Alain hadn't noticed that Reese's clothing was merely one of many things splashed by flaming oil; the other things being dry hay bales. The bales were becoming engulfed.

Alain looked around for the girl. During the melee, she'd snuck behind Alain to the old man and was desperately trying to drag him to the door. Alain ran over to her and took the old man's body from her, slinging it over one shoulder. The girl launched herself at him, screaming and beating him with her fists. Alain used his free hand to grab her arm and drag her out of the barn.

The girl resisted, trying to pull away from him, back into the conflagration, but she couldn't break Alain's grip as he pulled her and the old man's body to a safe distance from the blaze. He let her go and put the body down next to her. The girl sat on the ground and cradled the old man's head in her lap.

Alain turned back to the barn, but by now it was engulfed. He'd wanted to see Vinnie burn, make sure he was dead, but he'd see nothing now if he went back. He wanted to sniff for Vinnie on the air, but the burning barn overpowered all other smells and most sounds. If Vinnie wanted to attack, the confusion of the fire would provide excellent cover. Alain had to assume that Vinnie was either burning or had run off to lick his wounds.

Everything inside the barn was ablaze and the flames were heading up to the roof. Alain went to the well pump, and became his own one-man bucket brigade. He wasn't going to save the barn, but his advantages in strength and speed allowed him to quickly douse the roofs of the main house, two henhouses, an outhouse, and the two sheds, making sure that stray sparks from the barn wouldn't set them alight too.

The barn's roof collapsed, sending up a shower of sparks, then the walls fell in. It resembled nothing so much as a bonfire now, a bonfire that smelled of wood tinged with burning flesh.

In the distance Alain could see lights and hear the sound of excited voices. People had seen the conflagration and were coming to help, or perhaps merely to watch. He thought about saying "wait, let me explain" in French, but decided it was time to go.

He picked up his pack from where he'd dropped it. The girl continued to cradle the man's head as she cried and talked to him, smoothing his cheek with her hand. Alain wanted to stay and try to comfort her, but right now he knew she'd be about as willing to let him do that as her neighbors would to let him explain how none of this was his fault.

He scanned around once more for any sign of Vinnie. He'd probably burned up in the barn, but you could never be too careful. Alain found no sign of him, took a last look at the girl, and then ran into the surrounding forest.

Chapter 7: A Burial

The next night, Alain entered the barn's wreckage cautiously. He hadn't seen anyone standing guard, but he wanted to be ready in case someone popped up.

He found Reese's bones close to where he expected. He was pretty sure Reese couldn't be brought back from being beheaded and burned, but he stomped the skull with his boot, breaking it into pieces. He took the jaw and a few of the larger shards and threw them as far as he could in different directions... for safety's sake.

He moved quickly through the remaining rubble. Most of the animals had been out in the warm night air, leaving not much else but wood and hay ash, and some half-melted metal from the bailing wire and the tines of the pitchfork. To his great disappointment, there were no more human skulls, particularly not the one he'd been hoping for.

In his time as either a vampire or human, Alain had not sat as still and as quiet for as long as he did the next couple of nights, watching to make sure Vinnie did not return for the girl. He had a small amount of lamb's blood in his canteen and that held him so he did not need to hunt.

It was almost meditative as he focused on the farm and the surrounding area, sitting in a tree and just watching. So intent on trying to catch any movement, any sound, it came as a surprise to him when he discovered he had another sense. Without hearing, smelling, or seeing her, he could sort of just tell how far away the girl was and in what direction. She was a pulsing presence, as if her heart were a beacon. Intrigued by this, he stilled himself further and tried to see if he could pick up more. Gradually he began picking up some of the other animals in the woods around him. The larger they were, the more strongly they registered, and each had its own sort of flavor... Human, boar, badger, hare, bird. This was another thing the Army had neglected to mention.

When Vinnie did not return after two nights, Alain became upset. Pig and sheep blood helped, but by now Vinnie would be starting to the feel the pain and need. And if he wasn't coming back for the girl, he was either stoically suffering among the trees or he had found a human to feed on. After six months of training and fighting together, Alain knew "stoic" wasn't in Vinnie's vocabulary. Vinnie was somewhere else, feeding on someone else.

Alain didn't know what he'd do now. He'd probably seek and harass Germans until they killed him or the war ended. But before he left, he had to apologize to the girl. Even though Reese had killed the farmer, the memory of the girl holding his head in her lap and stroking his cheek broke Alain's heart every time it came back to his mind's eye.

Alain's paternal grandmother had emigrated from France when she was about the same age as the girl in the farmhouse, dragged there by a husband who dreamed of streets of gold but ended up fishing just like he'd done in Marseilles. She'd moved in with his parents to help out when Alain was three and his mother took sick. Six months later, when his mother recovered, Mémère was planted in their house too firmly to be dislodged and French was the official language inside the home. Speaking English in front of Mémère would get your ear pinched. So would trying to get out of going to church on Sundays. Alain and his sister went to church every Sunday, Christmas, and Easter without fail.

It had been three or so years since Mémère passed away and his parents hadn't enforced the French-only rule after she was gone. He was afraid his French might be a little rusty, but as he knocked on the farmhouse door, he decided it would have to suffice.

The girl was much calmer than he expected when she opened the door. He expected fear or anger, but she just said "Oh, it's you."

She was about five-foot-four, wearing a plain dress that went halfway down her calf and covered her arms down to a few inches above the elbow, an apron protecting the front of the dress. The house was cooler than the night air outside, but still warm enough for her to go barefoot. Her long, dark hair was tied up in back. She was one of the most beautiful things Alain had ever seen.

She turned away and walked back into the simple farmhouse. "You can come in if you want."

"You're not afraid to invite me in?"

She continued walking toward the stove, not even looking back. "If you wanted to kill me, you could have left me next to my father and been gone before the neighbors arrived. Instead, you drew water and saved my home."

Alain stepped into the house, not knowing why. She was giving him a serious case of the heebie-jeebies. He expected her to be angry, frightened, perhaps even a bit crazed. Being calm and matter of fact made no sense to him.

The farmhouse was small, two small bedrooms off a great room that encompassed a sitting area, kitchen, and dining table. The house was at least two hundred years old, if not older. It smelled of accumulated cooking odors, of soap, of minerals from the well, of root vegetables in the cellar, and of old pipe tobacco.

"He was going to die soon anyway." In his reverie, Alain hadn't noticed her sit down at the small dining table. She was seated sideways in one of the chairs, an arm on the table, one resting in her lap. "My father. The doctor gave him six months back before the Nazis came. He hung on for over three years, but it was getting bad. Your friends probably did him a kindness by ending his pain."

Alain watched her composure flake away as unspoken thoughts crossed her mind. "I only wish he hadn't died in fear." She turned in her seat, lay her head in her arms on the table and began to sob.

He had no idea what to do. He knew what he wanted to do. He wanted to sweep her up in his arms like they were in some movie and tell her everything would be alright now that he was here. But he hadn't come to romance her. He hadn't even noticed how pretty she was the night he rescued her... and helped get her barn burned down... but she'd thrown the lamp... Alain stopped. She'd lost her father and barn because he hadn't stopped Reese and Vinnie sooner.

He walked over to her and put a hand on her shoulder. He didn't pat or squeeze. He just lay it there gently to try and give her some strength, some reassurance. She responded by turning in her seat, wrapping her arms around his waist, and crying against his stomach, her tears wetting his shirt. He stood there, letting her cry, and didn't make a sound.

* * * *

She was on her second cup of a tisane she made from some local herbs and flowers, and her third shot of brandy. She sat in her father's chair in the sitting area, her legs folded up under her. The sitting area was composed of two comfortable chairs set up near the fireplace, side tables beside each one. On the wall opposite the fireplace was a rough-hewn bookcase where framed pictures were displayed in front of rows of books on upper shelves, while lower shelves held brandy and liqueurs.

A few wall sconces held oil lamps, about half of which were lit, casting a warm glow around the room, but not bright. It was sort of like being in front of a dying fireplace, though the fireplace was not lit on such a warm night.

Her name was Marie, he discovered. She'd been near the end of her second year at university, studying to be a teacher, when the Nazis invaded. Her mother and stepfather in Paris had paid to have her smuggled out to her father, feeling she'd be safer out in the forests where there was nothing of any importance to the Nazis.

"This village had a vampire, you know," she said out of nowhere as if she'd just suddenly remembered. She sipped at her tea, found it too weak, and added another splash of brandy. "My father told me the story when I was a little girl."

"800 years ago, there was a priest named Lucien who had lost his way, grown corrupted and sinful. This weakened him and let him fall prey to a vampire who must have thought it a perverse joke to turn a 'man of God' into an undead beast."

"When Lucien awoke as a vampire, he thought it must be a punishment from God, and to repent for his sins, he swore never to drink blood, even if it meant great suffering or even death. He believed God had let the vampire change him as a test. He believed it was God giving him a chance to prove himself righteous and save his own soul."

"For six nights he suffered, each night worse than the last, but on the seventh day he was relieved. God took away his hunger and took away his pain, but God left him the strength of a vampire. He pledged to use that strength to do good and became the protector of the village. He kept it safe from marauders and robbers, even kept our livestock safe from wolves. Eventually the people trusted him so much, they made him

45

mayor and all the town council meetings were held after dark for his comfort. For 100 years, our crops came in, our livestock thrived, and the town was safe."

"What happened after 100 years," Alain asked.

"It was the time of the Inquisition and the Church finally came to investigate the tales it had heard of a vampire. He could have run off, but he knew the priests would have burned the village for embracing him. He bargained with them to be forgiving of the villagers. In exchange he let them lead him quietly and peacefully to the village's center where the priests made all the villagers watch as he was staked and burned. He forgave the priests just before they drove the stake into his heart."

Alain sipped at his tea. "Do you believe the story is true? That he never drank blood?"

"Perhaps," she said.

Pieces were falling into place in Alain's mind. The Army gave them blood on the sixth night. If the story was true and the Army had let them go all night, they would have woken up free of their addiction the next evening. They gave them blood just in time to keep them hooked, and he was pretty sure they knew that was the case.

He stood up from his chair and walked out the door into the night air. He wanted to yell, scream, break something. But he didn't want to fly into a rage in front of Marie. He just looked up at the moon, taking deep breaths and clenching and unclenching his fists. There was so little the Army had told him, and half of it seemed to be guesses or lies.

Maybe that part of the story wasn't true. The vampire had protected their livestock, but no one said he was 100% effective. It was possible a lamb disappeared now and again. Maybe he had his own flock. Perhaps he could have mixed the lamb's blood with brandy and salt, possibly some anticoagulant herbs like cloves, or even garlic, to preserve and extend it so he would only have to take a lamb every month or so. If it looked like he never took blood at all, it would help him maintain the image of a redeemed sinner. If he told the villagers he would just feed on lambs and not them, they would always wonder what might happen to them if he ran out of lambs.

Then again, it could really be true. But why would Hell allow a good vampire to retain its powers? Maybe that was part of the deal. Vampires couldn't exist if God didn't allow it, so maybe God gave vampires the free will to choose between good and evil just like mortals. Maybe. If he did stop blood for a week, what was the worst that could happen? Death? Eternal torture? He was probably in for them already. And if he fed to avoid them, what happened when he ran out of lambs?

He sensed Marie in the doorway and turned to her. "I want to try it."

* * * *

Alain pulled the zipper of the duffel bag to chest level and looked up at Marie, standing 6 feet above him. "Remember. Do not come back and dig me up. If all is well, I will have the strength to get out myself. If it is not, you will not be safe around me."

Marie nodded. She wasn't happy about this. She'd offered to let him stay in her father's room while he did this, but he'd refused. Having a warm source of blood so close by might make it too tough to resist the cravings. Having six feet of dirt on top of him and the thought of all the pain and effort required to dig out... it still might not stop him, but it would be harder than walking over to the next bedroom. Combined with his will power, he hoped it would be enough for him to see it through.

He zipped the duffel the rest of the way and Marie began the slow, methodic process of shoveling the dirt back into an unmarked grave in the woods.

Chapter 8: Rising from The Grave

Alain didn't crawl out on the seventh night. He'd had that sense of being okay at the start of the sixth night in the infirmary, and again this sixth night, followed by the most intense pain and craving he'd ever felt. When he woke feeling okay on the seventh night, he just wasn't sure he could trust it. He was afraid he'd get out, rush to tell Marie he was cured, and then be struck with a craving that put his prior suffering to shame. So, he waited, expecting the other shoe to drop, expecting the pain to start, expecting the craving to come.

But it didn't. When Alain finally slept, he fell asleep happy. And when he woke again, he decided he was ready.

Getting unburied wasn't easy. When you're digging a hole, you just throw the dirt to the side. When you're digging a tunnel, the dirt gets thrown behind you. But when you're completely surrounded by dirt, it's a matter of inches, even fractions of inches, slowly trading places with the dirt as you move up and it moves down to fill the space behind you. Even a coffin would have been a blessing, providing a structured empty space for some of the dirt to move into as he got a head start on digging upward. Thank goodness he'd been buried on his back so he had some idea of which way was up. Even so, he continuously feared he was digging to the side or even farther down.

One of the indications of going in the right direction was that the dirt above him gradually got lighter. When he was able to shove an arm through and feel open air with his fingertips, he felt elated. At that point, it became like swimming in very slow motion, pawing his other hand up as he tried to bend his legs and get some push-off against the dirt below him. Instead of getting pushed upward, the force of his push compacted the dirt, opening up space which the dirt around him flowed down to fill. On the other hand, it freed up some space around his head, chest and arms, allowing him to better dig out with his hands.

Even though it was mere forest dirt, trying to climb through it was like trying to swim upward through quicksand. Not breathing became a mixed blessing, because the dirt filled every crook and crevice, down his pants and up his nose. Packed into his nostrils and up against his sinuses, it felt like the worst head cold he'd ever had, and there was no breath in his lungs to snort it out. The first thing he did after rising from the grave was take a deep breath and sneeze.

Though he'd told Marie not to come back to the grave, fearing for her safety, he found her sitting on the ground a few yards away, napping against a tree, a shovel beside her. Every night at dusk she'd come out and pounded the shovel against the dirt to let him know how many days he'd been buried. If it was two days, she'd pound twice, pause, then pound twice again in a rudimentary code. Alain was thankful she'd thought to do that, because it was easy to lose track of time.

He hadn't thought about that before they executed the plan to bury him. He hadn't thought about breathing either. When she was shoveling in the dirt, as the weight of the dirt pressed heavier and heavier against his chest, he began to panic because it was getting harder and harder to take in breaths. He took a deep breath and held it, and held it, and held it. Nothing burned, nothing ached. The only sensation he felt was the weight of the dirt trying to press the breath out of him.

Eventually he let it out. He felt a brief panic again screaming at him to inhale, but he did his best to ignore it and eventually it went away.

He'd found a number of places where folklore and reality disconnected. Thankfully, in this one, they didn't. He couldn't suffocate. But it was small consolation when, under the crushing weight of six feet of dirt, his butt cheek itched. That was one part of the discomfort he hadn't paid attention to when the Army denied him blood.

Back in the infirmary, the itching was a minor irritant. He scratched, it went into remission, and he could concentrate on the pain in his joints and his muscles. Buried "alive," the itching added a whole new dimension to his suffering. When it was on his nose or hands, he could rub it against the silk in small movements. The butt cheek wasn't even the worst of it. He could flex it and get some minor relief. There was one spot, though, between his shoulder blades, that he could do absolutely nothing about. Somewhere during the fifth night, he swore that if he got through this, he was going to get a knife and carve out that section of his back, burn it, and piss on its ashes.

Despite the itching, despite the pain, he endured. Marie coming to pound on his grave each night helped in more ways than just keeping track of the time. It gave him hope. Each night he heard that pounding, it reminded him that she waited for him. If he could just make it through, he could be with her and she wouldn't have to fear him or be revulsed by him. He would be like a regular man, or at least as regular as he could be.

He nudged Marie's foot with his and she woke from her doze. She looked up at him, covered with dirt, a shadow of a shadow in the night. "Did it work?"

He nodded.

She held out a hand to him and he helped her up. As he tried to let go, she held his hand fast. She picked up the shovel with her other hand and led him back to the farm. She was quiet as they walked, but

51

occasionally, she would look back at him and smile, giving his hand a squeeze.

When they reached the farm, she took him to one of the sheds next to the farmhouse, opening the door to reveal a large bathtub and a pipe coming in through the wall to feed it. He could smell a wood fire burning behind the far wall, and when she turned the tap, the water that poured from the pipe was steaming. She took a rag, dunked it in the water, and wrung it out.

Slowly, gently, she wiped some of the grave dirt from Alain's face. Working down his neck, she reached his shirt and unbuttoned it one button at a time, cleaning each newly exposed area, periodically stopping to get a new rag and dunk it in the hot water. When he was completely nude, she got a bucket and filled it from the tub. She handed it to Alain, then pulled a stool over next to him and climbed atop it, holding out her hand for the bucket. Alain returned it and she dumped it over him, washing the dirt from his hair.

She repeated the process until she'd emptied the tub, periodically scrubbing him where he needed cleaning. Last she handed him a wet rag and told him, "clean your privates." Alain did as she told him, not comfortable being naked in front of this woman he barely knew. The one advantage of being a vampire was that he had the image of the nurse from Hell in his mind. Thinking about her was better than thinking about baseball, the bible, and shoveling a stable combined.

While he washed, she opened the tap again, hot water sloshing into the tub. "Get in," she said.

She took the cloth from him and he got in the tub. The hot water felt amazing. If it took being buried alive to make a bath feel this good, he was willing to consider another dirt-nap. He just closed his eyes and luxuriated in it, so lost in the sensation that he didn't know Marie was in the tub with him until he felt her flesh against his. Her hand stroked his leg while she kissed his chest. Her long hair flowed across his shoulders while her belly brushed his "privates," driving any thoughts of the nurse out of his mind, replacing them with a rush of alarm. Panic, unlike the nurse, did not prevent him from reacting.

She slid upward along him and began kissing his lips. He tried to think of all the reasons this was wrong. He wasn't forcing himself on her. In fact, she was technically forcing herself on him. Maybe it was too soon after her father's death. Maybe she was doing it out of a need for human contact. Maybe he was just a convenient stranger and it meant nothing.

She gently guided him into her, gasping briefly as she slowly slid down him until he was engulfed by her. Slowly she rose back up, then down, getting a rhythm and burying her face on his shoulder, her breath hotter on his neck. The rhythm of her moving up and down on him felt so good. Being clean felt so good. The hot water felt so good. He gasped out the one thought on his mind. "Why?"

She moved upward until just the very tip of him was still inside her, and she stretched to put her mouth near his ear. "Because you are mine," she whispered, "and I am yours for as long as you will have me."

She began sliding back down, slowly, but he wrapped his left arm around her and arrested her motion. Tilting his face down, he cupped the back of her head with his right hand and pulled her into a kiss. He kissed her with the hunger of his conquered need for blood, with the sadness of his stolen mortality, with the lust he had for her body, with the desire he had for her heart. He poured everything he felt, everything he was into that kiss and she returned it. He could taste her loss, her passion, her curiosity, her mortality... and her love. Her offer to be with him as long as he would have her was no mere pillow talk. She had chosen him.

When the kiss broke and they both drew back to stare at each other in awe, he reached forward and stroked her cheek, uttering just one word: "Forever."

Over the next sixty-four years he would regret that word only three times, and then only briefly. Marie died of a heart attack at the age of 86 in a basement apartment in Queens, New York, in the midst of a tirade over an "American Idol" result she thought patently unfair.

Alain had been out at the corner store buying her some Ben & Jerry's ice cream. She wasn't supposed to eat it. But at 86, her doctors didn't want her to eat anything that wasn't a shredded wheat biscuit mushed up in soy milk. So in defiance, or just out of her pure enjoyment of being alive and all its pleasures, she'd had half a ham and egg sandwich for breakfast with strong French coffee, goose liver and crackers for lunch with a glass of wine, and dinner was a simple salad nicoise that Alain had prepared for her, washed down with mineral water... a concession to the fact that there would be Ben & Jerry's for dessert.

When Alain returned home, she was gone. Her body lay on the floor, but her spirit had moved on. Alain knew that if there was any justice in the world, she'd find her way to Heaven.

He planned to join her there, and keep his promise of "forever," but there was something he needed to pick up first.

Chapter 9: A Second Chance

Manhattan, Modern Day

Kurt rocked with the subway, lost in self-pity. Was he that much of a loser? Was he uglier than he thought? Or was it just that he wanted what he couldn't have?

He wasn't anywhere near joining the "incel" movement. It's not like he never had girlfriends in his life. It's not like a couple of them hadn't been hot, or at least hot-ish. But they'd all been friends of friends, or somehow from within his extended social circle.

Probably the closest to "unusual" was when he dated Hadley in college. He met her while working on the literary magazine together. What had seemed to be an exciting artistic streak at first eventually turned out to be a combination of neuroses and pretentious bullshit. The sex was good, so he'd put up with it until she dumped him because she said he was "too passive" and "never going anywhere."

Maybe he was. Instead of writing the great American novel, he'd graduated into a junior copywriter job, writing the great American reason why this shampoo was going to change your life.

And perhaps that's why the last year or so had seemed so unsatisfying romantically. He was looking to his love life to make up for what was lacking in other areas. He had these romantic notions of a chance meeting... not a "meet cute," but something more intense and dramatic... turning into the kind of romance that would define a lifetime... his Annabel Lee... his Beatrice.

He'd seen the lust of his life, or at least his month, at a club this evening. The best way he could describe her was to combine the best features of Rosario Dawson and Dania Ramirez (a teenage crush from when she'd been on "Heroes"); skin like coffee with cream, full lips, glistening black hair, that jaw line above a neck that begged for your lips... He could feel himself getting visibly excited and started thinking about baseball to prevent any unsightly bulges.

He was six-foot-nothing, neither scrawny nor muscular, neither fit nor fat, neither rich nor poor (though closer to poor), neither strikingly handsome nor frighteningly ugly. His hair was so light brown it got sort of blonde in the summer. He wasn't even blonde or brunette. He wasn't really anything at all other than extremely, achingly in the middle.

The girl at the club hadn't even looked at him. She'd been dancing with two girlfriends, and when Kurt went up and introduced himself... eh. Her girlfriends talked to him, but she just danced in her own little world, looking everywhere in the club but at him. Her name was Jennifer, her friends Sofia and Tania. He talked to them as a group, shouting over the music, not wanting to single her out, not be so goddamn obvious. Sofia and Tania would answer his questions, even asked him some. They were plenty friendly, but he wanted her and she wasn't biting. He couldn't tell if she was truly lost in the music or if she was truly, pointedly ignoring him. Either way, he eventually gave up.

He'd been at the club with some people he knew from college— not really friends, but more than acquaintances—and went back to their place to get his backpack before heading home. Tomorrow would be another day at the bottom of the food chain on the agency's creative team for a whitening toothpaste that gave half its profits to Amnesty

International. His project in the morning would be figuring out how to tell the product's story in a 3-inch square rectangle on the product's "environmentally conscious" packaging. It was almost Zen to contemplate a conscious toothpaste box, but that was the approved wording from on high.

Now on the subway, he was pissed he hadn't been more bold with Jennifer. What did he have to lose by moving between her friends and being obviously focused on her, requiring her to reject him rather than give up when she didn't openly accept him? The problem was that it just wasn't who he was. He wasn't that guy. If he got what he even thought was an unspoken "no," he gave up. But he suspected that by not being more shameless with his attentions and trying to get to a more overt "no," he was letting the potential "yes" get away too often.

Kurt felt a force pushing him to the side, jogging him out of his thoughts. The train was stopping.

The doors opened and he was sure he was hallucinating. Jennifer and her friends got on. Talking and laughing, they didn't notice him, didn't seem to remember him from the club. They took a few seats against the wall, still engrossed in their private conversation.

What are you waiting for, a voice shouted in his head. *This is too good to be coincidence. God's giving you a second chance. Go for it!!!*

Kurt walked down the wide aisle of the car until he was standing opposite the three. "Sofia, Tania, Jennifer," he said casually, "good to see you again."

It was as if they hadn't even heard their names. They kept chattering on as if he'd never said anything. He wanted to slink away, let the night be over, let these girls disappear. But the more overpowering thought was that for once in his 23 years of life, he didn't want to get home and think "If I'd only tried harder..." Better to curse himself for something he did wrong than something he didn't do at all.

Louder now, "Jennifer, hey." The three stopped and looked at him. In the glare of six headlights, he felt not only like a deer, but like a deer that had been shaved naked and doused with ice-water. Yet somewhere within him he found the will to continue. "You were at Static tonight, right?"

Jennifer and her friends eyed him. "Yeah," she said. "And you were the geek who tried to join us."

If Kurt had been armed, he probably would have pulled out a gun and shot himself in the head right there and then. "Gotta give you credit, though," she said, "you were the only one with the balls to try."

It sounded like a compliment, but still Kurt wanted to kill or be killed, just whatever would get him out of this amazingly uncomfortable situation.

Jennifer stood up. With a step, she was pretty much in his face. "But in the light, you're actually sort of cute. Particularly with that much blood in your cheeks, turning them so cherry red."

Kurt stood frozen as Jennifer kissed him on the cheek, then playfully grazed her teeth against it as if she were biting it. She moved around and planted her lips on his. It took a moment for the shock to disperse and the pleasure to register. When it did, he kissed back. She broke the kiss, pulled her head back and peered into his eyes, cocking her head as if searching for something in them. It took a few moments for her to find whatever she was seeking in his eyes, but she did find it, and then her lips were on his again.

Jennifer's hand came up behind his head, pulling him against her harder, and he felt a prick at the base of his skull, like he'd been stabbed with a thumbtack. He tried to pull back, but that only pressed the skin of his neck harder against the point.

The area around where he'd been pricked was quickly growing cold and numb, and the numbness was spreading, especially up the back of his head. He was no longer kissing Jennifer. She was kissing him. Her arm moved down from behind his head and went under his arm, propping him up as his knees went weak. He registered a mild surprise at the fact that she didn't struggle under his weight.

The numbness that crept up the back of his skull was in his limbs, his body wasn't responding. Jennifer's other hand went down to his crotch and started caressing. He could barely feel it. But to the other passengers on the subway, it must have looked pretty passionate.

The subway swayed to another halt. Kurt would have fallen down if Jennifer hadn't been holding him up. "Come on, lover" she said loudly, "let's get you home."

One of Jennifer's friends -- Sofia, Kurt thought, but the fog was deep enough that he couldn't be sure -- ducked a shoulder under his spare arm while Jennifer stayed under the one she was already supporting. The two lead him out of the train while the third followed. "Nawiheeyanawa," Kurt mumbled, the best protest he could muster.

As the girls pulled him across the platform and up the stairs, Jennifer or Sofia would go wide every few steps, swinging her leg out to kick his leg forward and make it look like he was making a feeble attempt to walk. Kurt tried as hard as he could to concentrate on making a protest, getting help. He was being drugged and kidnapped. This only happened in cheap spy movies. It didn't happen to normal people!

Reaching the street, Kurt saw a police car cruising by slowly. "Gawaagamooguhfuguh!!" The police car stopped and the driver shined a light on the four of them.

"What did he say?"

"Sorry officer." Jennifer smiled sweetly. "Our friend had a little too much to drink tonight. We're taking him home."

"Just get him off the street. Okay?"

"'Kay." Kurt could almost swear he saw a flock of butterflies come out of her mouth, the syllable was so laced with cuteness and sugar.

"Ahhhehsouee ayeeouayoo," Kurt said, instead of his intended "Arrest me! Take me to jail!" He tried for a shout, but he'd pretty much expended himself with the first one that got the cops' attention. This one was just a notch above conversational in volume.

"And lay him on his side with a bucket next to the bed," the cop riding shotgun called out from behind his partner. "He's pretty far gone."

"You got it," Sofia shouted.

"Yup," Jennifer said to Kurt as the cops pulled away, "we definitely have to give you points for balls. But you're going to be a good boy now, aren't you? In fact, you're feeling very sleepy."

Before Kurt could argue, he was out cold.

Chapter 10: Sacrifice

Alain looked at the back of the hooded head in front of him. He was in a room full of brown and black robes, about fifty people in all, gathered in the empty 20' by 30' storeroom behind an out-of-business adult bookstore in Brooklyn. He hung out in back. He was just here to watch. He didn't want to attract attention... yet.

Three women came in through the door off the alley, dragging some kid. He looked to be about 22 or 23, jeans, black leather jacket, backpack. He was limp in their arms. Whether his unconscious state was the kid's own fault or something they did to him, Alain didn't know.

On Alain's signal, George started working his way forward to get a better view of the proceedings. Meanwhile, the girls had stripped the kid to the waist and were laying him out on an embalming table on a stage against the wall, leaving his stuff in a pile below the head of the table. He was out cold, but just for good measure they tied his arms and feet down.

Finished preparing the kid, the girls donned robes and were joined by a fourth hooded figure, coming in from the store side, a wicked looking ceremonial knife in his belt and an unconscious chicken in one hand, held by the feet. He was 5'10" and solidly built. Even if Alain hadn't known who was in charge, he would have recognized Vinnie Rinaldi. Though neither Alain nor Vinnie was actively trying to kill the other at present, Vinnie wouldn't pass up the opportunity if it was dropped in his lap. "Bad blood," Alain chuckled under his breath, his nervousness making the pun much funnier to him than it would be at any other time.

Alain slouched down, trying to be harder to spot. It wasn't that he was afraid of Vinnie, but this ceremony was too important. He didn't want it disrupted until he had seen what he came to see.

As Vinnie took his place at the center of the table, facing the milling robed figures, two of the girls lit large braziers next to the table's ends and placed a bowl in front of him, setting it solidly on the edge of the table, its edge pressing into the kid's side, just under the ribcage. The cloying stench of the overly sweet incense in the braziers hit Alain's nose like a fist.

Vinnie pulled his knife and held the chicken over the bowl. Either it had been stunned or drugged, because it barely struggled or squawked, but it was alive. The blood couldn't be cold or artificially warmed. It couldn't be clotted or coagulated. It had to be recently pumped from a beating heart. Alain knew that much about the ritual. With a quick stroke, Vinnie drew his knife across its neck, sending its blood draining into the bowl. The crowd waited silently as the sanguine fluid trickled down.

When the blood's flow slowed to a slight drip, the chicken was thrown aside and the chanting began. A slow, rhythmic chant in a dead language. Most all in the room knew it and those who did not took it up after a few repetitions. Alain switched on the digital memo recorder in his pocket.

As the crowd chanted, Vinnie picked up the bowl and began painting on the wall in blood; two circles, one within the other, the inner circle holding a five-pointed star. In the ring between the inner and outer circle, he drew a sequence of symbols, an upside-down cross at the twelve o'clock position. It wasn't just the symbols that were important, but the sequence in which they were painted, even the order of the strokes to make them. Vinnie didn't know, but at least half-dozen of the people in the room were Alain's plants. Two of them carried hidden cameras and filmed the ritual to ensure every element was recorded.

Vinnie turned from the wall, picked up his knife from the embalming table, and turned back to the wall, raising the knife above his head and holding it in both hands.

Alain caught sight of George and made eye contact. A subtle nod from George let him know that everyone was on schedule and ready to go. Alain slid around the outer edge of the crowd, keeping an eye on the table and the people at it.

"Bright Angel," Vinnie shouted, "accept our offering and open a way so that we may deliver it unto you."

The lines of the five-pointed star glowed a sickly green, like cracks forming in the wide strokes of chicken blood. The light spread, filling the strokes, then the gaps within the star, then the gaps between the edges of the star and the circle, turning the interior circle into a dull pool of the green glow. Vinnie turned back toward the table, keeping the knife raised high, poised to stab it into the kid's chest and cut out his still beating heart to throw through the circle, and... "Now," Alain yelled!

Alain launched himself at Vinnie, distracting him from the task at hand. Vinnie dropped his knife hand into a defensive posture as Alain came in, throwing a flurry of kicks, driving Vinnie back while he slashed at Alain's leg.

Neither the kicks nor the knife made contact with their intended targets, but it moved Vinnie away from the table. On his yell, three of Alain's cohort had started shoving, throwing shin kicks, and rabbit punches, whipping the crowd up into a general melee. They moved quickly to the floor in front of the stage, dove in under the embalming table, grabbed the legs of the three girls, and pulled them out into the brawl. The girls were swung out into the crowd at knee height, toppling a dozen or so other robed attendees, creating wriggling masses of cursing angry people, ready to lash out at the nearest target even before they got to their feet.

George ran over to the table and freed the kid's hands and feet on one side before waving smelling salts under the kid's nose.

* * * *

Kurt grunted, jerking his head away from the sharp smell. "Wuzzat?"

A man slapped Kurt's face. "What's your name kid?"

Kurt tried to say "who are you," but still a bit sluggish, it came out more like "huryu?"

"I'm a friend," the man said, waving something under Kurt's nose, causing Kurt to flinch as the stinging scent jolted him back toward consciousness. The guy slapped Kurt's cheeks again. "What's your name?"

"Kurt." Just barely impinging on Kurt's dawning consciousness were the sounds of shouting and fighting all around him.

"I'm George," the guy said as he gave Kurt's hand a quick shake before undoing the wrist restraint. "I'll have you free in a sec. Then get the fuck out of here."

* * * *

Alain and Vinnie were slugging it out. An attempt to stab Alain resulted in Vinnie being disarmed by a blow to the wrist, the knife sliding along the floor of the stage just as George swung Kurt's feet off the table, helping him get standing. George felt the knife thud against his shoe and grabbed it. He put it in Kurt's hand. "Take this."

One of the robed figures had broken away from the brawl long enough to see what George was doing. He came flying toward George, tackling him and driving him off toward the side.

Vinnie's hood was down, revealing long brown hair pulled back into a ponytail and a somewhat attractive looking man. "You're dead meat, Beaudreaux," he snarled at Alain, his voice still thick with a Brooklyn accent. Alain didn't bother replying. He'd fought Vinnie enough times to know that it was pointless to engage in small talk like some pithy comic book hero.

Alain intercepted a right cross with a block and fired a jab to Vinnie's ribs. Between professional fighters of Alain and Vinnie's comparable sizes, each man solid and athletic in build, these punches would have packed a wallop. Between two vampires who really did not like each other, any one of these punches would have hospitalized a prize fighter.

* * * *

In the midst of all this, Kurt was looking for his backpack. He may have known his name, but he was still drunk from whatever was in his system, and though that guy had told him to get out, even given him this killer knife, he wanted his shirt, his jacket, and his backpack.

In the midst of the fighting and brawling, mostly oblivious to it, Kurt stumbled to the head of the table, saw his stuff, and picked it up, putting on his shirt and coat without bothering to close them, then slung the backpack over one arm. Straightening his pack on his shoulder, he saw the glowing circle on the wall. *Cool*, he thought. He went over to the circle and poked at it with the knife. Where the knife touched the circle, it went through the wall. "Like buttah," Kurt said, entertained by the novelty.

George had put down his opponent and looked over at the table. Seeing Kurt playing with the circle, he shouted "Kurt! Get the fuck out of here!!"

Kurt turned toward the direction of George's voice, the knife held out in front of him, just in time to have a kick to the chest from Alain send Vinnie stumbling backward, impaling himself on the knife in the small of his back. Vinnie reached around to grab at Kurt who dodged to the side, causing Vinnie to trip over his own feet as Kurt's grip on the knife wrenched it against his spine. He went falling backward toward the circle, Kurt pushed behind him. In desperation, one hand still on the knife in Vinnie's back, Kurt grabbed Vinnie's hood, trying to keep himself upright. Instead, they fell together through the glowing circle. Alain lunged for it, but a moment before he got there, thwip, the circle was gone and Alain slammed into the wall.

Alain gave the signal for retreat and his group disengaged itself from the fight, doing their best to leave the room a seething brawl from which they could slip away unnoticed. Alain ran with George, the three who had pulled the girls off the stage took off together, the rabble rousers and videographers in the crowd scattered. In a moment's time, it was just a room full of vampires and Satan worshippers beating each other silly for no reason.

Chapter 11: Taking Inventory

The trip through the green stuff was like a trip through a door. One moment he was falling toward the glow on the wall. The next he was tumbling out into a grassy meadow. He wasn't stretched, squeezed, dissolved, deconstructed, or discombobulated. It was like falling out of bed... sort of. Kurt had never fallen out of bed intertwined with a guy with a knife in his back.

Kurt was on his back and the guy in the robe scrambled around so that he was on top of Kurt, his knees on Kurt's arms. "Howdy do, pard," he said, a Brooklyn accent underlying the cowboy lingo. He was smiling, showing his... fangs? He reached around to his back and pulled out the knife Kurt had accidentally lodged there, wiping it on his robe. "This belong to you?"

Kurt began to struggle, but the knife was quickly at his throat. As he settled down, "Robe Guy" slowly moved off of him, keeping the knife at his throat. Robe Guy kneeled beside him, and looked at where the portal had been, the glow quickly fading.

When the circle on the rock wall had cooled to be the same reddish color as the rock surrounding it, Robe Guy let go of the knife, which fell to the grass beside Kurt's head. Kurt rolled, rising to his knees a few feet away. He may have felt a little drunk before, but his mind was clear now. Robe Guy was still staring at the rock wall, no trace of the circle left on its face, and his jaw was slack. "That son of a bitch," he said slowly, his face displaying total disbelief. "That son... of... a... BITCH!"

Robe Guy got to his feet and stared at the wall. Kurt looked at the knife on the ground. He wasn't sure where he was, but he had a feeling it would come in handy. On the other hand, he had to weigh the risks of trying to get it against the risks of trying to get away without it. He chose the second option. He rose to his feet, turned and ran. Robe Guy continued cursing at the rock wall behind him. Kurt didn't look back.

Kurt had no idea where he was going, but it didn't matter. The only direction he cared about was away. He didn't know if Robe Guy had noticed he was gone yet or if Robe Guy even cared. All he knew was that there was a tree line up ahead and it would provide cover where he could slow down and evaluate the situation.

Reaching the trees, Kurt ran into the woods, getting a couple of hundred yards in before he slowed from a mad dash to a jog. He zigged and zagged within the trees, trying not to keep to a straight path so he'd be harder to find. After another couple of minutes of jogging, he slowed to a walk, his chest heaving, his stomach threatening to expel its contents back up his throat. He stopped, half-crouching, his hands on his knees, and tried to catch his breath without vomiting.

Damn cigarettes. He'd always thought he was in fairly decent shape, but he hadn't put it to much of a test in the past few years. If he was anything, he was punctual, and that meant he'd never had to run to keep from being late. He'd used the gym membership his parents bought him last Hanukkah exactly twice. Each time he lifted way more than he should have, got so sore he could barely lift his arms high enough to feed himself, and didn't go back for months.

Kurt stood and leaned against a tree, reclaiming some control over his breathing, the fire in his legs dulling. He tried to take stock of his surroundings. The trees were a kind he couldn't identify, and that was no surprise since he didn't know much about trees, but he couldn't ever remember seeing this kind before. The leaves on them were six-pointed and had a reddish color to them. Or was that the light? Everything seemed to have a reddish tint to it, even his skin. It was minor, but it was noticeable. The leaf cover of the trees wasn't too heavy and he looked up at the sky. Perhaps it was sunset, he thought.

There was no sky. Above him there was only rock. It was a few hundred feet above the trees, but it was clearly visible. There were no clouds, no visible light source like a sun, just rock. He was in some sort of cavern, a very huge cavern. But there were trees growing, there had been grass in the meadow by the rock wall which was apparently the edge of the cavern. If he went back to it and traced it around, he might just find a way out. But Robe Guy was back there.

And now that he wasn't so panicked and was breathing through his nose again, he started getting the scent of the trees. They smelled like Vicks VapoRub. His chest began to itch as he remembered those colds as a kid when his mother would apply what seemed like an entire jar of VapoRub to his chest and he wouldn't be able to smell anything but menthol for a week.

Kurt kicked at the dirt and slapped his palm against the trunk of a tree. He was fucked. Better to be cursed for something he did wrong than something he didn't do at all? Wasn't that what he'd thought on the subway? God was giving him a second chance?

He shrugged off his backpack and sat down on the ground. It was a hard packed dirt, also fairly red, and remarkably free of leaves. He wasn't such a city boy that he'd never been out in the woods, and these weren't woods. They were way too clean and way too orderly.

He opened his pack and rummaged around inside, trying to get an idea of what supplies he had in case he was going to be here a while. He pulled out a pack of generic-brand menthol cigarettes, looked at it, turning it around, and then threw it, sending it on a long lazy arc to hit the trunk of a tree twenty feet away. He also had a pack of Kools that he rationed out. He was a year out of school with a degree in the humanities, working at a just-above-mailroom-level job with an ad agency, trying to cover a third of the rent on a shoebox living room and kitchenette with three closets they stuffed mattresses into. Of course, as it got more and more expensive with each passing sin tax or lawsuit against the tobacco industry, even generics were at a premium.

"I really oughta quit," he said quietly as he drew out a cigarette, leaving 12 in the box. He placed it in his mouth before dropping the box back into his pack.

Leaning back, he dug in his pocket and pulled out his Zippo, lighting the cigarette with it and then putting it away. As he slowly smoked the cigarette, he inventoried his backpack. His phone had about 2/3 of a charge and no signal. He had one toothbrush and one travel-size tube of toothpaste, because you never knew when you'd need a clean mouth. There was a hairbrush, a bandanna kerchief, and a hard salami sandwich on French bread in a Ziploc bag that he'd made himself for lunch, but didn't eat because he ended up having a way-too-expensive burger with some co-workers. There was an unopened 1.5-liter bottle of mineral water, a little piece of plastic with lighter flints, a spiral notebook, some folded printouts from work, and a pen. Normally he would have had his laptop, but he'd locked it in his desk at work since he was going clubbing.

In the front pocket he had some more pens, a reserve twenty-dollar-bill just in case he got foolish and spent everything in his wallet, and a couple of single use packs of ibuprofen he'd filched from the medicine cabinet in the break room. Kurt opened one of the packs and then cracked open the bottle of water. He drank just enough to wash down the painkillers and then one more mouthful for good measure. He was thirsty after the run, but since he didn't know where he was or how long it would be until he got more water, it was best to conserve his resources. He gave in and took a third mouthful before screwing the top back on the bottle and putting it back in the pack.

Kurt stood, buttoned and tucked his shirt, and slung his backpack over his shoulder. Then he dropped the cigarette on the ground and stamped it out. He looked down at it to make sure it was out. With no leaves or other detritus on the ground, the cigarette butt sat on the ground alone, a light coat of red dirt on it, so blatantly obvious that someone had been there and left their trash behind... he had an unused side pocket on his backpack. He opened it up and dropped the dead cigarette butt inside.

He looked up at the roof of the cavern. The cavern roof sloped downward to his right, back toward Robe Guy, and upward to his left. He turned to his left and started walking forward, sure he'd hit something sooner or later.

* * * *

Alain and George made it back to Alain's house in Queens safely. Neither of them had been followed.

George owned the house, but Alain lived in it. Alain was technically dead, so he couldn't legally own property, and thus it had been put in Marie's name while she was alive. Before she died, it was placed in a trust for George. George rented it back to Alain at market rates to keep the IRS from getting suspicious.

Though Alain was a vampire, George was not. George was adopted by Alain and Marie at the age of 15 when George's parents (their closest friends) died in an automobile accident 14 years ago. They'd made sure George finished high school with good grades and managed his parents' estate so he could graduate college with no debt and a nest egg to boot.

George had idolized Alain, and despite what the military had done to Alain, George enlisted in the Marines right out of high school, avoiding the Army as a concession. With a hero's heart, and a natural affability, he quickly got promoted to corporal, then he got a battlefield promotion to sergeant that stuck. But a man can only take so much, and when his term was up, he didn't re-up.

George was proficient with a knife, a variety of guns, minor demolitions, and held his own in hand-to-hand. He may not have been vampire strong, but Alain could rely on George to cover his back when needed.

They both sat at a table in the basement. George poured a shot glass of pepper vodka and downed it in a gulp. "Whoa."

Alain sat back in his chair, staring at an empty corner of the floor. "You got that right."

"What did we do in there," George asked, knowing the answer full well. They had gone to record the opening of a portal into Hell. Had they not interfered, the kid on the table would have had his heart cut out of his chest and thrown through while still beating. A symbolic gesture at best, since it was just meat and blood being offered up to Satan, not an actual soul. No other person can give your soul to the Devil.

That was a fact Alain had wished he knew in 1943, back when he awoke as a vampire: that he could say no. Alain cut himself off. His therapist said he had a lot of unresolved issues about how the Army had treated him. Dr. Schreiber did a booming business in vampires with betrayal issues dating back to their turning. Aside from a few vampire groupies who got turned because they wanted it, most were turned against their will. Dr. Schreiber told Alain he was not allowed to dwell on it. Alain couldn't change the past, but he could improve the future.

When the kid had fallen through the glowing circle, taking Vinnie with him, they knew exactly what had happened. The kid and Vinnie were now physically in Hell, corporeal bodies in the afterlife. On the one hand it was good. The reason Alain and George had been taping the ceremony was because Alain had planned to open just such a portal and go through himself. On the other hand, they'd accidentally sent an innocent kid through. "I've got to go after him," Alain said.

"But what about your plans?"

"I can do both."

George poured himself another shot of vodka and gulped it quickly before slamming the shot glass down on the table. "I'm coming with you!"

"No, you're not," Alain said calmly.

George slammed his hand against the table. "Why not?"

"Because I don't know if I can get you out. This was supposed to be one-person, one-way."

"Now it's two. If you can find this kid, you're going to need someone to ride herd on him while you do what you've got to do. Plus," George said with a wily tone, "I've got the videos. If you want them, going with you is my price."

George pulled out his wallet, pulled a card from it, and flipped it to Alain. "Anyway, I've got one of these."

Alain looked at the card, a parody of the "Get Out of Jail Free" card from Monopoly, offering the recipient an opportunity to "Get out of Hell Free."

"If you're going to come with me, you need to take this a lot more seriously than that," he said, dropping the card on the floor. "This isn't a camping trip with the boy scouts. This isn't Afghanistan."

"Of course not," George said, picking up the card from the floor and placing it in his wallet. "Afghanistan's hotter."

Alain scowled.

* * * *

In Alain's basement, six people had gathered. There were Alain and George, three of the other four party crashers from earlier in the evening, all of them vampires, and one additional vampire who had been singing at a small club in Soho during the festivities.

Alain and George both wore large hiking backpacks, each well provisioned with sleeping bags, food, water, some clean clothing, ammunition, two guns (an AR-15 in 5.56 NATO and a Glock 19 for George, a pair of well-cared-for Browning Hi-Powers for Alain), rope, climbing equipment, a hand grenade, a brick of C4 plastic explosive, and 3 detonators.

The farewells had been said before the chanting began. The incense was now lit. Using a brush and chicken blood obtained about fifteen minutes earlier from a sympathetic kosher butcher who kept odd hours, Alain re-constructed the circle and symbols Vinnie had painted on the wall. "Bright Angel," he shouted, raising his arms, "accept our offering and open a way so that we may deliver it unto you."

As the circle began to fill with light, two of the vampires grabbed George's arms. "Sorry George," one of them whispered, "we can't let you go."

The two vampires were Avery and his wife, Marina. If Alain and Marie hadn't taken George in, Avery and Marina would have. He knew they were holding him because they loved him. He also knew Alain gave them the idea.

The circle was nearly complete. George bit down on a pill he'd been hiding between his cheek and gum, a gram of pure garlic extract. He mixed it with his saliva, looked at Marina with an understanding look in his eyes, making his raspberry (a.k.a. a Bronx-cheer) take her by surprise as his garlic-tainted saliva sprayed out.

George quickly turned his head, spraying Avery. Garlic wasn't particularly harmful to vampires, but at that concentration, it stung like bejeezus if it got in your eyes. Avery and Marina released George's arms, wiping their eyes. George took off.

Considering the amount of weight coming at him with a running start, even as short as it was, Alain knew he wouldn't be able to deflect it enough to stop George from going through the portal. Either he could step aside and let George go through alone, or he could stand in front of the portal, let George tackle him, and tumble through the portal together.

He took the latter choice a split-second before George made contact. The two of them went falling through the glowing hole of light, and instants after their feet passed through, the portal was gone, leaving Avery and Marina wiping their faces as the other two attendees began cleaning the wall.

Chapter 12: Rollin' on The River

Checking his watch, Kurt saw that he'd only been walking for about ten minutes, even if it felt like an hour. He used the rising slope of the cavern's roof to guide him and he was still in the forest. Thankfully, there had been no sign of "Robe Guy"; no sound of a twig breaking nearby or Robe Guy yelling in the distance. In fact, it had been eerily silent. There were no bird noises. He'd seen no insects. It was as if the VapoRub trees were the only living things in the forest, save for him.

After another fifteen minutes of hiking, the forest came to an abrupt end, bordered by a grassy strip about 50 yards across, leading down to a rocky riverbank. The bulk of the river was shrouded in fog about 20 feet high that tracked the curve of the river. It ran away to both sides as far as he could see, following the curve of the cavern wall. The forest did too. It was like they'd been planned.

Directly in front of him, there was the fog, then empty air as the cavern's roof rose higher and higher, blurring in the far distance miles away. At what seemed to be the center of the roof, a giant jet of red flame shot down through a bank of clouds like the exhaust of a larger rocket than Kurt had ever seen. It was the light source for the cavern, and it burned almost as bright as the sun.

It was hot too. Kurt hadn't noticed the heat when he first fell into the cavern, but it had to be in the low 80s at least. He was tired, sweaty, and thirsty, even with his jacket tied around his waist.

He walked down toward the river. He'd get a drink from it and then follow it along until he came to a place where he could cross, perhaps even find some sign of habitation. Any sign of life would be nice, actually. It felt like he was the only living soul for miles.

As he reached the bank of the river, the idea of drinking from it became less attractive. He had no idea where he was and river water wasn't necessarily all that safe. With only the printouts in his backpack or those six-pointed leaves to serve as emergency toilet paper, he really didn't need to pick up a case of the trots. Still, if the water was cool, he could splash some on his head and neck.

He knelt down on one of the rocks and was lowering his hand toward the water when he heard a motor out on the river. He couldn't locate its source in the fog, but the noise was unmistakable. It was a boat. "Hey," he shouted, standing up and waving his hands. "Hey! Over here!"

Slowly the sound grew nearer, coming out of the dense fog, gradually turning into a canopied flat-bottom boat with a driver and no passengers. Kurt stood on the bank, waving his arm and watching the boat approach.

As the boat neared within a few feet, the boatman, a scraggly and dirty looking man in a robe, cut the engine and threw a rope. Kurt caught it and pulled, towing the boat into shore. As the old tires on the side of the boat bounced against the rocks, Kurt jumped into the rear. The boatman's back was to him and Kurt could see rips and patches on his robe as a hank of dirty, matted hair fell down from his head to just under his shoulders, looking more like a group of hair slabs than like individual strands. "Fare for crossing is one coin," the man said, turning in his seat to face Kurt.

As he saw Kurt, the man's jaw dropped, showing the five or so teeth in his mouth, and his dull eyes went wide. "Bouncin' Beelzebub," he whispered, "you're alive."

Kurt reached into his pocket, jingling the change. "Sure, I'm alive. Why shouldn't I be..." His look shifted to one of amusement. "Have I been on the news? Did they say those girls killed me?"

Kurt pulled a quarter out of his pocket and dropped it in the man's hand, looking at him expectantly, waiting for an answer.

The man's face was riddled with tiny scars, as if he'd had horrendous acne or a bad case of the Chicken Pox as a kid, and they had to be pretty bad to be visible underneath the layers of grime. There was a large boil under his left eye and the three hairs growing out of the mole on his right cheek looked like they might be longer than the scraggly beard that grew along his jaw. A slimy tongue dropped out of the man's mouth and wiped saliva across his lower lip. "No," he said.

Kurt laughed. The guy had to be pulling his leg. "Then why are you surprised I'm alive? Did you hear about that fight?"

The man's jaw slowly rose, closing his mouth as the tongue flicked out to wet his lips again. "You don't have any idea where you are, do you?"

"Not really," Kurt said cautiously.

The man licked his lips again. "What religion are you?"

"Why?"

"So I can name it with the name you use."

Kurt shrugged. "I was raised Jewish, but I'm sort of agnostic... guess I'm more spiritual than religious..." Kurt paused as the man looked at him impatiently. "Just tell me all the names."

The man shoved the quarter into the pocket of his robe. "Well, some called it Abaddon, Gehenna, Sheol, Hades... But most people nowadays just call it Hell."

Kurt stepped to the side of the boat and looked up, staring at the fire shooting down from the cavern's roof. "Your name's Charon," he said slowly, just above a whisper, as he looked at the flames and remembered a college mythology class, "the ferryman."

"Now you know where you are. Still want to cross?"

Kurt looked toward the cavern wall. "Is there a way out back there?"

"There used to be a tunnel, but the Greeks kept coming down and trying to rescue people, so they closed it off. The only way out is to go all the way through."

Kurt sat down slowly on the hard wood bench. He looked at his hands, turning them in front of him. "And I'm not dead?"

"No. Doesn't seem so."

Kurt sat in stony silence, his eyes unfocused. "Look," Charon said, "I've got a business to run. Are you crossing or not?"

"Might as well, I guess."

Charon kicked the engine into gear and began the slow trek into the fog.

The first touch of the fog on Kurt's skin wasn't cool. It was cold, close to freezing, and though they moved slowly through it, he could hear the wind scream past his ears as if they were racing. He couldn't think. He could barely breathe, the fog burning his throat with its chill each time he inhaled. He looked out into the fog, watching it swirl around him, blown by the same wind he heard but couldn't feel, just as the fog was cold but not wet. The eddies of the fog made patterns, and sometimes it would seem as if a swirl gaped open in the center, a hole appearing in it, issuing out the wind's mournful wail.

His jacket was quickly untied from his waist, put on, zipped up, and he put his hands over his ears, both for warmth and to block out the shriek of the wind. It was the saddest sound he'd ever heard, like a mother crying over her dead child, and it nearly broke his heart. Between the chill and that wind, Kurt just wanted to curl up into a fetal position on the floor of the boat, trying to preserve both his body heat and his sanity.

As the boat found its way out of the mist, the wind's wail fell behind them, the air warmed, and the whiteness turned to pink, then orange, then they moved into the open air. Kurt felt like he'd stepped out of a freezer and into an oven, the difference was so marked. But it was a relief. The shore ahead was a gently sloping dirt bank, another grassy meadow beyond it. And beyond that, signs of life... Kurt shook his head. They were signs of habitation. Signs of life would be too much to hope for.

"How do you stand that noise?"

"Oh," Charon said nonchalantly, "you get used to it."

Kurt shuddered. The human mind had a capacity for adaptation that let it get used to some pretty awful stuff, but getting used to that... Still, Charon was pretty much created for the job as far as Kurt knew. It's not like he got the job off Craigslist. Now there was a thought: "hades craigslist > men seeking women: ROLLIN' ON THE RIVER. I'm looking for a lady who likes seamen. JK. LOL."

He wasn't sure whether to laugh or cringe at that one, though the word "inappropriate" blinked on and off in his mind's eye. Kurt was tossed out of his mental amusement park when Charon cut the motor ten feet from shore, poling them in to the soft bank. "Far side," Charon said, smiling, his hand out for a tip as they nudged up against the shore.

Kurt stood and looked at the hand. The palm was as dirty as the rest of the man. He reached into his pocket and grabbed whatever coins were left, reaching out to drop them into it, and stopped. "No," he said, putting the coins back in his pocket, "I might need these for a return trip."

A sound came from Charon; a chuckle building slowly into a guffaw and then into a laugh. The laugh grew into a roar and he had to grip one of the poles holding up the tattered canopy to steady himself. Kurt leapt out of the boat onto the bank, making sure not to splash into the water, and walked away, Charon still in stitches behind him.

Chapter 13: Curiouser and Curiouser

Kurt headed up the bank, crossing the grass and coming to the edge of what seemed to be a town. The grass cut off at a crisp line and a packed dirt road stretched forward from it, wooden sidewalks bordering the road on both sides as it ran off into the distance.

Kurt hadn't looked at the grass much on the other side of the bank, but as he was about to leave it, he noticed that it was all a uniform length, like a golf course or a park. He wouldn't have been surprised if this was some genetic or magical property of the grass, yet he couldn't help thinking that there might be a lesser-known mythical figure like Charon, but who spent eternity on a riding mower.

The buildings on the main street were short, all single-story, and behind them ramshackle houses stretched as far as Kurt could see; shoddily constructed wood-plank buildings with flat roofs and almost no space between them. The main street seemed nice enough. The buildings along it were crafted with more care, the wood cleanly carpentered and cut in uniform slats, the corners of the buildings sharp. And people walked along the street, just like any other town, oblivious to his presence at their border.

Kurt walked over to the edge of one of the sidewalks and stepped onto it. The only time anyone seemed to walk in the street was to cross it and he didn't want to attract undue attention. The people ahead of him looked alive for all intents and purposes. A pallor tinged red from the ever-present flames gave them a pinkish color, almost as if they were blushing. Their clothing ranged from togas to high-necked Victorian garb, to even an Armani suit, but all of it was drab, all of it lacking the vibrancy of colors in the living world. It was whatever they were buried in, he guessed—the clothes of the dead.

He was wearing a pale golden orange shirt that his mother bought him because she said it would go great with a light-colored blue jean. Compared to the dull colors, it stood out like a flashing light. Even though it had to be over 80 degrees, he untied his jacket from around his waist and put it on, zipping it up to the neck to hide his shirt.

He kept his head down as he walked, glancing sideways into the windows of the buildings he passed. There was no glass in the windows, though it probably didn't matter in a place where there were no bugs and the weather probably didn't vary much. There was a library, a barber shop, a yoga studio, a storefront revival church, and a room where a group of people were playing Simon Says. The other storefronts contained a couple of tables and chairs each. One had card games going on, while people played board games in another, and a few rooms were unused.

Ten buildings up, the sidewalk cut off as he passed through an intersection only eight feet wide, giving him a chance to look down the narrow street into the mass of shacks, the term "shanty town" coming to mind. While the construction of the various shacks seemed haphazard, he could see streets crossing the one he looked down. Best he could tell, the disorderly squats were built on an orderly grid. "Curiouser and curiouser," he mumbled to himself.

Stepping up onto the other side of the intersection, he heard a voice shouting. It was female, young, and as he strained to hear what she was saying he realized it was one word being repeated over and over again. "Alive!"

Looking up from his feet he saw the girl, perhaps fifteen, another block down, pointing at him. "Alive! Alive," she shouted. Other people on the street began to notice, each pausing in their strolls or shopping to look where she was pointing, and as they noticed him, they began to approach.

Kurt twirled around. Behind him, people came out of the buildings. A group was forming and closing in around him. He backed off the walkway and down the side street as the people began to fill up the bottleneck between the buildings. They didn't seem particularly angry or excited, more curious than anything. Still, he was getting a serious zombie movie vibe he could not ignore. As the crowd grew bigger and closer, the urge to flee became more intense.

It didn't take long for the urge to become an imperative. Kurt turned and ran, the shouts of "Alive! Alive!" following behind him.

People came out of the doors of the shacks in front of him, clogging his path. Spotting another narrow intersection up ahead, Kurt slowed and whipped to his left around the corner, speeding up again as he got onto the straight road. More people had joined in the cry. "Alive! Alive!" voices called. Kurt sped around the next corner, turning right this time.

His heart pounded in his chest and the sweat ran down from his brow, but the sounds of the following mob were dwindling behind him. He turned at random, trying to make his trail hard to follow. Though his lungs burned from the running, he forced himself to pound onward, eventually slowing to a jog and then a brisk walk when his feet hurt and his breath became difficult to catch. Moving randomly through the warren of shacks, he put more distance between himself and the mob, and when he couldn't even hear a faint whisper of their voices, he finally allowed himself to stop.

There was no sidewalk on these dirt streets, but the house to his left had couple of feet of paving stones running along the front. Kurt sat down on the stones, slipping off his backpack before leaning his back against the wall of the shack with a thud, panting. He set the backpack down and unzipped his jacket, tearing it off, then unbuttoned his shirt almost to the waist. He gripped the lapels of his shirt and flapped it, forcing air to circulate around his sweat-drenched torso.

He wanted to throw up, could feel the bile rising in his throat, but held it down. Slowly he opened the backpack and pulled out his bottle of water, doing his best not to guzzle from it for fear that too much too fast would just all come back up.

After a while he settled down, his breathing slowing to nearly normal. He'd drunk about half of the water. He closed bottle and put it back in his pack. He had an urge to get out another cigarette, but after that run, he decided against it.

Kurt jumped to his feet as he heard a door open behind him, the backpack held by its strap in his hand, ready to be swung. The man who stood in the doorway was older, around his fifties or so, with a short beard and long curly hair, a tunic covering his body. Kurt stared at him, contemplating whether or not to run. The man stared back.

"You're alive," the man said, looking from Kurt's eyes to his sneakers and then back again. His posture loosened and he chuckled as if relieved. "You're alive."

"Yeah," Kurt said warily, still ready to run at the first signs of trouble, his hand tightening on the strap of the backpack.

The man looked down the street in both directions and then waved Kurt toward him. "Come in. We must get you out of the street before anyone else sees you."

Kurt stepped forward tentatively, trying to explore the man's eyes. He didn't know what he'd find, though. In living people, the eyes were the window to the soul. By all reasoning, this man was a soul, so what his eyes became a window to Kurt could only imagine. He seemed genuine enough. Kurt walked in quickly, letting the man shut the door behind them.

The house was small. The main room in which Kurt stood was perhaps ten by ten feet, curtains covering a doorway on the side. In the center sat a rough table of boards and posts with some similarly constructed chairs. "My name is Corynysus," the man said behind him.

Kurt turned, shouldering his pack. "Kurt Gray," he said, extending a hand. He'd done it out of reflex, but before he could withdraw it Corynysus had taken it in a firm grip. He was solid. Kurt didn't know what he'd expected. He'd never given that much thought to the manifestation of souls in Hell, but all the literature had portrayed them as specters, insubstantial wraiths. Corynysus, though, had substance, even mass. But it was lifeless mass. The hand, though solid, didn't seem to have bones, at least none Kurt could feel. It was more like rubber, somewhat hardened, or a stiff clay. The best possible comparison would be shaking the hand of a mannequin... and having it shake back.

"It is a pleasure to meet you, Kurtgray," Corynysus said, pronouncing Kurt's name all as one word. "I have been here so long that life was becoming like an old dream I was not sure I had ever dreamed. It is wonderful to be reminded that it really happened."

Corynysus was smiling broadly, his face lighting up so much that it was hard to reconcile the smile with the man's state and where he was. "Lyatea," Corynysus called, "come out and meet our guest, Kurtgray... from the world."

From behind the curtain a woman came out. She was short, slightly under five feet, but Corynysus was no giant either. Maybe it was just them, maybe the time they lived. Kurt recalled having read somewhere that the human race, due to better nutrition overall, was getting taller as the years passed. Corynysus turned, smiling proudly, to beckon Lyatea over to meet Kurt. She came to stand next to Corynysus and he put an arm around her, beaming proudly at Kurt.

"This is my wife, Lyatea," Corynysus said. "We were married 25 summers during life, but I passed before she did. When she passed, she spent hundreds of waking periods seeking me out in this maze. A better wife and greater love no man could seek in life or death."

Kurt's hand twitched forward before falling to rest at his side. He bowed rather than feel her hand in his. It wasn't that it disgusted him in a nauseating sense, it just gave him what could best be called the heebie-jeebies. "Thank you for having me in your home."

Corynysus waved Kurt to a chair and bid him to sit. Once Kurt did, Corynysus sat too, Lyatea standing behind Corynysus's chair. "Are you comfortable?"

"Yes, thank you," Kurt said. "If it wouldn't be too much of an imposition, though, would you have any water?"

Corynysus frowned deeply and Kurt feared he'd been too presumptuous. "I'm sorry," Kurt apologized. "I didn't mean to..."

Corynysus looked down and raised a hand. "No, no, no. There is no need to apologize." Corynysus raised his head and there was a genuine expression of sadness on it. "It is my shame not to be able to offer you, my guest, the full hospitality of my home. But I would be a worse host if I did. The food of this world is not for persons still of yours."

Kurt's eyes widened. "Is it poison," he asked, thinking of what might have happened if he'd had a drink from the Acheron, remembering suddenly that the rivers in the underworld were even dangerous to the touch.

"If it was only that," Corynysus said. "A man may enter Hades' realm, but if he eats its food or drinks its waters, he may never leave."

Kurt shuddered at this revelation. All the edible food and drinkable water he knew of in this whole damned place were in his backpack. And that was lunch, not provisions for what might be a long stay. "Holy shit," Kurt said. "Pardon my French." He should have remembered the tale of Persephone from mythology class. "You've been a great host. You saved me from making what could have been a terrible mistake."

Corynysus smiled and Lyatea behind him beamed, apparently proud of the compliment Kurt had paid to her husband. "Perhaps we can trade stories," Corynysus suggested. "It would be a way of showing friendship and I must admit that I am very curious about how you came here."

"That would be great, but..." Something had been nagging at Kurt and he felt like he would burst if he didn't ask about it. "How are you speaking English?"

"I'm not. We just all seem to speak the same language here. Some think it has to do with the Tower of Babel. In that story from the Jewish holy books, once men all spoke the same language, but the Lord of Creation scattered them and changed their languages because they became proud and tried to build a tower to reach Heaven.

"It is thought, perhaps, all those languages were a function of the flesh and once we became spirit we returned to the one original language."

Kurt considered the explanation. "Okay, but I'm flesh. How come we understand each other?"

"Perhaps the Tower of Babel concept is wrong. Perhaps it is an enchantment. Or perhaps there is some part of you that always spoke the one language and has awoken upon hearing it. I cannot say. Would you like to trade stories now?"

Kurt nodded.

Corynysus began the exchange, claiming it would be rude to let himself satisfy his curiosity first. He was a sandal maker from a village about three days' walk from Athens. How long ago he'd lived he could not remember. Corynysus had lived an uneventful life, and he believed that was the reason why he'd come to this place. He had not been hero enough to go to the Elysian Fields and rest in glory, nor had he been wicked enough to be punished. Instead he lived out a meager existence much like he had in the world. Lyatea sat and listened, sometimes nodding. She never spoke.

Kurt in turn related an abridged tale of how he'd arrived, leaving out the details of how he'd first struck out with Jennifer at the club and how he'd been a bit zonked when Robe Guy knocked him through the portal.

They talked longer, Kurt telling Corynysus about "The World," about technological advances and world politics, though it turned out Corynysus had heard much of it from new arrivals. When Kurt started yawning, though... He tried to control it, but it was hard to hide.

"You are tired," Corynysus said. "We have a bed in the other room."

Corynysus stood and Kurt followed him through the other curtain, grabbing his backpack off the corner of the chair where he'd hung it. The bedroom was smaller than the main room, containing little more than the bed, a small table, and a window that looked onto the wall of another shack less than a foot away. "It is not much," Corynysus said, waving his hand at the bed, "but it is all I can offer."

Kurt extended his hand and Corynysus shook it. "I really appreciate your generosity," Kurt said, smiling, the odd feel of Corynysus' hand in his not quite the disturbing shock it had been before.

Corynysus smiled in return. "Thank you. May you sleep peacefully and wake restored."

"Thank you," Kurt said. He watched as Corynysus left the room and let the curtain fall closed behind him. The bed was small and the mattress thin, but it didn't matter. He set his backpack on the floor, took off his boots, lay down, and was asleep within seconds.

* * * *

Kurt hadn't checked his watch before he fell asleep, but he was sure he'd slept at least ten hours. Waking slowly, he stretched his arms and legs, glad for having had the opportunity to rest. He'd been so fatigued the night before.

"Good morning," a voice said.

Kurt recognized the voice only vaguely. It was as if it had been in a dream of his, one which didn't bring back pleasant sensations. He'd dreamed of going to Hell, he remembered. Dreamed of being chased and ancient Greeks living in a shack. "Good morning," he replied in kind, turning on his side as he opened his eyes to look at the owner of the voice.

Seated in a chair not three feet from his bed was Robe Guy. "Sleep well," he asked, his voice patronizing, saccharine sweet. He'd lost the robe, and now looked like someone out of a Levis Dockers commercial, a pair of slightly wrinkled khakis and dark blue, cotton shirt covering his muscular frame.

"Shit," was all Kurt could say.

"Glad to see you too," Robe Guy said, standing. "You weren't easy to find. I had to sniff around this slum for hours."

Kurt sat up slowly so as not to make any wrong moves, and swung his legs over the side of the bed. "Sorry to put you to so much trouble," he said, rubbing his eyes. "Next time I'll leave a trail of breadcrumbs." As soon as he said it, he knew it was snide, but the fear was gone. What could the guy do to Kurt that was worse than the situation he was in now?

"You're a prince," Robe Guy said. "Clean yourself up, put on your shoes. You've got ten minutes. There's a piss pot in the corner if you need it." He turned to leave, and in the back of his shirt, Kurt could see a hole with a bloodstain around it where the knife had gone in... and come out.

Kurt waited until the guy was out of the room to use the bucket. Shaking off and zipping up, he scanned the room, trying to find an escape route. The window was very close to the next shack. Kurt would be lucky to be able to squeeze between them sideways. He sat down on the bed and quickly put on his boots, then he opened his pack and pulled out the sandwich and the bottle of water.

Not being sure how long he'd be in Hell, he needed to conserve his food. He ate half the sandwich, enough to kill the growling in his stomach, and he drank just enough water to wash it down without being too greedy. It left about a cup and a half in the bottle, which wouldn't last him very long. The human body needed three or four times that much liquid every day. He'd die of dehydration before he'd die of hunger, and then what? Would his soul go wherever it was supposed to go or would it be trapped in Hell? Was Hell the place it was supposed to go? Would he chicken out as death approached and drink the local water?

He put his stuff back in his pack and threw it over his shoulder. He'd have to go along for now, but escape would be on his mind, both from his current situation and from Hell itself. Kurt had meant to ask Corynysus if he knew a way out, but in the course of their chat he'd forgotten and now it didn't look like there'd be a chance. He was going to have to hope his captor knew the way out and was headed in that direction.

Robe Guy sat at the table as Kurt came through the curtain, Corynysus and Lyatea cowering by the door. "Ready to go," he asked, standing.

Kurt nodded, then turned to Corynysus. "Sorry." He wasn't sure, but he thought that Corynysus nodded to him, giving him absolution. At least he hoped that Corynysus could forgive him for leading this intruder to his home.

Robe Guy walked to the door and opened it, waving Kurt out. "Come on," he said, grabbing Kurt's arm and pulling him away. Kurt looked back at Corynysus and Lyatea's doorway and saw them peek out. Lyatea waved farewell, then Robe Guy dragged Kurt around a corner, and they were gone.

Robe Guy released Kurt a few minutes later when it became apparent that Kurt would follow without protest. They walked along the closest main street, following it toward the center of the cavern. If one of the souls noticed that Kurt was alive, they didn't make a big deal of it this time, crossing the street to avoid the vampire, who would snarl at anyone even remotely in their way.

Other than the snarling, they walked in silence for hours, keeping a moderate pace. Kurt looked around, trying to find an escape route, but each block was like the next, each intersection leading into a warren of shacks. The light never changed, the flames in the center of the cavern's roof a constant and unwavering source. And eventually, in the distance, an end to the main street appeared. It wasn't another meadow. It was a straight drop-off, a cliff leading out into space.

Kurt's feet hurt, as did his shins. His boots were advertised as being for walking, but still the miles they covered were more than his unconditioned city-living body was prepared for. He was sure his feet were blistered and he wanted to sit down and rest a moment, but Robe Guy seemed unwavering in his purpose. "You ever been here before," Kurt asked, breaking the long silence, the cliff looming a few hundred yards away.

"Once," Robe Guy said, "years ago, during the war. But I didn't get to see the sights."

"So how do you know where you're going?"

"All roads lead to Pandaemonium. We just follow them toward the center until we reach it."

"What's Pandaemonium?"

"Shut up."

Kurt did as he was told, walking silently, until they reached the end of the road. The last building, the sidewalk, the street all ended mere inches from the edge. A thin sliver of dirt and rock separated them from the open air. At the edge, Kurt could see down into the center. It was somewhat like Dante had described; concentric circles leading down, though Kurt could only really see the next, the rest blocked from his sight by patches of clouds and the pure distance. The next one down seemed to be at least a mile below, the tops of what appeared to be skyscrapers looking like pinpoints on a map, and he couldn't locate a stairway or elevator or ladder leading down.

"What's your name, kid," Robe Guy asked.

"Kurt. What's yours?"

"Vinnie. Ummm... Kurt?"

"Yeah?"

"Have a nice trip!"

Vinnie shoved Kurt over the edge of the cliff.

Chapter 14: Tracking the Prey

"Bouncing Beelzebub," Charon whispered, "you're alive."

"Yeah?" George dropped his pack on the floor of the boat. "So?"

"Pardon my friend," Alain said, distracting Charon. "He's not the most polite individual." He gave George a glare that caused George to lower his head, leaving Alain to deal with the boatman. "Have you seen any other living people recently," he asked, dropping a roll of quarters into Charon's hand.

Charon looked at the roll, whistled appreciatively, and pocketed it. "Yeah. I took one across nine degrees downriver... 'bout 5 hours ago."

"Was he with anyone? An undead person like myself, perhaps?"

Charon kicked the motor into gear, turning the boat away from the rocks and toward the fog. "No, he was alone. Got a vampire in the boat, crossin' about the same place he did right now."

"Right now," George said incredulously, "but you're here. That's physically impossible."

"Do you have any idea where you are," Charon asked.

George shut up and Alain sat down as Charon headed toward the fog.

Alain was relieved. Kurt had escaped Vinnie and had a five-hour head start on him. He and George had come out a fortieth of the way around the first circle from where Kurt had crossed. From his research, that would put Kurt about twenty-seven miles downriver. It would take him a few hours to make that kind of distance on his own, a day with George tagging along. He'd have to hope that Kurt had enough wits about him to find a place to lay low.

* * * *

Rather than risk the trouble involved with walking into the town, Alain and George headed down the riverbank in the direction Charon had pointed. As there was no day or night, Alain told George to just call stops when he needed a rest. Alain too would need a rest... eventually. He wasn't a machine, but he could go farther than George.

It had been a couple of years since George had served, but he was humping it like he was born to carry a pack. In five hours, they made 13 miles, which was a brisk pace considering that George was carrying a pack that weighed about a third as much as he did. Of course, some of that weight was redistributed every time they stopped for a drink, and some of it was left behind every time they had a latrine break.

At that 13-mile point, Alain called a halt for a meal break and some power napping. George had napped in the afternoon so he'd be 100% for the ceremony, and Alain had slept all day. But after the brawling, the running, the planning, the packing, and now eight hours of hiking, he could see that George had fumes in the gas tank. Two hours to eat and nap would make sure that George was at least functional for another few hours.

George slowly lowered himself to the ground. Alain opened one of the packs and pulled out a bottle of water, a Gatorade packet, and one of George's special field bars that were basically a serving of a paste of smooth peanut butter, salt, sugar, dried milk powder, and Irish sea moss powder stuffed inside a sugar cookie shell. They delivered 600 easily digestible calories, electrolytes, and vitamins in a small package. George had created them for his monthly camping trips because he said normal sports bars always left him feeling hungry.

"Thanks," George said, opening the bottle of water and dumping the Gatorade powder in. They'd packed a dozen 700 milliliter bottles each, nearly a third of their pack weight being water. A person normally needed around a liter a day, but with the amount of exercise they were getting, George was going to need closer to three. At that pace, they'd go through their water in six days, five if Alain used any for himself.

Alain didn't sweat, meaning he just needed enough water to help break down and wash out the food he ate, plus a little to prevent cotton mouth and general dryness. Maybe a bottle a day. He didn't need to eat, though. He got no benefit from it in terms of sustenance and power. But eating remained a comfort thing for Alain, even after all this time. His taste buds still functioned, perhaps even more acutely than before, and Marie had been such a good cook.

George finished his bar, and what he didn't drink from the bottle he poured into his canteen. Alain handed him the sleeping mat and George lay down on the grass, resting his head on it. He was asleep quickly, his breathing and heartbeat slowing.

Those were the only sounds Alain heard. As close as the town was, no sound carried down the hill from it and no one came out to investigate. Alain didn't suspect any trouble from it anyway. If Dante had been correct, the residents were good people; virtuous souls who hadn't had the opportunity to pledge their faith to God, or hadn't chosen to do so.

Alain had a hard time believing that. The bible had only arrived in some parts of the world recently. It just seemed unfair to be expected to play by rules you hadn't been told. A just God wouldn't condemn good people to Hell, would He? On the other hand, what was just about being made a vampire against your will?

Generally, Alain tried to believe in the "no one can know what's in the mind of God" philosophy: God was just and loving, and what Alain perceived to be unfair was just the part of God's plan that he couldn't understand. He had to believe that God made it all right in the end, that God did care, that God did love him. If he didn't believe that, this whole adventure was pointless.

He pulled out his wallet. The older pictures of Marie, back when they'd newly come to the states, were in an album in a self-storage unit, protected against the elements, against the tattering that would come from carrying them around, but he had more recent ones. The one he looked at was from the '60s and he'd laminated it to preserve it.

She was 41 in the picture, as beautiful as the day he'd fallen in love with her. He saw the beginnings of grey in her hair, only the slightest sagging in her cheeks, the beginnings of smile lines around her mouth and eyes. Every smile line represented ten thousand laughs and he felt like he could remember each one. Every one of her signs of age was earned from living — while he remained unchanged.

The last two Thanksgivings had been tough. It was her favorite American holiday and she laid down a spread every year that drew friends from miles around. Even at 85 you couldn't keep her out of the kitchen. After she died, everyone got together at Alain's and tried to throw a Thanksgiving party to make her proud, but it just wasn't the same. The next year they tried again. Most of them were so used to having Thanksgiving together, they still wanted to, which in a way was a tribute to Marie and the friends she had gathered close.

For Alain, he knew what was missing. The thing he was most thankful for was gone. Maybe it was silly, even sappy, but the song "Who Wants to Live Forever" from the Highlander soundtrack made him cry tearless sobs every time he heard it.

Alain shook his head. He was only making himself morose. He had a lot of things to do before he could even get to Heaven, and then he'd have quite a time getting permission to stay. He put the picture back in his wallet and put the wallet away. With the original plan, he'd have needed to be very lucky to succeed, but now with George and Kurt complicating things, the odds against his success multiplied by a thousand. He'd just do his best and hope it was enough. It was all he had.

* * * *

Alain woke George after 90 minutes and George made a few adjustments to his pack as they got ready to head out again. "Have you got a bead on Kurt yet," George asked.

Alain tried to sense Kurt. His human friends had loved playing hide and seek with him. Perhaps it was like throwing a ball for a dog, letting the tame vampire hone hunting skills he'd never need to use. But he'd become good at tracking people, sensing them. Of all the vampires he knew or knew of, he was the best tracker on either coast.

He stilled his breathing and opened himself up, trying to pick up any sense of a human nearby. George was like a huge, honking blip on his radar, but he was the only one. "No. We're still too far."

George unstrapped the AR-15 from his pack and held the shoulder strap in his teeth as he slung the pack onto his shoulders. He unfolded the stock, checked the sights, chambered a round, and flipped the selector to "safe" before slinging it over his shoulder for easy access.

"You're not going to need that gun," Alain said. "We shouldn't encounter anything dangerous on this level."

"You never know," George said, patting the AR-15, "and this thing packs a nice wallop. If I only knock 'em back a few steps it could mean the difference between getting away and getting dead."

Alain nodded. "You've got a point. But fire as a last resort only. Treat these folks like civilians."

"I gotcha."

* * * *

They'd been walking for about three hours when Alain got his first sense of Kurt. "He's on the move," he said, putting out an arm and stopping George.

"Where?"

Alain closed his eyes, expanding his senses, searching for the prey he sensed nearby, the beating heart like a sonar blip that smelled like a human. "He's near the edge. He's not moving as fast as we are, but he's got a good lead on us."

George took off running, but instead of running along the edge of the town, he headed straight for the closest main street. Alain started after him. "Where are you going," Alain shouted, speeding up to come even with George.

"We're not going to catch him in the first ring," George shouted, "and if we go toward his street, we're just running two legs of a triangle.

When we hit the edge, we'll be closer than if we followed his route and we can start moving sideways again once we're in the second ring."

"Lead on," Alain said, shifting his pack, preparing for the long jog ahead of him.

* * * *

"So," George said, peering down over the edge, no means of transport in sight, "how do we get down?"

"According to Phil, we jump," Alain replied, standing behind him, securing the AR-15 onto the pack.

George looked down again, estimating the drop to be at least a mile if not a little more, his stomach registering more than a touch of queasiness at the thought. "You're shitting me."

"Nope," Alain said, pulling the strap tight, tying it off, then pulling on the rifle to test his knot. "After you."

George felt the backpack press against him with Alain's weight behind it and then he was tumbling forward through space, beginning a mile-long dive toward the floor of the second ring.

Chapter 15: The Winds of Passion

Kurt expected to plummet, have the wind rush by his ears as he accelerated at 32 feet per second — a figure every freshman in Bonehead Physics had to memorize — until he reached terminal velocity, a speed at which he would continue falling until the ground or some other large object got in his way.

But it didn't happen. He was sort of floating down. This was terminal velocity, and it was no faster than a brisk walk.

Looking up he saw Vinnie, about 20 feet above him, go from a flat repose on the air into a dive, speeding up his fall to come even with Kurt then somersaulting over to come out lying flat on his back again, falling alongside Kurt at the same velocity. "The only way to fly," Vinnie said, spreading his arms out to his side.

"Wha... How... How is this possible," Kurt yelled.

"Physics, dumbass."

"No," Kurt said, realizing he didn't need to yell as the wind noise was negligible. "Physics says we'd fall much faster."

Vinnie chuckled, turning a lazy barrel roll. "Ya ain't in Kansas anymore, Dorothy. They play by different rules here."

Kurt winced. Where did he think he was? Another planet, another galaxy? The afterlife wasn't just another location somewhere in normal space. It wasn't natural. It was supernatural, as in beyond natural. He felt foolish. He felt insulted. But most of all, he felt relieved. He wasn't going to die; at least not yet.

Kurt began to relax as the fall continued, realizing that it would take a few minutes before he could expect the ground to get even reasonably close. When the tops of the buildings had come within a few hundred feet, Vinnie soared over to him, grabbing his arm. "We'll land there," Vinnie said, pointing at the roof of one of the skyscrapers. The roof was empty as far as Kurt could see, just a blank square with one small rectangle jutting up out of it.

As the roof closed to within a hundred or so feet, Vinnie yanked Kurt's arm, turning them both to a standing position. "Land with your knees bent," he warned.

The roof grew closer and Kurt bent his knees, bracing for a jarring impact. But as he landed, his knees cushioning the blow, it was barely harder than jumping off a table. "Welcome to the Second Ring Interdimensional Airport," Vinnie said, his voice high pitched and slightly effeminate. "The local temperature is hot and the local time is who cares. Thank you for flying Rinaldi Airlines. We hope you enjoy your stay in the second ring of Hell." Vinnie let go of Kurt's arm as he laughed.

"You crack yourself up, don't you," Kurt said petulantly.

Vinnie responded by ceasing his laughter and slapping Kurt in the back of the head... hard. Kurt stumbled forward and Vinnie aided him in his momentum with a boot in the rear. "Elevator's that way, Guido."

Kurt stumbled further, his balance thrown off worse by Vinnie's kick. Falling to his hands and knees to prevent himself from tumbling over, blood rushed to his face. As he stood, he shucked off his backpack and dropped it on the roof. Kurt turned to face Vinnie. "Go fuck yourself," he said, clenching his teeth and squeezing his hands into fists.

Vinnie cocked his head curiously. "What did you say?"

"You heard me."

Vinnie walked toward Kurt, an odd smile on his face. "Son, you're in a heap of trouble."

As Vinnie approached, he reached out to grab Kurt. Kurt figured that with Vinnie's apparent strength, it would be futile to try to knock his arm out of the way, so he came up with another idea. Lashing out with his foot, Kurt caught Vinnie squarely in the crotch and then danced back. Vinnie reacted as predicted, doubling over, a boot in the balls being more effective than a knife in the back. Kurt stepped in and sent a hard kick toward Vinnie's jaw, his toe stopping an inch from target as Vinnie's left hand wrapped around his right ankle.

Vinnie straightened up, yanking Kurt off his feet, catching Kurt's left foot in his other hand as Kurt went ass-over-elbows, his back slamming into the rooftop. Vinnie yanked Kurt's legs open wide, placing one foot in Kurt's groin and applying pressure.

"I gotta keep you alive until we get to Pandaemonium," Vinnie said, snarling, showing his fangs. "I gotta keep you in one piece. But I can get creative with pain."

He stretched Kurt's legs open wider, applying more pressure against Kurt's crotch. Tears formed in Kurt's eyes, but he only grunted. He just gritted his teeth and shut his eyes tight, doing his best to endure, hoping it would be over soon. Vinnie ground his foot against Kurt, causing new waves of pain to shoot out, and then let go, throwing Kurt's feet to the ground and stepping back. "Do we have an understanding?"

With his legs free, Kurt brought his knees up to his chest, rolling onto his side and curling into a fetal position, trying to weather the storm of pain that still besieged him. "I'll take that as a yes." Vinnie spit on the ground and walked away.

* * * *

Kurt wasn't sure what kind of misspent youth allowed him to identify the music blasting from the elevator's ceiling as Perez Prado's "Cherry Pink and Apple Blossom White," but the slow elevator ride was giving him a chance to reflect on it. The digital display had started off at the 216th floor, making the building enormously tall, taller than any building he'd ever been in, and was clocking off a floor about every five seconds in the slow descent. At the 180th floor it stopped and a damned soul got on. Unlike the souls in the first ring, this one was naked. He stood staring straight ahead and paid no attention to Kurt and Vinnie. A few floors later the elevator stopped again and a woman got on, also naked.

The bare bodies made Kurt think of his own. An icepack would have been very pleasant right about now, but there was an old cliche about a snowball's chances...

The song ended and "Papa Loves Mambo" came on at a volume a fraction of a decibel below earsplitting. Kurt sloughed off his backpack, catching a strap in one hand, and opened the front pocket, pulling out one of his packets of ibuprofen. Putting his backpack on the floor, he tore open the packet and shook out two pills.

"What are you doing," Vinnie shouted over the music, looking back over his shoulder at Kurt.

"Painkiller," Kurt shouted back, quickly popping them into his mouth.

"Yeah," Vinnie snickered and turned his head forward again.

Kurt grimaced, the sour taste of the pills on his tongue adding a little extra to the expression. He opened his pack and got the water out, taking just enough to swallow the pills, washing some of their sour taste away. He was tempted to pull out the half of the salami sandwich he'd left over from breakfast. His stomach was growling. But he didn't want Vinnie to know he had food with him. He poured another ounce of water into his mouth and swallowed, then quickly put the bottle back in his pack.

As the descent continued, the stops became more frequent, the elevator becoming crowded with naked souls. Some of the women were good looking, nicely proportioned, but Kurt wasn't responding down below. It wasn't necessarily that Vinnie had damaged him, at least not as far as he knew, but he'd felt that flesh when he shook Corynysus' hand. It would be like fucking a mannequin. He actually had to force himself to start thinking about other things, anything else, to keep his mind from racing forward with the connections that the thoughts of sex made: how these women would lubricate themselves, whether or not they would be warm... He shuddered and searched his mind for something, anything else to think about, oddly coming to rest on the 23rd Psalm. He didn't know why that had come to mind, but he concentrated, trying to remember it.

The Lord is my shepherd, he thought silently, *I shall not want... ummm...*

He maketh me to lie down in green pastures: he ummm, he ummm...

Yea, though I walk through the valley of the shadow of death, I will fear no evil. Kurt almost laughed aloud at the irony, biting his lip to prevent himself from making any sounds.

He couldn't remember much more, just something about dwelling in the house of the Lord forever and ever, amen. That didn't seem likely either. He searched his memory for something else to think about. This was getting depressing.

Bing. The elevator stopped again and the mass of people inside shifted, bringing them uncomfortably close to Kurt. Lowering his backpack down from his shoulder, he held it in front of his stomach, creating a protective barrier between him and them. He wondered what they had been damned for, what sins they had committed, but he wasn't about to ask. There was no conversation in the elevator anyway. The barber-shop quartet acapella "Ring of Fire" coming from the speakers in the ceiling would be enough to drown out all but the loudest shouting.

Bing again and the doors opened. The people started filing out while Kurt pressed himself back against the wall of the elevator, hoping Vinnie might just file out with them, not noticing Kurt's absence until the doors had closed again and Kurt could head back up. It was not to be, however. As the people walked out into the lobby, hundreds of others exiting from other elevators, Vinnie stood at the doors, holding them open for Kurt. "Move your ass," Vinnie said, snarling. Kurt did as he was told, throwing one of the straps of his backpack over his shoulder and exiting the elevator.

Following the throng of people out into the street, Kurt was assaulted by a strong wind. He hadn't felt a trace of it as they were falling, but this far down it was blowing heavily enough that he had to lean into it and follow Vinnie and all the others as they headed down the street toward the far edge of the ring.

The foot traffic on the street was amazing. Thousands of people entered and exited the buildings, some heading toward the ring's edge, some seeming to have come back. Those who walked toward the edge, like Kurt, leaned into the wind, occasionally getting pushed back a few steps by a strong gust. Those returning stumbled forward as the wind ushered them along.

The howling of the wind was too loud for Kurt to ask Vinnie what this was all about. He squinted his eyes, keeping a bead on Vinnie's back, and followed him down the street. Crossing the first intersection, Kurt almost fell over to the side, a strong cross wind meeting the wind blowing against him from the front, creating whirling eddies of rushing air, pushing him in one direction and then another. Kurt drove himself against it, straining to advance, each step threatening to topple him. An unfortunate soul rolled past, struggling vainly to stop, and barely missed knocking Kurt's feet out from under him.

The thought of giving himself up to the wind became more appealing with each tortured step forward, fighting against getting pushed back or to the side. He'd let the wind take him down a few blocks, then run back toward one of the buildings and hide in it. With 216 stories, they were huge and Vinnie would have a hard time finding him. Of course, he'd soon run out of food and water. Then he'd die or have to drink some of the local water, if he could find any, either of which would be disastrous.

Setting himself to the task, he kept on. His only choice was to get to Pandaemonium, find someone in charge, and plead his case. There had to be some rules. He was alive and he hadn't come voluntarily. They couldn't keep him. He was sure of it. They just couldn't.

Vinnie was waiting for him as he reached the far corner, making his way out of the cross-current. The beating of the unidirectional wind was almost a relief in comparison. Vinnie continued to wait, waving Kurt past him. As Kurt got in front, Vinnie got behind him, pushing on his back. Kurt didn't like acting as a wind break for Vinnie, but Vinnie's strength, adding to his own, made the going easier, particularly as they crossed through the intersections.

They made their way forward, fighting the wind for each foot of progress, occasionally ducking into the lobby of one of the skyscrapers for a brief respite. Even for all his bravado, Vinnie too seemed glad when they got out of the wind. During one such stop, Vinnie went off to recompose himself. Though Kurt was sure that he too looked a mess, he didn't waste the opportunity, scarfing down the half-sandwich in a few bites and stashing the bag back in his pack, wary of leaving any evidence. He drank more of the water than he should have and even squirted some into his hands, rubbing it into his wind-burned skin. He only had about two or three ounces left as he put it back in his pack. He wasn't going to make it. Judging by the width of the rings, it would take at least a day to cross each one, if not more.

Kurt sighed as he zipped up the pack and tied his bandanna around the lower half of his face, preparing to venture back into the wind again. Seven more rings meant seven more days. He'd be dead of dehydration before he got that far. He hoped God would have mercy on his soul.

* * * *

George fell about 30 feet below Alain and wished he could swoop up to take a swing at him. Even though the descent was mercifully slow and terminal velocity seemed to be about three miles an hour, he didn't like heights and he didn't like falling. As the roofs of the buildings approached, Alain yelled something to George. "What," George yelled back, attuning his ears so he could hear Alain's reply.

"Aim for the roofs," Alain yelled.

George looked down at the roofs, just more than a hundred feet below him. He was situated just about center between two of them over a wide avenue. Twisting in space, he tried to direct himself toward the one on his left. The distance closed and he grew nearer, but as it continued to dwindle, he realized that he was not going to make it. Frantically he struggled, trying to swim toward it, but it was no use. Five feet from the roof's edge, he passed it and continued falling toward the street, the side of the building slick, with no handholds he could grab and try to use for scaling his way up.

Still on an angled descent, he turned himself just in time to avoid bumping his head on a window, not thinking until he'd already bounced off that he might have tried to break it.

Looking up he saw Alain land just beyond the edge and within seconds he was diving off. In a straight dive, he sliced through the air, gaining on George until they were nearly even, twisting himself to lay flat on the air and maximize his resistance, matching George's speed. "Sorry," Alain said. "I should have told you sooner."

"We're not going that fast," George said. "Why did we need to land on the roof?"

A breeze brushed their faces, growing stronger as they fell. "That's why."

Within seconds the breeze grew into a wind. It seemed to be coming from the cliff wall, either originating off it or reflecting off it, pushing Alain and George along parallel to the avenue. "This isn't so bad," Alain shouted, the wind becoming noisy. "We'll gain some ground."

But the wind continued to grow in strength, accelerating Alain and George forward, falling on a diagonal toward the street. From this high up, he could see the edge as well. The second ring was perhaps a quarter of the width of the first, which would explain the skyscrapers, needing to house more people in less space. A large, Victorian style mansion sat at the terminus of the avenue, the drop-off just beyond it, and stretching back from its doors stood two lines of people, each at least a quarter mile long.

Still further down the wind grew stronger, pushing them faster toward the edge. They were actually over the lines of people when the wind ceased, though their forward momentum continued. Within another 50 feet, Alain began to feel a breeze pushing in the reverse direction, growing in strength as they fell. As the wind grew, it counteracted their progress until it was pushing them backward. Alain shouted to George. He knew George wouldn't be able to hear his words, but he got George's attention. Waving his hand and pointing to himself, he twisted so that he was positioned at an angle to the direction of the gusts, head up, feet down and pointed into the wind. George followed suit.

Like the flaps on the wing of a plane, the wind's force pushed them back less, but down faster. Nearing the ground, Alain could only hope that George was watching him. Twisting again, he lay flat on the air, spreading his arms out to brake himself. This increased the speed of his backward progress slightly, but slowed him vertically. When the ground was twenty feet away, he twisted once more, trying to get himself into a feet-first landing position. Unfortunately, he didn't count on the cross current. Hitting an intersection, he was twirled around, bouncing in the air, and continuing to fall as he was blown backward. There was no position he could assume that was to his advantage, so he curled into a ball and prepared for impact, getting blown out of the intersection moments before he hit the ground.

The angle caused the top of the backpack to hit first, the sleeping mat cushioning it fractionally before the frame hit, jarring Alain's shoulders and spine. Instinctively, he twisted so he lay flat on his stomach and then got up into a runner's crouch, leaning into the wind with his feet firmly planted. Slowly, getting a feel for the wind, he rose to his feet and turned around, moving back diagonally across it toward one of the buildings. Reaching the relative safety of the building's entryway, he stopped and turned back to the street.

George was stumbling toward him, limping a bit but otherwise looking none the worse for wear as the wind pushed him forward. Coming into the recess of the building's entrance, George stood up straight and pounded his chest. "Whoo," he shouted, shaking his head. "What a ride!"

Alain moved to the far end of the alcove, staring down the street without stepping into the wind. The ends of the lines were barely two hundred feet ahead, and a gap was visible between the mansion and the end of the last building on the avenue. "Let's go inside," he yelled over the wind.

Opening the door, he let George walk into the building's lobby, following him in. As the door shut, the roar and howl of the wind ceased. The lobby was still. Alain set the backpack down against the wall and closed his eyes, searching for Kurt. "He's behind us," Alain said, "about two miles back and two miles over, moving toward the edge."

"So, we can reach him," George said excitedly.

"I don't think so," Alain said. "Those crosswinds are blowing against us and trying to move forward through this wind is bad enough. I don't want to try sideways. Our best bet would be to get down to the third ring and try to intercept him there."

"We'll cut 'em off at the pass," George said eagerly.

"So to speak." Alain bent down and opened the pack. "But right now we'll eat and get some rest."

Chapter 16:

The House at the End of the Street

The lines leading toward the mansion were split by gender, women on the left side of the street, men on the right, each line feeding into the mansion through its own door. As they reached the back of the men's line, Vinnie steered Kurt around it and pushed him along until they reached the steps of the mansion where the wind suddenly and inexplicably stopped.

Vinnie came around Kurt and grabbed his arm, pulling him up the stairs, cutting in front of the first soul on line in front of the door. That didn't spark any protest from the souls, but it did from inside the doorway.

The doorman was humanoid. At least Kurt could say that for it. It had two arms, two legs, and a head. But that was where the resemblance pretty much ended. It was at least eight feet tall and its head was the size of an old twenty-inch tube television. Its skin was gnarled and brown, with thick veins crisscrossing it. Two small horns jutted out from the side of its head, which sloped down from them to a boxy jaw in a sort of upside-down isosceles trapezoid.

"Where do you think you're going," it said, stepping to the side of the doorway and extending an ape-like, overlong arm across it. Its voice was deep and rumbling, like someone had attached a big block muscle car engine to its vocal chords.

Vinnie flashed it a grin, his fangs fully extended. "V.I.P.," he said.

The doorman looked at Vinnie's teeth and nodded its huge head, moving its arm out of their way. "Of course, sir. If you'll just go inside, it's the second door on your right."

Vinnie took the lead, pulling Kurt behind him as they entered the hall. It was plushly appointed, a deep crimson wallpaper setting off a dark-stained wood floor. There were brass light fixtures spaced evenly along the walls and the first door they passed looked to be a heavy oak, stained a deep auburn and impeccably clean. The only things that ruined the beauty were the screams and moans filtering down the hallway, some suggestive of sexual ecstasy, others suggesting fear and pain. Reaching the second door on the right, Vinnie grabbed the brass handle and opened it, shoving Kurt in ahead of him.

The walls and floors were wood, stained a darker shade than the doors, with a creme wallpaper rising from a chair rail up to crown moldings. There were elegant furnishings interspersed around the room and a heavy wooden bar on the far side with a brass foot rail. It was like the coolest retro bar in the coolest private club Hollywood could have dreamed up. A damned soul stood behind the bar, cleaning a glass, and Vinnie headed straight for him. "Welcome sirs," the bartender said, putting down the glass as Vinnie pushed Kurt at a stool and then took one himself. "My name's Mick. What can I get you?"

"What ya got," Vinnie asked.

"Everything," Mick said, smiling, "and all of it imported from the world."

"Nothing from here," Kurt asked, surprised.

"This is a first-class establishment, sir. Only the best. We've got peanuts from the great state of Georgia; Coors beer, brewed with crystal clear water from the Colorado Rocky Mountains; and Evian water from pure springs in France."

"Let me have a Bud," Vinnie said, his mouth widening into a grin, "long neck."

Kurt cringed, but he knew better than to comment. "Got any Coke?"

"The kind you drink or the kind you snort?"

"The kind you drink."

Mick ducked under the bar and came up with two bottles, a dark glass one for the beer and a clear plastic one for the soda. He popped the cap off Vinnie's first, then twisted the plastic top off Kurt's. "Enjoy, gentlemen," he said, placing the bottles in front of them, then setting glasses down next to them.

Vinnie picked up his bottle and began drinking greedily, but Kurt looked at his cautiously. CA REDEMPTION VALUE, a copyright notice, even a 1-800 number for product information. Everything looked legit, and if it wasn't, he could plead deception... if a plea would even be possible. He wasn't sure what was going on, though he'd grown used to that recently. The bottle was mercifully cold and he raised it to his lips. With the first sip he relaxed. A Coke had never tasted better in his whole life. Satisfied that it wasn't going to kill him and not caring whether or not it would damn him, Kurt guzzled it, putting the empty bottle on the bar and accompanying it with a loud belch.

Vinnie finished his beer around the same time and set the bottle down on the counter. "Buddy," he said, motioning Mick over, "what you got that's imported?"

"Everything's imported, sir."

Vinnie belched at Mick. "What's not American?"

Mick started ticking off a list of beers from memory. He was about fifteen names into the list when Vinnie interrupted. "Fuck it," Vinnie shouted. "Just gimme another Bud."

"Another Coke for you sir," Mick asked Kurt.

"Sure," Kurt replied, his mouth watering at the thought. "And you said those peanuts were from Georgia?"

Mick bent below the bar again and lifted a large bag of shelled, roasted peanuts onto it. "Right out of the bag, sir." Mick poured some peanuts into a bowl and set it in front of Kurt.

Kurt sighed. He knew exactly where he was, but for the moment the bar was Heaven. Mick placed the drinks in front of the duo just as Kurt tentatively bit into a peanut. It was salty. It was oily. It was delicious. "So, when are the women getting here," Vinnie asked, breaking Kurt's train of thought.

"I've buzzed for them, sir," Mick replied. "They should be in any moment now."

Picking up his Coke, Kurt looked around the room, noticing things he hadn't picked up on when they entered. The couches were a deep burgundy leather and erotic art hung on the walls in old-master style. It dawned on him that this bar was in a house of ill repute.

As if he'd said the secret word, a door at the far end of the room opened and a group of women entered in a single file line. They were beautiful. Each wore some sort of revealing lingerie, perfectly designed to show just enough to tantalize and nothing more. There were about fifteen of them; tall ones, short ones, thin ones, full-figured ones, Caucasian, Asian, Black... you name it. It was like a cross section of the most beautiful women from around the world.

"Your preference, sir," Mick asked.

Vinnie scanned the line, his hand on his chin as if in deep contemplation. "Seventh from the end," he said, indicating a short, Mediterranean type. She had olive skin, long black hair, and beautiful dark eyes.

"Serena," Mick called. She stepped out of line and the remaining girls filed back out of the door as she came to stand in front of Vinnie.

Vinnie looked her over again. "Nice," he said, "but a couple of inches taller and a little bigger in the tits and ass."

Kurt's jaw dropped as Serena's body began to stretch and reshape itself, the breasts and rear swelling, her legs and torso elongating. Vinnie looked her over as the changes stopped. "Perfect." He turned to Mick. "You got any rope?"

Serena stepped forward and ran a hand over Vinnie's chest. "Oooh," she said, her voice sultry, "you're kinky. I like that."

Vinnie reached around and patted her ass as Mick reached under the bar again and came up with a coil of rope. "It's not for you, darlin'," Vinnie said, taking the rope from Mick with his other hand. "It's for him."

Kurt closed his mouth and gulped as Vinnie yanked him off the bar stool. A leather recliner sat in the corner of the room and Vinnie threw Kurt into it, pushing the back down and bringing up the padded footrest, laying Kurt out on it. With speed and skill, he wound the rope around Kurt's chest and tied it off. Then biting it with his teeth, he severed a length which he used to tie Kurt's ankles to the footrest.

Tied to the chair, Kurt could only stare at Vinnie, his mouth open in shock. "Yeehaw," Vinnie said, winking at him. Vinnie turned and walked back to Serena, putting an arm around her, then escorted her out through the far door.

Kurt turned his head to look at Mick, behind the bar. "What the hell was that thing?"

"Serena," Mick laughed, "she's a succubus."

"What is this place," Kurt moaned, turning to look up at the ceiling.

Mick laughed again. "You're pulling my leg. You come strolling into the VIP lounge with your vampire buddy and you're telling me you don't know where you are?"

"He's not my buddy," Kurt said, wondering if the guy noticed he'd been hogtied to the chair. "I'm his prisoner."

"You're not kidding, are you?"

Kurt turned his head to look at Mick again. "No."

Twenty minutes later Kurt had told Mick his story and got the scoop on where he was. The second ring was for the lustful; adulterers, people who'd been promiscuous, sexual hedonists, etcetera. Each day they had to brave the "winds of passion" and walk down the street to the house at the end of their avenue where they were forced to engage in the most excruciatingly painful sex acts imaginable, things even masochists wouldn't enjoy. The succubae who serviced the men and the incubi who serviced the women molded themselves into the most disgusting, horrific, and distorted shapes imaginable, adding to the horror of the experience.

Besides telling his story and getting the information, he'd been able to convince Mick to put a few bottles of water, a couple of cokes, a few candy bars, and some more peanuts into his backpack which sat on the floor near his stool. But now came the hard favor to convince Mick to do, untie him.

"Sorry," Mick said, "can't do that. I got a room here, a cushy job. Sure, I gotta go for servicing once a day, but I don't have to go out in the wind and if it's a girl I know, sometimes she's a little more gentle with me so it doesn't hurt as much."

"They take pity on you," Kurt asked, not able to believe that a demoness could feel an emotion.

"Nah. It's a tradeoff. I was a writer when I was alive, and trust me, if there's anything a demon likes more than messing with you, it's a good story, especially when they're in it. They're vain as all get out."

Kurt filed the fact away in his memory for future reference. "Anyway," Mick continued, "I wouldn't be doing you much of a favor if I let ya go. Your best bet of getting out of here is at Pandaemonium..." His voice dropped a notch, a hint of somber realization entering it. "That's if they don't kill you first." He paused. "And your best bet of getting there is with that vampire..."

"If he doesn't kill me first," Kurt said, finishing the sentence for him. Mick nodded.

"Hello, Mickey," a sultry feminine voice said as the far door opened, a succubus entering the room. She was tall, near six feet, blonde, and had curves in all the right places, her lingerie showing them off perfectly. If Kurt didn't know her nature, she'd be extremely appealing. But knowing what she was made Kurt feel a touch of nausea.

"Hey Lil," Mick said, busying himself behind the bar.

Halfway to the bar, Lil stopped, turning toward Kurt. "What have we here," she asked.

"Don't mess with him, Lil," Mick warned.

Lil turned her head 180 degrees on her neck. "Don't presume to tell me what to do, barkeep," she hissed. "Remember your place."

Mick looked down at the glass he was cleaning and polished it with a new fervor as Lil turned her head back to Kurt. "Are you mortal," she cooed, looking him over. "Oh, how delicious."

Walking over to the recliner, she sat on its arm and ran a hand through Kurt's hair. "You're so cute," she said, licking her lips. "I could just eat you up."

Kurt struggled against the ropes; afraid she might mean the last comment literally. Her hands caught his head, stopping its motion as she looked down at him. "Oh," she said, chiding him, "don't be such a naughty boy. Give momma a kiss."

As she lowered her face toward his, Kurt shuddered, part in fear, part in anger, part in disgust, but he couldn't stop her and her lips pressed against his, warm and flesh-like, her tongue pushing between his lips. He clenched his teeth to keep it from getting inside his mouth, but she just ran it over them.

As she released him from the kiss, he spit. "Such a spirited boy," she said, releasing his head. "Let's see what kind of six-gun this cowboy is packing."

Standing up from the arm of the chair, she stepped to the side and bent over his crotch, delicately unbuttoning his pants and lowering the zipper. He tried to move his hips to shake her hands away, but ceased when he heard her squeal with glee as if his gyrations were exciting her.

With a yank, she pulled his pants and underwear down to his knees. He was limp, the fear and revulsion keeping him from becoming aroused by her, something which did not escape her notice. "Let's see if we can make this soldier salute," she said, licking her lips.

Placing her hand on his chest, she ran it down along his shirt, her fingernails scratching softly, reaching his penis and beginning to slowly stroke it. Her head followed her hand as she took a light grip on his penis

119

lifting it up to circle the head with her tongue. "Ooh," she giggled, "looks like we're getting some results."

Kurt couldn't deny it. As much as he wished it was otherwise, he was beginning to get hard. He tried thinking of baseball, the cafeteria lady with the hairnet and perpetual sneer, even sumo wrestlers. Nothing worked against the effect of Lil's mouth on his stiffening prick. It was warm, soft, wet... As much as he hated to admit it, it was the best blowjob he'd ever had (not that he had many for comparison) and he almost regretted not being able to enjoy it, having to try to fight against it. But the fight was futile. Lil stepped away, his penis standing at full attention.

"That's a good little private," she said as she removed her lingerie.

Kurt hated this and closed his eyes. He kept them closed as he felt Lil step up onto the seat, swinging one leg over him, and grasp his penis as she lowered herself onto it. Her vagina was like her mouth--warm, moist--and just as talented. Kurt tried to think of baseball, sumo wrestlers, but it was no help.

Suddenly, as she began her upstroke, Kurt felt weak. It wasn't a sexual euphoria or wave of pleasure. As she'd moved up, she pulled something out of him. Kurt opened his eyes and stared up at her face. The beautiful facade was gone and in its place was something... It was like her face had been made out of wax and someone had heated it, melting the features until they ran into one another, the drippings collecting on her breastbone, leaving stringy trails down from her chin. She moved down and then up again, drawing more out of Kurt.

He turned his head toward the bar. Mick was pretending to arrange the bottles at the back of the bar, though Kurt knew Mick could see them in the mirror. "Mick," he called, "help me."

Mick paused a moment, but then started back to his task. "Mick," Kurt called again. "Please."

Mick turned around, approaching the bar, placing his hands on it. "Keep out of this, barkeep," Lil hissed, turning her hideous head toward him, the strands between her chin and chest stretching with the movement. "Don't worry," she said to Kurt, her head snapping back to look at him, "it'll all be over soon. When you come... you go." A laugh issued forth from the gaping hole where her mouth used to be, the misshapen tongue inside wiggling in concert with the sound.

Another downstroke and then up. He felt the next bit of his strength flee. "She's killing me, Mick," he pleaded, his voice now no louder than an emphatic whisper.

Mick lowered one hand under the bar, but made no other move. "Don't," Lil said, her head turning toward him. Mick raised his other hand in a gesture of submission and Lil turned back to the task at hand.

Another drop, another rise. Kurt felt too weak to move his head and it lolled to the side, staring emptily at Mick. He couldn't tell what Mick was doing, but it looked like he was staring at himself in the mirror, talking quietly to himself. Then, as if he'd made up his mind, he turned. Steeling himself, Mick placed his hands on the bar, one of them holding a large knife, and he leapt over.

Lil reached out for him, her arm stretching across the room straight for his throat. Mick paused in his approach, catching her wrist in one hand, the fingers stretching to grab him. Raising the knife, he brought it down on her forearm, slicing through it like butter. The hand dropped to the ground, still and lifeless, and the remainder of her arm snapped back to her like elastic. Mick launched himself into a run as she screamed and put up her other arm to defend herself, leaping as he got close to the recliner, catching her across the chest. The impact knocked her off Kurt and carried both Lil and Mick over the other side of the chair.

The moment she was off of him, Kurt could feel his strength flooding back. He could hear her screaming and Mick grunting, but couldn't see anything. The scream was quickly cut off and all he could hear was Mick grunting. Moments later, Mick was standing at his side, cutting the ropes that bound him to the chair. "I'm gonna catch Hell for this," Mick said, a wan smile on his face.

The ropes around his torso cut, Mick set about to freeing Kurt's feet as Kurt shifted himself to look over the side of the chair. Lil was in pieces on the floor, her head the only part of her left reasonably intact. She stared up at him, her tongue wiggling, her contorted lips moving as if she were trying to say something, but without lungs to provide breath, there was no speech.

With a final snapping sound, Kurt felt the ropes around his feet release. He quickly got up from the chair, pulling up his pants as he backed away. As he zipped up, he stared at the recliner. He'd almost had the life fucked out of him and the perpetrator of the deed lay in pieces on the other side. He shuddered, opening his mouth as he felt the soda he'd drank and peanuts he'd eaten beginning to come back up.

"Hey," Mick said, grabbing his arms and shaking him. "You've got to go."

Kurt came back to reality. "Uh, yeah," he said, running over to the bar stool and grabbing his backpack. "What's the best way out?"

Mick pointed to the door through which Lil had come in. "Go through there, stay to your right and follow it all the way back. There's a door at the end that leads out to a verandah right on the edge. Hop the railing and you're gold."

Kurt walked toward Mick, stopping a foot away, and clasped his arm. "I wish I could repay you..."

"You can," Mick said eagerly. Stepping back, breaking Kurt's hold on his arm, Mick raised the knife and swept it down, slicing through his left pinky, severing it just below the middle knuckle. He winced in pain as he picked it up off the floor and offered it to Kurt. "Take this with you," he said, his voice strained.

"Mick," Kurt protested, grimacing in sympathetic pain.

"I'm betting you can get out of this place," Mick said, forcing the severed digit into Kurt's hand, "and if a piece of me can get out of here with you, maybe the rest of me can follow." Kurt closed his hand around the piece of Mick's pinky. "Now go," Mick shouted, putting his hand in his armpit and bending over from the pain. "Go!"

Kurt shoved the finger into his jeans pocket and ran for the door, opening it and running down the hallway. There was no time to look back.

Chapter 17: Who's a Good Boy

Alain and George stood by the cliff face, staring up. "You're sure he's gonna come down here," George asked.

"He's near the edge, right above us. If he's going to jump off, this is as good a place as any."

George was carrying the rifle again. They hadn't slept on the second ring, only taking an hour and change to get some food and let their muscles rest. They needed to sleep, or at least George did, but they weren't going to be caught napping when Kurt came down with Vinnie.

They continued to stare up expectantly as Alain extended his senses upward, keeping a lock on Kurt's heartbeat that served as their homing beacon.

"He's moving," Alain said. "He's coming down."

"Where," George asked, peering up at the empty sky.

"Right here."

* * * *

Kurt lay on his back as he fell, staring up at the edge of the cliff, waiting for Vinnie to notice that he was gone and come leaping after him, but there was no Vinnie so far. Whatever he was doing was taking a while.

Kurt tried to will himself to relax, but he couldn't. Until he was out of this place, until he was safe at home in his apartment with a shotgun under the bed and a stake under his pillow, he wasn't going to be able to relax, constantly looking over his shoulder, waiting for Vinnie to catch up with him.

It wasn't until he was so far from the top that he wouldn't be able to spot the speck of Vinnie diving after him that he dared to look down. Below him he saw two figures looking up, waiting for him.

"Shit," he cursed. "Shit!"

Spreading his arms out to his sides he tried to angle his descent, sweeping to the right, but the fall was slow and his horizontal movement was similarly laggard, the entities under him merely walking along, tracking him as he fell. The temptation to give up, to just lay flat and fall into their arms was strong. He was tired; tired of fighting, tired of struggling, tired of being scared. But he couldn't let himself be caught now. After what he'd been through, he couldn't let it all have been in vain. Twisting, he steered himself into a standing position, falling feet-first toward the ring's floor, his knees bent, his hands clenched into fists. They wouldn't take him without a fight.

Hitting the ground, he took the impact with his knees and leapt to standing, fists in front of him, turning to take on the welcoming party. Before he could act, one of them had their arms around him from behind, pinning his arms against his sides as his attacker whirled him around and set him down in front of the other...

"You," Kurt yelled, trying to kick out at George. "I should have known you were involved."

"Whoa, whoa," George cautioned, stepping back, his left hand up and open, the right hand pointing the rifle in the air. "We're the good guys."

Alain let go of Kurt and stepped back. Though Kurt direly wanted to lash out and hit the guy in front of him, his previous fight with Vinnie led him to believe it might not be such a bright idea to go picking another fight until he was sure what he was getting into. "You were there... when I was pushed here..." Kurt was confused as to the exact sequence of events, but he remembered George quite clearly and the statements, albeit fuzzy, came out in an accusative tone.

Alain spoke up from behind Kurt. "If you'd listened to George and got out when he told you, you'd be a little cold, but you'd still be in New York. Without us... you'd be dead now."

Bits of the previous night came back to him. George untying him, telling him to get out. It was hazy, but he could remember that much. "What's your name," Kurt asked, turning to Alain. Alain told him, sounding it out like "Uh-lawn."

Kurt looked him over. Though not as bulky as George, the man seemed to pack a decent amount of muscle on his frame. He looked to be about Kurt's age, a few years younger than George. His black hair was short, but reasonably stylish. Not a guy you'd want to meet in dark alley, but he seemed to be trying to convey friendliness at the moment.

"And you're both vampires?"

"I am," Alain said. "George isn't." Alain looked up at the ring edge above them. "We have to get moving."

Kurt looked up too. He couldn't see Vinnie, but he knew Vinnie would be coming after him eventually. "Yeah," he said, looking back at Alain.

"George," Alain said, "you take point. I'll take flank. Kurt's in the middle."

George moved into formation. "Gotcha."

"Hold it," Kurt said, waving a hand and shaking his head as he stepped out of formation. "You guys go that way. I'll take off on my own."

"What," George asked.

"You were there when I was pushed here. Now you're here. And you," he said, turning and pointing at Alain, "are a vampire. Do the math."

"You really think you're going to be safer on your own than with us," Alain asked.

"You bet your..." Kurt was interrupted by a tap on his shoulder from behind. He turned and found himself face-to-face with Alain. "What the..." He looked back over his shoulder at where Alain had just been a split second earlier.

"I," Alain said, "am one of the less dangerous things you'll encounter in Hell." Alain pulled a pistol from his belt and placed it in Kurt's hand. "If this'll make you feel safer."

Kurt hefted the pistol, feeling its weight. "How do I know this thing is loaded?"

Alain pointed at a tree about 20 feet away. "Shoot it. Just remember to flick off the safety."

Kurt looked at the gun. He had no idea where the safety was. He'd never even fired a gun before. But he wasn't about to say so. "Just flip that down with your thumb," Alain said, pointing at a small lever on the side, near the hammer.

"I know where the safety is," Kurt said angrily. Flipping it, he turned, took aim at the tree and fired... hitting another tree, a bit left of it, about twenty feet farther away. He could tell George and Alain were trying not to laugh at him.

Kurt knew when to admit defeat. "Okay," he said, handing the gun back to Alain. "We stick together."

* * * *

Vinnie stood facing the bar. With his left hand, he applied pressure to the back of Mick's neck, pressing Mick's face against the bar's surface. In his other hand, he held a telephone receiver.

"So, what do I do now?"

The voice on the other end of the line was so scratchy it made Vinnie's ear itch. "Wait where you are. We'll send an extraction team."

"But what about the punk?"

"He is not your concern. Be ready to leave in 90 minutes."

"I wanna..."

"90 minutes," the voice said. There was a click and the line went dead.

He put down the receiver, then tightened his grip on Mick's neck and shoved him back over the bar, Mick tumbling to the floor behind it. Vinnie turned his back to the bar, leaning against it, supported on his elbows, as he looked around the room.

Lil's hacked-up body was in the chair, roughly pieced together and slowly melting back into a whole. She winked at Vinnie and wiggled her tongue, following it with a come-hither nod that was more like a convulsive jerk. Vinnie shuddered. Then again, he did have 90 minutes to kill.

"Bartender," he shouted. "You got anything stronger than beer back there?"

* * * *

They followed the edge of the ring wall for a mile before cutting inward, making random course adjustments, trying not to give Vinnie or any other pursuers a straight path to follow. During the walk, Kurt told Alain and George the story of what had happened to him since being thrown through the portal.

The third ring was a forest of more of those VapoRub trees, but in a less precise pattern and less uniform in their sizes, VapoRub ferns and brambles providing random ground cover. Volcanos, about 150 meters high and 300 meters wide, poked up out of the forest at regular intervals, demons ringing their edges and throwing things inside, their hoots of glee mixing with the screams of the damned. Nearing one of the volcanoes, George halted. "You two stay here," he said in a quiet voice. "I'm gonna do some recon."

"George," Alain called after him, his voice quiet but harsh. It was too late, though. George was gone.

Taking shelter under a tree, Alain put his pack down. "You might as well get some sack time," he said to Kurt. "I'll stand watch."

Sitting down, setting his own pack aside, Kurt was still uneasy about falling asleep around these guys. So far, they'd done nothing suspicious, but he couldn't trust them completely. Where they'd been, where they were. Normal, decent people weren't to be found in these places; not voluntarily anyway. Taking the rolled sleeping mat Alain

129

handed him, he placed it under his head and lay down, trying to keep his eyes open and be on alert.

Within sixty seconds, he was asleep.

* * * *

A white light pierced his eyelids, waking him. Kurt opened them slowly, finding he was laying on a street in the middle of a city. He stood up, rubbing his eyes, and looked around. The city was empty, not a single person in sight. The buildings rose up around him, most seven or eight stories tall, all in white concrete with gleaming mirrored windows. There were no signs on any of them and the bottom floors sat empty, their interiors devoid of furniture or fixtures. The trees in front of them, spaced evenly along the sidewalk, were green, thankfully, but no birds sang in them, no bees buzzed around the flowers at their bases.

"Hello," Kurt shouted, his voice echoing along the corridor of buildings.

"Hello yourself," a voice said behind him.

Kurt whirled to face the owner of the voice. A hundred feet away, leaning lackadaisically against one of the buildings stood a man in a brown sports coat and slacks, sporting a white turtleneck. As he approached, Kurt could see that he was in his fifties, thinning brown hair on top of his head, and he had the beginnings of a drinker's nose.

"Where am I," Kurt asked.

"Ever heard of nowhere," the man asked, stopping a few feet away.

"Yeah."

The man put his hands in his pants pockets. "That's where you are."

Kurt made a tsk'ing sound, scrunching up his face. "Nowhere's a concept, not a place."

"Yeah," the man said, smiling. "That's what you used to think about Hell, wasn't it?"

The man pulled one hand out of a pocket and started walking toward the sidewalk, motioning for Kurt to follow him. Kurt did, watching him warily, taking a seat on the sidewalk a few feet from where the man sat down. "Everyone ends up here eventually," the man said, waving his hand around in an arc. "Some people come here a lot. Ever heard of a guy who runs everywhere but gets nowhere?"

"Uh huh."

"This is where he ends up, most times in the middle. But as soon as he realizes that he's nowhere, he knows where he is. Then he's somewhere and he's not here anymore."

"That doesn't make sense."

"Not supposed to," the man said, putting a finger on his temple. "In the mind, location is always subjective. Like Disneyland. If you're of the right mind, you really are at the 'Happiest Place on Earth.' If, on the other hand, you're a miserable son of a bitch... you're not."

"So, what does that have to do with me?"

"Nothing... and everything."

"What's that supposed to mean?"

The man stood, but Kurt remained seated, looking up at him. "That's the secret of eternity, Kurt. Everything is full of nothing. Nothing is full of everything."

"I don't understand."

"You're not supposed to... for now. Think about it too much and you'll just get..."

"Nowhere," Kurt said, finishing his sentence.

The man pointed at Kurt, winking. "You're catching on."

"So how do I get somewhere?"

The man reached down and put a hand on Kurt's shoulder. "Just wake up, Kurt." He began shaking him lightly. "Wake up."

* * * *

Kurt woke to find Alain standing over him. "George hasn't come back yet," Alain said. "I'm getting worried."

Kurt sat up and rubbed his eyes as Alain backed away. "How long have I been asleep?"

"About three hours."

Despite the short rest, Kurt felt refreshed, though hungry. Standing, he threw his pack over one shoulder. "You want to go find him?"

"Yup." Alain grabbed the mat Kurt had been using as a pillow, secured it to his own pack, and put the pack on. Wordlessly, Alain started off into the trees.

"I'll stay right here in case he comes back," Kurt called after him.

Alain kept walking. "If Vinnie finds you, tell him I said hello."

If Alain was trying to scare Kurt into following along, it worked. Alain and George may have been unknown quantities, but they were benign so far. Vinnie was malignant.

As they walked, Kurt slipped off his pack, opening it and digging out a handful of peanuts. "Want some," he asked Alain.

Alain put out his hand and Kurt dropped the peanuts into it, then got another handful for himself and ate them. Chewing, he reached in and pulled out one of the bottles of mineral water. He unscrewed the cap as Alain tossed a few peanuts into his mouth and chewed... something was wrong here. Kurt stopped dead in his tracks and swallowed.

"Wait. You eat," he said to Alain, accusatively.

Alain continued walking. "Of course I eat. You'd prefer I drank your blood?"

Kurt took a swig from his bottle of water and capped it, then caught up with Alain. "I just thought vampires have to drink blood."

"'Have to' is a subjective term," Alain said.

"Like 'The Happiest Place on Earth?'"

That stopped Alain dead in his tracks. He turned back and looked at Kurt with bewilderment, then shook his head and let it go. "Do you 'have to' smoke those cancer sticks in your backpack?"

"No," Kurt said as comprehension dawned on him. "You mean blood is an addiction, like cigarettes?"

"Right, only about a hundred times more intense."

"Wow," Kurt said. "I just always thought it was food... something you needed to survive."

Alain stopped and looked back at him. "It's a sort of Catholic thing. It's all about the motivation, the impurity of the act. If you needed it to survive, then there would be some excuse. If you just need it because you're addicted, because it feels good, then each time you kill for it, the act is just that much more wanton, that much more evil. It was designed that way... more evil in the world, more evil on your soul. You understand?"

Kurt nodded.

They walked on a while longer in silence, Kurt drinking another half-liter from his water bottle before putting it back in his pack, both watching for any trace of George. Alain sensed him up ahead, but his location was fuzzy.

"So," Kurt posed the question he'd been wanting to ask, "you're not addicted to blood anymore?"

"Does an alcoholic stop being addicted to alcohol? Does a smoker stop being addicted to tobacco?"

"A friend told me you never stop being addicted to alcohol. You just stop giving into the urge to drink. You know the next drink could kill you."

"Exactly."

"But drinking blood won't kill you."

"It would kill a part of me I want to keep alive."

"What's that?"

"Whatever's left of my soul."

* * * *

They walked a half-hour without any physical trace of George, going just on Alain's senses, when they heard a howling in the distance... then some gunfire.

"George," Alain said. They turned toward the sound, correcting their course each time a howl hit their ears. Kurt had a fleeting thought of an African American comedian talking about how white people in horror movies get killed because they go toward the sounds of people getting murdered. He considered that this might be a perfect time to take off on his own, but he didn't want to find the source of the howl alone.

When the howling seemed fairly close, they saw George come running at them, dodging around trees. "Run," he shouted, speeding toward them. Kurt looked at Alain quizzically, but Alain kept looking in George's direction as he came closer. The howl resounded again and Kurt looked back at George, seeing the source of the howling break out of the cover of the trees, following a few yards behind him.

It was a dog... sort of. It had the body of a dog, but three heads bounced in front of it, extending off of a large neck and a broad body. At its shoulder it was as tall as Kurt's navel and the tail behind it seemed to be scaly.

"Run," George shouted again.

Twice was enough for Kurt, who turned and started running back the way he'd come, looking back to see Alain, George, and the dog hot on his heels. Alain caught up with him quickly, placing a hand on his pack, pushing him forward as the beast howled behind them.

At first the push helped speed him up, but as the dog seemed to gain on them, George catching up and passing them, Alain's push became stronger, more urgent. Unfortunately, Kurt couldn't run any faster and the push overbalanced him, sending him stumbling forward, turning as he fell. He hit the ground and skidded stomach-first into a tree, stopping abruptly as his body wrapped around the trunk and the air whuffed out of him. He scrambled, turning to get up, and came face to face to face to face with the dog.

Less than a foot away, all six eyes stared at him, all six ears laying flat back against the heads, the three mouths turned up in snarls, low growls issuing from the wide throat. "Heh-heh," Kurt laughed nervously.

The dog wasn't advancing, wasn't snapping, but Kurt expected it to come soon.

Don't show fear, he thought, trying to remember everything he knew about dogs. It's probably as scared of you as you are of it... Yeah, right... Don't look it in the eyes. That's an aggressive behavior. Show it that you're not a threat, but a friend. Slowly, doing his best not to make any sudden moves, Kurt began shrugging off the backpack. He couldn't even look to see if Alain and George had stopped. He wasn't going to look the dog in the eyes, but he didn't want to turn his head either.

As the pack fell to the ground, the dog growled, one of the heads emitting a quick bark. Kurt froze, letting things settle and then slowly pulled the backpack around. As he got the backpack onto his lap, one of the heads closed its lips, turning curiously, though the ears remained set flat against its head. "Good boy," quietly, trying to sound reassuring as he got the pack in front of him, beginning to open the zipper. The sound of the zipper made the curious head snarl again, but it didn't attack.

So gradually, as if he was pulling it across one tooth at a time, Kurt opened the pack halfway. He reached in, taking painstaking care not to move too quickly, and took hold of the bag of peanuts inside, pulling it out. "See," he said as the bag crested the opening, causing all three heads to growl in unison. "Yum-yums."

He got the bag out and moved his hand forward, half closing his eyes, waiting for one of the heads to bite it, but they didn't and he turned the bag over, spilling the peanuts onto the ground.

One of the heads lunged forward and Kurt dropped the bag, jerking his hand back, holding it against his chest as he closed his eyes and cringed in terror. He heard some snarling sounds, then the crunching noises of the peanuts being eaten, and then felt the breath of one of the heads against his face as he heard the three heads sniff at various parts of his body. Its breath smelled awful, like rotten meat with a slight under-scent of peanuts. Kurt waited for the bite, feeling the breath of the other two heads arrive at his face, one on each cheek. They had his head surrounded on three sides and he pressed his head back against the tree, expecting at any moment that each mouth would begin tearing at his face.

Three tongues licked his face in unison. Slowly, he opened his eyes. The head in front of him was licking him, its ears no longer flat against its head, but relaxed. Kurt reached up and tentatively patted it. It responded by licking him again.

"Looks like you've made a new friend," he heard Alain's voice say, approaching.

All three heads snapped around in Alain's direction, growling. "No," Kurt said, scratching the middle head behind its left ear. "Friend. Friend."

The middle head looked at him as the other two continued to growl. "Friend," Kurt repeated. The other two heads stopped growling and looked at him, cocking questioningly. Kurt stopped scratching the middle head and reached out with both hands to scratch the other heads. The eyes on the two heads closed and the mouths opened, the tongues shaking as the heads panted happily and the snake-like tail wagged.

When Kurt had played with friends' dogs, he'd said stupid things to them like "you're a good dog, yes," or "what a big puppy," talking in baby talk and patronizing tones. With this monster, as dog-like as it acted, none of that felt appropriate. "Good boy," he said, his tone as normal as if he'd been saying it to Alain. The dog responded, though, the middle head nuzzling his chest as he scratched the other two.

In the distance a high-pitched whistle blew. All three heads snapped up, looking in its direction, then looked at Kurt, low whines escaping their mouths. "It's okay," Kurt said, nodding his head in approval. "Go."

The left head darted in, licking his cheek, and then the animal took off running, following the repeated whistle, barking and howling like... like a beast of Hell.

Kurt let himself fall back against the tree, going limp as all the tension bled out of him. "Whoa," George said, breathing a sigh of relief. "That was a big rub on Buddha's belly. What was that thing?"

"Cerberus," Alain said, walking forward and crouching next to Kurt. "Dante's Inferno, third ring, where the gluttonous lay beneath a hailstorm, of stones I believe, while Cerberus, the three-headed hound of Hell barks and rips them limb from limb... You okay, Kurt?"

"Yeah," Kurt said, inhaling a deep breath and exhaling slowly. "Probably need a change of underwear, though."

"Hail," George asked.

"Yes," Alain said. "I guess it's not so far from a storm with those demons throwing rocks at them."

"They're not rocks," George said, reaching into one of the voluminous pockets on his cargo pants and pulling out a round object about the size of his fist. "I found one near the base of one of the volcanoes before that thing... E Pluribus or whatever you called it... came running down the side and started chasing me. They're heavy, but they're not rocks."

He handed the object to Alain who stood and inspected it, sniffing it then breaking it apart and sniffing inside. "Hah," Alain said, chuckling. "Stale dinner rolls." He tossed a half to Kurt so he could inspect it. "Makes sense."

* * * *

138

They reached the edge without further events, even taking a few hours to rest, eat, and take turns napping. Kurt looked back at the volcanoes, hearing Cerberus howling and barking again as he ran from one to another. He wondered how much real dog was in that beast, whether there really was a "good boy" under all that snarl and scales. It was a futile thought, however. He would probably never know and continued wondering would get him nowhere. Not wanting to go nowhere again, he jumped.

Chapter 18: The Great Hero

There were shouts—challenging one another—as they fell toward the fourth ring. There were too many to make out any distinct words, but as they drew closer, they could see the almost honeycombed surface was actually composed of many arenas in which damned souls stood behind lines of cars, one car occasionally jumping out of line, pushed by a mass of souls toward the other, impacting and pushing the opposing line back, like a bizarre game of Red Rover. Some of the impacts were accompanied by cheers, possibly meaning that a car had broken through. All the impacts were accompanied by the anguished screams of souls.

The fourth ring, Alain thought, *where the avaricious and prodigal are divided into two camps and roll stones against one another.* "Steer toward the walls," Alain shouted to Kurt and George. Each arena butted up against the other and no passageways between them were obvious. If they fell into one, Alain wasn't sure they'd be able to get out.

Kurt and George followed him, angling their descent to come down along the top of one of the walls, which appeared to be 10 feet wide. Alain didn't stop for pleasantries as they landed. He moved out immediately, taking point as George ushered Kurt in behind him, then fell in behind Kurt. "Keep together, move fast, and don't fall off," Alain told them.

The roof of the cavern was now so far above them that figuring out its slope was going to be difficult. But the big red jet of flames could be seen directly ahead. All they had to do was aim for it.

As they moved along the wall, Kurt peered down into the arenas. The cars were luxury models — BMW, Lexus, Mercedes Benz — and the screams they heard came from the hapless souls who were strapped to their fenders and grilles, getting crushed as the cars crashed into the opposing lines.

Every time Kurt or George stopped to watch the cars roll, Alain came back and ushered them along. He didn't like being on top of the wall. There was no cover, making them sitting ducks, three dark spots moving along a white path. They were moving at a good clip when George called a halt. They stopped and George pointed behind them. "What in Hell is that thing?"

Approaching them was the unholy offspring of a street sweeper and a snowplow, fed growth hormones since birth. It was tipped in front with two eight-foot-tall push broom heads, angled into a flying wedge. And it was coming at them... fast.

To Kurt, its purpose was obvious. It made sure any stragglers got swept off into the arenas. He was already five feet past Alain before Alain thought to shout "run!"

Alain and George were faster than Kurt was, but this thing was faster than any of them, and Kurt knew he wouldn't win in a race of pure speed. At the very first corner, he slowed, whipped around it, and sped up again. He figured a zigzag along the arena walls was going to be the only way to slow it down, because if that thing took the corners at speed, it would flip over.

Kurt looked back and watched Alain and George speed past his corner, staying on the straightaway. Then came the horrendous contraption, turning the corner without slowing down, and coming straight for him. He poured on as much speed as he could, hearing Vinnie's voice in his head, jeering "physics, dumbass" as Kurt ran for his life.

* * * *

Alain noticed as soon as the sweeper turned the corner. He and George had sped down the straightaway specifically to lure the machine off Kurt. The math made no sense. He and George were two targets. Kurt was one. Why did the machine go after Kurt?

He didn't have time to ponder it. He stopped, shucked his pack, and took off running as fast as being a vampire would allow. Despite the urgency and panic of the situation, pushing himself this hard felt good. The more he used his power, the stronger he felt, and this was giving him an exercise high.

From behind the sweeper, he leapt up into its open-air cab. There was a readout screen showing Kurt within crosshairs, but there were manual controls too. The problem was that the machine was a few seconds from hitting Kurt and Alain didn't know what any of the controls did. Sometimes the simplest solution is the best, he thought to himself, grabbing the steering wheel and yanking it to the left.

The steering wheel was tight, the autopilot fighting his pull. Alain pulled harder, summoning every ounce of strength he had.

He felt the wheel move a fraction of an inch, but that was enough. On the straight, narrow walls, the wide sweeper's wheels began to move over the edge, just a few inches at first, but once one wheel lost contact with the concrete, the process sped up rapidly. Alain jumped clear of the machine as it fell sideways over the wall and into one of the arenas below, followed by a wild chorus of shouts.

Kurt slowed down, hearing the crash, and came back to stand next to Alain who stared at the carnage he'd caused below. Kurt reached sideways and patted Alain on the arm in an almost absentminded gesture of thanks, more of his concentration going to trying — once again — not to barf.

* * * *

"Bouncin' Beelzebub," the boatman said, "you're alive."

The remainder of the fourth ring was uneventful and the trio had reached the edge. Unwilling to wait for another sweeper to show up, they jumped quickly. Now, on the banks of the Styx — the river running through the fifth ring — they found themselves getting in another boat piloted by another boatman.

If you took Charon, fed him a couple of sandwiches, sandblasted him clean, washed and styled his lice-ridden head, and put him in a pair of canvas deck pants with a heavy wool sweater, he might look like someone this boatman had taken pity on. Phlegyas had the build of a professional wrestler and his observation that Kurt and George were alive was followed by him wrapping them up in a huge three-way bear hug, bouncing them up and down on the floor of the boat.

"Nice to see you too," Kurt said as Phlegyas released them.

"You do not understand," Phlegyas said, laughing. "The last mortal to pass this way who wasn't some sort of black mage was an Italian poet. That was centuries ago. It is so boring here. Who am I going to talk to? The burbling bastards who were so angry in their lives they ended up in this ring?"

Alain coughed, getting Phlegyas's attention. "If you don't mind, how did you know we were alive?"

Phlegyas waved a hand as if this was something everyone should know. "For the first thing, you are all the wrong color. Eh? The souls are dull and pasty. Second, how many souls have you seen with backpacks since you got here? Third, if you have a soul inside you instead of merely being a soul, you glow."

"You," he said to Alain, "not so much. You're a vampire, right?" Before Alain could reply, he was on to George.

"You," he said waving a hand at George, "more."

He turned to Kurt, spreading his arms open wide with joy. "But you! There is so much life in you! You are a great hero, right?" Phlegyas wrapped Kurt up in another bear hug and then kissed him on the head. "You have the soul of a mighty warrior!" He released Kurt and turned back to Alain and George. "You two are his servants? You carry his packs while he performs a great quest?"

"Yes," Alain said quickly, "we are his servants." George tried to contradict him, but Alain reached out and pinched George's arm, following it with the universal just play along hand gesture and eye bulge.

"Tell me," Phlegyas asked, "what is this noble quest? Do you come to rescue a comrade in arms, perhaps your lady love? There have been far too few rescues since they sealed the tunnel."

"His lady love," Alain said quickly. "If you will begin our journey across the river, I will tell it as we travel. I am his troubadour. I record his deeds so that I might someday compose an epic poem of his quest."

144

Phlegyas clapped his hands together and rubbed them with glee. "Start your tale, vampire," he said, kicking the engine into gear and guiding it out into the waters of the Styx.

* * * *

"And that is how my master defeated the evil den of thieves known as Al Qaeda."

"Magnificent," Phlegyas boomed, slapping his hand against the steering wheel. The boat bumped against something that scraped along its bottom as the boat passed over. Kurt had no need to look out the back of the boat to know they'd just run over another soul. Apparently, the newer ones weren't sunk deep enough in the mud, so they got bumped and bashed by the boat as it passed.

It was a slow boat and a wide river. George lay asleep on the bench, but the repeated bumps kept Kurt awake, plus he was finding Alain quite the entertaining storyteller. In the last story, Kurt seduced a beautiful Pakistani girl to get her to betray the whereabouts of Osama bin Ladin, then led Alain and George on a daring daylight raid that ended in the death of bin Ladin and twenty of his closest lieutenants. If you believed Alain, Kurt was a perfect gene splice of Chuck Norris and James Bond. Kurt just had to smile and play along, trying to look aloof, as if these tales of his deeds bored him.

"There's the far bank," Phlegyas announced, a hint of sadness in his voice as he swung the boat around to butt up sideways against a small, rickety dock. Alain shook George awake while Phlegyas wrapped an arm around Kurt.

"You're a hero after my own heart," Phlegyas said, thumping his chest with his free hand.

"I'm afraid Alain may have exaggerated a bit in his stories," Kurt said, sheepishly.

"Oh," Phlegyas said, leaning in conspiratorially, "you've as much killed a terrorist as I've fondled Aphrodite's breasts. But heroism is subjective."

"Like Disneyland," Kurt said.

"Exactly! In the coming days, you will be called upon to make hard decisions, my friend." Phlegyas put his hand on Kurt's chest. "Trust this hero's heart."

"Now," Phlegyas said, releasing Kurt so he could step back and address the group. "When you get to the bank, you two mortals strip, pour some of your water into the dirt, and coat yourselves in mud: feet to follicles. It'll hide your color and hide your glow. You'll need it to cross the rings between here and Pandaemonium."

"What is Pandaemonium," Kurt asked.

Phlegyas hunched in on himself like he was telling a campfire ghost story. "It is the lair of the king of Hades," he said in an almost awestruck whisper. "They say not even the palace of Caesar could match its grandeur and opulence."

"Well, thank you," Alain said, shooing Kurt and George out onto the dock. "You've been a great help and a great friend."

Alain stepped onto the dock and Phlegyas kicked the boat into gear, swinging it back out toward open water. "Remember me, my friends," Phlegyas shouted as he waved broadly. The boat dissolved into mist and it was gone.

Chapter 19: Gorgon World

They camped in a grove of VapoRub trees on the far bank of the Styx, spending nearly 12 hours sleeping, eating, and taking care of other necessities. George and Alain were generous with their food and Kurt shared from the stash of imported snacks and beverages that Mick had packed for him.

After the food and the rest, George and Kurt stripped to their underwear and made a puddle of mud with some water, rubbing a thin coat of mud on their bodies. "I never would have pictured you as a tighty whities guy," Kurt said.

"You pictured me in my underwear?"

"No, I..."

"You said you never pictured me as a tighty whities guy, so you must have pictured me some other way. Boxers? Commando?" George paused. "Were you picturing me going commando?"

"I..."

A flying dirt clod whacked George in the side of the head. "Stop screwing with him," Alain said.

George chuckled and continued applying his mud. Kurt followed, the redness in his face fading. He felt a little stupid, but he also realized George was treating him like one of the guys instead of some outsider, and that made him feel better. Even so, he'd be damned if he asked George for help spreading mud on his back.

* * * *

Kurt's clothes and boots were either in his pack or tied to it, and he held it by the strap in one hand as he fell. The mud had been thin and wet, and it had been decided he and George would air-dry on the way down rather than wait it out before jumping. Kurt hadn't been too keen on that, thinking that if demons awaited them at the base of the next cliff, he'd be trying to fight in his underwear, but he got outvoted two-to-one.

He yelled "cannonball" as he jumped off the fifth ring and fell for a while in a standing position to maximize speed and the amount of air blowing on him. As he rolled out into a prone position to get more airflow across his chest, he got his first view of the sixth ring.

The object that grabbed his attention first was small from this distance, but he could swear it was... No, he thought, rubbing his eyes and looking down at it again. Nothing had changed. It was a ferris wheel. A little to the side of that, a dot sped around a mountain, running in and out of it. A roller coaster? Kurt's mouth opened, the slight wind rushing in. They were dropping into Hell's amusement park.

As they got closer, Kurt saw a large pavilion containing three statues, each at least fifty feet tall, all on one large pedestal. They were women with snakes for hair and what looked like a multi-headed snake wrapping around each of their waists. Their hands were at their chests and their fingers dug into their breasts, the nails piercing the skin, fountains of red liquid falling and pooling below them in a pond that surrounded the pedestal's base.

Landing just outside the walls of the park, Kurt looked up to see the name of it inscribed on an arch above an entry gate. "Welcome To Gorgon World," it said. "Abandon All Hope Ye Who Enter" was written below it in smaller letters. The gate was open and no ticket taker stood guard.

"Everybody okay," Alain asked, shrugging off his pack.

Kurt moved his joints to get a quick status report from his body. Everything reported back normal. He got dressed.

Alain looked Kurt and George over once they were dressed. "Rub some dirt on your clothes. It looks weird with your skin covered in dirt and your clothes being clean."

Kurt and George did as they were told. Now they not only felt grubby, they looked it too. It wasn't too uncomfortable, though. The thin mud of the 5th ring had dried dusty instead of hard, so there was very little cracking and flaking to contend with.

Once Alain was satisfied that they looked dingy enough, he had Kurt trade packs with him. Now they were just a vampire and his damned-soul servants out for a stroll, and Alain led the way through the gate.

The entry into the park was like a museum of grotesquerie. Damned souls were arrayed in mini dioramas, tortured in all sorts of ways. There was the traditional flaming pitchfork and boiling in oil at the beginning of the walkway. Midway, a diorama featured a damned soul being rotisserie cooked, while another displayed a man with his feet pushed up behind his head, a red-hot poker repeatedly invading him through a very sensitive orifice. Closer to the end was a soul coated in honey and fire ants, and another soul lay on what looked to be a bed of nails, though the nails turned out to be lit cigarettes.

Some of the weight from Alain's pack had been shifted to George's. Still, it was damn heavy. Kurt thought the red dirt made them look more like Martians than damned souls, but as they entered the midway, the demons who pitched the games didn't give them a second look.

"Agonize the apostate of Freedonia," one of the demons shouted, waving a cane. "Three fireballs for a coin."

"Ignite an irresolute skeptic," another called. "One measly coin for a quiver of flaming arrows. Test your skill. Shoot out an eye and win a prize."

Each booth featured damned souls, their heads poking through openings in the back, macabre stuffed animals hanging on the walls. Kurt thought the demons, unlike the hulking doorman on the second ring, looked like huge versions of the evil Mogwai from Gremlins. Ridged brows topped teardrop shaped eyes with cat-like irises. Ears like bat wings extended out from the head. Spindly limbs branched out from narrow chests and ended in claws. And the whole package was covered in weather-beaten lizard skin. They were the unholy offspring of a tequila-fueled affair between a chimp and a velociraptor. Completing the unnerving effect, each demon wore a red and white striped coat and a straw hat, like an early 20th century carnival barker.

"What's going on here," Kurt whispered out of the side of his mouth.

"Sixth ring," Alain said, pausing to think. "They burn heretics here."

"Sir," a demon shouted from a booth, calling to Alain. "Sir."

"Oh shit," George said under his breath.

Alain put on a brave front, smiling at the demon as they approached. "Yes?"

"Sir," the demon said, leaning forward over the counter, a curtain hiding the back of his booth. "How'd you like to warm up a witch's day? We've got one, just newly arrived from Earth. You'd be her first. Just one coin." The demon winked knowingly.

Alain didn't want to inspire suspicion, so he pulled out a quarter and handed it to the demon. The demon lay three water balloons on the counter. "Napalm," he said, winking again. "Highest quality. Ignites on contact with air."

Alain picked up one of the balloons, seeming to test its weight as the demon went back and took hold of the curtain string to reveal some unfortunate soul. Kurt felt sadness and fear for the poor woman who looked pleadingly at Alain, his arm moving back to throw the balloon. Heaving his arm forward, the balloon hit the wall, four feet to the left of the woman's head, and bounced off unbroken, splattering on the floor and making the demon dance back as smoking trails of liquid reached for his feet.

"Oh, sir," the demon said, picking up another balloon and handing it to Alain, "that couldn't be your best, could it?"

"Sorry," Alain said, looking bashful. "I was beating my servants during the fall from the fifth circle, wasn't looking where I was going, and landed on my shoulder. It's still a little tender."

"Of course, sir," the demon said as he looked at Kurt and George. "I fully understand. Perhaps you'd like me to throw the balloon for you?"

"No," Alain said, hefting the balloon as if he were testing its weight "I'll get it this time." Alain stepped back into a baseball pitcher's stance and launched the balloon like a rocket. It hit even farther to the

151

left, near the corner of the booth, its contents splattering away from the witch and igniting a couple of the closer stuffed mutations. The demon grabbed a fire extinguisher from under the counter and rushed over, putting out the flames quickly.

"Sir," the demon panted as he returned, "I would really suggest that you let me throw the balloon for you this time." The demon put the fire extinguisher away and straightened up. "You do want a prize don't you," he asked, waving a long arm at the row of plush monstrosities.

"Are you implying I can't throw a simple balloon at a fucking witch," Alain asked angrily, picking up the balloon and holding it like he was going to throw it at the demon.

"No, no," the demon said, bowing and retreating a few steps. "I suggested nothing of the sort. It was just my concern for your shoulder. Perhaps you'd like to rest a few minutes while it finishes healing. I'll be more than glad to wait."

"No," Alain said determinedly as he turned to the side and set his jaw, squinting as he aimed. Kurt thought he was overacting, but the demon bowed and nodded some more, believing every bit.

As Alain brought his arm forward, he let the balloon go too soon, sending it high. It hit the tent's top three feet before the witch and drops of blazing liquid showered the floor as the roof caught fire. The demon grabbed his fire extinguisher and tried to put the fire out at an angle, the napalm that dripped from the tent's top making it impossible to get right below the blaze as it gradually ate a hole in the cloth. "Whoops," Alain said, adjusting the lapels of his coat and clearing his throat. "I guess you were right." He turned and waved Kurt and George forward. "Come along, you miserable pieces of shit."

"I think he's enjoying this," Kurt whispered as they walked.

"No talking," Alain said, loud and imperious, "or I shall beat you both again."

Kurt and George both pressed their mouths shut, more to keep from laughing than anything else.

* * * *

Crossing through a concert plaza about a mile out of the midway, Alain spotted a demon running toward them. Actually, it wasn't really running, more like a strange kind of limping lope. Unlike the other demons, it was fully clothed in a dark suit and it sported a set of horns, somewhat like those of a ram, but a young ram at best.

"Sir," it shouted as it ran, waving an arm over its head, pointing its index finger in the air. "Sir!"

Alain stopped, Kurt and George stopping behind him. "What is it," he asked as if annoyed, straightening his posture and standing at least half a head taller than the demon.

"Sir," the demon said in what sounded like a clipped British accent, though it was partially obscured by his panting. "I'm so sorry to bother you, but I need to speak with you about a small... ummm... fire you caused earlier." With it standing in front of them, they were able to get a better look at its clothes. The black suit was ill-fitting, covering a white shirt and a thin black tie.

"And who are you," Alain asked, looking down at him.

"Ahhh," the demon said, extending a hand, "Nybras. Executive assistant to Lord Asmodeus."

Alain looked at Nybras' hand and then back at Nybras. "What can I do for you?"

"Well, there are many matters at hand, the most pressing of which would of course be the fire. Ummm... Would you mind accompanying me to the park office? I promise... it'll only take a little bit of your time."

Alain looked at his watch and made a show of weighing the decision, stroking his chin as he scowled at Nybras. "Well, I can spare a few minutes, but make it quick."

"Of course, of course," Nybras said. "If you'll just follow me, Mister... ummm..." Nybras cocked his head.

"Stark," Alain said. "Avery Stark."

"Of course, Mister Stark. If you and your... ummm... bearers? If you'll all follow me, please."

Nybras stepped to the side, turning and waving Alain ahead, taking up position beside him as he walked deeper into the park. "If I might ask... ummm... where did you get your bearers?"

"I picked them up in the first ring," Alain said. "You don't think I'm going to carry my packs this whole way, do you?"

"Oh, no," Nybras said with an overly apologetic laugh, "but it's... it's just a rule we have here... ummm... well, it's... generally prohibited to remove condemned souls from their native rings... but, ummm... of course, exceptions can be made. If you don't mind my asking, though... ummm... Why are they red?"

"They looked too clean, so I dirtied them up a little." Alain looked straight ahead, never dignifying one of Nybras' questions enough to look at him as he answered it.

"Of... of course," Nybras said, seasoning it with another one of his laughs, "of course. Perfectly sensible. Perfectly sensible... ummm... just a little farther now."

Reaching the edge of a building, Nybras put a hand on Alain's back to guide him around the corner, eliciting a growl from Alain. Nybras quickly retracted his hand, clasping his hands behind his own back.

Ahead of them, Alain saw a golf cart, complete with the striped top. "Ummm... we can take this the rest of the way," Nybras said, stopping and waiting for Alain to get in. "Your... ummm... bearers... can run behind us if that's all right."

Alain walked around front, getting in on the passenger's side of the front bench. "I'd prefer they ride. You know how clumsy these souls are. If one of them tripped and damaged my possessions..."

"Of course, of course. Get in there you lot," Nybras shouted at Kurt and George, raising a menacing hand. "Don't dawdle. Don't dawdle."

Kurt and George scrambled into the back seat, taking off their packs and holding them between their legs. Nybras got behind the wheel and flicked a switch on the dash. "Ready, are we," he asked. "Then let's proceed."

The cart took off with a jerk, but then accelerated into a smooth glide, whizzing through the park. Nybras was quiet, apparently intent on his driving, and Alain was glad of it. He'd gotten himself into some deep shit and taken Kurt and George with him. Right now he was pulling it off, but what about when they checked on Avery? Avery was clean, not one kill. As far as Alain knew, Avery had never even tasted blood.

Alain caught himself. It was no time for memory lane. He had to set his mind on extricating himself, George, and Kurt from things present, namely this situation. He was too close, too much lay in the balance to get tripped up now.

"That's the office, up ahead there," Nybras said, interrupting his thoughts, pointing toward the giant fountain with the three gorgons. As they approached, Alain could see that there was a door in its base, a thin concrete path leading across the pool of blood to it. Nybras screeched the cart to a halt in front, causing them all to lurch forward. "And we're here."

Stepping out, Nybras waited for Alain, George, and Kurt to get out of the cart. "It's just this way please," Nybras said, walking off toward the path. Kurt gave Alain a questioning look as he slipped the backpack on, but all Alain could do was shrug. Setting himself back in his imperious composure, Alain strode forward, Kurt and George trailing him.

The blood in the pool moved thickly in small waves, falling from the wounds in the Gorgons' breasts and draining into holes in the pool's rim. A strip of concrete about five feet wide ringed the base. Reaching the door, Nybras opened it, allowing Alain into the hallway beyond, and then stepped in front of the door. "Your bearers can wait here, please," he said.

Stepping inside, Nybras shut the door, leaving Kurt and George outside without waiting for permission from Alain. "If you'll just come this way, I'm sure we can have everything taken care of shortly," he said, walking around Alain and further down the hall.

* * * *

"We're fucked," Kurt said, removing his pack and sitting down, leaning his back against the wall. George removed his pack and sat next to him.

"How many Cokes do you have left," George asked, ignoring Kurt's doom-and-gloom pronouncement.

"One, but it's in my pack and Alain's got it."

"Snickers too?"

"Yup."

"Damn." George rummaged around in his pack. "Thank Jesus and the Jeezettes," he said as he seemed to find whatever it was he was seeking.

George set his prize on the concrete between him and Kurt. Two cans of Starbucks Doubleshot Frappuccino and a bag of peanut M&Ms. He popped open a can and handed it to Kurt, then opened the bag and held it out. Kurt held out his free hand and George poured a few candies into it.

They sat there, sipping their drinks and chomping their candy. There were so many questions Kurt wanted to ask. He was curious about George, about all the things George knew about Alain, about all the things George knew about this trip, but George seemed in no mood to talk.

Kurt looked into the distance. It was frustrating to wait like this, the situation out of their hands. All they could do was wait and hope Alain pulled it off. George didn't seem too concerned. Kurt hoped it wasn't an act.

* * * *

The hallway terminated at a curved, almost bulging wall; a door in its center with a large golden A on it in an angular gothic script. The door to Nybras's office was 10 feet before it on the left side.

His office was small, but not absurdly so. A curved wall ran along the right-hand side as one entered, a door in it leading into the center office. Nybras walked to the far end, taking a seat behind an orderly desk.

"Please sit." Nybras tapped a couple of keys on a computer keyboard with one hand, waving at two chairs with the other.

Alain sat, laying his hands in his lap, trying to appear nonchalant.

"Now..." Nybras turned toward the computer, his fingers clacking away on the keys. "Stark, was it? Avery?"

"Yes."

Nybras typed a few more characters, looking intently at the screen. "Here we go... Stark, Avery. Undead inception date, July fourteenth... Ah, Bastille Day... nineteen hundred and sixty-two... in the," Nybras paused to giggle, "year of our Lord." Nybras paused again, peering at the readout on the screen. "This can't be right. It says 'kills, zero.'"

Nybras punched a few keys and squinted. "No... that's right. Zero kills." Nybras turned and looked at Alain expectantly.

This was the moment of truth. Alain realized his fate rested on how he reacted. His original thought was to leap up, shouting about how preposterous it was, but he stifled it. Liars protested vehemently. "Your computer's wrong." His voice was cool and even. He relaxed in the chair, crossing one leg over the other.

Nybras turned back to the screen, inspected it, and turned back to Alain. "It says zero kills."

Alain uncrossed his legs and sat up in the chair. "Are you accusing me of lying," he asked calmly.

"Ummm... no," Nybras said, "but..."

"Can you honestly tell me you've never received a wrong answer from a computer?"

Nybras hunched his shoulders, his fingers tapping nervously on the desk. "Well," he said, pausing and thinking, "we're in the midst of switching over from Windows to Macintosh. Apparently, Satan got an iPhone for his birthday and now he's all Mac this and I that." Nybras stifled a low growl. "Ummm... we could be having problems with the... transition, or migration, or transmigration of the data... whatever it's called."

"There's your answer," Alain said, leaning back in the chair, re-crossing his legs.

"Of course," Nybras said emphatically, banging his hand against the desk. Standing, Nybras leaned forward and bowed his head. "How silly of me. I do apologize."

Alain nodded his head and waved his hand dismissingly. "These things happen. Not your fault."

"I should say not," Nybras said, straightening his posture.

"Now," Alain said, "as to the matter of the tent I damaged."

"Oh, yes... yes... of course. Tent and stuffed novelties." Nybras sat down. "I'll only be a moment." Reaching under his desk, Nybras pulled out a large three-ring binder and started flipping through the pages. "Now you do understand, of course," he said as he scanned through the book, "ummm... we're very well off in terms of precious metals... gold, silver, that sort of thing... iron, aluminium, concrete, rocks... rocks..." Nybras looked up from the notebook, staring at the door, a look of disgust forming on his face. "Lots of rocks... piles and piles of rocks..."

"I see," Alain said, interrupting his reverie.

Nybras buried his attention in the notebook again. "Yes... umm... as I said, we're very rich in those things but..." He looked up from the book, turning his head toward Alain. "Most textiles have to be imported."

"So, I'm not going to get off this one cheap, huh?" Alain gave Nybras an amused smile.

"I'm afraid not," Nybras said. Turning back to the book, he flipped another page, drawing his finger along a column of figures, eventually stopping about three quarters of the way down. "Here we go," Nybras said, running his finger horizontally across the page. "Item sixty-six fifty-two. Carnival tent, red and white... striped." Nybras punched a few keys on his calculator, then flipped a few more pages. "Booth novelties, stuffed..." he punched in another figure, then hit the total key a couple of times.

"What's the damage?"

Nybras cringed, lowering his head between his shoulders. "One hundred and thirteen dollars... ninety-seven cents... American."

Alain had deliberately not brought his wallet. He didn't want to have any identification on him that might contradict whatever lie he told if caught. But he had brought a money clip, figuring that money might come in handy even in the afterlife. He'd loaded it with $2300 (20 hundreds, 13 twenties, and 8 fives). He peeled off a hundred and three of the fives and casually tossed them onto Nybras's desk. "Keep the change," he said.

Grabbing the bills while Alain put his clip away, Nybras took them and counted them quickly, laying them within easy reach before he pulled out another notebook. With a few quick strokes of his pen, he made some notations on one of the pages, then put the notebook back under his desk and opened his top drawer, sweeping the bills inside. "There," he said, slamming the drawer shut, "all finished."

Alain cleared his throat to get Nybras' attention. "My receipt?"

Nybras cocked his head and smiled a demonic smile. "Can't slip anything past you, can I?" He pulled a receipt book from the desk, scrawled out a receipt, tore it from the book and handed it to Alain.

Alain stood, folded the receipt, and put it in his coat pocket. "If there'll be nothing else."

"Well," Nybras said, standing, "I have an appointment at Pandaemonium early tomorrow. If you were not adverse to missing some of the... ummm... sights, you and your bearers could travel with me."

"Well," Alain said, acting as if he was considering his options. "I was looking forward to seeing the Phlegethon..." He didn't want to spend any more time with this demon than absolutely necessary.

"Yes, of course," Nybras said. "Perhaps I could at least give you a lift to the edge of the ring."

Alain couldn't think of a reason to turn him down. "You're too kind."

"I am not kind!" Nybras slammed his fist on the desk. "I was being polite, following the rules of etiquette and offering you my hospitality, and you insult me by calling me kind?!"

"I'm sorry. I didn't know."

Nybras did not seem mollified by the apology. "Politeness is done out of obligation, rules of conduct! Kindness is done out of the goodness of your heart! How dare you accuse me of having goodness in my heart? How dare you?! Get out of my office! Get out now! I have no more obligation to you!"

Alain casually buttoned his coat, took one last look around the office, and left.

Chapter 20:

And the Scales Fell from His Eyes

Unlike the clean high-rises of the second ring, the seventh was post-industrial urban squalor: large blocks of buildings blackened from burnings, clouds of smoke over parts of the ring, streets littered with trash and the burned-out husks of what appeared to be vehicles. It was essentially an urban war zone, and as they got closer, they could hear eruptions of gunfire below.

A bullet whizzed by Kurt. He wasn't sure what it was; like having a fly or an angry bee go by you at high speed. When a couple more passed, following the sound of cracks of gunfire from below, he put two and two together. "They're shooting at us," he yelled.

George had been carrying the rifle as they jumped. He wriggled around to get a bead on the shooters and returned fire, each shot moving him slightly upward in the light gravity of the fall. Rather than take cover and engage in a firefight, the shooters ran. They weren't brave defenders. They were just taking pot shots.

The group angled down toward one of the rooftops. Alain landed first, sweeping the perimeter as George and Kurt came in to land. Once all of them were down, Alain ushered them through a door into the stairwell that led up from the ground.

"Fuck," George said, seeming as if he was just catching his breath.

"Seventh ring," Alain said. "The violent."

"Wonderful," George sighed. "How do we get across this one? We going to fight our way across fifteen miles of armed turf?"

"Freeze," a voice shouted in the darkness below them. "I'll put a bullet in your damn heads."

The voice didn't seem deep enough for a man or high enough for a woman. As the gun-wielding figure approached them, it entered the shaft of light coming in from the open doorway behind them. They were at the mercy of what appeared to be a fourteen-year-old boy.

"It's a kid," George said, laughing as he relaxed. His relaxation was cut short as a loud bang resounded in the cramped stairwell and a bullet buried itself in the wall next to George's head, showering him with a spray of plaster. Kurt's ears rang and he wiggled a finger in his right ear, trying to clear the feel of the loud sound. He could see the kid shake his head as if his ears hurt too, but wasn't going to make a show of it.

"A kid with a goddamn gun," the boy said, motioning George to close ranks with Alain and Kurt. George obeyed. He and Alain held their guns at their sides, but didn't let go of them. Kurt stood behind them, a stair up.

"What's your name, son," Alain asked calmly as he took a step down the stairs.

"I ain't your son," the boy said, leveling the gun at Alain's head. "Now you got three seconds to tell me what the fuck you're doing up here before I cap you."

"We jumped down from the sixth ring," Alain said, taking another step down, putting him four steps from the boy.

"Bullshit."

"I'm going to reach into my coat." Alain moved his free hand toward his breast pocket. "I'm just getting a kerchief. Don't shoot." Pulling a white handkerchief from his coat, he reached behind himself. "One of you take this and clean yourself up a little."

Kurt stepped forward tentatively, watching the boy with the gun. The barrel was still zeroed in on Alain, but the boy's eyes were tracking motion, not his target. Taking the kerchief, Kurt spit on it and started wiping the red dirt from the fifth ring off his face.

As Kurt's cleaner skin was revealed, the boy's eyes went wide and his voice was almost reverent. "You're alive."

With the boy's attention on Kurt, Alain took advantage of the distraction to step forward and swipe the gun out of his hand. The boy put up little resistance. Disarmed and shocked, they expected him to run, but the boy composed himself. "Shit, we've gotta get you out of here. Kolya and his boys will be up any minute."

"Who's Kolya?" Alain put the boy's gun in his belt and took a more active hold of his own.

"Later," the boy said hurriedly, turning to look down the hall. "Follow me."

The kid took off down the hall, but the three paused, George and Kurt looking to Alain for their cue. Alain shrugged and took off after the boy, Kurt and George following.

The boy led them down a hall, peering down a stairwell at the end. Voices could be heard far below and they were approaching. The boy put a finger to his lips, cautioning the three men to be quiet, and then crept down the stairs, his shoulder against the far wall. Alain, George and Kurt followed, doing their best to make as little noise as possible.

Slowly, they made their way down as the approaching voices got closer. Three flights down, the boy crept out into the hallway, the men following as he went to door after door, trying the knobs until he found one that was unlocked. Standing at the open door, he motioned the men inside, indicating that they should hurry. The three hustled in and the boy followed them, shutting the door quietly behind them. Another finger to his lips signaled to them to remain quiet. The men stood in the hallway of a small, unfurnished apartment as the boy put his ear to the door.

When the boy was apparently satisfied with whatever he heard, he opened the door quietly and peered out. Holding up a hand, flat, palm out, he motioned to the men to stay as he crept into the hallway. Not sure exactly what they were up against, the men didn't find themselves feeling too scared, but whatever they were up against sure scared the boy and that was enough for them to take it seriously.

A few seconds later, the boy returned and motioned for them to follow him. The three crept into the hallway and followed the boy down ten more flights of stairs. A flight from the lobby, the boy stopped and motioned for them to stay and be quiet. Rather than creep, the boy steeled himself and sauntered down the stairs. They couldn't see what was happening, but they could hear it.

"Hey," the boy said.

An adult male answered. "Wazzup, Ty?"

"Kolya said the shipment's big this time. He wants you to get Curly and Moe to help."

"Cool."

About thirty seconds later, the boy was back up at the landing, motioning for the men to come with him. Following his lead, the three crept down the stairs, but rather than go out the lobby doors, they crossed to the side and headed down another two flights into the building's basement. The boy led them through a maze of halls and pipes, stopping about 20 feet from the end of the hall they were in, opening a door to his left and leading them inside.

Pulling a chain, he lit the bare bulb hanging from the ceiling. The room had boxes piled along the walls, leaving a small rectangle of space extending from the door. The boy went to the far wall and slid some boxes to the side, exposing a hole about three feet in diameter, and waved the men into it.

This time they didn't follow his instructions. Alain nodded toward the hole. "Where does that lead?"

"'Nother room like this." The boy waved them forward.

"And what's there?"

The boy's voice and wave grew more impatient. "'Nother hole like this."

Alain didn't budge. "Where are we going?"

"To see Albert."

"Why would we want to see Albert instead of Kolya?"

The boy's face was twisting into a mask of anxiety. "'Cos Kolya'll kill you."

"And Albert won't?"

The boy nodded his head violently. "Works for me," George said as he moved around Alain and headed for the hole. Alain looked back at Kurt, who shrugged. Alain shrugged in return. They both headed for the hole.

With the frame pack preventing him from crawling on his hands and knees, George slid in on his stomach and pulled himself forward with his elbows. Pausing at the hole, Alain reached down to the boy's gun in his belt. After inspecting it a moment, he turned back and handed it to Kurt. Kurt reached around toward his back to put the gun there, but Alain shook his head in the negative. Kurt took this to mean he should hold onto the gun. He gripped the pistol, finger on the trigger, ready for action.

Alain grabbed Kurt's hand gently and pulled his finger off the trigger, out of the trigger guard, and left it pointing forward against the side of the gun. "Always keep your trigger finger indexed. You only put your finger on the trigger when you have your target and you're ready to shoot. Gun Safety 101. Also, try not to point it at George as you crawl. Never point the gun at something you're not willing to destroy. So, keep it pointed up as you crawl... Actually, you know what, I'll take it back."

Alain stepped aside as he put the gun in his waistband with one hand and motioned Kurt into the hole with the other.

His backpack being the book-bag type rather than a frame pack, Kurt was able to crawl on his hands and knees with a couple of inches of clearance between his pack and the top of the tunnel. This allowed him to catch up to George fairly quickly as Alain followed and the boy came in after him, using ropes attached to the rears of the boxes to pull them back into place.

The tunnel extended about forty feet before George, very carefully and very slowly, slid a box aside, peering out into the room. The room was dark, so he listened, but all he could hear was Kurt's breathing behind him. Figuring it was okay, he slid the boxes aside even further, giving himself enough clearance to get out, though the pack made it rather awkward. Getting to his feet, he swung his hand around for a chain near where he thought the light would be. He pulled it, filling the room with light from the bare bulb.

The room was almost a clone of the one they'd just left, empty except for boxes. George gave an all-clear signal with his hand, motioning Kurt out of the hole.

Kurt crawled out, followed by Alain and the boy. The boy quickly pushed the boxes back into place and then went to the wall to his right, moving more boxes to expose another hole. This time there were no questions. George took point, Kurt followed, Alain came next, and the boy crawled after them.

In the next room, after the boy had moved the boxes back into place, he moved to the door and put his ear against it. Satisfied, he opened it and peered out, then motioned the men out the door. Stepping back inside, he shut off the light, came out, shut the door and then led them through another maze. Rather than go to the stairs that led to the lobby, they veered off to one side, up a short set of stairs to a steel door. The boy opened it and peeked out as the flame-light filtered in. He motioned to George to hold it open as he crept out for some recon, back a few seconds later, motioning for the men to follow him.

The door was at the bottom of a recessed stairway in an alley. The boy led them up the stairs, across the alley, down two buildings, and then down another set of stairs to a steel door. This door had a camera above it and the boy smiled at the camera. A few seconds later, they heard locks click in the door and the boy pulled it open. They followed him in and the door closed behind them.

* * * *

The basement they entered wasn't the twisting, turning maze the other basements had been. Instead, many of the walls had been knocked down, creating a large open space, albeit with supporting columns spaced around them. There also weren't any stairs leading into it. Every possible exit had a large steel door covering it.

There were tables laid out with what appeared to be weapons or security projects in varying stages of completion. Against a far wall was a desk with a computer, a few video monitors, a control panel and a heavyset, balding old man sitting in a desk chair. "Hey, Albert," the boy said.

Swiveling around, he smiled at the boy, his bushy moustache turning up with his lips, the smile standing in contrast to the nasty-looking Mac-10 automatic pistol in his lap, aimed at his visitors. "Morning, Ty. Who're your friends?"

"They're alive," was all Ty said. Albert's smile disappeared and with his free hand he put on a pair of glasses that hung from a chain around his neck.

"If you'll excuse me," he said as he stood and moved closer, the pistol still aimed at the new arrivals. "I probably don't need these anymore. Don't seem to make a difference. But my mind is convinced that I do. My back doesn't hurt anymore and the senility that plagued my last years is gone, but I still feel like I need my glasses."

Stopping about 10 feet from the group he peered at Alain and Kurt. George was still covered in red dirt, though sweating from the recent exertion had caused it to run in places. "So they are," Albert said. "Doesn't mean anything. Why are you here?"

"Long story," Alain said.

"I've got time," Albert replied. "Why don't you boys put your guns down on that table, shrug off your packs, pull up a chair and tell me all about it?"

"And what if we don't want to?" George asked.

"I'm the only one who knows how to open the doors and I've got more booby traps rigged up around here than you can find, even if you knew how to disarm them. You're not leaving until we're all friends."

* * * *

A half hour later, friendship was achieved. The story of how Kurt had entered Hell and how Alain and George came after him was told. In turn Albert had explained the seventh ring to them.

"It's not just criminals, warmongers and soldiers who enjoyed the killing a bit too much. We've got child abusers, wife beaters, rapists, people who facilitated fighting..."

"Like Don King?" Albert cocked his quizzically. George expanded. "Boxing promoter."

Albert smiled and straightened his head. "Naw, I'm talking about the political hawks, the men who'd send a few thousand boys off to die to keep the price of bananas or oil down... or the guys who employed me."

"And who would they be?" Alain asked, his voice flat and serious.

"The arms makers, arms dealers, arms designers... all of us wonderful people who made a living from coming up with new and more effective ways to kill people, then made sure they got manufactured and distributed so they could get used for their intended purpose."

George took a deep breath. "So that's why you're here?"

Albert shook his head sadly. "I wish it were that simple. Then I could feel angry with God, never accept responsibility, and shake my fist in righteous indignation. I could say I was defending my country, claim it was righteous."

He paused and removed his glasses, massaging the bridge of his nose as he looked at the floor. When he looked up, his face displayed a look of such sadness, all three men could feel it. "I beat my kids... physically, mentally... occasionally took a swing at my wife..."

Kurt didn't know what to say. For all intents and purposes, Albert seemed like a nice old guy. Up on the first ring, when he'd met Corynysus and Lyatea, even Mick on the second ring, there'd been some sense of cosmic injustice, of an unfair God. But now... "Why did you...? Didn't you know it was wrong?"

Albert shook his head and smiled a sad smile. "Told myself it was my duty to keep them in line, but mostly I was punishing them for my short temper. That's one of the few blessings you can get here if you really want it... clarity, understanding. If you're willing to let go of your rationalizations, they can get the wings you can't and fly away."

"So why were we running from people?" Kurt asked. "Why were people shooting at us?"

"If you're willing to let go of them. Most of the people here cling to their anger, their insecurities. Everything that made them bad on Earth gets worse here. It's just easier to be mad at God or someone else. You have to be willing to get desperately honest with yourself to see the truth of your own evil. And that honesty is amazingly frightening, scarier than even the Devil himself to some people.

"You know the story of Paul of Tarsus... from the Bible. He was a persecutor of early Christians following the crucifixion. On a trip to Damascus, Jesus came before him and blinded him. For three days he couldn't see, didn't eat, didn't drink. This changed Paul, and in his blindness, he saw the error of his ways and prayed for forgiveness. I'm not exactly sure how it's phrased in the Bible... 'and the scales fell from his eyes.'"

"I was never much for religion, but to me it's an allegory. Jesus took Paul's blind hatred and made it manifest as a physical affliction. Only after he let go of that hatred, was he given the ability to see again."

Albert paused as the men took in what he said. "Did you meet anyone besides Ty here before you came to me?"

They all shook their heads in the negative. "Tell them, Ty."

"Kolya's blind. So're most of the folks on this ring."

"But you're not," Kurt protested.

"He sees shapes and shadows," Albert said, "some blurred colors, little more. Hasn't let go of all of it yet. Running with Kolya doesn't help."

"Then how..."

"How did I know you were alive," Ty finished.

"Yeah."

"You glowed."

* * * *

Taking advantage of the safe haven, Alain, Kurt and George cleaned up and ate a bit of their dwindling provisions. Alain and Kurt had around the same waist size and shoe size, so he loaned Kurt a pair of boxers and some fresh socks. Albert had them pee in buckets which he covered and kept. "You'd be surprised at how many useful chemicals you can get from piss."

The trip through the sixth ring hadn't been too hard or taken too long. Their ride to the gorgon fountain in Nybras's golf cart cut 60% off the walking they had to do. Still, neither George nor Kurt refused the opportunity for a nap.

He wasn't sure how long he'd been asleep, but when Kurt woke, George was still sacked out on the cot next to him. Kurt felt reasonably refreshed, so he sat up on an elbow on the cot. Alain was over at Albert's workbench, talking with Albert. There was no sign of Ty as Kurt scanned the room.

He got up from the cot and padded over towards Alain and Albert, feeling the cement floor through his socks. Despite being in a basement, it was warm. Everything in Hell seemed to be warm.

There were no more swiveling chairs, but there was a stool at one of the tables. Kurt lifted it gingerly and set it down close to Alain and Albert with similar care. "You woke up just in time," Albert said. "Your friend here was about to tell me how he became a vampire."

"Cool," Kurt whispered. The story sounded very interesting. He was about to sit when the standard post-sleep pressure in his bladder decided to make itself known. He went over and grabbed a bucket.

"That one's George's," Albert said.

"Does it matter," Kurt asked.

"Humor me."

Kurt wasn't in a mood to argue. He lifted the top off his bucket and emptied his bladder. When he was done, he replaced the top, jogged back, and took his seat on the stool.

"You done?" Alain asked.

Kurt nodded and Alain took that as his cue.

"It was World War II," Alain started, "and I was in the army. Hitler wasn't the only one with a fascination with the occult, and the Army had captured itself a real live vampire..."

Chapter 21: I Call it a Slingshot Chair

During the telling of Alain's tale, George woke and quietly joined them. Kurt had no doubt George already knew the story and had heard it many times before, but he sat, listening with as much attention as Albert or Kurt paid.

Albert was the first willing to speak. "So, how does that story end with you being here?"

"I found out Dante wasn't just creating a flight of fancy when he wrote his *Divine Comedy*. Turns out it is possible to get to Heaven by passing through Hell and Purgatory first. I just have to pick up that piece of soul they took from me, get through Purgatory, and make my case to stay once I get to Heaven."

"And your odds of that working are..." Albert trailed off.

Alain nodded grimly. "Somewhere between slim and none. But what are my chances if I do nothing? Where do I end up if I do nothing? I end up here."

"I'm not saying you're wrong," Albert countered, "but let me play Devil's advocate for a moment." He paused and made a chuckling grimace, as if he realized he'd just made a bad joke. "So, you end up here. But if you fail, you end up here soon. If you stayed on Earth, you could put it off for decades, possibly centuries."

"No." Alain shook his head. "You're assuming I'd want those years on Earth, living alone and knowing I could never be reunited with her. Even if my chance of being with her again is one in a trillion, I'm willing to bet those years on it. If I lose, the heartbreak is the same either way."

Albert posed a counterargument. "They say if you loved once, you can love again."

"Not like this."

Kurt stood up. "'Not like this.'" He mocked Alain. "Cut the mopey emo shit. You're what, 97? This isn't 'The Princess Bride'. You're not the Dread Pirate Roberts. You're acting like a 15-year-old who thinks that their love is like no love ever before seen in the history of mankind and that no one understands it."

Albert raised his hand. "I understand it."

George raised his hand. "Me too."

Alain looked at Kurt, not with anger, but with a mixture of pity and concern. "Tell me you never looked for that love Kurt. You're a young man."

He'd looked for it. He'd been feeling discouraged. Getting kidnapped off the subway sure as Hell hadn't helped. "It's a fairy tale."

"Kurt, before you got here, didn't you believe Hell was a fairy tale?"

"Yeah but..."

"But now you know it's real. Isn't there a possibility true love is real too?"

"You're asking me to accept that true love is as real as Hell?"

"I wouldn't use those exact words... I'm not asking you to believe anything, Kurt. Just accept the possibility it's true instead of dismissing it out of hand."

Albert broke in, affecting a mock British accent. "'There's no use trying,' Alice said, 'one can't believe impossible things.'"

"'I daresay you haven't had much practice,' said the Queen of Hearts. 'When I was younger, I always did it for half an hour a day. Why, sometimes I've believed as many as six impossible things before breakfast.'"

Kurt, George, and Alain all looked at him, confused expressions on their faces. Albert chuckled. "Alice in Wonderland. I lived through the 60s and was a huge believer in the Apollo program. When people would ask me how I could believe that men could ever step foot on the moon, I'd pull out that quote."

Albert's interruption seemed to have taken the wind out of the sails of Alain and Kurt's debate. Kurt offered his hand. "I'm sorry. Just having a pity party."

Alain shook it. "It's all right."

Albert rubbed his chin in consideration before seeming to make a decision. "Let me show you something."

He walked to one of the tables and motioned to George to come over. "Help me move this."

George took one end and Albert took the other, sliding it up against its neighbor. In the concrete floor, there was a sheet of metal with holes at both ends. As Albert bent down and grabbed the sheet through one of the holes, George did the same on the other end. With small grunts on both their parts, they lifted it and slid it aside, exposing a deep hole in the floor.

"It's a tunnel," Albert said, slightly out of breath. "It leads to a man-made cave in the side of the cliff wall between this ring and the 8th. In the cave there's a... well... I call it a slingshot chair."

"What's it do?" Kurt asked.

"I found out that Dante was right too. You pick up information here and there. The portal to Purgatory is somewhere in the 9th ring. The chair should be able to shoot a few men to Pandaemonium. I would have tried it already, but I wanted to get a better bead on the portal's exact location, so..."

Albert was interrupted by a loud buzzing. One of his video monitors flipped on automatically. It showed Ty, very disheveled and looking as if he had been beaten. Apparently, though souls could not bleed, they could bruise.

Albert ran over to his bench and flipped a switch as George ran toward the door. The door opened, letting Ty fall through. George grabbed him before he hit the floor and dragged him from the doorway. "Clear," George shouted. Albert flipped the switch back and the door swung shut quickly.

Before Albert could run to the boy, the buzzer sounded again. Looking at the monitor, Kurt could see a group of men in Albert's stairwell. A large, burly one seemed to be their leader and he looked up in the direction of the camera. "You know what we want, old man," a voice came over the loudspeaker, rich, Russian, and full of anger.

Albert ignored it, running over to Ty. The boy lay on the floor, his head at the knees of George, who knelt next to him. Albert kneeled at the boy's side and ran a gentle hand over his forehead. "What happened?" he asked.

"Kolya," the boy said, his breathing ragged, his words coming in individual short breaths, "found out I lied... No demon drop... Hurt me... Made me tell him about the lifers."

"Damn," Albert said, "they must have let him escape so they could follow him. He wouldn't lead them here on purpose."

"Send them out," Kolya's voice came over the speakers. "All of them."

"What does he want with us," Kurt asked.

"Ransom," Albert said, rubbing the bridge of his nose. "The demons sometimes drop weapons and ammunition onto the roofs so the angrier souls can keep up the level of violence in their turf wars. Matter of finders-keepers. But if a gang can catch someone passing through and hold onto them, sometimes they can leverage a couple of direct shipments, maybe even bigger or better guns. One of the gangs that caught a black mage got themselves a rocket launcher. Pretty much leveled one of the buildings in the third district before they ran out of rockets."

"I'm giving you to the count of three, old man," the menace in Kolya's voice came through loud and clear on the speakers. "One..."

"We've got to get you out of here," Albert said. He rose, grabbing George's arm, trying to pull him off the floor. George rose to his feet and followed, Alain behind him.

Kurt hesitated. Ty had risked his life... no, that was bad thinking... he'd risked a lot of pain for them and already suffered quite a bit of it. Kurt put his hand on Ty's forehead.

"Two..."

"You're a good kid, Ty," Kurt said softly. "Get better."

"Three..."

Kurt got up and ran to the hole as the clanging sound of bullets peppering Albert's steel door rang throughout the basement.

Albert waved the three men into the hole. "The catapult is simple. Press the green button to wind it. Pull the lever to release it. Go!"

George ran to the corner in which their packs lay and dragged them all over. George and Alain quickly shrugged on their frame packs while Kurt put on his smaller backpack. "Good luck," George said to Albert before dropping into the hole.

"You're next," Alain said to Kurt.

Kurt looked at Albert. "Thank you," he said, then dropped into the hole.

The clanging of the bullets against the door stopped and was replaced by a loud thumping sound, as if they were trying to break the door down with brute force.

As Alain prepared to drop into the hole, Albert grabbed his arm. "That kid you're with... Kurt. There's something special about him."

"I haven't known him all that long," Alain said, "but yeah, he seems like a good guy."

"No," Albert said, shaking his head. "When he glows, it's not like George. He's brighter. It's not normal." Albert paused. "Keep an eye out for him. I've got a feeling you're going to need him."

Alain clapped his hand on Albert's arm. "Thank you... for everything," he said, and then dropped down the hole.

Albert grabbed the metal plate and started dragging it back into place. It was slow going, until suddenly it got lighter. Albert looked up and saw Ty at the other end of the plate, helping him shift it into place.

Silently Albert and the boy got the plate settled and the table back over it, and then went back to Albert's desk to watch the monitors showing Kolya's men trying to break down his door.

"It'll hold, won't it?" Ty asked.

Albert nodded. He looked at Ty incredulously. The boy was whole and healthy again. "How did you..."

"That guy," Ty said. "He put his hand on my head, and he was glowing, glowing real bright. Just about hurt my eyes. He said, 'get better' and it was like... BAM! The bruises started getting smaller, the pain started getting smaller, and then all of it was gone."

Albert looked over at the metal slab under the table. Lot had sheltered two angels from an angry mob and proved himself worthy of being saved from the destruction of Sodom. He didn't know exactly what Kurt was, but Alain's chances at Heaven didn't seem as far-fetched or as impossible as they once had.

* * * *

Albert had apparently taken great care and great time with his tunnel. It was tall enough that none of them had to stoop and wide enough for two men to walk abreast without crowding each other. It was reinforced with metal poles or latticework every 10-20 yards and electrically lit. And it was long.

Judging by where they landed and the tunnels Ty had taken them through, Albert's place wasn't more than a couple hundred yards from the wall down from the sixth ring. And the 7th ring was at least 15 miles wide. In however many years Albert had been in Hell, he'd established his workshop, established its defenses, established an independence from the gangs that ruled the ring... It was quite an achievement. As a matter of fact, to get the materials and dig the tunnel, either Albert had recruited a lot of help, or he just happened to locate his workshop right above a tunnel someone else had dug.

There were some things about Albert that just didn't add up, but Alain wasn't planning to go back and ask about them.

The trio went down the tunnel, single file, walking as fast as they could. Alain and George, being non-smokers and in much better shape than Kurt in general, allowed him rest stops every mile or two or slowed the pace for him. They were small favors, to be sure, but even Kurt felt a sense of urgency. The possibility of armed men behind them was, at least to Kurt, not as powerful as the possibility of the portal ahead of them. It didn't represent the way home, not directly, but it was a major step in the right direction.

There was little talking as they moved along except to communicate rests and changes of pace. Between the jogging, walking, and rest breaks, the trio made it to the end of the tunnel in around 4 hours. They ate and drank from Alain and George's provisions, leaving Kurt's supplies as "emergency" rations.

At its end, the tunnel widened into a cave mouth about 25 feet wide by 15 feet high and 30 feet deep. Bolted into the rock of the cave floor was a contraption looking like Albert had ordered it from the same ACME company that sold Wile E. Coyote all his gizmos. At the back was a large box, ostensibly containing a motor that cranked two grooved wheels. Cables led from the wheels to a bench on a sliding track, and the bench was connected to the box by a very large spring.

As per Albert's instructions, there was a lever on the chair and a green button on the box. Alain pressed the button and the wheels started turning, cranking the chair farther and farther back, compressing the spring.

The bench was wide enough for the three of them, but just barely. Kurt headed over to sit down. "Wait," Alain said, heading over to the mouth of the cave. At its edge, he picked up some dirt clods and crushed them to dust. Kurt and George walked over, trying to figure out what he was doing. Alain took his canteen, opened it, and poured some water into the pile of dirt he'd just made.

"What are you doing," George asked.

"You boys need to fix your makeup."

* * * *

The one thing Albert hated about these calls was the voice. Just the sound of it made him feel like things were crawling on him.

"You are sure it was them?"

"A vampire and two mortals. They fit your description. How did you know they would come to me?"

"We did not." Albert itched as it spoke. "Why do you think your competition was so interested in them as well, Mr. De Santos? We just count ourselves lucky you were so uniquely poised to guarantee their safe passage."

Albert cringed. They knew about his tunnel. On the other hand, they'd done nothing about it.

"Anyway," he said, trying to draw the conversation to a close, "they're on their way."

"Thank you, Mr. De Santos. Your assistance is most appreciated. We will deliver your shipment in a few days."

The line went to a light static hiss, indicating the party on the other end had severed the connection. Albert had never seen the demon that he'd just spoken to, only hearing its voice on a rare occasion, and he was glad of it. If the demon looked anything like it sounded, he'd probably tear his own eyes out.

He'd actually liked Alain, Kurt, and George. They seemed like nice guys. He sort of felt bad about the heads-up to Pandaemonium. On the other hand, Pandaemonium was offering three shipping containers of assorted equipment, delivered directly to prevent hijacking.

He got them through the ring safely. He earned the shipment. The heads-up was merely a courtesy. There was little that happened in Hell without the princes of Pandaemonium knowing about it.

* * * *

The three men squeezed onto the bench, their packs on their laps, hugged tight to their stomachs with their arms through the straps.

Alain sat on the left side, next to the lever, Kurt sat in the middle. "Ready," Alain asked.

Kurt adjusted himself in his seat. He nodded. "All systems are go," George said from Kurt's right.

"Then we're off to see the wizard," Alain said and pulled the lever.

Chapter 22: Why Should I Fight You?

The bench shot forward, making Kurt feel like he was in astronaut training, the acceleration pressing his body into the bench and his pack into his chest. The sensation was mercifully short as the bench came to a sudden stop and he was flung out of the cave mouth, only barely keeping a grip on his pack.

He tumbled head over heels, one arm and both legs flailing in an attempt to gain some sort of control, the remaining arm holding his pack tight to his chest.

Slowly, gradually, he oriented himself so that his head pointed forward and his body remained relatively parallel to the ground. At this point he was able to look around him. Alain and George were ahead of him — Alain by about 15 yards, George by about 10 — both already composed.

They were heading down toward a castle that was larger than any building Kurt had ever seen. Made from stone and crowned in precious metals, the walls formed a giant square at least 6 miles on each side. Soaring towers rose up along the walls, glittering bridges connecting them a kilometer or more to towers rising up from the gigantic main hall below. Kurt had seen pictures of the newest hotels in Las Vegas and Macao, huge monstrosities that were supposedly the largest ones in the world. They paled in comparison to Pandaemonium.

Ahead of them, Kurt could see a set of cables running down toward a platform at the top of one of the taller interior towers. Alain pointed to the platform and George and Kurt angled themselves to try to reach it. As they got within a few hundred feet of the platform, Alain yelled something, but his voice was drowned out by the sound of something coming down the cables. Kurt looked back and saw a large cable car bearing down on them. It swooped over them and came to a stop at the platform. Alain and George hit the platform running, coming to a stop before going off the other side. As Kurt joined them on the far edge, the car's doors opened and Nybras stepped out.

Nybras loped over to them and took Alain's hand, shaking it heartily. "Mr. Stark, what a magnificent landing. That was outstanding."

"Thank you." Alain tried not to show his disgust at being touched by a demon, instead turning it into a mild disdain, as if he was being touched by someone who did not deserve to touch him.

"Please let me apologize for overreacting earlier. I understand you were not trying to accuse me of kindness, but were just being polite, as I had been. I truly... ummm... I hope you won't think too harshly of me."

Alain pulled his hand from Nybras's grip. "These things happen."

Opposite the platform was an elevator which made a binging sound as the doors opened.

"Shall we enter?" Nybras asked.

"You go ahead," Alain said. "I'm enjoying the view."

"I could wait."

"No, no." Alain put a hand on Nybras' back and gently pushed him toward the elevator. "You have business to attend to."

"Really," Nybras said, looking over his shoulder at Alain. "It's no bother at all. I... I could give you a tour."

With a little extra force, Alain pushed Nybras into the elevator, reached in, and pushed the "L" button. "Thank you, but no."

None of them had seen a demon be sad before, but the way Nybras deflated just before the door closed looked about as sad as anything they could imagine.

Alain walked back across the platform to where Kurt and George stood, questioning looks on their faces. "Shit." Alain shrugged off his pack and sat, leaning his back against the railing.

George's eyes were wide. "Jesus H. Christ! Man, I thought we were goners."

Alain ran a hand down his face. "You thought?"

Alain smiled only briefly, then got serious. "We're in it now. One screw-up from here on in and we are the main course at the weenie roast."

George shrugged off his pack and sat down cross-legged facing Alain. "So, what's the plan?"

Kurt followed George's lead, sitting as Alain ran his hand over his face again. "According to the information I was able to gather, they keep the soul segments in the dungeons under the castle. We're going to have to find the way in..."

"So that's what's going on!" A look of comprehension grew across Kurt's face. "We're stealing back your soul."

Alain felt angry and took a deep breath to center himself. "It wasn't supposed to be we. It was supposed to be me and me only."

Kurt shrugged. "Well, we're here, like it or not. So, what can we do?"

"Nothing. Just follow close, act subservient, and don't slow me down."

* * * *

Alain and Kurt had swapped packs again, Kurt carrying the frame pack and Alain slinging Kurt's small pack over one shoulder. Kurt couldn't help but notice that he'd gotten into the habit of long elevator rides with vampires. At least this one hadn't kicked him in the crotch and the elevator music was at a moderate volume, though the selection was a marching band version of "Dead Man's Party" on a permanent loop.

As the doors opened onto the ground floor of Pandaemonium, Kurt's senses were assaulted by a host of stimuli. Bells rang, lights flashed, and an air-conditioned breeze blew in through the doors, a relief after the August-like temperatures outside.

"Shall we," Alain said under his breath. He stepped out first, Kurt and George following.

The carpet they walked across was a vibrant crimson, extending throughout the giant hall under a grid of grand chandeliers in gold and crystal. Any visible exit was hundreds of yards away with a maze of gaming tables and slot machines covering the floor in between. Demonesses cruised the floor in short cocktail dresses, barbed tails waving lasciviously behind them as they trucked their trays to waiting players while other demons walked with whips, lashing damned souls who pushed change carts.

To the side of the elevator, a sign advertised the entertainment on tap. A demon that looked like Jabba the Hutt with horns wore a white jumpsuit with gold sequined highlights and held a microphone. Gilded letters proclaimed that he, Behemoth, could be seen nightly in the Cocytus room.

George stage-whispered to be heard over the background noise. "Holy shit."

"We need to find a way down to the dungeons," Alain said through closed teeth as he pretended to smile, looking out over all the wretched excess. "We'll follow along the walls. Look for a door marked Security or Employees Only."

Alain led them off to the right, walking along as if he owned the place, nodding jovially to the patrons as he passed. Kurt, on the other hand, could feel his heart thumping in concert with every step. He kept waiting for someone, something to stop them and question Alain. But they kept moving.

Not all the patrons they passed seemed to be demons either. Some appeared to be living and human, their skins healthy and in good color, their clothes in the latest style, but Kurt had no chance or desire to do any detailed examinations to confirm his judgment. He just plodded along, keeping his mouth shut and trying to keep his eyes straight ahead, ignoring whatever whoops of joy or screams of pain assaulted his senses.

Kurt could catch glimpses of all sorts of devious gaming tables. A damned soul lay strapped to a wheel of fortune, his head tilted back and to the side in an unnatural position, his nose smacking against each pin as it passed through zones that represented the prizes to be won. At another table a damned soul was being cut open, its mock intestines scooped out and thrown in the air over a play area, the gamblers laying bets on how they'd fall. There was a table where a damned soul lay face-down over a piece of cheese, its back and chest marked into quadrants as gamblers lay bets on which sections a starving rat would gnaw through to get to the cheese.

Kurt bordered on becoming physically ill as Alain called their first halt. Moving in front of a door marked Private, he ushered Kurt and George behind him. Kurt stood just behind and to the side of Alain, blocking George as he knelt in the space between them and the door and picked the lock. Kurt looked straight ahead as he heard the door click open and then shut again. "Nothing," George whispered harshly.

Alain began walking again, Kurt and George following close behind. They made a circuit of the room, checking two more doors in the same manner as the first, then turned into a shopping concourse, heading for an exit. Even though the air was cooler, Kurt was sweating lightly, surreptitiously wiping away the moisture in circular motions, spreading the dirt on his torso and face around, trying to keep it from leaving trails.

The shopping concourse featured shops selling everything from sundries, to clothing, to jewelry. Kurt paused in front of one shop, staring incredulously at the wares in its window. "Jesus died for my sins and all I got was this lousy t-shirt" sat under a Pandaemonium logo on a t-shirt. Another shirt featured the bleeding statues with the slogan "Gorgon World: Come on Baby, Light My Fire."

Alain growled from five feet away, "Kurt, come on." Kurt looked at the damned souls modeling the shirts, hanging from stands by hooks that pierced their skin, their faces masques of pain. He shuddered, feeling the bile rising in his throat, and made an effort to keep it down as he jogged over to join Alain and George.

Kurt felt inconsolable. "This is monstrous."

"This is Hell!" Alain glared at him. "Get over it."

Walking further along the hall, Kurt kept his head down, watching Alain's feet, unable to look up for fear of seeing the displays in other windows. Alain halted. Moving his gaze up, Kurt saw another door.

189

He went to his usual position as George worked the lock behind him. The door opened with a click. "Stairs," George whispered.

"Go," Alain said through gritted teeth, his arm swiping out to the side and pushing Kurt toward the door. Kurt backed through and stepped to the side, Alain backing in after him. Once in, Alain shut the door and breathed a visible sigh of relief.

George slipped off his pack and untied his rifle. Alain moved to the top stair and put a finger to his lips, looking down into the stairwell. "I've got point. Kurt, you're in the middle."

Alain moved to the wall of the stairwell and walked down cautiously, Kurt following with George behind him. They made their way down flight after flight, going deeper into the recesses of the castle until the stairs bottomed out in what seemed like a service tunnel, pipes and cables running along the top and sides. It was hot down there and Kurt was now sweating more than he could cover with simple wiping. It didn't matter, though. If they were caught now, pretending to be a lost guest with his two damned souls in tow wouldn't cut it. "Hold it," Kurt said.

Getting behind Alain, he opened a side pocket of his backpack, pulling out two Snickers bars. "I was saving these for an emergency." He handed one to George, then offered the other to Alain.

Alain took the one Kurt offered and then snatched the other from George who was raising it to his mouth to tear the wrapper with his teeth. George protested, albeit quietly.

Alain put one in his coat pocket and then tore the wrapper on the other. "We'll split one. Save the other for our victory dinner." He smiled wanly, trying to convey confidence, but it didn't seem to take as he split the Snickers bar in thirds and each consumed their portion in a dismal silence.

* * * *

Alain walked down the hall, Kurt behind him, George behind Kurt. He hadn't thought to prepare himself for nearly as much as this was turning out to require. The whole plan had been nuts to begin with and was only getting nuttier. He was supposed to slip in and out, blending into the shadows, find the portal into Purgatory in the wall of the ninth ring, dive through with his soul, and make his way to Heaven where he'd plead his case before God. But even if he didn't have Kurt and George with him, it wouldn't have been that easy. He was a fool to have believed otherwise.

He had no idea what to expect when he found the part of his soul they'd removed 78 years ago. He didn't know exactly where he was or how to get to the portal into Purgatory. From here on he was winging it.

There was a cross tunnel about fifty feet up. He approached it with caution, motioning for Kurt and George to stay back. Peering around the corner, Alain saw it was empty. To the left it led farther down nearly as far as the eye could see. But to the right... About thirty yards down it ended in a door. He was tempted to go on and ignore the door, believing that finding the dungeons couldn't be that simple, but it bore investigation. Motioning Kurt and George forward, he skulked around the corner, heading toward the door.

The door was made of metal and it was heavy, a steel lip preventing it from being kicked in. Alain took the rifle as George got to work, watching behind them. Five agonizing minutes later, George tapped him on the back. "Not going to happen," he said. "I'd have to drill it, possibly blow it, but I don't have the equipment."

Alain looked at the lock. The handle was steel, heavy, no screws or bolts visible. Taking a grip on it, he began to pull. Even with his vampire-enhanced strength, it wasn't budging. He put a foot against the

191

wall, pushing himself backward as he pulled. The handle mechanism jerked, pulling out partway, a loud squeak accompanying the movement. Alain let go and shook his hand, the imprint of the handle pink in his palm.

"That's good," George said, pulling a screwdriver out of a toolkit on the floor. "I can work with that." Prying under the circle of metal around the handle, he popped it out, the ring shooting down the handle and clattering onto the floor. George reached into his pack and pulled out a spray can with a long plastic nozzle and a heavy glove. Putting the glove on, he picked up the can and inserted the nozzle into the gap exposed by the ring's removal, spraying for a good while. Putting down the can he picked up his screwdriver again, orienting it carefully, and then smacked its end with the heel of his palm. Alain heard something shatter inside and the handle fell to the floor.

George cleaned up his tools and put them all back into the pack with the can, keeping only the screwdriver. George inserted it into the lock, taking great care with where he put it, and tapped the end a bit. Scooting to the side of the door frame, George grabbed the handle of the screwdriver and pulled it toward himself. The shaft of the screwdriver flexed, seeming almost on the verge of bending, and then the end moved, a click sounding inside the door's lock. The door swung open.

Alain caught it and held it open a crack, exchanging places with George. The door led into a grid of crisscrossing hallways, sitting at the intersection of a T, with hallways extending away from it to the left, right, and straight ahead. Along the walls of the hallways, there were prison-like barred doors every ten feet or so. "I see cells," he said, turning back to Kurt and George, moving the door so the steel lip pressed his fingers against the frame.

"You think that's it?"

"It's gotta be it."

Alain shushed them. "I don't like this. It smells like a trap. It's too easy."

Kurt raised an eyebrow. "They knew you were coming so they built a fake dungeon?"

Alain remained serious. "Anything's possible."

"So, what do we do? Turn around and go exploring in this labyrinth until we find the minotaur? We might never find our way back here."

Alain had to admit Kurt had something. As much as he distrusted the whole scenario--finding the dungeons so quickly, and finding them unguarded on top of that--it would be nearly as stupid to walk away as it would be to check it out.

"Alright. We're going in, but there are no heroes here. First sign of trouble, you two take off running. There's a portal out of here somewhere in the cliff wall, I think. Find it, get out of here, and if anyone or anything tries to get in your way, just shoot it and keep running."

Alain looked at Kurt and then at George, each one nodding his assent. "Okay then. Stay close and stay low."

Turning back to the door, Alain took a firm grasp on the steel lip with one hand, removing the screwdriver with his other and dropping it into his coat pocket. Opening the door a crack, he looked down the hallway again. It was empty. He opened the door further, sticking his head in partway and looked up and down the hall. Still empty. Taking a deep breath, he opened the door further and moved inside, taking a quick right and crouching against the wall. He motioned Kurt and George in and they both snuck through the door, quickly joining him.

Alain pointed to his right, planning to make a circuit around that block. Rising up from the crouch, he walked down the hall, his knees bent. Kurt and George followed. Passing the first cell, Alain looked in. "What the..." George exclaimed in a loud whisper. "There's a kid in there."

George was right. Sitting on a bed that hung down from the far inside wall was a child, looking at them, a forlorn expression on its face. Its skin was pale, and though it was possible the lack of color came from being down in the dungeon instead of up in the sun, Alain knew that wasn't the case. The child was a part of some vampire's soul. Alain was tempted to try and open its cell and free it. It was abominable that it was being held here. But it was a risk he couldn't take. As much pity as he felt for the child, he had a task he had to complete. Alain raised a finger to his lips as he raised his eyebrows. The child acknowledged it with a sad nod that tore at Alain's heart.

Moving down the row, the next seven cells held the same. In each sat a child, some slightly less pitiful than the first, some more, all of them breaking Alain's heart as he passed, unable to help them. When he reached the corner, he looked around it. The hall stretched away into the distance, no one visible along it. He turned left around the corner, Kurt and George following, passing by five more cells, each with a child in it.

He turned the next corner just as easily. Perhaps there were no guards because they had nothing to fear from a dungeon full of children who seemed to have no desire or ability to escape.

The opposite side of the block was like an E. Passing the first two cells, Alain found a gap opening into a short hall that dead-ended at a cell, four cells running along each side. He turned in, walking along the center, looking into each cell. At the third cell on his left, he stopped.

It was like looking through his mother's photo album. Sitting on the bed was a child almost exactly resembling him at the age of six. Running to the door of the cell, he grabbed the bars, staring between them at the child. The similarity was amazing. "What's your name?" he asked the child in a loud whisper.

As if it were waking up, the child focused on him, seeming to just be noticing him at the door. Alain asked again: "What's your name?"

"His name's Alain," a voice came from his left, shouting triumphantly in a Brooklyn accent.

Alain, Kurt, and George all whirled to face the owner of the voice. At the hallway's exit stood Vinnie, four very large bouncer demons moving in to flank him, two on each side. "Howdy, Kurt. See you met my old Army buddy." Vinnie smiled, his fangs extended.

Alain slid the backpack off his shoulders and dropped it to the floor, advancing on Vinnie, his fists up. "Let them go, Vinnie. You and I can settle this right now."

Vinnie raised his hand and placed it on a demon's shoulder, leaning against its muscular arm as he patted its chest with the other hand. "I don't think my friend here would like that. Anyway, why should I fight you? I got you."

George rushed the line, his rifle peppering it with bullets. "Bastard!" Vinnie was knocked back as bullets struck him in the jaw and throat, but the demons didn't even move, the bullets embedding in their thick hides. Five feet from the line, George came to a halt as the demons moved in to close the hole left by Vinnie. Standing there, panting, George stared at the demons. They didn't move to hurt him, didn't say a word. They just stood there, blocking the exit. "Shit!" He lowered the gun and backed up, coming to a halt next to Alain.

There was nowhere to go. Slowly, Alain raised his hands.

Chapter 23: At Hell's Mercy

In the cell, Alain sat on the bed next to the younger version of himself, staring into the boy's eyes. "He's in shock."

Kurt sat on the floor, leaning against the wall as George paced in front of the bars. "That's what they took out of you?"

Alain looked at the boy. He was still amazed at the resemblance. He'd been so busy running and fighting through panic the last time... "Yeah. I guess."

"Congratulations, you're a mother."

Alain didn't dignify the statement with a reply. George grabbed the cell bars and pulled against them. "Bastards!"

Kurt shook his head. "You're just wasting your time."

Alain couldn't agree more. They were at Hell's mercy. Their packs had been confiscated, the guns taken. They'd be let out when someone saw fit, though who that someone was... Alain turned back to the child on the bed as George gave up his vigil by the bars and sat down against the wall opposite Kurt, brooding. Alain looked back into the boy's eyes. "Do you know who I am?"

The child stared blankly. "What do we call him," Kurt asked.

George shrugged. "Alain?"

"That's too confusing." Kurt stood and walked over to the bed. "We've got an Alain. Maybe we can call him Junior or something."

Alain continued staring at the boy. "Junior's fine."

Kurt leaned over Alain's shoulder and looked at the child. "Hey, Junior. You can wake up now."

Junior didn't respond. Alain looked away. "It's no use. He's put up walls to protect him from his reality here. We can't break through."

Kurt looked into the child's eyes. "Let me try."

Alain scooted back on the bed, letting Kurt sit down next to the boy.

Kurt turned to Alain. "You still have that other Snickers?"

"Yeah," Alain said, reaching into his coat pocket. It was one of the few things that hadn't been taken. He pulled out the candy bar and handed it to Kurt. Kurt tore open the paper and turned back to the boy.

"You like candy?" Kurt showed him the Snickers bar. The boy was unresponsive. "Come on... Chocolate, caramel... packed with peanuts?" Nothing.

Kurt tore off a small piece, then took a bite from the bar. "Mmmmm," he said, "this is really good. You try a little." He put the piece to the boy's lips. Slowly the boy's mouth opened, allowing Kurt to put the bit of candy bar inside. "That's right. Now chew it."

The boy sat there, unmoving. Kurt pointed to his own jaw. "Chew." He made exaggerated chewing motions, moving his jaw up and down. Gradually the boy's jaw began to move in little increments, moving down, then stopping, then down again, then up, until a gentle, regular chewing motion had been achieved. After a while the boy's throat moved, indicating that he'd swallowed.

"Good, huh?" The boy nodded slowly. "You want more?" The boy nodded again. "Okay, but you gotta say the magic word." The boy stared at him. "What do you say when you want more candy?"

The boy's head dropped and he swallowed again. Slowly he raised it back up and opened his mouth. "Please," a tiny voice squeaked out.

Alain had never been more overjoyed to hear a single sound in his life. Leaping to his feet, he moved around Kurt and lifted the boy off the bed, sweeping him into an embrace. "Yes!"

"How sweet," a voice called from the door, destroying Alain's joy in an instant. "Figures you would have a family reunion here."

Alain set Junior back on the bed and turned to the door, placing himself between it and the boy. Reese threw Alain a sarcastic smile. "Nice to see you again. I trust the accommodations are comfortable."

Alain seethed, glaring at Reese. "What are you doing here?"

"Well, you sort of sent me here. Or is old age getting to your memory?"

"That's not what I meant."

"In due time." Reese pulled Kurt's pack of Kools from his pocket and drew a cigarette from it, lighting it with Kurt's lighter. He seemed to shiver as he took the first drag, a small gasp of pleasure escaping his mouth as he drew it away from his lips. "Goddamn, it's been a long time. Want one?" He waved the pack at Kurt.

"I just quit."

Reese mocked him with another smile. "That's too bad. Then you wouldn't mind if I keep these?"

A strained smile crossed Kurt's face. "Knock yourself out."

"You are too kind." Reese took another drag, exhaling the smoke in a tight stream toward Alain. "Well," he said, dropping the cigarette on the floor and stubbing it out with the toe of his boot, "I just wanted to stop by and say hello."

"Why?" Alain hands clenched into fists.

"Besides getting to see you locked up in a cage? That's not enough?" He paused and then shrugged. "Guess you're gonna have to wait and find out."

Alain remained tense, staring at the bars as Reese turned and walked away, his laughter echoing back to the cell.

* * * *

They were taken to an interrogation room, looking like something out of a Hollywood set storeroom. Alain sat calmly at the table while George paced by the door. Kurt sat in a corner with Junior, talking to him.

Further attempts by Alain to get through Junior's walls had made no impact. It seemed that the only one who had any rapport with the boy was Kurt, which seemed strange considering that the boy was literally a part of Alain. But he trusted Kurt. When the demons had come to collect them and take them all to the interrogation room, Junior had taken Kurt's hand, not Alain's.

Kurt knew this must be disturbing to Alain and he had some theories on why it was playing out this way, though none he could confirm. Most of his conversation with Junior was one sided, talking in consoling tones, just trying to make contact.

"Do you like baseball?" Kurt asked.

Junior sat staring at his hands.

"I do. I used to love the Mets when I was your age." Kurt felt sort of silly saying when I was your age. By all accounts, the boy was over seventy years old and had been imprisoned the entire time. Forever stuck at a physical appearance of six, with a six-year-old's understanding of things, all alone in a prison cell with scary monsters watching over him. Kurt could only imagine the kind of experiences that had built up the walls he was trying to break through.

"It isn't fair that you're here, is it?" The boy looked up at Kurt and shook his head slowly. "I know how you feel. I was going home when these bad women dragged me to this scary place, and then there was a big fight, and then I was here. It's not fair that I'm here either."

The boy nodded his head and Kurt saw that he'd hit something. "Do you know Peter Pan?" The boy shook his head in the negative.

"Well, there are these kids who got lost in Never Never Land. And they banded together to keep each other safe. They called themselves the Lost Boys. I think we're Lost Boys too."

"George," he called, "come here."

George stopped his pacing. "What," he asked, a surly note in his voice.

"Just come here."

George walked over and sat down next to Kurt, facing Junior. "Junior. George is lost too. Aren't you, George?"

"Yeah. Whatever."

Kurt put a finger under Junior's chin, lifting the boy's head so he could look in his eyes. They weren't as blank as before, he noticed as he took Junior's hand. Kurt could see that he was listening, that he was

200

paying attention to what Kurt said. "See," Kurt said, "you're not all by yourself anymore. We're a club, the three of us. We're Lost Boys."

"What a pile of horse..."

"Shut up, George," Kurt chided out the side of his mouth. "You know, though," he said to Junior, "we can't be a real club until we take a club oath. You wanna take the oath with us?"

Slowly, Junior nodded. "Okay. Give me your hand, George."

Grudgingly, George gripped Kurt's hand. "Now take Junior's." George took Junior's small hand.

"A circle of three is strong, but a circle of four is stronger. Alain is lost, just like us. Can we invite him to join our club?"

Junior shook his head in the negative. "Okay. Maybe later. Right now, we'll do our oath. Repeat after me... I, say your name..." Kurt said his own name while George said his. Kurt looked expectantly at Junior.

"I, Alain Beaudreaux," the boy said in a quiet voice.

"Do solemnly swear..." Kurt paused to allow George and Junior to repeat his words, "that at all times and in all places... I will be loyal and faithful... to my Lost Boy brothers... and I will do right by them... and I will trust them to do right by me... and if I break this oath... I'll turn into a dirty bug and eat dog poop forever." Junior smiled faintly as he repeated the last line.

"Now all we have to do is spit on it." Letting go of George and Junior's hands, Kurt spit in his palm, then rubbed his hands together and put them back out. George and Junior did the same and they linked hands again. "We're a club," Kurt said as the door opened behind them.

Kurt and George stood quickly, taking protective stances in front of Junior while a demon, about the same size as Nybras, but standing more confidently and wearing a smartly tailored suit, walked in. "Good afternoon, gentlemen." The demon put a briefcase down on the table. "My name is Mammon and I'm here to help you."

Alain sat up in his chair, taking his arms off the table and crossing them in front of his chest "What are you supposed to be? Our lawyer?"

Mammon sat down opposite Alain. "Better." He popped open his briefcase. "I'm your agent."

"What do we need an agent for?"

"You haven't heard," Mammon asked incredulously. He pulled out a stack of papers. "I forgot. You've been down here the whole time."

"Heard what?"

"A huge extravaganza." Mammon waved his hands. "The grudge match of the century. A no holds barred, tag-team fight to the death. Vinnie Rinaldi, the Hackensack Hacker, and Tommy Reese, the Michigan Mauler, versus Kurt Gray and Alain Beaudreaux, the Pillagers of Pandaemonium!" Mammon shuddered with pleasure. "I love it... though I am still workshopping the titles."

Kurt winced. "Hey!"

Alain put up a hand to silence him. "What's in it for us?"

Mammon flipped through his papers, stopping at one and running a finger across a few lines. "Well, since Gray didn't come here voluntarily, we can't technically keep him. But if you win..." He gave George a quick glance. "We'll let Miller go too."

Kurt stepped forward. "And what if we don't fight?"

Mammon moved his finger lower on the page, scanning the text. "We let you go, Gray, but we publicly execute Beaudreaux and Miller."

"Execute?"

"Look..." Mammon threw up his hands as if there was nothing he could do about it, "they're demanding a show. A fight would be preferable to an execution, but..."

"What about the boy," George asked.

Mammon leaned to the side, peering around George's legs at Junior, then sat up. "Him? Well, we're going to kill Beaudreaux anyway, win or lose. So, when he dies, the two parts of his soul will be merged back into one and he'll go to the sixth ring to burn with the heretics."

Alain had grown strangely still with that comment, but George seemed to take up the fight. "No!" He turned to Kurt. "We gotta be able to do something... Ah!" He turned back to Mammon. "A side bet. They win, we go on into Purgatory and through to Heaven, with the boy, and plead our case. They lose, you get my soul."

"No," Alain said, turning in his seat. "George, you can't. I won't allow it."

"It's not your choice," George said.

Mammon pursed his lips and nodded his head, considering the proposition. Flipping through a few more pages, he ran his finger along a few lines. "Sorry, but it's a no go. Says here your soul is balanced right now; seventh ring here, third ring Purgatory. Fifty-fifty that we get it anyway. But that gives me an idea."

As Mammon scanned down the page, Kurt looked at George, recalling the clouds of smoke and gunfire on the seventh ring. He couldn't imagine George being destined for there. He didn't see George as evil. Violent, perhaps, but not maliciously so. He put a hand on George's shoulder as George's head dropped.

Mammon reached into his briefcase and pulled out a smart phone. "Hold on," He tapped its screen with a claw, then turned away from the group, placing a finger in his large, pointed ear as he held the phone to the other, occasionally mumbling something. Less than two minutes later he took it from his ear, tapped the screen, and turned back to them. "This is interesting." He chuckled softly. "Seems that when he first got here, Gray was set for the first ring... non-believers... but since then his balance has changed."

Kurt's hand dropped from George's shoulder and fell limply to his side. "I'm going to Heaven?"

"Well..." Mammon shook his hand side to side. "You've got a little fucking around and some other minor things to pay for in Purgatory first, but... yeah. With your present balance, you'd get there... eventually."

"Huh." Kurt tried to think through the implications. What had changed about him that shifted the balance? The first ring was for non-believers. He hadn't much thought about it, but whatever doubts he'd had about the existence of God were pretty much gone. In a sense, he'd gotten religion. It didn't seem fair, though. Other humans had to take it all on faith, but he'd been shown proof.

"And that leads us to the bet." Mammon clapped his hands. "Gray puts his soul on the table too and it's a go... with the following conditions, of course. You guys lose, he goes to the sixth ring. If you win, Gray and Miller get to go with the boy while we keep Beaudreaux, but... if they make their way to Heaven, they have to get an audience with," Mammon paused and made air quotes with his fingers, "'The Lord, Our God' within seven days, win their return to the mortal plane, and win forgiveness for Boudreaux's sins. Fail in any of those provisions, you all come back here and," Mammon chuckled, "suffer the consequences."

Alain and George both looked at Kurt. The decision rested with him.

Reaching for the wall, Kurt leaned until his hand rested against it, then walked himself over and slid down it, sitting at the base. He had a lot of choices. The easiest one was to run away. That was the only option that didn't require him to risk death or damnation. But could he do it? According to Mammon, if Vinnie had killed him on that table, he'd have ended up on the first ring for the rest of eternity. But now... he had a shot at Heaven and he vividly remembered the tortures they'd seen on the sixth ring.

If he fought and won, but didn't bet, Alain would die, Junior would be reintegrated into his soul, and the amalgam of the two would spend the rest of eternity as a target for napalm balloons. The only choice that had any chance of full success was betting his soul, and that was a long-shot at best.

I will be loyal and faithful to my Lost Boy brothers, and I will do right by them, and I will trust them to do right by me, and if I break this oath I'll turn into a dirty bug and eat dog poop forever. He looked at Junior. He'd just been trying to break through the walls, lessen the boy's pain. But the boy had taken the oath, had recited it and even sealed it with spit. When Alain died, Junior wouldn't exist anymore. Even if Alain's soul was saved, he would be reintegrated, he guessed. Junior wasn't a real boy. He was a figment, a half-soul. But reality didn't matter, did it? The only thing that mattered was whether or not Kurt believed in the oath. And looking inside himself, he knew: if he ran out, if he compromised a single bit to save his own skin, he'd be a bug... a dirty, shit-eating bug.

Kurt brought his knees up and wrapped his arms around them, staring blankly into space. "Tell your boss he's got a bet."

"Wonderful!" Mammon clapped his hands in front of his face like a happy child. He gathered his papers and put them back in his briefcase. "The fight's in two days and I'll negotiate you every advantage of course. First-rate guest suites, soft beds to sleep on, weights if you want to work out, first-rate food and drink imported from Earth so you can carbo-load or fat-load or protein-load... Whatever! Ooooh, I could just kiss you guys."

Mammon slammed his briefcase closed, picked it up and walked to the door. "Give me an hour and I'll have everything worked out."

A demon opened the door and Mammon left, stopping and giving them a smile and a victory sign before the door closed behind him. Alone together, George walked over and stood in front of Kurt, looking down at him. "You're one crazy motherfucker, you know that?"

Alain rose from his chair, gently pushed George out of the way, and sat down next to Kurt. "I want you to know, Kurt, that I really appreciate this. I really do. But when Mammon comes back, I want you to back out, tell him you've changed your mind. I can't let you go through with this."

Kurt squeezed his knees tighter, resting his chin on them and looking over at Junior. "It's not your choice."

Chapter 24: You're First

Mammon was true to his word. Within an hour, a cadre of demons came and escorted them upstairs, taking them through the casino as hushed whispers circulated, no one daring to shout any encouragement or abuse. They went up in one of the elevators to the eighteenth floor where George, Alain, and Kurt were each given a large suite with all the amenities. Junior was put in with Alain, but within minutes of the demons leaving them to their preparations, Alain brought him over to Kurt's suite. The boy wanted to stay with Kurt.

It hurt Alain that Junior didn't want to be with him, wouldn't communicate with him, but Kurt had hit it on the head with his Lost Boys thing. Junior had waited nearly 80 years for Alain to rescue him. While Alain spent his years basking in the glow of Marie's love, this little boy had been in a prison cell, literally surrounded by monsters.

Sitting in his suite, Alain couldn't rest, couldn't sleep. He was consumed with guilt. After all he'd gone through, he'd considered himself brave, fearless. He'd spent the last seventy-plus years with this unflappable image of himself as a righteous and caring person, and the sight of that one little boy, as unquestionably a part of himself — a part of his soul — as anything in his life, sitting there behind his walls of pain and fear, had shot that image to shreds.

After Kurt and George had rested, because rest was what they needed more than anything, the whole group gathered in Kurt's suite to eat. Anything they wanted was available and it was all imported. The one thing about demons was that they'd lie to you ten ways to Sunday, but when they made a deal, they stuck to it. You had to look for the loopholes in the deal because they'd exploit every one to its fullest, but this was a simple deal. Mammon had presented them the conditions, stated explicitly in writing, for final approval. Apparently Hell was so confident of victory, it didn't need to hide gotchas in a mountain of legalese.

The meal was heavy, but simple. The first course was a salad of tomato, cucumber, and onion with a light vinaigrette. The second course was a hearty chicken soup with lots of noodles, chunks of chicken, and big slices of carrot. This was followed by a main course of steak, mashed potatoes with gravy, and corn on the cob. And it finished off with apple pie for dessert. It was traditional fare, something to remind them of home, but the only one who might have had a chance of it truly being a homey meal was George. For Alain, home was Marie's roast chicken. For Kurt, home was a plate of Dad's brisket with Bubbe's potato latkes. Still, stuck in a luxury suite in Hell, the meal somehow said "America" and gave the three men a sense of pride and unity despite their different backgrounds.

Alain had primarily steered it to that because he didn't want the three of them ordering last suppers. If they spent these two days acting like condemned men, they were going to lose the fight before it started.

Junior didn't join them at the table, sitting in a corner by one of the stereo speakers, slowly eating a Snickers bar Kurt had ordered him and drawing with some crayons. They'd returned the packs, sans weapons, and Kurt had connected his phone to the stereo and his "Chill" playlist was on.

As they pushed their plates away, settling back to give themselves a bit of time to digest the steaks before dessert, the silence weighed heavily on Alain. No one had talked during the meal. They'd all eaten slowly and somberly, each one seeming afraid to broach the subject that was on all their minds.

"Kurt, have you had any training in hand-to-hand combat?" The sentence hung in the air like a bad fart.

"A little Karate at the Y when I was a kid. Made yellow belt."

"Shit," George mumbled.

"Well," Alain said, "Reese and Vinnie both have. I'm not going to force anything on you, but if you want, George and I are both more than qualified to give you a few pointers."

Kurt pushed his chair back and stood up. "Why? Vinnie's a vampire, like you. I tried fighting him before and he kicked my ass."

"The bigger they are, the harder they fall," George said.

"What's that supposed to mean?"

"What it means," Alain said calmly, trying to counteract the frustration that was apparently boiling in Kurt, "is that Vinnie's overconfident. He thinks he'll take you easily. I'm hoping to be the one who does the dirty work and keep you out of it altogether if I can, but if you end up in the ring with him, that attitude is going to be his Achilles heel. It may not win the fight for you, but it could keep you alive long enough for me to get in there."

Kurt tensed, his volume going up a notch. "And what if I'm in there because you've already been killed?"

Alain hadn't wanted to think of that possibility, but now that Kurt aired it, it had to be dealt with. "Then you may just be screwed. But if you go down without a fight, you're a punk, and you'll have to remember that every time someone shoots a flaming arrow at your eye... for eternity. You have to put up the best fight you can, even if it seems hopeless, and George and I can help your best become better between now and then."

As Kurt considered the proposition, Alain looked beyond him. Junior had stopped coloring and was watching them intently, his partially eaten Snickers bar resting on the table next to his crayons. Alain tried to smile at him, but it came out wrong, the seriousness of what was going on making his smile into something more like a grimace. Junior turned back to his paper and hastily picked up a crayon, leaning over and setting himself to the task of coloring. Alain's attempted smile disappeared.

"Okay," Kurt said. "I don't know what good it's going to do, but I might as well give it a shot."

"Thank you," Alain said sarcastically. "Your show of confidence is overwhelming."

* * * *

The roar of the crowd didn't energize Kurt. It made him cringe. Standing behind a curtain at the edge of a ramp leading down into the center of the arena, Kurt felt like an idiot. He'd been stupid to accept the bet. He'd been stupid to even hope that they might have a chance of winning. And he'd been stupid not to back out when his costume was delivered to his room.

It was a silver, sleeveless unitard, gold stripes coming down from the shoulders and merging into a lightning bolt on his chest. He wore lightweight golden boots and a gold belt, and he felt ridiculous. He hadn't even been able to laugh at Alain when he saw him dressed in the same outfit, his embarrassment had run so deep. Luckily, George had been there to do enough laughing for the both of them.

Music began to echo through the arena, slightly muffled by the curtain. They'd been allowed to choose their entrance music, and they'd debated various songs on Kurt's iPhone for about an hour. Kurt had eclectic tastes, often listening to a song and thinking how it would soundtrack a movie scene, so he collected songs that fit various themes.

After a number of rejects, ranging from the "Hallelujah Chorus" to "We're Not Gonna Take It" to the theme from *The Last Starfighter*, George had suggested AC/DC's "Big Balls" in honor of the huge balls it was taking to go through with this. Kurt and Alain had both shot that down, but it made Kurt think of AC/DC's "Thunderstruck", which got the consensus vote.

Kurt couldn't help but think the thunderbolt on his costume was because of the song choice and he could only wonder what the costumes would have been like if they'd gone with "Big Balls."

On the first chorus of "Thunder!" the curtains opened and Kurt looked out on the arena. Twenty thousand demons, damned souls, and assorted other denizens of the netherworld packed the house, screaming and yelling. The ring seemed so far away and the path was lined on each side with crosses, buried in the concrete upside down, a damned soul crucified on each one. Mammon set the pace, striding forward into the fray, Kurt and Alain following behind.

George and Junior sat somewhere in the crowd, but Kurt couldn't locate them. As he shuffled down the ramp, the demon behind him gave him a two-handed push in the back. "Keep it moving," it shouted as the crowd screamed happily in response. *Nothing like the home-field advantage,* Kurt thought miserably, moving closer to the ring.

The heavy music thumped out of speakers all around and there were succubae dancing a lascivious ballet in the ring, writhing around one another, their hands running over each other's bodies in slow syncopated movements. It wasn't the kind of ring he'd seen on television. The posts were wooden and the ropes were actual rope, tied directly to the posts. There was no padding, the canvas looking like there was nothing but hard floor beneath. There would be no theatrics here, Kurt thought. Wrestling might be fake, but this was fatally real.

Approaching the ring, Kurt saw something just before it that horrified him. He ran ahead and knelt in front of one of the crosses. "Mick!" he shouted at the soul on it.

Mick stared blankly at him. His arms stretched out to the sides, Kurt looked at his left hand. The pinky hadn't grown back, a wrinkled nub where it had once been. "Move it," Kurt heard as a large demonic hand grabbed his arm and jerked him to his feet, shoving him forward. Kurt looked back over his shoulder at Mick. He'd kept Mick's pinky in the pocket of his jeans and it now rested in the side pocket of his pack back in his room. So many people were relying on him and Alain to win this fight; Mick, George, Junior, even Alain.

The succubae parted as a demon held up one of the ropes for Mammon to enter the ring, Kurt and Alain following him. The demonesses moved to greet them as they stood and waited. Kurt shuddered as the tongue of one flicked at his ear while another ran her hand slowly down his chest, cupping his genitals and massaging them roughly. Gritting his teeth, Kurt reached down and grabbed her by the wrist, jerking her around in front of him. Releasing her wrist, he put his hands on her shoulders and shoved as hard as he could, sending her flying back, bouncing along on her ass before coming to a stop.

The audience went into a frenzy, cheers and angry shouts mixing into a wall of white noise. "That was beautiful," Mammon shouted, patting him on the shoulder, "incredible showmanship."

Kurt whipped around and shoved Mammon, sending the demon stumbling back. The two larger demons stepped in, grabbed Kurt's arms and restrained him, but the audience was already insane with shouting, so loud that no one noticed when the music switched to Inner Circle's "Bad Boys," no one watching as Vinnie and Reese entered the arena. The majority of the crowd only spotted them when the duo was already halfway to the ring.

The succubae ran to the other side of the ring, seductively beckoning them forward. Vinnie and Reese were dressed in matching black robes, cowls covering their heads and obscuring their faces. They looked like the avenging monks of a mad god and the crowd cheered them forward. The audience wanted blood. Lots of it.

Entering the ring while the succubae held the ropes for them, Vinnie and Reese moved to the center, throwing off their robes in a simultaneous set of grand flourishes. Each was bare-chested, wearing black stretch pants and black boots. They waved to the crowd, smiling as it cheered them on, chants of "Vinn-eee, Vinn-eee," arising from pockets of the audience.

The demons released Kurt and stepped out of the ring as the announcer stepped in, walking to the center. Wearing a white tuxedo, he was human, or perhaps a vampire. He grabbed a microphone that lowered from the ceiling and shouted into it. "Ladies and Denizens! Mammon Enterprises, in association with the Azmodeus Arena and Hades Box Office, presents the Grind in Gehenna, the Prosecution in Perdition, the Havoc in Hell! A no-rules, no-referee, tag-team fight to the death with damnation on the line."

The audience shouted and clapped, thumping the floor with their feet, raising a loud din. "Fighting out of the white corner, at a combined

213

weight of three hundred and forty-four pounds, wearing silver with gold trim, Kurt Gray and Alain Beaudreaux, the Pillagers of Pandaemonium!"

Loud boos rose up from the crowd. Crumpled pieces of paper and plastic cups were thrown toward the ring. "And fighting out of the black corner..." The announcer paused as a round of cheers went up. "At a combined weight of three hundred and fifty-eight pounds, wearing nothing but black, Vinnie Rinaldi and Tommy Reese, Hell's Avengers!" The cheering grew louder, the foot-thumping beginning again.

"And now... let's *gird our loins for baaattllle!!!*"

Letting go of the mike he exited the ring, followed by the succubae. "All right, Kurt," Mammon shouted in Kurt's ear, slapping him on the shoulder, "you're first."

Chapter 25: 100% Captain Kirk

First?

Kurt turned to protest, but Mammon was already leading Alain out of the ring. Turning back, he saw Vinnie stretching against a ring post as Reese slipped through the ropes and took up a position on the other side, smiling confidently at Kurt.

Ding! The bell rang and Vinnie let go of the post. The audience was shouting, but the volume was noticeably decreased as Kurt stood planted in his spot and watched Vinnie come toward him. *Run*, his mind shouted at him, but his legs didn't seem to want to move. Swiveling at the hip he saw Alain behind him, standing at the ropes, waving him over. Suddenly his knees buckled and Kurt almost fell to the mat. He caught himself in time, exerting control over his body, and ran toward Alain, hand out, reaching for the tag. Alain leaned over the ropes, stretching his arm toward Kurt. And that's when Kurt felt Vinnie's hand on his shoulder.

His progress halted, he was spun around to meet a right cross that sent him staggering to the side. Unconsciously he put a hand to his jaw as he steadied his legs, waiting for Vinnie's next approach. Vinnie stood between Kurt and Alain, and as Vinnie came close, Kurt feinted to the left and then drove to the right, trying to get around him. Vinnie threw up an arm, clotheslining Kurt and sending him to the canvas flat on his back.

Kurt didn't have time to regain his bearings. As he struggled to get up, he saw Vinnie's face above him. Vinnie took a grip on the chest of his costume, hoisting him to his feet. Grabbing Kurt's arm, Vinnie began running, dragging Kurt with him, then stopped, whirling Kurt around and throwing him into the ropes. He bounced off, heading straight for Vinnie's outstretched arm, another clothesline in the making. Letting his body go limp, Kurt dropped to his knees and slid beneath Vinnie's arm. He fell forward onto his hands and immediately began rolling, moving out of the way as a leap landed Vinnie in the spot where he'd just been.

Kurt scrambled to his feet and circled as Vinnie came toward him, dancing out of reach as Vinnie tried to grab him, keeping Vinnie always in front of him. As Vinnie made another lunge in, Kurt moved to the side and dropped to the floor, bracing himself with his hands and swinging his legs in an arc toward Vinnie's, a move he'd been practicing with George and Alain. Connecting, he toppled the vampire, sending him falling forward into the ropes.

Kurt was up immediately and was on Vinnie before he could turn around, punching him in the kidneys twice before he whirled to the side, connecting an elbow to the back of Vinnie's head. Kurt danced back and waited for Vinnie's next approach, beginning to feel confidence stealing up on him.

As Vinnie turned, the smile was gone, a look of determined anger now on his face. Kurt's confidence dropped. He should have taken the opportunity to tag out, but he was stuck. As Vinnie approached, a hand out to grab him, Kurt grabbed it, whirling to try a judo throw he'd practiced with George and Alain. Rather than rolling Vinnie over his hip, though, Vinnie pulled him up, wrapping an arm around his throat. "Play time's over, bitch," Vinnie shouted in his ear, loud enough to be heard over the renewed cheers of the crowd.

Pulling upward, Kurt's throat caught in the crook of his arm, he shook Kurt like a toy. Kurt grabbed his arm, trying to break his hold. Vinnie was as strong as ever and Kurt pulled futilely at his arm as Vinnie squeezed tighter, cutting off his breathing.

Things began to get blurry and Kurt realized he was going to die if he kept pulling at Vinnie's arm. Shooting his hands back over his head, he connected with Vinnie's face, groping desperately for Vinnie's eyes. One thumb connected and Kurt pushed with all his might as Vinnie jerked his head around, loosening his hold on Kurt's neck.

Kurt sucked in a gulp of air, and as he exhaled, brought down his other arm, digging his elbow back into Vinnie's stomach. The air rushed out of Vinnie and the arm loosened further, allowing Kurt to slip out. It was tempting to bounce back and try to inflict more damage on Vinnie, but Kurt knew better now. Stumbling forward he turned and ran for Alain, tagging his hand before crashing into the ropes and falling to his knees.

Alain was up and over the top of the ropes almost instantly as Kurt fell flat on the floor and rolled out of the ring beneath the bottom rope.

Vinnie had already recovered by the time Alain reached him, but Alain bulled into him, pushing Vinnie back until he slammed into one of the posts. The post bent with the force and Alain backed up a few steps, slamming into Vinnie again. The post bent again and Kurt could swear he heard a crack, even above the sound of the roaring crowd. Alain backed up again and leapt forward, but Vinnie rolled out of the way, turning to the side along the ropes and Alain hit the post with full force.

The post snapped, a jagged wooden edge pushing up into Alain's stomach as the top ropes on both sides sagged. Alain fell back, a tear in his costume fraying through the lightning bolt, a bleeding cut running up along his abdomen. Vinnie took advantage of this to rush Alain, throwing punch after staggering punch at Alain's head, pushing Alain back. "Come on Alain," Kurt yelled, pounding his fist against the mat.

Alain staggered backward, pummeled by Vinnie's blows. He was feeling every one and the pain wasn't receding. The gash along his stomach wasn't closing up. A punch hit him in the mouth and he fell back another step, tasting blood from a cut on his lip. Another jab caught him and the cut opened wider, his mouth filling with blood. This wasn't supposed to be happening. He tried to drop his fangs, but nothing happened.

Vinnie pushed him back against the ropes, one arm going around Alain's neck while the other arm pounded his abdomen. "This one's for France, and this one's for 'sixty-two," Vinnie yelled, punctuating the statements with body blows. Alain wanted to bend forward, but Vinnie held him up. "Yeah," Vinnie hit him again in the upper abdomen, "it hurts, doesn't it." Vinnie punched him again and Alain coughed, spitting blood in Vinnie's face.

"Oh yeah," Vinnie said, his tongue darting out and licking off some of Alain's blood. "Tastes good." Vinnie hit him again. "Didn't think you were gonna win, did you?" Another punch and Alain's knees quivered. "The fix is in. I'm gonna finish you off nice and slow and then they'll throw that punk of yours in with me. I'm gonna make him scream."

"No," Alain protested, coughing, little flecks of blood spraying out.

"What are you gonna do about it?" Vinnie asked, following it with three quick jabs to the ribs. Alain could feel one crack. Satan had given and Satan had taken away. He was mortal, the curse of being a vampire gone.

Vinnie let go of him and Alain crumpled down on his knees. "Come on, hep-cat," Vinnie shouted, the crowd around them going crazy, "give me your best shot."

But Alain couldn't concentrate on him. He could feel his face swelling, the cut on his stomach had been opened wider, the blood trickling in rivulets down the silver of his costume. It was over. The life without living, the being with people without being close. All the pain of the last seventy-plus years welled up inside.

"What are you waiting for," Vinnie shouted. "Come on. Stand up and take it like a man."

Alain began to cry. His throat grew thick and his eyes started to water. It was almost a shock as the first tear rolled down his cheek, followed by another and another. Slowly he reached up and wiped one away with a finger, bringing the finger to his mouth. Even through the blood he could taste it, the salt, the sorrow. Crying was a biological process that stopped when he became a vampire. Even when Marie died, he'd been unable to cry. All the decades of losses, disappointments, and pain welled up in those tears.

"Whatsa matter," Vinnie yelled. "You a pussy? Can't take it? Come on, motherfucker! Come on!"

Putting a hand on the mat, Alain crossed himself with the other. He tensed his legs. *Twenty-three*, he thought, shouting it out in his mind, *twenty-three! Hut! Hut! Hike!* Alain launched himself forward from the crouch, catching Vinnie in the stomach with his shoulder, wrapping an arm around him and driving forward with his legs. Pushing with all his strength, with everything he had in him, Alain accelerated their progress, knocking Vinnie off balance as he pushed him backward across the ring. And then they stopped, Vinnie stiffening.

219

Alain let go and stumbled back. Vinnie was standing at the broken post, the shard of wood protruding out through his chest. Vinnie's eyes were wide as his hand went up to the jagged point. Drawing it away with his fingers bloody, he stared at them. "You son of a... bitch. The fix..."

Vinnie's eyes glazed over, still staring at his hand. His arm went limp. His bloody hand dropped to his side. As his legs gave out, he slid off the broken post and crumpled to the mat.

Alain dropped to his knees and fell forward onto his hands. Coughing again, he watched the flecks of blood dot the mat. "Now it's my turn," a voice shouted behind him. "I'm gonna enjoy this!"

* * * *

Kurt had watched in horror as Vinnie battered Alain, seeing Alain bleed. He'd thought Alain was immortal, but something happened. His strength was gone, his invulnerability gone, and though he'd beat Vinnie, he was nearly incapacitated, on his hands and knees, spitting blood as Reese entered the ring. "Alain! The ropes," Kurt shouted. Turning to run around to the corner closest to Alain, Kurt found Mammon blocking his way.

"Can't go there," Mammon said, putting out his arms to create more of a barrier. "That would be cheating."

"And you don't call what you guys did cheating?"

"That's immaterial," Mammon said.

Kurt threw a hard right, catching Mammon on the jaw and knocking him off his feet. Clutching his hand in pain, Kurt looked down at Mammon. "Then sue me, you fuck."

Kurt ran to the end of the ring and took a sharp turn around the corner, running to reach Alain. Alain had crawled within a foot of the ropes as Kurt reached them, Reese stalking forward just a few feet behind him. Kurt leaned over the edge of the mat, grabbing Alain's outstretched arm with both hands and threw himself backward, pulling Alain out of the ring. Alain slid under the bottom rope, leaving a smeared trail of blood on the mat, and tumbled over the edge, falling to the floor. Kurt didn't have time to check on him, though. The fight wasn't over yet.

Grabbing the middle rope and lifting a foot to the mat, Kurt pulled himself up. As he clambered over the rope, Reese grabbed him by the hair and pulled him the rest of the way through, dragging him to the center of the ring. Bent over, his hair in Reese's hands, Kurt tried another move. This one wasn't from George and Alain, though. This one was 100% Captain Kirk.

Grabbing Reese's forearms, he threw himself backward, raising a foot as he fell and planting it in Reese's stomach. Reese went up in the air, letting go of Kurt's hair as he somersaulted over him, landing on his back.

Turning quickly, Kurt scrambled to get on top of Reese before he could get up. He got a knee on Reese's left arm, but not his right. Catching Reese's right arm as he swung it up to defend himself, Kurt held it away and rained down punch after punch at Reese's head. Reese tried to dodge, but Kurt was berserk, unable to be stopped, connecting each punch, slowly beating Reese's face to a pulp. When Reese finally lost consciousness, the crowd was screaming.

Looking to the edge of the ring, Kurt saw that Alain had raised himself to standing, leaning on the edge of the mat. "Kill him!" Alain shouted.

Kurt had never killed anyone and the thought of it made the berserker rage drain from him, leaving him suddenly feeling weak. The man below him was technically already dead, but the killing blow had to be delivered. He didn't look evil, though. Unconscious, his face dented and smashed, he looked pathetic. He was no longer a threat. He was just pitiful. "Kill him!" Alain shouted again.

Kurt remembered everyone who was depending on him, everything that rested on this fight. If he didn't kill Reese, Satan won by default. Slowly, reluctantly, Kurt moved off Reese and rolled him over onto his stomach. Straddling Reese's back, he took Reese's head in his hands, one on his chin, one on the back of his skull. Kurt took a deep breath, steeled himself, and jerked Reese's head around to break his neck like they did in the movies, falling back in shock as Reese's head came off in his hands.

From the stump of Reese's neck something seemed to bleed out, a pool forming in front of the soul-corpse. It had no color, as if light entered it and disappeared instead of bouncing off. It was like a pool of black nothingness. It grew to nearly five feet in diameter, extending out from the stump. Kurt rose to his feet, dropping Reese's head, and moved back as a tendril rose up from the edge of the thing. Waving in the air, it seemed to be looking around, orienting first on him, and then Alain.

The tendril vibrated and then shot out toward Alain, wrapping around his torso. Alain clawed at it, trying to pull away, trying to escape as it pulled him forward. Kurt ran around the thing, careful to avoid its edge, and grabbed the tendril. His hands let go reflexively as the dire cold of it burned them. Looking at his palms, Kurt could see red marks of frostbite running along them where he'd made contact with it. Alain was halfway up onto the mat, struggling to break loose as it dragged him toward the gaping hole of nothingness it had become.

This was why Reese had been so easy. It wasn't him that they had to kill, but the emptiness, the nothingness inside him, and Kurt didn't know how.

Ignoring the pain of the cold, Kurt renewed his assault on the tendril, grabbing it and trying to break it loose from the mass, but it kept retracting, sliding through his hands without friction, pulling Alain ever closer to its edge. Kurt let go of the tendril, giving up on struggling futilely against it, and ran around the edge. He grabbed Alain's feet and planted his own, digging his heels into the mat and pulling, fighting the thing for possession of Alain.

But Kurt hadn't counted on Alain's blood. The smeared fluid made the canvas slick and Kurt found himself being pulled with Alain toward the edge like a water-skier behind a slow boat. The tendril retracted into the gaping emptiness, disappearing as it pulled Alain's head and shoulders in, the rest of him following slowly.

Kurt fought against the thing's immense strength, scrabbling his feet, trying to gain a solid purchase he could use to leverage himself and put up more resistance. But he was pulled inexorably forward, more of Alain disappearing into the pit. As Kurt's feet reached the edge, he let go, stumbling backward and falling to the mat a few feet away as he watched Alain's feet slip beneath the surface of the seeming pool of emptiness and disappear.

The arena was silent; the crowd's shouting was non-existent as Kurt stood and stared helplessly at the void. No tendrils rose up to come for him, but they would eventually. He knew that much. If the pit of nothingness wasn't beaten, it would do whatever it was doing with Alain and then come for him. If he left the ring, tried to run away, he'd find himself in a carnival booth on the sixth ring.

But how to beat it? It didn't have any substance. If he hit it or kicked at it, his hand or foot would just sink in and he might not be able to get it out. There was no way to attack it from the outside. The only way, he guessed, was to attack from within, assuming that it was even possible to survive inside it. *Well*, he thought, *one way or another, I'm gonna have to find out.*

Pinching his nostrils closed, Kurt ran forward, leapt up in the air, took a deep breath, and closed his eyes...

Chapter 26: Say Your Goodbyes

It was bitterly cold inside. That was Kurt's first thought. Opening his eyes, he saw nothing, just blankness. He heard nothing. He tried inhaling through his nose to see if he could smell anything, but he couldn't inhale. There was no air. But there was no sensation of a pull on him, not like how he'd seen guys explode in the vacuum of outer space in sci-fi movies. *I'm going to suffocate*, he thought, his lungs beginning to burn as he held his breath.

There was a tingling along his skin, growing quickly into pain. It was a sensation of unraveling; his body falling apart, the cells being unknit by the nothingness in which he was immersed. He didn't have to worry about suffocating. His body would dissolve into oblivion before the lack of oxygen could cause brain death. Fight against it, he shouted at himself in his mind. Fight, dammit!

Kurt tried to will his cells back together, hold himself in one piece. Getting an image of a cell in his mind, remembered shakily from Biology class, he concentrated on each part of it — the mitochondria, the vacuoles, the nucleus — trying to make his body conform to the manifestations in his mind. It was no use. The pain grew as the void took him apart bit by bit.

He exhaled his breath, the air in his lungs escaping into the emptiness. He was a goner. *No*, his mind protested, *there has to be something.*

I've tried, he thought, answering himself. *The nothing is too strong. I can't beat it.*

Then join it.

Give up? It'll eat me alive!

You're trying too hard to be something. Become nothing.

Kurt didn't understand, or perhaps he did. There was some part of his mind that did, some part that understood enough. Emptying his mind, Kurt relaxed and opened up to the nothing, welcoming it, joining with it. He felt the tendrils of nothingness sneak into his mouth and nostrils, in through his ears, unraveling him from the inside as it continued to pick him apart from the outside. The pain blurred, dimmed, and was replaced by fascination as his body became a flimsy shell, a dim outline of what he once had been, now only a few cells thick, and like a dissipating cloud of smoke, he was gone, absorbed by the emptiness.

Yet though his body was gone, though his brain cells no longer existed to make thoughts, he was still conscious in that nothingness, as if some essential part of him could not be reached by it, could not be unmade by it. A kernel of what was him had remained, had held form, or whatever it was, but it was helpless, floating in the void of nothingness. Without his body, he felt lost.

Become nothing, he thought. Slowly, he let go. He relaxed even further, like falling asleep, but with no eyes to close, no shallow ragged breaths to grow deep and even. He gave up his will and the seeming shell that enclosed his consciousness, impervious to the nothing, dissolved on its own accord. That which was Kurt, that which was something, dissolved in the nothingness, spreading out from the center and growing diffuse.

He saw a light, not with any eyes he knew. Almost as if it had been too large to see in his kernel form, but as he expanded, losing form and spreading out in all directions at once, that last tiny bit that was Kurt did not lose cohesion, did not lose perception. It was nothing, it grew without gaining mass, stretching like the skin of a drum being drawn taught around the head of the barrel, and at any moment he expected his consciousness to snap, to reach its breaking point and tear, and then it would all be over.

It continued to stretch, though, blossoming out like a ball of fire from an explosion, and he was in all parts of it at once, staring out at the edges from the center while he stared in at the center from the edge. He feared it was enough to drive him mad, but how was he to know that he wasn't mad already? Perhaps he lay in some cell under Pandaemonium, his mind snapped, this his own personal Hell.

The light became three; red, green and blue whirling around each other, condensing to form white dots as he expanded and watched from within and without. The white dots joined with others, which joined with others, some of them bouncing around as other smaller ones whirled around them. The larger dots joined with others at the borders of the orbits of their satellite dots, sharing satellite dots in bonds which held them in positions relative to each other.

Kurt's field of perception grew to encompass more dots, whirling and bouncing in more complex patterns until there were so many that the individual dots merged into something other. All the information coming in would have overwhelmed him, but he was relaxed, letting himself fall away as he seemed to dissolve, minute bits of him being consumed by each thing that entered his perception. Kurt saw strands of grey tinged with red, becoming a tiny patch of the blood stained canvas as the ends of him drifted farther apart.

The canvas expanded. It became the ring and Kurt was over it, under it, and within it. Every fan in the crowd, every piece of trash they'd thrown, every speck of dirt on their shoes consumed a piece of Kurt, absorbed him, absorbed his perception. He felt as if soon there would be nothing of him left, as if the finite being that he must be would eventually run out of bits of itself to give to these tiny bits of matter, and it was okay because he had given himself over to becoming nothing, to dissolving.

Yet still the ends of him drifted farther apart, passing through the arena's roof and floor until the whole of Pandaemonium lay within him, each denizen in the casino visible even though the roof covered them, each gambling chip, each child-soul in the cells. He drifted outward, into the rock and into the air, the ninth ring opening to the eighth, the eighth to the seventh. He could count every soul, every stone. He felt every joule of the heat, smelled every molecule of oxygen, nitrogen, and sulfur in the air, leaving to each particle he passed a tiny bit of himself. The seventh ring opened onto the sixth, the sixth onto the fifth. He could taste the foul water of the Styx, hear the pop of every air bubble passing up from the damned souls gurgling below its surface.

He engulfed the jet of flames and still he was not consumed, he didn't run out of bits of himself to give to the heat, to the fire, to the rock. He expanded through the miles of rock that composed the roof of the cavern.

Eternity spread out before him like slices in a pie. The landscapes of Heaven, Purgatory, Hell, and thousands of vistas revealed themselves to him. He could see every soul, every cloud, offering each a bit of himself as the ends of him passed. He saw galaxies as the natural universe entered into the scheme. It was amazing, level upon level, all seeming to occupy the same section of space at the same time, all vibrating to a different frequency. There was a sound to the vibrations. All the atoms and molecules moving, all the voices of all the beings, all the waves crashing against all the shores. And there were more than the planes of natural and supernatural. The universe opened onto another universe and another, each filled with wonder, each filled with sound, each taking and incorporating a bit of him as he stretched, waiting for the final bit to be consumed, waiting for nothingness to settle upon him with an end to his perception.

As Kurt moved toward the apex, the shell of the multiverse which contained all that was, the sounds blended into an amazing harmony, into a music unlike any he'd ever heard, growing to a crescendo as every bit moved into the realm of his consciousness...

And then it was gone. Kurt sat on a curb, in the middle of a city street. The perception was gone, limited to the distance his nerve endings stretched from his brain as he found himself once again trapped within his body, looking out through two eyes. The buildings rose up around him, blank. The leaves on the trees sat still, no breeze to move them. "Congratulations," a voice said beside him.

Turning his head, Kurt saw the man. Same brown coat, same drinker's nose. "I was..."

"I know," the man said.

"Am I dead?"

"No, you won."

Kurt looked around, incredulous. He was half-in shock from the whole experience. "How?"

"You filled nothing with everything. They cancelled each other out."

Kurt was so confused, so lost, he almost wanted to revert to childhood and cry like a little kid. He remembered being in the pit, feeling it slowly unraveling him, and then he'd thought to become one with the pit, become nothing... "Nothing is everything and everything is nothing," Kurt muttered to himself, comprehension coming in small shards like a broken mirror reassembling itself. "But how did you know what I did?" he asked, turning to the man.

"From here, one sees quite a bit. We're at the origin point. Before the universe was anywhere, it was Nowhere."

Kurt reached out a hand to touch him, but pulled it back. "Are you God?"

"No," the man said, chuckling. "I'm just an old friend of Alain's."

Kurt shook his head in confusion. "What? I... don't..."

"I don't understand it either," the man said, cutting Kurt off. "One day I woke up and I was here. I couldn't leave. So, I just dangled my feet over the edge, where the sidewalk ends, and started watching... But I can't keep you here to listen to me ramble. You have to go back now."

"How?"

"Just realize where you are. When you know that you're Nowhere..."

Kurt smiled as comprehension dawned. "Then I have a location, and I'm somewhere, and..."

"Tell Alain that Jean Louis says hello," the man said, and then everything disappeared.

* * * *

"...I'm not here anymore," Kurt said, feeling the mat under his rear end. The crowd roared as he looked around. He was in the arena. Reese's lifeless husk lay a few feet away, Alain lying next to it, face down, and Vinnie lay crumpled next to the broken post.

Kurt crawled over to Alain, putting his hands underneath Alain's shoulder, and rolled him over. Alain's mouth had swollen, there was a dark swelling over his right eye, and the gash along his abdomen remained, though the bleeding seemed to have stopped. As Alain took in a strained breath, Kurt sighed in relief and shook him lightly. Alain's eyes flickered open, not seeming to focus on anything. "Did we win," he asked, the words coming out weak and breathy.

Kurt smiled, his throat growing thick and his eyes misting. "Yeah," he said. "We kicked their butts."

Alain closed his eyes and his body relaxed further. "Cool."

* * * *

Kurt sat in the hospital room as Alain lay in bed. They'd only been given an hour to talk before Kurt, George and Junior would have to leave. Alain was conscious, whatever they'd given him helping keep the pain at bay for the time being, his wounds wrapped and bandaged. He had spent the last forty-five minutes filling Kurt in on what they could expect in Purgatory. "Now remember," he said, "Dante seemed to have the general gist, but there was a lot he got wrong or left out. Maybe on purpose, maybe things have changed... I don't know. Just don't expect everything to conform to what I told you."

Kurt nodded, scribbling a last note in his journal. "What do I do when I get to Heaven?"

"I don't know," Alain said, a small wince crossing his features. Apparently, what they'd given him was wearing off. "Marie will be there. Find her. She'll help you."

"Okay," Kurt said, closing his journal. "That seems to be it." He stood from his chair, putting the notebook in his pack.

"We've still got a few minutes left," Alain said, tiredness in his voice. "Stay and talk to me. It's going to be a lonely wait while you and George take care of business."

Kurt zipped the backpack closed and sat again. "Do you honestly think we're going to succeed?"

"I have to. It's the only hope I've got."

A silence filled the room and grew with each passing second, becoming uncomfortable. "You never told me how you beat that thing," Alain said, breaking it.

Kurt recounted the story in as much detail as he could. Much of the memory was already getting hazy. "There was a man there," Kurt said, the memory coming back to him. "He said he was an old friend of yours. His name was," Kurt paused, trying to remember, "John something. No, like John... Jean Louis. He said to tell you that Jean Louis said hello."

Alain laughed, a small chuckle that caused him to wince as it aggravated his broken rib. "It figures," he said, smiling.

Kurt stood and moved his chair closer to the bed. "I don't want to pry, but who is he?"

"You wouldn't believe me."

Kurt looked into Alain's eyes. "I've pretty much had the cynicism beat out of me on this trip. You'd be surprised at what I'm ready to believe."

"Jean Louis Kerouac," Alain said, "Jack Kerouac."

Kurt's eyes went wide. "You knew Jack Kerouac? You were friends?"

"Yeah," Alain said. "Dangling his feet off the edge of eternity and watching absolutely everything." Alain smiled. "I could see him enjoying that... for a while at least."

A million questions formed in Kurt's mind. Who else had Alain known? What other Beat authors had he been friends with? How... "Time's up," Mammon said, coming through the door. "Say your goodbyes and let's go."

Kurt stood and leaned over Alain, clasping his hand. "I won't let you down," Kurt said.

Alain squeezed back. "I'm counting on it."

* * * *

Kurt looked at the green glow on the cliff face of the ninth ring. It was circular, about ten feet wide. He was in his own clothes again, his backpack slung over one shoulder as he clutched the strap with his right hand, holding Junior's hand in his left.

"Now don't forget the deal," Mammon said. "You have a week to get to Heaven and get an audience with... that guy... and plead your case. If you fail to win Beaudreaux's salvation within that time, you come back here."

"You don't need to remind me," Kurt snapped angrily. Mammon retreated, an arm raising as if to ward off an attack.

Kurt turned, leading Junior toward the glowing portal on the wall. George joined them, making the last adjustments to the straps of his own backpack.

"You ready?" Kurt asked. George nodded. Junior looked scared, but he nodded too.

"Then we're off to see the wizard." Kurt smiled, squeezed Junior's hand, and stepped through.

Chapter 27: You Will Do Penance

It was impossible for Nybras to sweat, but his neck felt hot just the same, and the collar of his shirt itched around the gnarled, nut-brown skin. He stood, trying to build up his confidence, in the city of Dis on the sixth ring of Hell, in a hallway within the hollow pedestal under a statue of three Gorgons, in front of a door with a large golden A on it. The door opened.

"He sees you now," a yattering imp said, bouncing up and down on its spindly legs while it held the door for Nybras. "Oh, he's not pleased, not pleased at all," the imp's voice was high pitched and raspy, a heavy note of derision in it. As Nybras walked through, it jumped up on his shoulder and took hold of one of his large, pointed ears between two bony fingers, digging its sharp nails into the flesh and bending the ear towards its mouth. "You're fucked. Oh, you are so fucked. They're going to sing songs about how fucked you are."

Nybras ventured slowly into the darkness, a circle of light ahead of him, his neck itching like crazy as the imp sang in his ear. "There once was a demon named Nybras, Nybras, who screwed up so royally. They cut off his head and put shit in his neck, then washed it all down with some pee. There once was a demon named Ny... urrrk."

The imp's song was cut off by Nybras' hand wrapping around its throat and yanking it off his shoulder. With a grunt, he threw it off into the darkness, taking pleasure in hearing the thud of its small body impacting against an unseen wall. His gloating was quickly cut off as the circle of light ran across the floor and surrounded him, placing him in its center. "Ny-bras," a booming, deep voice said. It was an awful, flatulent voice, like a chorus of a thousand tubas made flesh.

A ring of fire sprung up on the border of the circle, keeping Nybras from moving more than a few inches in any direction unless he wished to get burned. If he was mortal and this was the world, the flames might have been a welcome exit, but the flames would only char the suit from his body and singe his skin. A lost cherub, warped by the world in which he lived, Nybras had been created of stronger stuff than mere flesh. Even the damned souls might have some respite as they slowly healed their wounds, their pseudo nerve endings going numb with the shock their minds so mercifully allowed, but for Nybras, pain was a concept that had meaning beyond anything men could imagine. Pain could become his life; never-ending pain, constant and in full bloom, like the sting of salt rubbed into a wound that was forever new. Nybras shrank into himself, hunching his shoulders and moving as much of his body away from the flames as possible.

"You... ummm... wanted to see me, sir," Nybras asked, stuttering out the words, his voice breaking and pausing abruptly, making obvious his knowledge that this wasn't just a casual meeting with the boss.

"You will do penance," the unseen voice said.

"But -- " Nybras wanted to defend himself. He hadn't been privy to the knowledge of the vampire and the two mortals gaining entry to Hell. He had no way of knowing that the man's name was Beaudreaux and not Stark, and the concept of a vampire with zero kills was such an unlikelihood that it was easy for him to be convinced that the computer was malfunctioning. How was he to know that the real Avery Stark actually did have zero kills? It wasn't fair.

"You will do penance."

Nybras braced himself for what would come next. The shackles that would wrap around his body and carry him off to a special pit in Pandaemonium exclusively reserved for disobedient denizens, a place where all the tortures in Hell combined into a storm of pains, into a rage of anguish so terrible the suffering could not even catch their breath long enough to scream. "You know of the wager?" the voice asked, the shackles hovering into view just beyond the circle but not venturing past the flames.

Nybras had heard. He'd watched the pre-fight show on a monitor in one of the Pandaemonium bars. "Yes," he said meekly.

"You will see to it that they lose."

Nybras shook his head in disbelief. "B-but... how?"

"Are you not hellspawn? Are you not a demon?"

Nybras wanted direly to shout "no!" He was spawned in Heaven, as were they all, all the major players. He'd been a cherub, good with numbers, and one day Satan had come upon him walking the halls of the celestial palace. Oh, Satan was beautiful then, such light, such wonder. Nybras' fall had come from eventually loving him more than God. He had been so beautiful... "I... am."

"Then be it," the voice rumbled, the reverberations making Nybras shudder. That had been the downfall. Lucifer, oh, he'd been beautiful, and cunning, and sly. But the rest; big brutes with more muscle than brains who all fawned upon him, praised his beauty, convinced him that they could gather their strength and defeat the holy host. And Nybras, lucky Nybras who was so in love with that beauty that he was

236

blind to anything else, let himself be stuck with keeping books for Azmodeus, the morale officer of the new armies.

The flames rose up with ferocity, closing over his head like a dome. "You are hellspawn," the voice reminded him, "serve for the love of your master." And in the flames, for a moment, he could swear he saw Satan as he'd once been — the brightest angel in Heaven. Then the floor opened up to swallow him and he fell.

Chapter 28: Settle Down!

This time there was no stumble, no fall. Kurt walked through, stepping in one side of the portal and stepping out the other. He held Junior's hand in a firm grip, but he didn't have to drag him through. The boy came willingly, wanting to be out of Hell, trusting that whatever lay on the other side of the portal would be better, trusting in Kurt to take care of him.

Kurt had never had someone trust in him like this, so completely, putting their fate in his hands. He'd heard stories about dogs, the animal trustingly licking its human's hand as the moment approached when the veterinarian would put it to sleep. And now Kurt felt almost in the same position with Junior, leading him into God knew what with the boy trustingly holding his hand.

I will be loyal and faithful to my Lost Boy brothers, and I will do right by them, and I will trust them to do right by me, and if I break this oath I'll turn into a dirty bug and eat dog poop forever. Junior believed in the oath, or it seemed he did, and Kurt had come to believe in it to the extent that he felt he owed that allegiance to Junior. It was almost as if he'd become the boy's father, or at least an older cousin with guardianship.

"All right, Fearless Leader," George said, standing on Kurt's other side, "what now?"

George... Older than Kurt, bigger and stronger than Kurt, with military training, yet he was deferring to Kurt's command. Technically Kurt was the youngest of the group. George was almost 30, and Junior... well, even though he had the appearance of a young boy and acted much like one — a very traumatized one — he'd been a prisoner in Hell for over seventy years. Kurt wasn't even twenty-four yet. He didn't feel ready to lead, capable of leading. But Alain had briefed Kurt on what to expect in Purgatory, had put his faith in Kurt to save his soul. Alain had anointed Kurt as the new leader of the expedition, passed the mantle to him. It made Kurt want to sit down and become a rock, just turn to stone and not have all this responsibility heaped upon him, but there was a lot riding on the outcome of this quest or whatever it was. George's soul, Alain's soul, Junior... and Kurt's own soul.

He took stock of his surroundings. They seemed to be in a small, almost circular antechamber, a seven-sided shape about fifteen feet across. The walls were white concrete, the ceiling about ten feet high, and the floor was covered in reddish-brown heptagonal tiles with white grouting lines between them. It was spotlessly clean and a gleaming chrome escalator tirelessly rose to whatever lay above. "The only place to go is up," Kurt said.

Kurt was wearing a pistol in a holster on his belt. With his free hand he unsheathed it and passed it over to George. "Be ready for anything, but don't be conspicuous about it." George took the pistol and put it in his waistband, untucking his shirt to cover it.

Kurt stepped onto the escalator first, drawing Junior on with him. It seemed to rise about thirty feet, concrete bordering both sides, and it was odd, Kurt noted, that there wasn't one beside it, going in the opposite direction, as if no one was ever expected to go down from where they were headed. Breaking through into open space, Kurt got his first glimpse of Purgatory, so shocking that he tripped on the metal plate where the escalator ended. He let go of Junior's hand as he stumbled forward, regaining his balance and looking out at the vista before him. For miles and miles, curving over the horizon, stretched the most immense... was it an office plaza? A shopping mall?

Kurt closed his eyes and shook his head. Purgatory was supposed to be a great mountain with ledges where the penitent souls learned the lessons of the sins they had committed, expiating them before they could move on to Heaven. But this...

He was in the center of one end of a main plaza. Twenty feet above, a mezzanine stretched out along one side, about thirty feet wide, no stairs leading up to it, and above that, maybe two hundred or more feet, levels began, great long balconies that circled the immense length, overlooking the main plaza. "Junior," George shouted behind him.

Kurt turned back. Junior was floating in midair and George had a tenuous grip on one foot, keeping him from floating higher. Kurt took a couple of running steps, leapt up, catching a better grip on Junior's leg, and pulled him down to the floor, then pushed on his shoulders to keep him anchored. It wasn't a hard task to keep him on the ground. The pull wasn't great, but Kurt could feel a light straining against the pressure he put on Junior. "George," Kurt said, "hold him."

Kurt took off his backpack and emptied its contents. Putting in one bottle of water, his iPhone, and a notebook, he gingerly slipped it over Junior's shoulders and adjusted the straps. The fit wasn't perfect, considering the backpack had been made for someone Kurt's size, not Junior's, but it was good enough not to fall off too easily. "Let go," Kurt said.

George took his hands off the boy and they watched. He rose slowly, his heels leaving the floor first, then his toes, an expression of fear on his face. Kurt pushed lightly on Junior's shoulder, bringing Junior back to the floor, and put another bottle of water in the pack. He let go again and watched. Junior stayed on the floor. "Walk a little," Kurt said, waving Junior away.

The boy hesitated, looking at Kurt with a pitiful gaze as if to ask *do I have to*, as if it scared him to put distance between himself and Kurt, but a reassuring nod got him to do as Kurt told him, walking about ten feet away and then back. "Now jump as high as you can," Kurt said. The boy squatted and then sprang up, his little hands holding onto the straps of the backpack. He went nearly six feet in the air, then came down slowly, looking like an astronaut on a moon walk. Kurt walked over, patted his shoulder and tousled his hair. "Good," he said. "We had a close call there."

"What in the... what was that," George asked.

"When the souls arrive in Purgatory, they're weighed down by their sins. As their sins are expiated, they can move up higher toward the pinnacle, toward Heaven. Junior apparently has no sin..."

"So, he was floating up to Heaven," George said, completing Kurt's sentence.

Kurt looked upward, trying to spot the ceiling. There was one, maybe three-hundred and fifty feet up, paned with glass skylights, and light came in through it, ostensibly from some sort of sun. There didn't seem to be any artificial light sources that Kurt could spot, but Alain had warned him that Purgatory did have day and night. Kurt didn't know whether or not to believe it though. Dante's description was far from the mark on this one.

"Let's put the rest of this stuff in your pack, George," Kurt said, bending down to pick up the remaining contents of his own, strewn across the floor. He spotted the bandanna in which he'd wrapped Mick's pinky and picked it up. The final image he'd had of Mick came unbidden into his mind, the man crucified upside-down along the ramp into the arena, the stub on his hand where the pinky had once been, the catatonic, unblinking stare. Mick had saved Kurt's life and the crucifixion was his reward. Kurt put the bandanna into his pocket, wanting to keep the pinky close.

George slipped off the large frame pack and put it down near the pile of stuff, opening it and helping Kurt pack it all in; the ibuprofen packets, more water... There were no cigarettes.

They untied the rifle from the pack and George slung it over his shoulder, allowing Kurt to holster the pistol on his belt again. When the items were all in George's pack, they zipped it back up and George took it up, hooking the straps over his shoulders. Kurt took Junior's hand again, and they walked forward into the plaza, looking for a way up.

The plaza was as long as the eye could see and then some, easily fifty yards wide, but Kurt couldn't spot an escalator or elevator or stairs anywhere. The walls on this level were blank, just tall expanses of white, leading more than a hundred feet up to the first concourse on one side, to the mezzanine on the other. Yet none of it was familiar. He'd seen the entirety of existence, everything, including Purgatory, Heaven, Hell, all the planes of eternity, but it was all hazy, it was all fading...

About a mile in, they came to the edge of a pool. Raised three feet from the floor, tiled along its edge with the same reddish-brown brick and white grout, it stretched on into the main plaza, disappearing over the horizon. It was wide, maybe 30 yards with thirty-foot aisles on each side between its edges and the walls, containing clear water and a blank white bottom. Kurt and George sat down on the edge, Junior standing in front of them.

So far, they hadn't seen a single soul, hadn't heard a single sound. It was as if the mall were abandoned. "So, what now," George asked, turning to look farther in.

Kurt followed his gaze. "I don't know. This isn't anything like I'd expected. We've gotta go up. I know that much."

"But how? I don't see any stairs, any escalators..."

Kurt brought his feet up and stood up on the ledge. "Junior," he said, reaching down to the boy, "come up here."

Junior took his hand and Kurt helped him up onto the ledge. "I'm going to put you up on my shoulders and I want you to tell me what you see. Okay?"

Junior nodded. Placing his hands under Junior's armpits, Kurt lifted him up to sit on his shoulders. "What do you see?"

Junior was silent. "Stand up if you can." Kurt felt Junior's hands on his head and he held Junior's ankles for balance. The boy was amazingly light, only a couple of pounds, the backpack's weight being partially offset by Junior's buoyancy. "See anything now?" Kurt asked.

"Yes," Junior replied, his voice quiet and meek.

"What?"

"People."

"Sit down and hold on tight," Kurt said, tugging gently on Junior's ankles as George stood up eagerly. Junior did as Kurt said. Holding onto Junior's legs as the boy gripped handfuls of Kurt's hair, he jumped down from the ledge and took off running, George keeping pace beside him.

They jogged down the right side of the pool, the mezzanine above them. They couldn't spot anyone yet, but as they ran, they began hearing faint shouts in the distancer. With every step, the shouts grew louder, slowly growing into a distant roar, sounding like thousands of people shouting excitedly. Cautiously, Kurt slowed his pace, George slowing alongside him, but the shouts continued to grow louder at a quickening pace. And then, in the distance, two images became clear to Kurt. On the water a large boat chugged forward, and on both sides of the pool, huge masses of people ran alongside it, shouting and cheering. They were still hundreds of yards off but they ran forward at an inhuman pace, nearly as fast as speeding cars on a city street, somehow achieving incredible velocity as they tried to keep up with the boat.

It looked like an enlarged version of the amphibious troop transports from World War II movies, a few shades darker than battleship grey, and the mass of people extended back, continuously pouring forward over the horizon like a flood of water breaking loose from a dam. Kurt backed up as they approached, not showing any signs of slowing, their shouts becoming an excited roar.

"We'd better move," George shouted over the noise of the approaching mass as he tugged on Kurt's shoulder. Kurt took hold of Junior's ankles and turned, running back toward the pool's edge. As they passed it, they stopped and pressed themselves against the wall, poised to move if the flood of people became dangerous.

The people rushed past them, gathering in the plaza in front of the pool's end, jostling each other as they jockeyed for position, eagerly awaiting the arrival of the landing craft. It slowed as it neared the edge, stopping ten feet from the tiled border, its front panel dropping forward to become a gangplank. The front of the crowd surged forward onto the gangplank as a mass of new arrivals were seemingly pushed out, looking confused, afraid. Most of them started rising the moment they came out into the open air and the waiting souls grabbed for them, wrapped them in embraces, lunged for their legs, trying to catch a grip on them. Souls thronging onto the platform got pushed off the edges and fell into the water, floundering there while others beat at each other and fought to get at the new arrivals.

As the arrivals rose, some of the souls clung on, slowly moving upward with them, most losing their grips within ten or twenty feet, falling back into the surging mass of people only to be crowd-surfed along the top of the throng and thrown into the water, or seemingly denting the mass, knocking down other souls as they fell from greater heights.

Looking up, Kurt could see the rising figures, the luckiest ones having lost their hangers on, reaching the lowest levels. As they reached the apexes of their individual rises, each seemed to shake like it was caught in the grip of a rushing wind and was blown onto the walkway of its level, disappearing from sight. Those hangers-on who had been tenacious enough to retain their grips on their hosts were shaken loose and fell back to the plaza, impacting against the hard floor, splashing into the water, or taking down portions of the crowd like dropping bombs. And when the new arrivals had all been expelled, the gangplank dissolved, dropped the remaining throng on it into the water, and reappeared as a closure over the entrance to the landing craft as it chugged backward, going to pick up its next load of souls.

The seething mass of people hooted and cried and charged back down the aisles in hot pursuit, leaving the few dazed new arrivals who hadn't floated up and some unfortunate stunned dropped souls and victims of the violence. Kurt watched the bulk of them leave, feeling a severe disgust. The whole incident had taken no more than minutes, but it felt like it would take years to get rid of the foul taste it had left in his mouth.

The new souls who hadn't been too severely injured stepped out of the pool and looked around. Most wore suits or dresses, some in various states of undress. They were of every race, every nationality, all pale and sickly white under the filtered sunlight from the roof panels, no red flames to tint them closer to flesh. A woman, seemingly Caucasian, in a light dress, saw Kurt and George and walked toward them. She stopped five feet away and stared at them. "Is this Hell?" she asked, her voice frightened, her body trembling.

"No," Kurt said. Slowly he lifted Junior off his shoulders and set him on the floor. "This is Purgatory," he said, stepping forward.

The woman looked at him, then looked behind her. "You're not dead, are you?"

"No."

The woman's expression was blank, then she fell to her knees, weeping into her hands. "I'm so sorry. I tried to be good. I tried." She clasped her hands in front of her. "Please bless me."

"Ummm," Kurt hesitated, looking back at George. Junior had taken George's hand and was watching everything with his normally blank stare, not as if interested but not with disinterest either.

"You're alive," the woman pleaded. "You're alive and you're here. Are you a saint?" She looked at George and Junior. "Are they your wards? Are you escorting them to Heaven? Can you take me with you?"

"Ummm..."

"Help me," she shouted, attracting the attention of the other souls behind her. "How can you be so cruel," she cried. "Bless me... forgive me..."

"Bless me too," another soul shouted from near the pool's edge as it approached. "Yes, bless me too," another soul chimed in, the others joining it as they all approached. Kurt tried to think of why they were there. Alain had explained it. The late repentant inhabited the beach, well at least Dante had described it as a beach. They were those who had "found" God too late in their lives, too apathetic to give care to the status of their souls until they had reached their deathbeds or their final years. Kurt didn't like the concept. As far as he was concerned, if someone was good, they should go to Heaven. Just as he'd considered the first circle of Hell unfair, this too sucked royally.

"Bless me," the chorus of souls called, more and more of them approaching. There were perhaps thirty in all who were coming toward him, maybe another ten who lay too stunned to move. Some limped or hobbled, their legs damaged from the falls, others shuffled, half in a stupor from the shock of arriving where they had. "Bless me, please. Bless me." They moved in closer, some falling to their knees and clasping their hands in front of them. Others were more bold, trying to touch Kurt, dropping down on their hands and knees to grovel at his feet.

Kurt moved back, pressing against the wall next to Junior and George. "What do I do?" he asked, looking helplessly at George, his hands up protectively, trying to fend off the souls who reached for him.

"I can shoot them," George replied, slapping at hands with one of his own while he held the rifle at the ready with his other, "or... you can bless them."

Kurt hadn't been to synagogue very often, neither of his parents being strongly religious, only taking him on the occasional Saturday or the High Holidays. How was a secular Jew from Manhattan going to bless a bunch of half-damned goyim? "Settle down!" he shouted, needing some quiet in which to think.

The souls obeyed, only a few whimpers coming from them as the few stragglers dropped to their knees and looked expectantly to him for his blessing. If he told them he was no saint, that he couldn't help them... He'd seen the throng go after the new arrivals. These souls might try to tear him apart. George could shoot them, but then what? It wasn't like he could kill them. "Dear Lord," he intoned, the sound of his voice quieting even the whimpers. But what to say next? "Ummm... Dear Lord, I beg You to forgive these sinners. Ummm... Grant them relief from their... from their... from the weight of their mistakes. Let their hearts be their merit..." He paused, amazed at his cool turn of a phrase. "Let their hearts be their merit and let them rise up from this degradation into the light of Your love. Amen."

Kurt looked at the souls, afraid of what would happen when the benediction had no effect. They weren't floating upward, but they continued to wait as if he could do something more. "What's your name?" he asked the woman in front of him, the one who had first called him a saint.

"Ariana Guerra," she replied, her head still down, her hands still clasped in front of her.

Kurt really did feel sorry for her. In life she must have been a beautiful girl, perhaps happy and full of joy, but here she was only slightly better than damned, and it weighed heavy in his heart to see her suffer. He wanted to do something. If he could help her rise, even up to the first level, she'd be that much closer to paying her debt and moving onward. "Give me your hand, Ariana."

Cautiously, almost afraid to touch him as if she would get burned, she reached out and took his hand. He pulled gently on it, prompting her to stand up. "That was all the blessing I can give," he said sadly, placing his other hand on her cheek. "I'm sorry. If it helps any, I forgive you."

Ariana clasped the hand he held against her cheek, turned her face and kissed it. "Thank you," she said.

Kurt felt her hand tugging from his grip, but she wasn't backing away. She was moving upward. Her hand slipped out of his and he watched her slowly rise from the floor, her speed gradually increasing, moving diagonally away until a hundred feet up she was in the middle of the plaza and continuing upward at an increased pace. At the last level before the ceiling, she shook and was blown to the side, disappearing from sight.

Kurt continued to watch until after she was gone, complete silence surrounding him, and then all chaos broke loose. George was quick to respond, firing two shots in the air from the rifle. The souls fell back, afraid, but they were like a dog on a chain, straining, just waiting for the right moment to break free and rush forward. Kurt, on the other hand, was in shock. Did he do that? Was it his blessing, his forgiving her? Was it Ariana's willingness to thank him for trying? He didn't know if he could take responsibility, but if he could... He shook his head and moved back to stand by George and Junior. "Saint Kurt," George said with sarcastic deference, a chuckle following it.

"Shut up," Kurt snapped, then cringed. "Sorry."

"S'okay," George replied.

Kurt looked down at Junior to see how he was handling all this. "You okay?" he asked, putting a hand on the boy's shoulder.

"You saved her," Junior said, looking at Kurt with awe.

"No," Kurt said, shaking his head, "I don't think so. I think she saved herself."

Junior reached up and pulled Kurt's hand off his shoulder, gripping it with both hands. "No. You saved her."

Kurt stared at the boy. What had Junior seen that he hadn't? And how had he saved her? He couldn't understand it. His blessing hadn't made anyone else rise and he couldn't believe that his forgiveness meant anything. He pulled his hand from Junior's grip and stepped away from the wall again. "You," he said, pointing to a meek-looking man, "come here."

The man looked around as if Kurt had to be pointing to someone else, then tapped his chest while looking questioningly at Kurt. "Yes, you," Kurt said, waving him over. The man detached from the small crowd and shuffled over, his head bowed.

"What's your name," Kurt asked as the man stood before him.

"Leon... Leon Jackson," The man mumbled staring at the floor.

"Where ya from, Leon?"

"Alabama, sir," Leon said, still refusing to meet Kurt's eyes.

"What did you do for a living, Leon?"

"I was a pipe fitter, sir."

"Give me your hand, Leon."

Kurt put his hand out and the man slowly, tentatively, put his own hand in it. "Look at me, Leon." The man raised his head and looked into Kurt's face. It was obvious he was frightened of him. Reaching forward, Kurt cupped his other hand against the side of Leon's jaw. "I don't know if I can help you, Leon, but I'm going to try... There's a weight in your soul, Leon. Can you feel it?"

Leon nodded. "When I move my hand away from your face, Leon, I want you to imagine that I'm pulling that weight off of you." Leon nodded again. Kurt was amazed at this blind trust, this willingness to believe that he could actually do any of this. Kurt didn't believe it. He was talking out of his ass, making this up as he went. He didn't feel an obligation to these people, not like he did to Alain, or Junior, or Mick. But, still, there was some boy-scout instinct in him that made it hard for him to just turn his back on them, to tell them to go screw off when they'd seen him save someone else. Slowly, Kurt pulled his hand back. "I forgive you, Leon."

Leon looked at him for a moment and then began rising. "Thank you," Leon said as his hand slipped out of Kurt's. Kurt watched him rise slowly, gaining speed, until he reached the last level, like Ariana, and was taken by the wind.

The crowd of people started shouting again, pressing forward toward Kurt. "Me next," they called. "Save me!" George fired off another shot from the rifle and they drew back. Kurt knew it wouldn't work indefinitely. Eventually they would swarm him and George without heed, the gun meaning nothing to them as they realized all it could do was cause temporary pain. Kurt stepped back to join George and Junior against the wall.

"I've got an idea," George said, slipping his pack off and setting it on the floor. Opening it up, he reached in, dug around a bit, and came out with a coil of thin orange rope. "Hundred and fifty feet," he said, handing it to Kurt as he bent down to re-zip the pack.

"Jesus," Kurt exclaimed. "What are you, Felix the Cat? Lock picking stuff, first aid kit, food, flashlights, ammo, rope... What else you got in that bag of tricks there?"

"Not much," George said, standing up. "Some rock-climbing gear, a short-wave radio, matches, some fishing wire and hooks. Basically wilderness survival... and then some."

"If you find a pretty girl and a steak dinner in there, I've got dibs." Kurt paused, waiting for George to laugh. George didn't. "So, what do we do with the rope?"

"Well..."

Chapter 29: You Sure You're Okay?

George stood against the wall, holding the end of a knotted length of rope while Kurt stood out in the plaza, holding the end of another piece. Both ropes were attached to a soul, a Greek fisherman, who floated upward toward the edge of the mezzanine level. Kurt's rope kept him from floating off, while George played out his rope to try to keep him from floating too far toward the middle to be any good to them. As the man reached the edge of the Mezzanine, George gave a tug on his rope to pull him over so he could grab the railing. The man grabbed it and clung to it, wrapping his legs around it to keep himself from floating away. Untying George's length of rope from his waist, he knotted the end around the railing. "Done," he shouted.

George yanked on the rope to test the knot. It seemed to hold, so he leapt up, grabbed it just above one of the knots they'd tied for handholds and swung out from under the mezzanine into the uncovered portion of the plaza. "It's good," he shouted.

The fisherman waved to them and then untied Kurt's length of rope from around his waist, letting it fall to the floor. Releasing the railing, he floated up and out, rising to the top before he was blown over.

George let go of his rope and stood next to Kurt out in the plaza. Junior remained back against the wall, but a call from Kurt brought the boy jogging out to stand between them as Kurt went about the task of forgiving each of the remaining souls in quick succession, watching the air above the plaza fill with floating bodies.

George was amazed by all this. He'd grown accustomed to magic at an early age; his parents having a vampire for a best friend helped. Yet nothing could have prepared him for all this. He'd seen dead bodies, seen the undead, but the demons, these souls... God forgive him, but they gave him the willies. Even Junior. For all intents and purposes, he seemed like a little boy, but he wasn't. He was older than George and he'd never even been alive. He wasn't a boy. He was a thing. George couldn't help feeling a little spooked.

Even with Alain's vampirism, George had never really believed in Hell, or demons, or the Devil, not deep down. But now... Now he was trying to physically make his way to Heaven, his soul bet on whether or not he could. And when it came down to it, every dirty fighting trick he knew, every bullet he'd brought, none of it would help him when he got there. This guy, Kurt, some kid who ended up here by accident... He'd watched this guy jump into that pit and somehow beat it from the inside. Now he was literally saving souls, speeding up their voyages to Heaven, and it was like nothing to him.

Kurt didn't seem extraordinary. He had a good fighting spirit when he got charged up, but he was a kid. Half of the time he seemed like a helpless baby, totally ignorant of the harsh realities of the world, of all the ways it tried to kill you. And then when it reared up its ugly head and came after him, Kurt turned reality around and kicked it in the ass.

"Ready to go?" Kurt asked, the last soul floating off toward whatever destination. George nodded. He'd follow Kurt anywhere, if only to see what was going to happen next.

* * * *

George had climbed the rope, the loose length going up coiled over his shoulder. Then he lowered it. One end of the loose rope was tied around Junior's waist as George stood on the mezzanine, holding the other. Kurt slipped off the backpack and Junior began to rise. Somehow, watching Kurt send those souls floating upward had attached the boy to him even more strongly, had opened him up. As Kurt had been releasing them, relieving them, whatever the heck it was he'd been doing, Kurt had snuck a glance at the boy now and then and he could swear he'd caught Junior smiling.

George pulled in the slack on the rope, keeping Junior in tow, pulling him toward the mezzanine as he floated upward. As he pulled the boy over the edge, with nothing to weigh him down, he tied the rope off, letting Junior float there like a helium balloon.

Kurt adjusted the straps on his backpack and put it on, then tied the bottom of the knotted rope to George's pack. The rope was thin enough that the knots didn't give the best purchase, but slowly Kurt made his way up it, thankful for the physical exertion, thankful for feeling like he only weighed thirty pounds, thankful for something to absorb his concentration so he didn't have to think about what he'd just done. It confused him, and as a matter of fact, scared the shit out of him. As he crested the edge of the mezzanine railing, George began pulling the rope up, his backpack along with it. Kurt used the time to pull Junior down to the floor and put the other backpack on him. Once the two lengths of rope were coiled, the unknotted one was put in George's pack while the knotted one, now too bulky, was wound and strapped to the outside.

George walked point, rifle at the ready, while Kurt took flank with the pistol back in its holster. Junior walked between them. This wasn't the Yellow Brick Road and it wasn't wise to walk abreast of each other, arm in arm, singing. The running crowds of the lower level had proved that Purgatory was not a safe place.

From up at this height, Kurt still couldn't see the far end of the mall. It had to stretch on for miles, and with his luck, the stairs or escalator or whatever it was that led up to the first walkway was probably at the other end. The mezzanine that they walked on now was just covered with the same tile, a four-foot wall along its periphery, a chromed metal tube running along the wall's top as a rail.

Something sort of pink lined the wall ahead to the right, almost like a padding a foot or so thick. Coming within about thirty feet from it, George stopped. "What's up?" Kurt asked, moving around Junior to stand next to George. George seemed green around the gills, half ready to vomit. Holding on to the railing for support, he waved his rifle at the padding.

Kurt stepped closer to examine it. The surface was uneven and the padding was segmented, with lines running down the middle of each segment. Kurt moved closer. The lines were zippers, and the padding's plastic lining was semi-translucent from a closer distance. "Body bags," Kurt mumbled in disbelief. Running a few miles ahead of them, the wall was covered three to four high in body bags, every one of them full. He heard the roar of the crowd in the distance, the mass of souls running at inhumanly breakneck speed.

Peering at the closest bag, one without any above it, he didn't see movement, but there was something inside, a human shape darkly outlined in the plastic. He was tempted to open it, inspect what was inside, talk to the person. The roar of the crowd grew louder, nearly

255

below him as he reached forward for the zipper. He drew his hand back like he'd been shocked as the shape inside reacted violently, thrashing in response to his closeness. Kurt stepped away, moving back until the soul inside the bag settled down.

The crowd had passed below him now. The souls were probably just being pushed out. He turned to look out over the plaza and see the bodies pass. They rose in ones and twos, sometimes a hanger-on making it past the mezzanine level, and then one paused. Shaking, it blew diagonally toward Kurt. He ducked as it passed over his head and smacked into the wall with a thud. Two sheets of plastic shot out from the wall and surrounded the unfortunate soul, meeting in front of it and zipping up, sealing it in. It thrashed a moment, but soon fell still.

Kurt racked his brains for what Alain had told him of Dante's description of Purgatory. These were the late repentant who had died violent deaths; essentially believers who had died unexpectedly and had only repented with their dying breaths. Kurt felt a rage growing inside him. He might believe in God now, but he still thought God was an asshole. Knowing he could possibly save these people, he was tempted to start unzipping bags, start the whole process he'd gone through on the last level. But how long would it take? There were thousands of bags.

He felt frustrated. He had never expected to be able to help these people, but he could. But the more time he spent helping them, the more he risked his chances to get to Heaven, get an audience with God, and plead Alain's case. People were going to die faster than he could forgive them, anyway.

Kurt's knees went out from under him and he sat down on the floor with a thud, suddenly unable to stand. These thoughts were so alien, so incredible. It was like they were registering on him for the first time. He was going to walk through the gates of Heaven, up the steps of the celestial palace, and ask for an audience with God. When he was in college, he couldn't even get an audience with the Dean of the English department without making an appointment two weeks in advance. The magnitude of the whole thing was outrageous.

Even Moses had been told "don't call me, I'll call you." Who was he? A junior copywriter from New York? He wasn't a prophet or saint. He hadn't been selected by God. He'd literally fallen into this when Vinnie knocked him through the portal. He'd seen all of existence, been to Nowhere...

"You okay, Kurt?" George said.

Kurt jumped, surprised by George being next to him, not having noticed him approach, but the shock helped knock him out of his stupor. "Uhh, yeah," Kurt said, looking up.

George put out his hand and Kurt took it, letting George help him to his feet. Kurt was still dazed, but at least his legs would support him again. "You sure you're okay," George asked, inspecting Kurt's face.

What was Kurt supposed to say? No, I'm not okay. I can't do this. What the fuck ever made me think I could? Junior was over by the wall, seemingly too afraid of the body bags to come forward, but Kurt was sure Junior would come if he called him. "Yeah, I'm fine," Kurt said in a low voice, his breathing so shallow he had to inhale before he could say another word. "Take point and keep close to the rail. We don't want to disturb the bags."

George looked surprised. "You're not going to do anything to help them?"

"What do I look like to you," Kurt snapped, his face bunching up, his eyes squinting, "the fucking messiah?" He walked to the closest bag, the soul in it thrashing in response to his approach. Kurt brought his arm back and drove his fist into where he suspected the soul's stomach was. "Stop it! Stop it!" He turned to George. "They knew the rules," he shouted. "It wasn't like every priest didn't tell them to repent every Sunday before he went and fucked an altar boy up the ass. It wasn't like every pompous born-again on the street corner didn't wave his Bible with his slicked-back hair and shit-eating grin, telling them 'Repent before it's too late,'" Kurt waved his hand above his head like it held an imaginary book, then brought it down, extending his hand toward George, an accusative finger pointing at his chest. "Hellfire and brimstone, George. That's what they got promised. Fuck that it's not fair! So, it's hard on Earth. Fuck them!"

Kurt turned to the bag he'd punched, reached up, and grabbed the zipper, yanking it down. The soul inside was dazed, confused as Kurt took a grip on its arm and jerked it out of the bag. "Smile, you fucker," Kurt said, dragging the disoriented soul across the mezzanine, "you're being saved."

Reaching the edge, Kurt pushed the soul, a man, against the low wall. "I forgive you!" Kurt smacked it in the jaw with his open palm, impacting hard and then sliding his hand off slowly. "Fly! Be free!" Kurt bent down, grabbed one of its legs, and lifted it, pushing it over the railing. The soul went over the edge and paused in space before a wind rose up and threw it back against the wall with an audible thud, a bag wrapping around it and sealing it in. "I am not the light! I am not the way! And I don't have time for all this shit!" Kurt paused, breathing heavily, then stared at George. "Now take point."

George didn't move. Reaching down to his belt, Kurt drew the pistol from its holster and leveled it at George. "I told you to take point," Kurt said, his voice hoarse and heavy as he flipped off the thumb safety and squeezed the handle, his index finger tight on the trigger.

"You gonna shoot me, Kurt?" George asked, his voice almost a whisper.

Kurt's hand shook, tears blurring his eyes. "I'm not a fucking saint," he shouted. "I can't save everyone! I can't even save myself!"

George reached out, putting his hand on the barrel of the gun. "Let go of the gun, Kurt."

Kurt released his grip on the handle, letting George slide the gun out of his hand. "I can't do it, George."

George set the safety, put the gun in his belt and stepped forward. He put his hand on Kurt's and gently pushed it down to Kurt's side where Junior took it in his. Kurt looked down at Junior, expecting the boy to be frightened or nervous, but the boy looked up at him with a reassuring smile.

"It's okay, buddy," George said, softly. "Why don't we sit down and take a break?"

Chapter 30:

Merrily, Merrily, Merrily, Merrily

A few miles farther into their walk, George was at point, Junior was in the middle, and Kurt silently pulled up the rear. George couldn't imagine the burden that Kurt carried as they passed along the rows of body bags, each enclosed soul a silent accusation. He shouldn't have pressed Kurt to do something. The kid had been taking everything in stride only because he'd somehow minimized it, only because he had been able, in all the confusion and activity, to ignore it and concentrate on the task at hand.

George felt guilty. When he'd asked Kurt to do something for all those souls, he'd forced Kurt to confront it all at once, to let everything come up from whatever pit he'd held it in. He hoped the kid would get over it soon. Whether Kurt was still the leader of this expedition was in doubt, but whether he was necessary to it was clear.

One hand running along the railing, George looked over the edge of the mezzanine at the pool below. Something seemed different. It looked like they were farther above it than they'd been a mile back. "Hold up," he said, stopping, Kurt and Junior stopping behind him. Slipping off his backpack, he opened a pocket and pulled out one of Kurt's ballpoint pens. It was a cheap plastic thing, but when you took off the cap it was a round cylinder that would roll fairly well. Putting it on the floor, he sent it rolling back the way they'd come.

Normally it would have rolled a few feet and stopped, but it went farther, rolling nearly twenty feet before the small bumps from the caulked gaps between the tiles bounced it enough out of alignment to turn it and cause it to stop. They were on a slope. Very gradually, almost imperceptibly, the mezzanine was rising. They'd only gone up about twenty feet over the last two miles which would make the slope less than one percent, but they were going up.

He saw Kurt staring at the pen, then Kurt leaned over the railing. "Well, shit," Kurt said quietly, not so much in amazement as in mere observation. George smiled, waiting to be complimented on his discovery, but Kurt took Junior's hand and walked forward, leaving George standing behind them, wearing a fading grin.

* * * *

Twisting as he fell, Nybras saw a pool a few hundred feet below him. Some small boat, or one that looked small from his height, had stopped at its edge and things were rising from it.

The fall wasn't like the slow drop in the rings. This place had higher terminal velocity and Nybras was dropping quickly, gaining speed as he did. It would hurt when he hit, and he looked for something to grab onto.

He was in the center of the giant ring. He'd never be able to swoop far enough to the sides to grab onto one of the ledges. He was in a near panic, but he retained enough lucidity to notice that many of the things that were rising up from below were ceasing their ascents, getting caught by sudden winds that blew them to the sides.

Nybras looked for one that was getting close and tried to angle his fall toward it. Growing closer at an increasing velocity, he saw now that the thing was a soul. Grabbing the corners of his coat, he tried to increase his wind resistance, allowing him a little more rudder control, swooping toward the soul. As he grew near, the soul stopped in its ascent and began to shudder. Nybras closed his coat and tried to go perpendicular, falling as fast as he could. He wasn't directly above the soul, but that became an advantage as it began flying off to the side, right into his path. He hoped that his timing and position were correct. That hope was confirmed within hundredths of a second as the soul smacked into him, its force carrying both it and Nybras over the railing and into a jarring impact against the level's wall.

A demon could not be knocked unconscious, but as Nybras slumped against the wall, every inch of his body aching from the hit, he closed his eyes and tried to fake it.

* * * *

Kurt walked almost unconsciously, like driving on autopilot, but rather than letting his thoughts consume his attention, he had let himself go blank.

Kurt stumbled. He'd put his foot out to step, but suddenly the ground wasn't beneath it. He would have toppled forward if George hadn't grabbed his shirt and pulled him back. Kurt shook his head, re-orienting himself on the situation around him. Ahead of him sat a wide gap, stretching on perhaps a mile or more, and below him there were steps leading about twenty feet down into it.

The floor of the gap was hidden mainly by treetops; short, stunted trees, though mercifully green in the few places they had leaves. They were half-barren, each looking sickly and frail, the visible branches and trunks thin and grey. And among the trees there were flashes of movement.

George put the pistol in his belt and checked the straps on his pack before unslinging the rifle. Kurt watched him preparing for battle or whatever oddness lay ahead. "George," he said quietly. George didn't respond. "George," he said with more volume. George turned his head and looked up at Kurt. "I'm sorry," Kurt said.

George nodded solemnly. "Why don't we take a break first," Kurt suggested. "Eat, get some rest, then we can head down." George agreed with another nod.

They'd been supplied with some imported provisions before leaving Hell, but nothing better than MRE's, sodas, water, candy bars, and trail mix. Kurt and George each hungrily consumed a pack of almost-food and washed it down with a Coke while Junior nibbled quietly on a Snickers. The silence was amazing.

Kurt sat, licking the last bits of gravy off a finger he'd stuck inside the pack, trying to figure out some method of breaking the silence without it feeling awkward.

A noise caught his ear. Off against the wall, now thankfully bare of body bags, Junior sat with his knees up, picking at the candy bar with little bites, savoring each one, and he was humming. Kurt concentrated on the sound coming from the boy, trying to pick out the tune.

"Da, da-da, da-da, da-da..." It came slowly, but it was familiar. Kurt wrapped his mind around it, trying to put words to the notes. There was a syllable for each one.

"Up above the world so high," the words came into Kurt's mind. "Like a diamond in the sky." Kurt began humming quietly as well.

When the song ended, Junior didn't start again. Instead, he looked at George. Kurt followed his gaze and saw George looking at Junior. "Row, row, row your boat," George began in a low voice, still looking at Junior, "gently down the stream." George's voice picked up some volume. "Merrily, merrily, merrily, merrily, life is but a dream."

George stopped and turned his head as Junior's gaze oriented on Kurt. Kurt immediately felt the spotlight of their gazes and racked his mind for a song. "I'm a little teapot, short and stout," he sang tentatively, raising one arm while bending the other and placing his hand on his hip. "Here is my handle. Here is my spout."

He looked expectantly at the two, first Junior, then George. As his eyes met George's, the man's face began to contort, then George broke into laughter. Kurt felt puzzled as George snickered, but then realized how he looked, imitating the teapot, and began to laugh too. "When I'm hot and ready, hear me shout," Kurt tried to sing through his laughter. "Tip me over and pour me out."

By the time he was done, George was on his side, laughing. Kurt looked over to Junior to see what his reaction was, but the boy only smiled at him and went back to his candy bar and humming.

* * * *

Nybras recalled the first time he had fallen.

The banners lay strewn among the wounded. Michael and his armies, victorious, had bound the rebels hand-and-foot and hung them on spits, like game. For every rebel, two angels shouldered the spit and carried the defeated to the edge of a giant portal, opened on the highest mountaintop in the ranges surrounding the blessed valley that was Heaven.

Like a volcano, green magma glowing still just beneath the edge, each spit was staked into the ground, the bindings cut. The thrones of Lucifer, Beelzebub, and Belial had been torn from the walls of the celestial palace and mounted on pyres of stones where Michael, Gabriel, and Ariel sat in them and cast down judgment.

Raphael stood defense for each rebel, singing the praises of his past, singing his glory and his right to salvation. But each time the judgment came down. "Guilty," said three times from three mouths. And even though they could not die, Azrael placed his hand against their heads, letting them each know the touch of Death before they were pushed through.

Nybras had felt the cold of that touch suffuse his body, saw a tear fall from Raphael's eye, as he toppled backwards into the abyss.

It hadn't been evil that warped their bodies. It had been rage... anguish. Their ears grew large and pointed, listening for the forgiveness that would never come. The anger at its denial thickened and gnarled their skins. The gnashing of their teeth sharpened them to points. The weeping in contrition turned their eyes red. And even Lucifer had grown ugly. He had been loved best among all angels and thus he missed that love more than any other. All the denizens of Hell hated God for this abandonment. And this was the true source of Hell's evil — not amorality, not pride, not greed — but the most deep-seated and dutifully harbored spite, because their father no longer loved them.

Nybras' eyes shot open, his entire body shuddering from the memories. For a moment he didn't remember where he was, but a look around quickly reminded him. The two mortals and the portion of Beaudreaux's soul were coming and he had to prepare their reception.

Chapter 31:

You're Stronger Than You Think

George led the way down the stairs. They were each nearly two feet high and four feet deep, more like the seats of some amphitheater than a stairway. Kurt and Junior walked next to each other, Kurt helping Junior down each step.

At the bottom, the trees extended from side to side between the walls. Predominantly fruit trees, half appeared to be dead, the others weren't bearing fruit, not even a stray piece of rotted fruit on the dirt floor. There was no undergrowth, no brush to obscure the dark packed soil. A faint sound of voices could be heard up ahead. It wasn't the shouting of the mad, rushing hordes from the main plaza. Instead, it sounded like... singing.

After his adventure on the third ring of Hell, George wasn't so fired up to go investigate. He remained at point, but he proceeded cautiously, making sure Kurt and Junior were following. George tried to stay alert as he pushed forward, but the singing distracted him. It grew louder faster than it should, but when they stopped moving, it stayed at the same volume. It was as if the singers only moved when they did or the trees acted as a mute.

The trees had been planted in neat rows, and though the treetops were no higher than twelve or thirteen feet, George didn't have to duck beneath any low branches, noticing the scars of the carefully amputated lower limbs along the trunks. Someone had once tended this garden with a lot of care, but lately the trees had been neglected.

A few hundred feet up, the garden opened into a clearing. George pulled back behind a tree and motioned Kurt and Junior to take cover. Peeking out, he could see human shapes moving in the clearing. They were definitely the source of the singing. He moved forward cautiously, making sure that Kurt and Junior stayed at least a few rows behind him. As he got closer, he saw the men in the clearing moving round a large wooden structure, climbing up and down ladders. They all wore robes, some wore crowns.

The lack of undergrowth proved to be a liability as George felt a surprising tap on his shoulder. Whirling, he shoved the barrel of the rifle up under the chin of the man behind him. The man, bearded and in a purple robe, froze. George glared at him, but the man merely raised a mug into George's field of view. "Wine?" the man asked.

* * * *

Sitting under a tree in view of the giant vat in the center of the clearing, Kurt and George each sniffed tentatively at a mug as many men in robes gathered round them. "You are from the world," one said incredulously before taking a generous quaff from a wooden mug.

"Yeah," George said, "we've been through this before. We're from the world, we're heading up, and we came from down."

"No one ever gets out of down," one of the men said, an effeminate and slightly built specimen wearing a robe of purple with golden fleur-de-lis on it, his eyes wide in an incredulous look.

"We did," Kurt said, watching them warily. These men weren't harmless drunkards. They were kings, all of them. These were men who spent their entire lives plotting and scheming to stay in power. He trusted them about as much as he trusted a politician who said this is for your own good.

One of the kings left the circle without excusing himself and walked toward the giant vat, mug in hand. That was where all the fruit had gone, fermenting in a giant mash into a barely palatable brew. Kurt looked at his own. He hadn't tasted it, fearing the native food in Purgatory might have the same effect as the native food in Hell, to trap one there. He'd cautioned George against drinking as well.

One of the kings eyed Junior. He was a Richard or a Henry or a William, Kurt couldn't keep them straight. "And this is a pure soul you are escorting?"

Junior, sitting between Kurt and George, moved closer to Kurt, leaning into him. "Yeah," George said, his eyes darting around the circle as Kurt put a protective arm around Junior.

"Then you must be a saint," one king said. "Would you be willing to bless us?"

"Oh, I cannot disrupt God's plan," Kurt said quickly. "It wouldn't be right."

"God's plan has already been disrupted," a voice shouted from outside the circle. The kings all jumped, not so much in surprise as in fear, and the circle parted at the side. Striding toward them from the large vat was a huge soul. Rather than the royal purple robe, he wore furs. His crown was a Norse helmet, replete with horns. Pale, as a soul should be, his mane of red hair had an almost pinkish tint, but he was an impressive figure of a man, nonetheless.

"Eric the Bold," the man said by way of introduction, "terror of the frozen wastes, and about thirty other meaningless titles." He bowed, doffing his helmet, then stood up straight. "At your service."

Kurt and George stood, following the example of the other kings. Once standing, they realized that Eric was barely five and a half feet tall, but he was broad-shouldered and wide-chested, making him an imposing figure despite his lack of height. Kurt put a hand on Junior's shoulder, pushing Junior behind him. "What do you mean, God's plan has already been disrupted?"

Eric glared around the circle, causing some of the kings to shrink back. "When I got here, this garden was in full flower. Heaven it wasn't, but it was still a nice enough home. Each night a giant serpent came to ravage the garden, but an angel of God would descend with sword in hand and fend the beast off."

Some of the kings nodded in confirmation, far-off looks in their eyes as if remembering the good old days. "Then, a few hundred years ago, the angel stopped coming. A few of us gave fight, but even our best warriors were laid waste by the magnificent strength of this beast. Slowly, over the decades, as more of these weak pantywaist kings joined our lot and built this vat, more of my force went soft and we have given up this garden, row by row. A hundred yards on," Eric motioned behind him again, "is where the battle line lies, the garden beyond it in a shambles."

"Now, Eric," one of the kings, a Juan Carlos or Ferdinand, said, "if there were hope, we'd fight by your side. But a wise man knows when a fight is futile."

"Would you have the serpent ravage the whole of the garden? When it finished with the garden, what would become of us? Take it from a man who has spent centuries in this fight. Just because you can no longer die does not mean you can no longer suffer."

"We've heard it all before, Eric," a voice piped up from the far side of the circle. "Have you ever tried diplomacy? Have you ever tried negotiating? What if you had given the serpent a portion of the garden at the outset? It might have been satisfied. But every night you roil its blood with battle and incite its lust to conquer the whole place."

"Ah, yes," Eric laughed, "a word from our British friend. Beware of him, lads. His version of diplomacy is to throw all of his compatriots into a pit of serpents, hoping the monsters will eat him last."

Eric locked eyes with George, then let his gaze drop to the rifle, still gripped loosely in one hand. "You three are not men of inaction. You do not belong with these sycophants and schemers. You belong with me and my men. Join us in battle tonight. Perhaps with your powers behind us, we'll be able to defeat this beast."

"And what if we don't join you?" Kurt asked, not relishing the thought of a battle.

Eric's gaze shifted from the rifle to Kurt. "The only way out of here is to go past that damned snake. You can fight your way out or sit here with these fools and drink yourself silly while you wait for an angel to come. It is your choice."

Turning, Eric left the circle and walked toward the tree line. Kurt looked at George, but the only advice George could offer was a shrug. The circle started condensing, the drunken kings gathering in around them once again, a number of them eying Junior in a way that Kurt did not like. "Eric," Kurt shouted, dropping his mug, "wait up."

As dusk fell, George cleaned and oiled both the rifle and the pistol. They had no reason to doubt Eric. Even the other kings had confirmed his tales of the serpent. There were no fires in the garden, but as dusk grew into night, large light panels in the roof of Purgatory came on, keeping the place in a dusk-like light.

"How go the preparations?" Eric asked boisterously as he plopped down to sit next to George, his voice still only slightly quieter than a shout.

George finished screwing the barrel back into the rifle until it clicked into the locked position. "Just fine."

"These are magnificent weapons you possess, these guns," Eric said. "I have heard of them from the others. I look forward to seeing them in action tonight."

George slapped a loaded magazine into the rifle and chambered a round. "I don't."

"Ah yes," Eric said, "I almost forgot. You are still alive. Death still holds some fear for you. Well, it's not so bad really. In fact, since that angel stopped coming, the dullness has been taken from it and it's quite bearable."

"Do you really enjoy all this fighting?" George asked, putting the rifle down as far from Eric as he could reach without being conspicuous. "You said that you can still suffer even if you can't die. Doesn't the thought of that suffering bother you? Doesn't it bother you that you lead other men to it every night?"

Eric didn't reply immediately. In the distance George could hear some of the drunken kings still singing, otherwise it was quiet. No birds, no insects, none of the natural sounds he'd grown to expect in this kind of setting. "Pain is just pain," Eric finally said. "It goes away. This too shall pass."

Eric turned and put a hand on George's shoulder. "I put the affairs of maintaining my rule before the affairs of my own soul and my own heart, and I regret that. But these battles I do not regret. My comfort will return in time. It always does. But my home... my honor... they are not so easily regained."

"Yes," Eric said, standing, "I look forward to seeing those weapons of yours in action tonight. If we are lucky, the serpent will be defeated. And then none of us will have to court pain."

* * * *

There were few swords in the garden. Only those kings who died with a sword in their hands had one, and most of those had gradually joined the group around the vat. The remaining kings brandished clubs or spears made from tree branches, some sporting sharpened tips or small rocks embedded in the ends. "The snake's scales are as hard as iron," Eric said, standing by the stairway with Kurt and George.

"Are there any vulnerabilities?" George asked.

"None that I know of," Eric said. "It is my hope that your guns will be able to pierce its skin."

"And what if they can't?" Kurt asked.

"Then we are lost."

A shout in the distance announced the approach of the snake and the men got ready. The trees at this end of the garden that had not been broken into stumps were stripped of leaf and fruit, bare except for scrawny branches that weren't thick enough to be used as weapons. The broken trunks had been used to create the wine vat. There was no cover, no place from which to ambush. The men stood at the bottom of the stairs in a loose battle line, waiting for their adversary.

A king, stripped to his britches, bounded down from the top of the stairs. "It comes," he shouted before tripping off one of the lower stairs, diving forward and plowing into the dirt below. He scrambled to his feet quickly, picked up a club from against a stump, then joined the battle lines.

"To victory," Eric shouted, waving his club above his head. The other kings, only about twenty in all, raised their weapons and shouted in response. George checked the weapons as Kurt turned and looked for Junior, hidden behind a trunk about fifteen yards back. Kurt heard George call his name as George handed him the pistol. "We don't have a lot of ammo," George said. "Maybe a couple of mags worth for each. Fire no more than a couple of shots. Aim for the head. If the bullets don't penetrate the scales, then drop back. Wait until the snake opens its mouth and then try to fire inside and hit the soft tissue."

"And if that doesn't work..." Kurt asked, his voice dropping low enough so Eric couldn't hear.

"Grab Junior. While the kings are busy with the snake, we'll try to get around it and get up the stairs."

The snake's head crested the stairs and the kings renewed their shouting, throwing rocks and clumps of dirt at it.

It was a huge head, easily four feet wide, with a jaw big enough to swallow a man whole, and a large body followed it. At a shout from Eric, the vanguard of the motley battalion ran forward, five in all, charging up the stairs, spears pointed forward. On the stairs, with its large body, the snake didn't have enough room or purchase to bring its tail into play as a weapon. Instead, it thrashed its head side to side as it moved forward, the sheer bulk of the moving weight knocking kings out of its way as spears were blunted on its hide.

More kings rushed forward as the snake moved down the stairs, confronting it before it reached the bottom. One got around it, up a few stairs, and attacked from the side, trying to pry the point of his spear under the scales and pierce the flesh below. The snake turned its head back, taking a couple of club blows to the skull, but also knocking two kings flying into the side wall where they slumped to the ground. The king with the spear dodged away as the snake's head came at him, but it didn't go after him. Grabbing the spear which was lodged in its scales, the snake whipped its head forward, releasing the spear at the apex of the arc, sending it zooming like a javelin into the trunk of a tree.

With the kings out of the way, George leveled his gun and took aim. The constant thrashing of the head didn't give him a great shot, so he waited, timing the thrashes, and as the head was mere feet from him, he fired two shots. Both ricocheted off the scales. "Shit!"

Kurt too had taken aim and was about to fire, when a sound distracted him. It was hard to hear over the shouts of battle, but it sounded like Junior. Turning his head, he saw the French king, the gold fleur-de-lis reflecting a small bit of the artificial light, pulling Junior back toward where the drunken kings had gathered.

"Junior!" Kurt yelled as he turned to chase after the fleeing king. Hearing him, the king stopped and looked back. Seeing Kurt coming after him, he did what apparently had been his plan all along. Stripping the backpack from the boy, he took a good hold of Junior, wrapping his arms around the boy's neck as Junior rose.

Junior's buoyancy lifted the king from the garden floor. Kurt kicked in every ounce of speed he had as the pair lifted through the trees. Coming within a few feet, he leapt, catching onto the king's feet.

Kurt's weight, being solid and living, was more than enough to drag the pair down, but the king let go of Junior. Kurt and the king fell to the dirt as Junior rose farther into the air. Kurt got up and made a leap for Junior, but it was no use, the boy was already too far above him and was rising upward and out into the open atrium with increasing speed. All Kurt could do was watch him float away.

His short reverie was broken by the king's voice. "Bless me," the king whimpered, tugging with one hand at Kurt's pant leg. Kurt had dropped the gun before leaping after the two and now he found it pointed up at him. "Bless me," the king said again, more loudly now, waving the gun at Kurt.

Kurt looked down with contempt, then spat in his face. The king's finger tightened on the trigger, but surprise registered on his face as the gun refused to fire. Kurt grabbed the barrel with his left hand, clocking the king with a downward straight-right to the nose. The king released the gun and fell, sprawling out on his back. Standing over the King, Kurt leveled the gun at his head. "You forgot about the safety," Kurt said, flicking the safety off. The gun jerked in Kurt's hand as he put a bullet between the king's eyes. "Consider yourself blessed."

With his attention back on the battle, Kurt noticed that the sounds of it had diminished behind him, being replaced by the screams and moans of the injured. He ran back to see most of the kings laying around, unconscious or severely incapacitated. Eric, George, and a few others held the snake at bay, lunging forward with spears. George moved to dodge the head as he patiently waited for opportunities to shoot into the snake's mouth. Another advance of the snake and a whip of its head knocked Eric flying to the side. Everything seemed to slither into slow motion as Eric's shout distracted George while the snake whipped its head around, opening its mouth and catching George around the midsection.

George dropped the rifle and screamed as the snake whipped its head side to side, its teeth grinding into his flesh. Kurt stopped and leveled his gun, but there was no clear shot without the possibility of hitting George. With a final thrash, the snake let go of George, flinging his bloodied body into one of the walls.

A blind rage filled Kurt. Rather than fire, he ran forward, and as two kings distracted the snake, he made a run past its head and leapt onto its back. It took the snake a moment to register his presence as he climbed toward its head. It began thrashing, trying to throw him off, but Kurt wrapped his legs around it, grasping the dull edge of a scale as he used his thighs to inch himself up the snake's body.

It was almost impossible to hold on and retain his grasp on his gun, but somehow, he managed, moving farther up the snake. Its head led the thrashing of the upper body, and the closer to it he got, the more force there was trying to shake him off. Shoving the pistol forward, Kurt lodged the barrel under a scale on the snake's head and fired.

The thrashing stopped almost instantly as the snake slumped lifeless to the ground, blood oozing out of its mouth. Kurt fell off to the ground beside it, and lay on his back, spread eagled, his breath coming in rasps. The few kings that remained conscious tried to raise a cheer, but they were as tired as Kurt. There would be time for celebration later, when all the wounds had healed.

Kurt sat up quickly. Not all the wounds would heal so easily. "George!"

Running to the wall, Kurt found Eric kneeling by George's body. He had lain George out so as to be comfortable, but the trickle of blood on George's lips and the blood pooling around him were clue enough that the wounds were fatal. Kurt pushed Eric out of the way and knelt by George's side.

George stared up into the dusk, his eyes unfocused. "George!" Kurt slapped his cheek. "George! Come on, buddy!"

George's eyes seemed to focus slightly. "Kurt," he rasped.

"Yeah, buddy. I'm here. We got the sucker."

George smiled a moment before his body was racked with coughs, causing more blood to bubble up from his mouth. His eyes lost focus again. "George," Kurt shouted, shaking him. "George!"

George seemed to come back, but only slightly. He was almost dead. Kurt was desperate. Junior was gone; George was almost gone. He was going to be left alone. As much as the thought of George dying pained him, the thought of being left alone here was even worse. "George, ask me to forgive you," he said.

George didn't respond. "George," Kurt shouted, shaking him again. "Ask me to forgive you!"

"Forgive me," George said in a voice barely audible.

Tears were streaming down Kurt's cheeks as he put his hand on George's jaw. "There is a weight within you," Kurt said, his voice growing thick. "It is the burden of the wrong choices of your life. I draw it away from you and free you from it. I forgive you."

As Kurt slid his hand off of George's jaw, George lost focus for the final time, his eyes glazing over and his breathing coming to a halt. Kurt wanted to pound on his chest, do CPR in desperation like some dedicated doctor on a medical show, but he knew it was useless. George was dead, his soul probably materializing on the seventh ring of Hell like Mammon had said was his destiny.

There was no strength left in Kurt and he slumped over George's body, Eric's comforting hand on his shoulder. But though George's blood was supposed to be warm, Kurt began to feel an icy chill against his chest and face. Sitting up, he saw a form rising from George's chest. Like a thick rope obeying a fakir's flute, it rose from George's body, writhing and expanding, taking human shape... taking George's shape.

As the face became discernable, it smiled at Kurt. The mouth moved, but no sound came from it. And then it began to rise. Desperately, Kurt grabbed for the legs. Still not fully formed, they had substance, but were almost squishy, yet Kurt held on, refusing to let go, feeling them fill out and become solid in his hands. George's hand reached down and took hold of Kurt's arm, pulling him to his feet, and Kurt wrapped his arms around George's chest, resolving not to let him go.

* * * *

They walked along the walkway, the far wall still a few miles ahead in the distance. George wore his pack to keep him from rising upward. "How ya doing there?" Kurt asked, looking straight ahead. Kurt had stripped down, washed with a bottle of water, and replaced his bloodstained clothes with spare clothing from George's pack. He'd rid himself of most signs of the battle, at least on the outside.

"I'm okay," George said. The walking was difficult, balancing the backpack against his buoyancy. Without a counterweight on his chest, the pull was one-sided and he had to lean into each step to keep from toppling backward.

His body felt strange to him, almost alien, yet he was strangely at peace with it. He had sensations from the weight of the pack, the temperature of the air, even a tinny taste in his mouth, but none of it was the same as before. It wasn't as localized. Rather than feeling the pack's straps cutting narrow paths across his shoulders, the touch was diffused, like there were two wide hands pushing down and back. He kept on touching his body as they walked, pinching his arms, tapping his chest with his index finger. He didn't seem to have any bones, any distinct nerve endings. It was like he was all cartilage and subcutaneous fat, even where his muscles should have been on his arms and chest, like a thin layer of padding beneath vinyl, covering a solid plastic structure that was exactly the same shape as his body, but just smaller.

He bent the same way, moved the same way. His strength felt like it was the same as when he was mortal. Yet there were no muscles for locomotion. When he stretched, he didn't feel anything stretch. He would move his arms out and to the sides, but in the chest, back, and shoulders there was no sense of pull or compression. His arms just moved within a certain range and could not go beyond it. He didn't have any ribs. His chest was just that same padding over a plastic mold.

"You know," he said, "this could speed things up."

"How so?" Kurt asked, still staring ahead.

"We don't have to find ways up. You just tie a rope to me and let me float up to the next level. I tie it off and you climb up. We could get through the levels in a matter of hours instead of days."

"The next level is too high," Kurt said. "We don't have enough rope. And even if we did, I'm not strong enough to climb that far."

You're stronger than you think, George thought, their walk continuing on.

Chapter 32: One Nightmare Ends...

Ever since being pulled out of Alain, Junior had spent most of his time under psychological attack. During the 70-plus years in the cells, the demons hadn't just been a presence, they'd been actively hostile. They would shout at the child souls, grab them and shake them, rake their claws across their backs or arms. Then they would laugh. If they didn't actually feed on the fear and pain of the child souls, they definitely got high on it.

During the first few years, Junior had been like a child in an orphanage, hoping against hope that his real parent would come and rescue him, take him off to live in a warm home with love and no more monsters. But that was the last torture. There were so many times that Alain had come to his cell, told him everything was going to be okay, that he was going to take him away from all this. He would open his arms for Junior to come hug him, but when Junior accepted the invitation and the arms wrapped around him, the being he thought to be Alain would turn into a demon and hurt him.

Eventually, when Alain would come to his cell and beckon him, Junior just curled into a tighter ball, putting his hands over his ears so he couldn't hear Alain's voice. So when Alain came with the two men, Junior wanted to retreat. But Kurt, he glowed so bright. Junior had never seen anything like it. He almost believed Kurt was an angel, and deep in the recesses of the maze of walls and blockades he'd created in his mind, Junior allowed himself the faint hope that maybe Kurt really was there to save him.

Kurt was so nice to him, so kind, so gentle, it was hard to fight the sneaking suspicion that Kurt was an angel, that this wasn't just some elaborate and especially cruel trick, now that he'd stopped believing in Alain ever coming to rescue him. Yet Alain was with Kurt. He didn't try to lure him, didn't make any false promises. He just seemed sad. Junior could almost believe it was really Alain. But it had been such a perverse deceit so many times.

The oath had helped him trust Kurt more. He couldn't say why, but it made him feel better, made him feel connected to Kurt. And then, when Kurt made that bet, when Kurt beat that pit of nothingness, when Kurt took his hand and led him out of Hell, when he saw Kurt actually save souls, all of it made him feel like Kurt was honestly and truly his personal guardian angel, that there was nothing that Kurt could not do.

When the king released him, Junior didn't float up happily or peacefully. He turned and tried to swim downward, he willed himself to be heavier, and when that didn't work, all the hope he'd allowed himself to feel in the past few days turned around on him and punched him in the stomach. He'd never felt pain like this. Junior curled up into a ball and waited for the demons to come again.

When he reached the top of his rise, he felt a wind shake his body and blow him over the railing. He'd seen souls smack into the walls, and he began to tense up, closing his eyes tighter so he didn't have to see the wall he'd be hitting. But he never hit a wall. He was gently lowered to the ground.

Junior opened one eye. He was in a very big room, but not like Purgatory. It was white, like clouds. Other children flew in from out of the mists and were set gently down. At a far end of the room, three beautiful angels with wings stood before three doorways. The children would walk up to them, an angel would take a child in its arms, kiss it on the forehead, and walk it through one of the doors as another angel flew in to take its place.

Junior so wanted to go to the angels, be wrapped up in their arms, be kissed on his forehead. But in his mind's eye, he saw the angel picking him up, wrapping him up in its arms, its teeth growing long and sharp, horns sprouting from its head as its skin turned into a leathery tree bark. He curled up tighter and closed his eyes. He just wanted to wake up back in his cell. It was horrible there, but it was a horrible he knew.

He was lifted into the arms of some being, but he stayed curled up, his eyes shut tight. He couldn't look. He just couldn't.

Junior felt the slow vibration of the angel's wings flapping and felt the cool air across his face as they moved. They flew for maybe 10 or 20 seconds, and then they set down, the angel walking a bit before it came to a stop.

Junior heard a door open. "This is the one you were seeking," a beautiful voice said.

The angel moved its arms and he was put into the arms of someone smaller, softer. "Thank you," the person holding him said, a voice sounding like a woman with a French accent that reminded Junior of Alain's grandmother.

"I could be cast down for this," the beautiful voice said.

The person holding Junior shifted her stance a bit. "You know it was the right thing to do. God will approve."

"I hope so," the beautiful voice said.

Junior felt the breeze and heard the sound of the flapping wings, and then they were gone. The woman who held him walked with him a bit, then sat down and rested him on her lap. She smoothed his hair and kissed his forehead. "Alain," she called to him softly. "Open your eyes, Alain."

Junior opened his eyes a sliver, trying not to let her see that he was peeking. The woman who held him wasn't a demon. She wasn't an angel either. She was simply a soul like he was. And she was smiling at him.

He opened his eyes wider to get a look at her beautiful smile and she caught him peeking. Her smile broadened with an infusion of joy. "Hello Alain," she said, her voice soft and welcoming. "My name is Marie and I have been waiting a very long time to meet you."

* * * *

Reaching the very end of the mezzanine they found no stairs, no elevator leading up.

Kurt looked out over the railing, the wading pool below extending into a glass wall with a beach beyond. The water in it remained as part of a wide creek that fed into or from a sunlit ocean over which the troop transport ships apparently travelled.

"It's too far for the ropes," George said, looking at the next level up, hundreds of feet above them.

Kurt stared at the water. "Tell me something I don't know."

"I could try floating up with a partially empty backpack," George said, "just enough to slow the rise so I could control my motion. Maybe there's a rope on the next level that I could lower down to you."

Kurt turned away from the railing. "And what if there's not? Then we're separated. You have no way to get to me. I have no way to get to you. We're screwed."

George looked at Kurt's eyes. They were glazing over from fatigue, but he wouldn't admit to it. The last time either of them had slept was before going through the portal, and that was maybe 30 hours ago. They'd walked through the ersatz night, into the dawn, and kept going. They were easily into the late afternoon of their second day.

Kurt refused to sleep, insisting on walking, and George's new form wasn't showing signs of getting tired, at least not yet. Combine that much time with the amount of physical and emotional stress Kurt had undergone... "Why don't we make camp here," George suggested. "We'll eat something, get some sleep. Maybe a new day will give us a new perspective."

"A new day," Kurt said, snorting. "When the overhead lights dim and that sun that probably isn't really a sun comes streaming back in through the window? And we're that much closer to losing the bet and giving up our souls?"

George didn't know what to do. He knew Kurt needed rest, but Kurt was too afraid to sleep. "Let's at least eat."

Kurt nodded and sat down, staring at the wall with a look that half-said he was going to throw up and half-said he was two seconds from kicking the wall's ass.

Absentmindedly, George slipped off his pack so he could get some rations. Immediately he began rising. He grabbed the pack, but his body continued to rise, making it look like he was doing a handstand off its frame. "Kurt," he squeaked. "Little help?"

Kurt bounded over and pushed George to the ground, then helped him slip the pack back on. With George seated, Kurt took things out of the large frame pack and stuffed them in his backpack. Hanging one loop of his backpack around George's neck, he helped George slip off the large frame pack.

The weight was enough to keep George seated on the ground, but since it was in a more compact space, hanging off his neck, it took a careful balancing act, using whatever passed for muscle control in his new soul body to keep himself from flipping ass over elbows and rising feet first. George kneeled as Kurt came around behind him and pushed down on his shoulders, allowing George to slip the pack off his neck and onto his back. That gave George a firmer hold on his balance, especially when they tied the straps around his waist. Most of his lightness seemed to be in his chest, almost as if his heart literally pulled him upward, and securing the torso seemed to create a workable center of gravity.

"You good," Kurt asked.

"Yeah," George said, breathing a sigh of relief.

Wordlessly Kurt walked off and sat down in his previous spot, resuming his staring contest with the wall.

As George rummaged through the rations, he found a bottle of sleeping pills he'd packed. He figured one would knock Kurt out for four hours, more if there weren't any stress nightmares. He crushed it into a pouch of military almost-food before handing it to Kurt. He followed it with a bottled water, rather than a Coke, not wanting to give Kurt a caffeinated counterpoint to the pill. Kurt didn't complain.

During the meal, George ate slowly, watching to make sure Kurt ate everything in the pouch and remained seated. After finally finishing his meal, he told Kurt he was tired and needed a lay-down. The smaller pack held him to the floor as he lay on his side, but his feet still wanted to lift, so he tucked them under the frame pack and actually found a small comfort zone.

While George pretended to sleep, he watched Kurt sit eerily still, eerily silent, staring at that wall with a look that couldn't decide between vomiting or picking a fight. It took a while, but the expression began to crack as Kurt tried to stifle a yawn. He succeeded a few times, but eventually they were coming freely. His lids drooped, then would snap open; his head nodded forward, then snapped back.

It was like those internet videos of kittens trying not to fall asleep, only not cute. But eventually, just like the kittens, Kurt succumbed.

* * * *

Kurt woke in a familiar place; the empty streets, the blank nondescript buildings. "How ya feeling," the man in the brown suit asked, kneeling beside him.

Kurt looked around. "How did I get here again?"

"George drugged you."

Kurt rubbed his head. "That son of a bitch."

The man just smiled. "He was right, you know. You were being irrational. You needed the rest."

Kurt shrugged. He was pissed, but there was nothing he could do about it right now. "Alain told me who you are."

The man stood up. "Walk with me."

Kurt stood up and began following the man down the street. "Alain said you're Jack Kerouac."

"Yeah," the man said, continuing to walk.

Kurt jogged a few steps to come abreast with him. "You mean you really are Jack Kerouac? The Jack Kerouac?"

"Yeah," Jack said. Raising an arm, he pointed into the distance. "The sidewalk ends about another hundred yards up."

"But, but," Kurt stammered, "you're *Jack Kerouac*."

"Uh huh."

Kurt was amazed. He was in the presence of one of the great American authors of the 20th century. Somehow, he was expecting Jack to be as excited to be Jack Kerouac as he was to meet Jack Kerouac, but apparently it didn't work that way.

As they continued, the street seemed to fade, until abruptly, it cut off and nothing but blank space extended off in front of them. Jack walked forward and sat down on the sidewalk's edge, dangling his feet into the void, but Kurt stayed a yard back, just staring.

"Come on," Jack said. "Sit next to me. There's nothing to be afraid of."

Kurt inched forward, each step tentative, and then sat down a couple of feet from the edge, scootching forward on his behind until his feet dangled off the edge and he sat even with Jack. "What do you see?" Jack asked.

Kurt stared out into the vast void, but it was all white with some faint points of color. "Nothing really."

"Try to focus on one of the colors," Jack said. "Just stare at it. Don't blink. Let your eyes lose focus until it's a blur. Sort of like those stereograms they used to have in the Sunday funnies."

Kurt did as Jack said. He picked a point and watched it, letting his eyes slowly relax and watching the light turn from one point into two and then three. But it kept expanding, kept increasing in numbers. It was like a computer screen, with one pixel turning on at a time, randomly expanding the pattern until the screen filled.

Slowly, the pixels coalesced like a haze in front of Kurt's eyes, then the whiteness began to change, colors fading in, an image starting to form. It was blurred, the forms and shapes indistinct. There was a large patch of blue, some green, some grey. A larger dark patch was a sort of mottled brown. Then, by reflex, Kurt blinked and it was all gone.

"What did you see," Jack asked, placing a hand on Kurt's shoulder.

Kurt described what he saw and Jack laughed. "Yeah," he said, "it takes a little practice. Plus, physical eyes can't stay open too long. That's an advantage of being dead. Your eyes don't burn."

"What was I supposed to see," Kurt asked.

"Dunno," Jack replied. "It's not really the point. You're not supposed to see anything in particular. You're just supposed to watch. You just look, and focus, and watch until you get bored. Then you watch something else."

"What do you see?"

Jack patted Kurt's shoulder. "I've seen lots."

Chapter 33: The Assistant Angel

Kurt woke with a slight headache, probably a hangover from whatever George had slipped him. He'd spent a few hours with Jack, staring at the points of color, watching them expand. He'd finally had a blurry vision of a man in a boat before his physical body had moved up from the deep recesses of unconsciousness enough for his knowing where he was to take him out of Nowhere and back to Purgatory.

Sitting up he rubbed his eyes. "Hullo," a voice said.

Kurt dropped his hands and opened his eyes wide. The voice wasn't George's. As he looked around for the source of the greeting, he realized he was no longer on the walkway. He was in an office, a bank of video monitors covering one wall. In fact, he wasn't laying on the floor. He was on a couch. "Hullo," the voice came again.

Kurt snapped his head around in the voice's direction. Across the room, sitting behind a large desk, was... Kurt was sure he must be dreaming. Blue shirt, patches, badge, raising a donut to his mouth. "Where am I?" Kurt asked, seeing George sitting in a chair near the desk.

The walls were that fake wood paneling common to cheap construction and the carpet a dull industrial gray.

The man took a bite of his donut and chewed it slowly, then sipped something from a paper cup to wash it down. "This here's the security office," he said. "Name's Duke. Why don't you come have a seat with your friend?"

Slowly, Kurt got up from the couch, walked across the room, and sat in a chair near George trying to shake off both his sleepiness and bewilderment. "You fellas mind if I ask you your business here?"

Kurt looked at the man again. He had more color than your average soul. "Are you an angel?"

Duke took another bite of his donut. "Only an assistant," he said through his mouthful, then swallowed. "But I'm the tops of the assistants. I'm in charge of this whole place." Duke got up and walked around from behind the desk. He was wearing dark pants, about an inch too short, with white socks and black rubber-soled shoes. "Now, if you don't mind answering a few questions. Your friend here wasn't too helpful."

Kurt looked over at George, who merely shrugged in response. "Your friend here," Duke continued, "said you two are just passing through on your way to Heaven."

"Yeah," Kurt said warily.

"But you're not dead." Duke leaned forward and poked Kurt's shoulder. "Are you a saint?"

"Get many passing through," Kurt asked.

Duke reached back for his donut. "Not really. Don't get much of anyone but souls for the past few hundred years. Not even angels. You know, my shift was supposed to change three hundred and seventy-two years, one hundred and sixty-eight days, and 5 hours ago... give or take. But no one came to relieve me."

"That's terrible," Kurt said, trying to muster as much fake sympathy as he could. "What happened?"

Duke shoved the rest of the donut into his mouth, chewing noisily. Reaching back for his cup, he knocked it over, spilling its contents over the desk. "Oh, fink," Duke said through a mouthful, turning around and grabbing some papers to mop up the spill.

After swallowing the rest of the donut and throwing the coffee-soaked papers into his trash basket, Duke turned back to Kurt. "Now if you'll please state your business," he said, leaning back against the desk, then hopping forward. As he turned around and grabbed some more papers, Kurt could see a wet stain on the back of Duke's pants. Duke finished mopping up the rest of his coffee and threw the papers in the basket, then grabbed some more and spread them around the edge of the desk before turning and leaning back again, making a slight crinkling sound as his rear met the paper-covered desk. "That's better."

"You're an assistant angel, huh," George asked.

Duke snapped his head to look at George in surprise, almost as if he'd forgotten George was there. "Yeah," Duke said.

"And what do you do around here?"

Duke waved his hand at the video monitors. "Mainly I watch for fires and guard the gate."

"The gate," Kurt asked.

"Yeah," Duke said. "This here's the antechamber to the gates of Purgatory."

Kurt looked around, spotting a double door behind and off to the side of the desk. "So, beyond that door are The Gates?"

"Those are The Gates," Duke said.

"You're kidding me."

"Nope," Duke said, walking over and opening the doors to expose a view of a small corridor leading to a stairway going up. "These are The Gates. That stairway there goes up to the first level."

"Weren't we on the first level?" Kurt asked.

"That was the mezzanine," Duke said, shutting the doors again and turning to face them. He placed his hands on his hips and glowered. "Now what is your business in Purgatory?"

George stood and glowered back. "Like I said. We're just passing through."

Duke shook his head. "Uh-uh. No one just passes through except for holy people and we haven't had any of those in my whole shift."

"Well then," Kurt said, getting up and standing next to George, "I'm holy."

Duke looked at him incredulously for a moment, then quickly turned and marched to the cooler. Stooping, he pulled out a paper cup, filled it with water, and walked back to Kurt. "No thanks," Kurt said. "I'm not thirsty."

"Bless it," Duke said, shoving the cup at him.

"What?"

"Bless it. If you're holy, you can turn this into holy water."

"Fine," Kurt said, getting a little tired of the whole charade. "In the name of God, I bless this water." Kurt waved his hand over the cup. "Amen."

Duke turned away and marched over to a cabinet as George nudged Kurt. "That's a blessing?" George whispered.

"What do you expect? Latin," Kurt replied.

Over at the cabinet, Duke opened the doors to expose a large box with a funnel on top. Flipping a switch, he set some lights to blinking and poured the water into the funnel. As the water dripped in, Kurt could swear the machine was talking. "Ouch... Hey... Ow Ow! Owwwwww!!!!"

"Duke," Kurt yelled over the noise. "What the he-- What's that noise?"

"Holy water tester," Duke said as the voice grew more insistent and more pained.

"Why's it talking," Kurt shouted louder as the screams grew to earsplitting levels.

"The only way to really test holy water is to pour it on a demon!"

Kurt started to suspect that he was very holy as the machine shot out a slip of paper just before bursting into flames. Duke grabbed a fire extinguisher from the wall and put it out, then put the extinguisher down and looked at the paper.

As Duke looked at the paper, his eyes widened. "I'm very sorry for detaining you, sir," he said, suddenly bowing on one knee before Kurt. "Had I but known... Please. I'm just an assistant angel. I'm not even that smart."

Kurt was taken back by Duke's sudden obsequiousness, but George merely reached down and snatched the paper from Duke. "Holiness rating of 9.4. What's that mean," he asked, waving the paper in front of Duke.

Duke didn't answer. He merely whimpered, reaching for Kurt's hand and placing it on his head. "What does 9.4 mean," Kurt asked.

Duke continued kneeling, his eyes staring at the floor. "It's a log 1000 logarithmic scale," he said shakily. "God's a 10, which is a thousand times holier than his top archangels, who rate a 9. Seraphim and cherubim are in the low sevens. Some saints can get as high as 5. Average human is a 1 or 2."

"What's your score," Kurt asked, unsuccessfully trying to pull his hand out of Duke's iron grip.

Duke's head bowed lower. "Four point seven."

"Four point seven?"

"I'm only an assistant angel," Duke cried.

"But a 9.4? That's like hundreds of times holier than any angel."

"Yes sir," Duke whimpered. "I know sir. I hope you will forgive me for not recognizing you at once, sir."

As calm as Kurt tried to be on the outside, he was like a boiling pot on the inside, thoughts rising to the surface like bubbles. His holiness rating explained so much; how he'd been able to bless the souls, how he'd been able to beat that void that bled out of Reese. But while it answered those questions, it opened up a whole book of new ones. How could he be that holy? He'd had premarital sex, taken the Lord's name in vain, lusted, indulged in gluttony... he was a common twenty-first-century secular sinner.

He wanted to ask Duke, but as Duke kneeled before him, he decided to put that thought out of his mind. "Duke," he asked, "what's the quickest way to the portal to Heaven?"

"The elevator," Duke said, hopefully.

"How do we get to it?"

Duke stood up, snapping to attention. "It would be my pleasure to escort you to it, sir." Turning on his heel, Duke headed out the door of the office. Kurt grabbed the frame pack rather than risk George turning into a Macy's Thanksgiving Day Parade float again while they tried to swap packs. Duke came back in the door, apparently having realized they weren't following and waited impatiently for George to help Kurt secure the pack.

With all the weight they'd shifted to his smaller pack, the frame pack's bulk was less heavy than when he'd carried Alain's on the 6th ring, though it was still a bit unwieldy. Kurt and George followed Duke out quietly. He walked to the base of the stairs, turned ninety degrees on his heel and opened a door. "After you, sir," he said, holding the door open and bowing as he motioned Kurt along. Kurt wasn't sure which was more freaky: being in Purgatory, being holier than an archangel, or having this archangel wannabe bowing and scraping before him. As he walked down the hall, he wondered if he was as holy as Jesus. Duke hadn't even mentioned him.

"Duke," he asked, his pitch rising at the end of the name. "Just for shits and giggles..." Kurt paused, wondering if it was okay for a guy with a holiness rating of 9.4 to say 'shit'. "What's Jesus's holiness rating?"

"Who?" he heard Duke call out behind him.

Kurt stopped, turned and looked past George at Duke. "You know. Jesus? How holy is he?"

"How holy is cheese?" Duke approached Kurt and George. "I hear Swiss cheese is pretty holy." Duke bent over and slapped his knee as he made a sound that sounded something like a guy with a sinus condition who couldn't decide if he was laughing or gagging. When Kurt and George didn't share his enthusiasm, it ended abruptly.

"Jesus," Kurt repeated, his voice flat and bordering on angry. "How holy is he?"

Duke shook his head. "Never heard of the guy."

"Jesus," George blurted out, exasperated. "Son of God. Lived on Earth about 2000 years ago."

"Ohhhh," Duke said, nodding in comprehension. "I wasn't around then."

"Wasn't around then," Kurt asked. "I thought God created all angels at the beginning of time."

"He did," Duke agreed, "but you don't go to the show until you're ready. I paid my dues in three different galaxies before I got promoted to one of Earth's afterlives."

"One of Earth's afterlives? How many are there?"

"Oh, a bunch."

"How many is 'a bunch'?"

"I don't know. Lots? Supernatural Geography wasn't my best subject in angel school."

"What was?"

"Volleyball." Duke gave a satisfied nod and turned around, heading toward the elevator with his back to Kurt and George.

"Volleyball?" George mouthed the word silently to Kurt.

"He's only an assistant angel," Kurt whispered. One hand on George's pack, he gave him a gentle push forward and they walked briskly to catch up with Duke.

* * * *

The walk to the elevator took another ten minutes and Duke paused at the doors, waiting for Kurt and George to make up the last few yards they'd been trailing. "And we're here," Duke said.

The elevator doors looked like regular elevator doors; two half-doors with a semi-reflective steel finish. "You fellas mind if we stop on the fourth level on our way up? Got some guard business to take care of."

"What kind of business?" Kurt asked warily.

"Demonic intrusion. Seems one snuck in a few hours before I found you fellas."

"I don't know..." Kurt said, not eager to meet any more demons.

Duke's face fell and he dropped to one knee again, grabbing Kurt's hand and putting it on his head. "Please!"

Chapter 34: A Once & Future Angel

Kurt's first thought was that the elevator music in Purgatory might be worse than the music in the second ring of Hell. While the volume was a lot more tolerable, what sounded like the overemoting tots from an episode of "Barney" singing "Anything You Can Do, I Can Do Better" grabbed his nerves and ran a cheese grater across them. Thankfully the trip was short and he nearly leapt out of the elevator into the fourth ring of Purgatory, glad to be free of that noise.

Stretching away, he saw rows and rows of big-screen televisions, a couch facing each one. And on each television, perky aerobics instructors exhorted the viewers to go for the burn. As Kurt walked around the first row of couches, he saw the souls that were being subjected to the perk-a-thon. Each one was grotesquely overweight, their faces like the heads of butterflies poking out of cocoons of fat. These were the slothful, the lazy, and the weight of their sins manifested on them as real weight. Only when they got off their behinds and exercised it off would they be light enough to rise.

"Mr. Gray," Duke called, "we've got to go about a mile that way." Duke pointed in the opposite direction.

Kurt tapped the soul in front of him on the shoulder. "You wanna come with us," he asked. "You know, a walk would do you worlds of good."

The soul continued staring at the TV. "Nah, I'm good."

"Suit yourself," Kurt said, walking off to join Duke and George. He didn't feel so bad about not helping this soul or pretty much any soul on this level. They had the means to help themselves, but they didn't feel like it. So let them sit. *Sometimes, people have to save themselves*, he thought.

He, George, and Duke walked down the rows and rows of televisions, seeing the people enmeshed in their couches. It took a while before they saw someone actually exercising; a woman who looked to have dropped about two-thirds of the weight she needed to lose before she'd rise. Kurt stopped at her row and wondered aloud about blessing her and speeding up her trip, but Duke advised against it. "Let her finish what she started," he said.

"Pretty wise for an assistant angel," George said, nodding approval.

"Well, I don't plan to be an assistant forever," Duke replied.

And that's when Nybras struck. Leaping out from behind a row of televisions, he rushed forward, pushing Duke aside, making a beeline for Kurt with his hands reaching for Kurt's throat. George put a foot out.

Nybras went down, his chest hitting the floor and then his chin, skidding to a stop with his hands eighteen inches from Kurt's boots. Before he could get up and scrabble toward Kurt, Duke had a knee on his neck and was cuffing him like they were on an episode of "Cops." Kurt almost expected Duke to start reading the demon his rights as he stood him up and shoved him up against the ring's outer rail.

What Kurt didn't expect was for Duke to look to him. "So what do we do with him?"

"How should I know? You're the angel."

"Assistant angel," George corrected.

"If I may... ummm... interject," Nybras said from his position against the rail. "Standard operating procedure would be to cast me down."

"What," Kurt asked, "you mean like throw you over the rail?"

"Unless you are able to open a portal into Hell, that would probably be best. Once I recovered, perhaps I could find the portal into the ninth ring."

"Wouldn't that hurt?"

"Ummm... immensely. But remember that I did try to kill you and cause you to lose your bet, thus committing your soul to the sixth ring."

"He's got a point," George said.

Duke reached down with one hand and grabbed the leg of Nybras's pants, preparing to throw him over.

"No," Kurt snapped. "No throwing anyone over the railing. Just hold him still."

Kurt walked up to Nybras, placed a hand on the side of his face, and then drew it away. "I forgive you."

Nybras turned away from Kurt, jerking Duke off balance and doubled over, a howl escaping his lips to rival the howling of the imp in the holiometer. Kurt felt terrible. He hadn't done it to punish Nybras or cause him pain. He didn't know why he did it. It just seemed the thing to do. But he was sure he hadn't done it with malice.

Fortunately, the howling was brief. Nybras seemed to run out of air and didn't wind up for another outburst. He just stood there, bent over and panting. But when he stood up and turned to face them...

"Holy shit," escaped George's mouth.

"What he said," Duke concurred.

Nybras's horns had shrunk to nubs. His large, pointed ears had shrunk to the size of a movie elf's or a "Star Trek" Vulcan's. The cuffs clanked to the floor behind him and he brought forward actual hands, not the oversized claws he'd so recently tried to wrap around Kurt's throat. He needed a manicure and his skin was still gnarled and nut-brown, but his demonic features had definitely been reduced.

Nybras looked at his hands, then raised them up to touch his head and face. His eyes went wide and he fell to his knees before Kurt, wrapping his arms around Kurt's legs. "Please," he cried, "forgive me again! Forgive me again!"

Kurt reached down, hooked a hand under one of Nybras's arms, and lifted him to his feet. He reached out, touched Nybras's jaw, and said "I forgive you."

Nothing happened.

Kurt touched Nybras's jaw again, envisioning himself drawing away the demon's burden. "I forgive you."

Nothing happened again.

Nybras began to cry. "Why didn't you just throw me over the edge? Do you know how long it's been since I was cast down? Do you know how long it's been since I heard God's voice, felt God's love? Then you give me hope! Hope! Hope that I could be redeemed, that I could be *loved*!"

Nybras fell to his knees and sobbed. "Why didn't you just throw me over the edge?" He fell over onto his side and curled up into a ball, his body wracked with sobs.

He was a demon. Even with the changes Kurt's forgiveness had caused, there was no denying it. Yet, even so, Kurt pitied him. He'd had hope dangled in front of him and yanked away. Nothing on this level, but girls in junior high could be pretty cruel... *Okay*, he thought, *this isn't about me.*

This was not the kind of things Jews knew, particularly secular Reform Jews. Salvation and redemption weren't big elements of the faith. You followed the rules, you loved God, you loved your family, you loved your community... Kurt stopped. Nybras had said that Kurt took his hope that he could be loved. Kurt had given Nybras his forgiveness, but had he given him his love? Kurt looked at him. How could you love a demon? It wasn't like this was a bad human who could change. This was a demon. They couldn't change.

But Nybras had changed. He had changed from an angel into a demon, and now Kurt had changed him part of the way back. But just saying "I love you, man," wasn't going to cut it. If he didn't mean it, it wouldn't work. He looked at Nybras again. This was once an angel, beloved by God, but he had been cast down into Hell and abandoned. In a way, he was lost... a lost boy. Kurt looked down at him and the pity ebbed away. He felt sad for him, but it was a new kind of sadness, the sadness you feel when someone you care for is hurting. Kurt knelt down next to Nybras and put a hand on his shoulder. "You are loved."

There was no howl this time, just a blinding burst of light, and when the spots cleared from Kurt's eyes, the demon had been replaced by what looked to be a 13-year-old boy. He wore Nybras's suit, but his skin was smooth, his ears round, his hands perfect. A shock of curly brown hair topped his head draping down in ringlets. The boy sat up, looking at his hands, then touching his face, his hair. "How...?"

302

Duke stood there with his jaw dropped. "Amazing," George said, chuckling in disbelief.

Nybras jumped up and threw his arms around Kurt, then dropped to one knee and took Kurt's hand, kissing it.

Kurt just stood still, thinking two words over and over and over: "holy shit, holy shit, holy shit."

* * * *

Alain turned off the TV. They got every channel in Hell that was playing on Earth, plus a few more they made themselves, and still he couldn't find anything he wanted to watch.

There was a knock at the door of his hospital room. "Ya decent in there," a voice asked as the door opened a crack.

Alain straightened himself up in his bed. "Sure, come in."

The door opened wide and in walked a tall man in jeans, a denim shirt, bolo tie, white sportcoat, and white cowboy hat. His blonde hair was tied into a ponytail in the back and he wore a neatly trimmed beard and moustache. Lying in bed, Alain couldn't get an accurate read on the man's height, but he guessed it to be about the same as his. "How the heck are ya," the man said with a cowboy twang, stepping forward and extending a hand.

Alain shook it cautiously. "As good as can be expected, I guess. Can I help you?"

The man smiled. "Question is, can I help you?"

"I don't know," Alain said. "Who are you?"

"Oh," the man said, taking off his hat. "Allow me to introduce myself. The name's Deuce... Deuce X. MacKenna and I'm your court-appointed guardian angel."

Chapter 35: Gobsmacked

The British have a way with words sometimes, and it was a British idiom that best hit the mark when used to describe Alain's reaction to meeting Deuce: gobsmacked.

"I've secured your release from this hospital," Deuce said, pulling some papers out of his coat.

"But I'm injured," Alain protested weakly.

"No, you're not. You have been restored to full health and had all your vampire powers restored as well. I've filed a breach of contract suit on your behalf for that bit of shenanigans. If Gray doesn't make it, we may be able to invalidate the contract on that alone."

Alain stuck a hand under his bandages and felt his stomach. The gash from the other night was gone. He willed his fangs to drop... and they did. "How do I know this isn't a trick?"

Deuce straightened up, putting a hand over his heart. "'Our Father, which art in Heaven, hallowed be thy name; thy kingdom come;

thy will be done, in Earth as it is in Heaven.'" He paused to let it sink in. "Now, can a demon say the Lord's Prayer?"

"I don't know," Alain replied. "Can they?"

"Touche," Deuce acknowledged. "What can I do to prove to you I'm an angel?"

Alain thought. "Demons are bound by their contracts. Get a piece of paper, write 'if I'm a demon, I'll burst into flames right here and now' on it, then sign it."

Deuce nodded. "Nice." Deuce pulled a notepad and pen out of his other coat pocket, scribbled furiously on it, then signed it with a flourish. He tore the sheet off and handed it to Alain, who inspected it and shrugged.

"I guess you're on the level," Alain said, getting out of bed. "Know where they put my clothes?"

"Under the bed."

Alain looked under the bed and found his travelling clothes; cleaned, mended, and neatly folded. After his time in the army and 60+ years of marriage, Alain had pretty much given up on modesty. He stripped out of his hospital gown and bandages and put his clothes on as Deuce gave him the rundown.

"I'm going to escort you out of the hospital wing. I'm supposed to escort you back to the hotel wing, where you'll be given a suite and run of the casino while we wait for the outcome of the wager. But if you're amenable, while we walk through one of the outer courtyards, you're going to give me the slip. You'll run around the outside of the next tower to a staging area where they're preparing a weapons drop for the seventh ring."

"There you'll find a large crate with a quad bike, and some gas cans. You'll go inside, close the crate from within, and hitch a ride. When you get there, you'll recruit a raiding party of about ten guys who can take orders, then you'll come back here and make a lot of trouble."

Alain finished tying his boots and stood up. "And why would I do that?"

"Because if you want Kurt to succeed up there, we're going to need a distraction down here."

Alain walked to the door and opened it for Deuce. "Then let's get to work."

* * * *

Kurt stood before the portal into Heaven with George and the two angels: Duke, the assistant angel, and Nybras, the once and future angel. Nybras and Duke were arguing about who would go through the portal first to sing Kurt's praises and prepare Heaven for his arrival.

"I met him first," Duke shouted. "I am his messenger."

"Ah, but I am his miracle," Nybras countered. "I should be his messenger."

Kurt only half-paid attention. He was still thinking "holy shit, holy shit, holy shit." He'd just gone on autopilot and followed the three back to the elevator, then out of the elevator to the portal. George put a hand on his shoulder.

"They're about to throw down, buddy. You gotta put an end to this."

Kurt shook his head, clearing the clouds, blowing the holies to the right side of his brain and the shits to the left. He pinched the bridge of his nose as he listened to each angel shout "no, I am his messenger."

"Neither of you are my messenger," he said quietly. The two angels stopped shouting and turned to him, giving him sad puppy-dog eyes. "We want to do this quietly, if at all possible. I may be the biggest, baddest thing to hit Heaven since... well... since Lord knows, but if I walk in there, swinging my big holiness dick, I might just piss off someone we need not to be pissed at me." Kurt sighed. "Let us exemplify humility."

"Humility," Nybras exclaimed. "Why didn't I think of that? It's perfect. And may I say, it's so in tune with your 'vibe'."

Kurt closed his eyes. *So, this is what having hot air blown up your ass feels like*, he thought. *Sort of sucks.*

"So," George interrupted, "what can we expect on the other side of the portal?"

"I've never been through this way," Nybras said.

"Me neither," said Duke.

"Hold on." Now it was George's turn to pinch the bridge of his nose. "Duke, how is it that you've never been through this way?"

"I used the portal in the security office."

George pinched the bridge of his nose tighter. "Why didn't you just let us use that portal?"

Duke nodded his head sideways at Nybras. "I didn't want to face the emon-day alone-ay."

Nybras sighed in exasperation and George was about to say something rude, but Kurt spoke up. "Okay, this is how it's going to go. George and I will step through the portal first. Duke, you and Nybras will count to ten — a slow ten — and then follow us. On the other side, if I do not call you over to us, we've determined it's too dangerous to be seen together. Only join us if I call you to us. Is that clear?"

Nybras and Duke nodded their heads. Before anything else could go wrong, Kurt grabbed George's arm and escorted him through the portal.

* * * *

Kurt and George found themselves in a very large semi-circular room, souls feeding out of portals spaced about every twenty feet along the walls. Velvet-roped pathways funneled the souls from their portals to a set of moving walkways in the center of the far wall. Kurt heard Duke's voice say "ten" as Duke and Nybras popped out of the portal behind them, immediately coming over to join Kurt and George.

"Oh, I know this," Duke said. "Standard arrivals lounge set-up."

"I thought you said you hadn't been this way before," George said, accusatively.

"Not in Earth's Heaven, but this is a pretty standard configuration." Duke looked around and seemed to find what he was looking for off to their right. "Follow me."

Duke stepped over the velvet rope bordering their pathway, crossing three more paths and making a beeline toward a blue door set in between two portals. The lettering on it was alien to George and Kurt. They hadn't seen any alphabet like it on Earth. Duke saw their confusion. "Angel script," he said. "Says 'employees only.'"

Duke unclipped his ID badge from his chest pocket and swiped it across a black pad at the side of the door. There was a beep, then a click, and Duke swung the door open. "After you," he said, ushering the other three through. Duke stepped inside and closed the door behind them. "Follow me," he said.

Duke led them down a stark hallway, the walls that same dull white with dull yellow floors that seemed to be symptomatic of older civic buildings. They walked for hundreds of yards before the hallway terminated at another door with a black pad beside it. Duke swiped his badge again, and opened it, ushering the other three out.

They exited into another large hall and Kurt could see what Duke had led them around. The moving walkways fed into lines, each leading up to a gate where an angel greeted each soul, typed a few things into a computer terminal, and then either let it through or had another angel escort it away. On the other side of the gates, souls who got through were greeted by other souls who hugged and kissed them, then led them joyfully from the hall.

"Did you just sneak us around the gates of Heaven," Kurt asked.

"I got the feeling you didn't want to attract attention," Duke said. "If a mortal showed up at the gates with an angel who was cast down... it would have attracted attention."

"Gold star for Duke," George said, patting him on the back. Kurt smiled and nodded. "Now let's get out of here and find someplace less conspicuous to figure out what we're going to do next."

Duke led them to the closest exit, coming out on the right-hand side of a 200-yard-wide staircase leading down from the reception hall to a grand avenue. Kurt stopped and looked around, getting his first view of Heaven. He'd always pictured it would be something like the touristy part of Washington D.C. on one of its best days; great monumental buildings gleaming in the sunlight, cherry trees covered in pink blossoms, lots of gleaming metals, white marble, and sunshine reflecting off of all of it. And it did not disappoint. His first view of Heaven showed him a combination of nature's beauty and grand architecture that made him feel good inside. It was beautiful in the way Botticelli's Venus was beautiful, but even more so.

"Wow," he said.

Nybras's eyes teared up. "It's been so long."

The four of them stood there, basking in the view, when their almost trancelike joy was broken by a voice shouting one word. "Kurt!"

Chapter 36: Reunions

The voice had come from their right side. Everyone looked to the right, but there was no one there. Then a woman peeked around the side of the building and waved to them, gesturing them toward her. Kurt and the angels stood rooted to the spot, but George took off at a dead run.

A group of people who know they're somewhere they shouldn't be are a bit like herd animals. If one takes off running, there is an instinctive urge in the others to follow. Not wanting to be quite as conspicuous, the three of them walked quickly toward the corner of the building, the two angels following Kurt's lead. George disappeared around the corner and they followed him about twenty seconds later.

George's backpack was on the ground and the woman who had waved at them was in his arms, swept up in a bear hug as George twirled her around. Peeking out from behind them was a little boy. When he saw Kurt come around the corner, he ran around them, made a beeline at Kurt, and leapt at him. Kurt caught Junior and hugged him ferociously.

Duke and Nybras watched the scene in bewilderment. Eventually, George put the woman down and walked her over to Kurt,

Junior, and the angels. "Kurt," George said, so joyful he paused and leaned in to kiss the woman's cheek, "this is Aunt Marie... Alain's wife."

Marie extended a hand, "Junior has spoken about you nonstop since he arrived."

Kurt shifted Junior's weight so he could hold Junior with one arm. Here in Heaven, Junior was no longer lighter than air, but he still only weighed maybe 30 pounds, a lot less than he would if he were a corporeal 6-year-old boy instead of a soul. He took Marie's hand and shook it as he looked her over. She wasn't as beautiful as Alain had claimed, but possibly no woman was. Yet she definitely had a zing to her and she definitely wasn't the 86-year-old woman who had collapsed while cursing Simon Cowell. She looked to be in her late twenties or early thirties, bold and confident. "Alain spoke of you often," Kurt said.

"And who are your friends," she asked, eyeing Duke and Nybras, who stood a few paces behind Kurt, looking uncomfortable.

Kurt turned and introduced the two as Marie walked up and shook their hands. "This is Duke, an assistant angel we met in Purgatory. And this is Nybras..."

Before Kurt could tell the lie he'd come up with for how Nybras joined the group, Marie jerked her hand from Nybras's. "One of the fallen," she exclaimed, recoiling. "How did he... how did you... what is he..."

Nybras bowed deeply. "My lady, I am but a humble angel who has been given a second chance by this miraculous being," he said, remaining bowed. He slowly raised his head, though he remained bent over. "Please believe that I am not the angel I once was. I am reborn from kindness and love." His eyes seemed to mist up and he launched into a falsetto rendition of "Amazing Grace".

Duke stepped up and cupped a hand over Nybras's mouth while helping him straighten up. "Easy there," Duke chided Nybras. He turned to Marie. "I may only be an assistant angel, but I know a miracle when I see one, and I saw Kurt redeem this demon. Believe me, you have nothing to fear."

Marie looked them over. "Come with me," she said, seeming to have made her decision. "We can't stand here talking all day. It's not safe."

* * * *

Deuce had been true to his word. He took Alain on the scenic route to the hotel tower, detouring to an outside path between two minor towers. As they walked the path he whispered to Alain, "this is where you run away."

Alain was pretty sure there'd be a video camera somewhere and he didn't want to cause any more trouble for Deuce than the angel was already causing for himself, so he resisted the urge to shake Deuce's hand before he took off running. He could hear Deuce behind him, making feeble sounds of protest at his "escape."

Although Deuce had told Alain what to expect, he was still surprised to see three shipping containers sitting unguarded and open in the courtyard on the other side of the tower. The security was so sloppy it made Alain a bit suspicious. It was almost this easy to find the dungeons and Vinnie had been waiting for them with a reception committee.

They couldn't just kill Alain in his hospital bed, he thought. Well, they could, but it wouldn't be kosher. But killing him while he tried to escape would be another matter entirely. He'd never thought to ask to see Deuce's wings or halo. He'd had Deuce prove he wasn't a demon in disguise, but never had him prove he was an angel. Maybe Deuce was a vampire, or a black mage, or some other business associate of Hell that would have allowed him to prove himself not to be a demon.

But Alain was at a loss for options. The portal to Purgatory was outside Pandaemonium's walls, and they were too high for him to scale. He'd have to find a way outside the walls, then find the portal before he was caught. It was nearly impossible. But as he looked at the cargo container, the biggest vibe he got was that he was walking into a giant roach motel.

Stop it, he silently shouted to himself. If he'd wanted to think this through, the time was before he ran away from Deuce. Now that he was off on his own, he was an escapee, and instead of doing something to preserve his life and freedom, he was crouched by the curve of a tower, frozen in indecision.

Slowly he crept toward the cargo container. Various alarms in his head screamed at him that this was a bad idea, but he couldn't shake the feeling that Deuce really was an angel. There was obviously something going on that was bigger than him. He was a guaranteed soul for Hell, George was 50/50, and Kurt was out of Hell's reach. That meant the bet Satan took was basically even odds. There was no house advantage. Satan wouldn't — or at least shouldn't — have taken an even-odds bet. There had to be some higher stakes on the line. And if there were, it would make sense for Heaven to take an interest.

Alain entered the cargo container. As promised, there was a quad bike, gas cans, and a number of crates. The closest crates contained Kalashnikov assault rifles. Alain didn't have time to read the rest. He pulled the container doors closed, manipulating the locking mechanism from within, creating a deep darkness within the crate. A few stray cracks let in enough light that his vampire-enhanced vision could make out shapes and outlines. He sat on the quad bike and waited.

* * * *

Even the back alleys of Heaven were nice. They reminded Kurt of the narrow streets of old Italian mountain towns that you saw in coffee-table books. Marie led them along a twisting route, avoiding major thoroughfares. Kurt carried Junior, who had refused to be put down, George carried both packs, and the two angels followed along.

Eventually, they came to the back gate of a small walled garden surrounding a two-story townhouse. When Marie opened it without a key, Kurt was initially shocked, but then he realized that if there was any place you should be able to leave things unlocked, it would be Heaven. Marie ushered them through the gate and into the house, leading them into the kitchen.

The kitchen was like something out of a magazine. It was not only large and well-appointed, but it had a nook with a table that could seat six. It was just large enough to be impressive, but still small enough to give off a sense of comfort. The range top was in a central island, and a cook at the island could feed people sitting on stools at the other side, or it was just a handful of steps to deliver a dish over to the nook.

Marie waved the group over to the table and dashed out of the kitchen. George set his pack down against the far wall of the nook and then sat down in the chair closest to it. Junior let Kurt put him down so Kurt could take the chair at the head/foot of the table, just around the table's corner from George, then climbed up into Kurt's lap. In the center of the far wall of the nook was a recessed window with a view of the walled garden and a bench below it. The two angels opted to sit on the bench rather than take seats at the table.

Marie returned, walking quickly into the kitchen. "Are any of you hungry," she asked, not waiting for a reply before opening a cupboard and starting to pick ingredients.

316

"Won't we be condemned to stay if we eat the food of the afterlife," Kurt inquired.

Marie paused in thought. "I don't know." She began picking ingredients again. "But I must cook. It's what I do when I'm nervous."

George smiled. "Truth. I gained 3 pounds the week before her IRS audit."

Kurt could understand why she was nervous, but what he didn't understand was... "what are we waiting for while you cook?"

"Friends," Marie said, pausing in her kitchen bustling.

"And what are these friends going to do?"

"Help us."

"How?"

"I don't know," Marie said. She walked over to the table, remembered the open cupboard, jogged over to close it, then crossed back to the table and sat down.

"Things are — how should I say it — bizarre around here. Heaven is not so heavenly. God has not been seen in centuries and there is some sort of junta of angels that has taken over to rule in his place. Everything looks heavenly on the surface, but it's sterile, overly clean. There used to be troupes of musicians and performers who roamed the streets and occupied corners of the parks. There were salons, choirs... I never saw any of this, but the old-timers speak of it in hushed whispers."

"Heaven was a celebration. But celebration of that nature was prohibited. Gatherings of more than four souls have been prohibited. Can you imagine the size of the extended families here? If two people had more than two children, they can't have the whole family over for dinner, much less their children, grandchildren, cousins... And those who complain openly have been known to disappear."

Kurt felt his face flush as panic began to set in. "God isn't here? What do you mean God isn't here?"

He moved Junior off his lap and got up from his chair, beginning to pace. "How could God not be here? This is Heaven! He has to be here!" He turned to Marie and grabbed her arm. "God has to be here!"

George stood and put a hand on Kurt's arm, pulling him loose from Marie. "Kurt, you need to settle down."

Kurt shrugged off the hand. "Settle down? How can I settle down? God is not in His Heaven! Mister God is not home at the moment! We bet everything! *I* bet everything."

A tap on the shoulder turned Kurt around. He turned to face Nybras who passed his hand over Kurt's eyes. Kurt stiffened, then slumped and fell backwards into George's arms. "I'm sorry," Nybras said, "but he might have hurt himself if he kept going that way. It should only last a few hours."

Marie stood up. "Let me show you where you can put him."

* * * *

When Kurt woke, he was in a familiar place: white buildings, empty windows, and Jack sitting next to him on the sidewalk.

"How..."

"Nybras slipped you an angelic mickey," Jack smiled. "He was right. You were going to hurt yourself."

Kurt remembered the rant he'd been on before losing consciousness. Oddly, he had a hard time getting worked up over it. "God's not there," he said very matter-of-factly. "We're going to lose the bet."

318

Jack stood up. "Walk with me," he said, heading off toward the sidewalk's end. Kurt got up and followed.

About 20 feet before the end of the walk, he stopped and turned toward the wall, pointing to a small box. Kurt looked at it and saw a fairly standard fire alarm pull, with the "in case of emergency, break glass" message written on it.

"There's one like this next to God's throne in the Celestial Palace. If you pull it, He will show up."

"But there's this junta of angels, and Heaven's on lockdown... How am I going to get in there? It would take a miracle."

Jack smiled again. "Says the guy who turned a demon back into an angel."

Kurt sat down on the curb, putting his elbows on his knees and his face in his hands. "But I don't know how I did that. I've got no idea how any of this works. It's like the force is strong with me, but I have no Obi Wan." Kurt lifted his head. "Could you..."

"Noooo," Jack cut him off, waving a hand in the air. "Not the right place, not the right guy. But you've met your Yoda already. Gentleman by the name of Michael Barlow wrote a short story about a man who got to be God for a week and had to learn how to use God's powers. Story wasn't that great. He never submitted it anywhere. But, oddly enough, his insights into the nature of holiness and how to focus it to create miracles... deadly accurate."

"So, he's in Heaven? I can find him?"

"No and yes."

Kurt leaned back and lay on the sidewalk, staring up. "A straight answer! My kingdom for a straight answer!"

"You know him better by his nickname, Mick."

Kurt sat up.

"The way you find him is you use that pinky in your pocket to bring him to you."

"How?"

"From a little acorn, a mighty oak grows."

"What?"

"Your friends are waking you up."

* * * *

Alain had been waiting for the door to open and a cadre of demon guards to storm in, but it never happened. He sat quietly in the dark for about an hour, then felt the cargo container move with a hard jerk, then it felt like it was swaying slightly, accelerating upward in regular, rhythmic motions, as if being lifted through the air by a great winged beast.

The flight was brief, maybe 30 minutes, before he started hearing bullets pinging off of the cargo container. The forward progress halted and the container bounced slowly up and down as if the great winged beast that carried it was hovering. There was a great roar and then a huge whooshing sound. Screams came from far below and then the forward progress began again. After another half hour the container began lowering, setting down with a thud. There was some muffled talking and then another thud as something large butted up against the far end of the container and shoved it forward, the metal grinding against the ground. Alain had no idea how far it was shoved, but it happened about 15 times and then stopped, leaving only the residual sound of the two other containers being shoved in on either side of his.

There was some more muffled talking, another beastly roar, then a rush of air, as if the winged beasts had launched back into flight. At the far end of the container, Alain heard clanking as the door was opened. He hopped off the quad bike and took a runner's crouch so he could bolt out and have the advantage of surprise. But when the door opened and he saw the figure in the doorway, the plan to run past him/it turned into an impromptu tackle.

Alain got his knees on the man's arms and sat down on his haunches looking down at the owner of the shipment. "How ya doin', Albert?"

Despite being on his back, his arms pinned, Albert tried to muster joy. "Alain," he exclaimed. "You survived. Thank the heavens!"

Alain heard the men approaching behind them, clumsy oafs who plodded so heavily it was like drumbeats to his sensitive ears. He preferred to focus on Albert, though, and did nothing as three rifle barrels were pressed up against his head. "Heavens indeed," Alain said quietly.

"What do you want we should do with him," a gunman asked in a voice Alain instantly recognized as Kolya's.

Albert looked up at Alain questioningly. "Alain?"

The gun blasts to his head might not kill him. The barrels were aimed too high. If you wanted to kill a vampire with a gun, you needed a shotgun blast that could separate the head from the neck. But three rifle shots to the head would slow him down.

Alain raised his hands and slowly got up off of Albert as the three men behind him shifted to keep the barrels of their guns against his head. Albert got to his feet and stood before Alain. "You know, I really am glad to see you."

"You have an odd way of showing it."

Albert's eyebrows raised. "You showed up uninvited and pinned me to the ground in front of associates who don't know you. What did you expect?" He waved a hand at the men behind Alain. "Put the guns down. This is all making me feel like we're in a bad James Bond movie. Kolya, open the crate on the left... no, your other left... There should be a case of scotch in it. Grab a bottle and meet us in my lab."

Albert turned and started walking. He looked back at Alain, "you coming?"

Chapter 37: Arrivals

Kurt woke up in one of the most comfortable beds he'd ever experienced in his life. The mattress was soft, but not too soft, the sheets and quilt were heavy enough to make him feel cocooned in pleasant warmth. Despite the gentle nudging and calling of his name, he really didn't want to leave his little pocket of bliss. Then someone reached under the sheets, grabbed his feet, yanked them out from under the covers, turned him perpendicular to the bed in the process, pulled them out, and set them on the floor, pretty much forcing him to sit up on the side of the bed. As he sat up, he came face-to-face with George. "You've got visitors," George said, smiling.

Kurt did a groggy physical inventory. They hadn't undressed him, but they had removed his boots. "Boots," he said to George.

"Entryway closet, by the front door." George put out a hand and Kurt accepted it, letting George help him to his feet. He wasn't weak, but he was still working at shaking off the grogginess from Nybras's angelic mickey. "Everyone's got their shoes off downstairs. You'll fit right in."

Kurt took that statement with a grain of salt. Fitting in because he was shoeless might be one thing, but being 23, scared out of his wits, responsible for multiple lives and souls, and possessed of enough power to turn a demon back into an angel... he didn't think he was going to find that club gathered around the punchbowl. As he came down the stairs, he gave George a pat on the shoulder and whispered in his ear "can you try to get me one of our Cokes? One of ours."

George gave him the high sign and headed off to the kitchen as Kurt descended into a room of mostly unfamiliar faces. He knew Duke and Nybras, of course, Marie, and then there was Elvis... Kurt stopped. Elvis — the young, pre-Army, Jailhouse Rock Elvis — was teaching Junior how to play "Blue Hawaii" on a ukulele.

The other people in the room were... "I'm sorry," Kurt asked. "Are you *the* Elvis?"

The man looked him up and down. "Actually," he said in a nasally voice, "my name is Herman Borowitz. You see they let us pick how we want to look when we get here. Oy, there are more Marilyn Monroes than you could shake a stick at."

"Really," Kurt asked incredulously.

"Of course not, son," Elvis said, slipping into his normal voice as he reached out a hand. "Elvis Presley, pleased to meet you."

Kurt shook Elvis's hand as other visitors created a sort of receiving line, passing by and introducing themselves. The four other visitors included Leonardo Da Vinci, King Arthur, Eleanor Roosevelt, and Barbara Greenstein.

As Barbara introduced herself, Kurt paused. All of the other visitors were famous. "And what are you famous for," he asked her.

"My noodle kugel," Barbara said, smiling demurely, and went back to her seat.

With everyone sitting again, all eyes were on Kurt and the silence was oppressive. He had no idea what to say, how to start, but everyone seemed to be expecting something of him. "Thank you all for coming," he said, unable to think of anything else.

George arrived with his Coke and handed it to him. Kurt stood there and sipped at it, hoping someone would jump into the fray. George did.

"They're all up to speed, buddy."

"The way I see it," Arthur said from his chair, "is we all need to find God. This is the common cause that draws us together. I propose a quest..."

Eleanor Roosevelt rolled her eyes. "Not another quest. This is not the round table, dear."

"Yeah, man," Elvis concurred, "how are we gonna go lookin' for him anyway? I can look behind the couch, but unless there's a guy back there who says 'hey, I'm God, nice to meetcha,' I got no idea what he looks like or where to look."

"What we need," said Leonardo, staring directly at Kurt, waving a hand as he spoke, "is a miracle. A few miracles, perhaps. This is what Mr. Gray brings to the table, eh. Armed insurrection is doomed. No war machine I could design can stand up to Michael's flaming sword. We need miracles. Force is not an option."

Leonardo's repeated insistence on miracles made Kurt remember the conversation in Nowhere. He was the young padawan to Mick's Obi-Wan. He was Daniel-san to Mick's Mr. Miyagi. But last time he saw Mick, he was crucified upside down on a walkway through the Asmodeus Arena. How could he get him here? *From a little acorn, a mighty oak grows*, Jack's voice echoed in his mind's ear.

As the rest of the group argued, Kurt put down his Coke, then quietly found his way out of the room and out of the house into the walled garden. Finding a patch of dirt that seemed big enough, he dug a small hole with his fingers. He reached into his pocket and found Mick's finger wrapped in his bandanna. He unwrapped it and dropped it into the hole, shoving dirt over it and patting it down.

Then he watched it... nothing happened. He wondered if he was being impatient. In every sword and sorcery book he'd ever read, when you planted something magical into the ground, you had to invoke it. Kurt turned phrases for a living, or at least he was a junior phrase-turner. He could come up with an invocation.

"Michael Barlow, I command you to rise."

Nada.

"We welcome you into the embrace of Heaven, Michael Barlow. Use this connection between its soil and your soul to find your way to us."

Nope.

"By the powers invested in me by a sick and perverse universe, I forgive you, Mick. I give you my love. I give your freedom. Come join us in this Heavenly garden."

Not really.

By now a crowd had gathered in the doorway to watch Kurt perform his latest miracle. Nybras had apparently elbowed himself into a prime viewing situation.

Kurt didn't know what else to say. "Mick," he mumbled under his breath, "stop fuckin' around down there and get your ass up here, now!"

"Maybe you need to water it," a small voice said. The crowd in the doorway parted and Junior walked out into the garden, followed by Marie who held a pitcher of water. Jack had said that a mighty oak would

326

grow from an acorn, so it made logical sense. Kurt took the pitcher from Marie and poured some of its contents on the spot where he'd buried the pinky.

Nothing happened. Kurt felt Junior tugging at his pants leg. When he looked at him, Junior beckoned him downward. Kurt knelt so he was on Junior's level and Junior leaned in. "Holy water," he whispered in Kurt's ear.

Kurt closed his eyes and put one hand over the pitcher. He'd done a half-assed blessing in Duke's office and it had worked, but he really wanted it to work this time. The problem was that the only Hebrew blessing he could remember was the blessing over the wine. It would have to be good enough. "Baruch atah Adonai, elohenu melach haolam, boray p'ree hagofen. Amen."

Kurt looked down at the pitcher and the water had turned dark. He sniffed it. It smelled like Passover wine. *Oh, fuck me,* he thought. He quickly poured it out on the dirt hoping no one would notice he'd just accidentally turned water into wine. On the other hand, he thought, there was probably no better way to invoke the soul of a bartender than with an alcoholic beverage.

It only took a few seconds before a pink shoot rose from the soil. Quickly, like watching a stop-motion animation of a plant growing, more shoots rose, twining into vines, growing upward. The stalks split, becoming legs, intertwining again at the pelvis and growing into a torso, sending out small shoots from which leaves unfurled. Stalks split at the shoulders to form arms as the main stalk became a skull, the leaves fleshing out the exoskeleton of branching vines, creating a man-sized topiary. As the leaves expanded and their edges touched, they fused together, gradually creating a seamless skin. More leaves sprouted from the skin and fused to become pants and a shirt.

Over the five or so minutes this took, everyone watched, transfixed, including Kurt. Despite it being a miracle — his miracle — he

327

couldn't avoid feeling like he was watching some reimagining of *Invasion of the Body Snatchers* and that instead of it becoming Mick, he was growing the pod-person version of himself. He stood up to peer at the face, and as he watched, he kept willing himself not to fall asleep... just in case.

But when the fusing stopped, the eyes opened, the mouth opened, and Mick gasped, falling forward. Kurt caught him and steadied him. "It's okay, Mick," he said. "Breathe. Breathe."

Mick leaned against Kurt, panting, gradually gaining control of his legs and arms. When he could stand on his own, he pushed off of Kurt gently and stood back. He stared at Kurt for a moment, then grabbed Kurt's head in his hands, kissed Kurt on the cheek, and still holding Kurt's head in his hands, Mick laughed. It started out light, but grew in intensity and joy. Mick let go of Kurt, leaned back, raised his arms toward the sky and just stood there, laughing until tears ran down his face.

* * * *

"Have a seat," Albert said, waving Alain toward a stool in his lab. "Can I get you anything? I believe there's some imported beer in one of the cargo containers."

Alain sat, watching Albert like a hawk as he kept his other senses at peak sensitivity so he could be sure where Kolya and his boys were. "And what earned you three whole cargo containers," Alain asked, figuring he already knew the answer.

One of Kolya's men walked in with a styrofoam cooler and put it down on a low table. Albert walked over, opened it, and pulled out a bottle of vodka, so cold you could see frost on the glass. "Kolya, why don't you share this with your men? I'll be safe with Mr. Beaudreaux here."

Kolya wasn't a loyal soldier, and the way he licked his lips, it seemed he hadn't had either vodka or a cold beverage in quite some time. He took the bottle and went back down the hall toward Albert's garage area, his men following behind.

"They move pretty well for blind men," Alain said.

"There are different grades of blind," Albert replied. "They're not so blind they see nothing but black, but they'd be considered blind for all legal purposes. Everything's a blur with moving blobs. Camouflage works really well. They're easily ambushed."

Alain realized they were getting off topic. "Back to my original question..."

Albert paused and dug in the cooler, pulling out a bottle of Canadian beer with a twist off cap. He popped the cap and took a long drag off the bottle before turning his attention back to Alain. "Someone in Pandaemonium was quite interested in making sure Kurt arrived intact. Word was put out that there'd be a big bonus for whomever found him and got him across the seventh ring safely."

"So you knew who we were when Ty brought us to you. Was he looking for us?"

"Yes and no." Albert settled down on a stool and took another sip from his beer. "I knew there was a reward for getting a vampire and two mortals through this level safely. But there's a little over 3,000 square miles of seventh level and about 8 million souls here. Putting out lookouts would be futile. Ty brought you to me because he thought Kolya would hold you for ransom and torture you for fun."

"And where is Ty?"

"Sleeping. You know Kurt healed him before he left, right?"

"Had no idea."

Albert put his beer down on the table and stood up from his stool. "Look, I'm not your enemy and I'm not your Judas. You're obviously not here with Hell's blessing and you wouldn't come back for fun. If you're just passing through on your way back up, I've got some rock climbing gear I'll be glad to give you. If you're here for another reason, maybe I can help."

Alain crossed his arms over his chest and leaned back as far as he could on a backless stool. "And what would be in it for you if you helped?"

"What part of he *healed* Ty was unclear to you? He beat that pit thing!"

Alain raised an eyebrow. "They broadcast the fight everywhere in Hell," Albert said with a dismissive wave. Albert began pacing. "They talked about the bet in the pregame show, how souls were on the line, how Kurt would get a chance to try to get through Purgatory to Heaven if you won... how he has to convince God to save your soul or he loses his."

Albert stopped pacing, standing rooted to one spot. "If he loses, I don't think it's just a matter of Hell getting another soul. I think if Hell gets him, it's a game changer, and it's going to change things in a very bad way. I'm not an altruist. I'm offering to help, because I honestly believe that if I don't, we're all screwed."

Alain thought for a moment. "So, let's say I decide to believe you. Let's say I let you help. All your guns are going to be no use against demons. What can you do to help?"

Albert smiled and walked over to Alain. "Well, first off, did you know your friend pisses holy water?"

Chapter 38: Lessons in Miracles

When Mick settled down, and it took a while, Marie brought him a glass of water. He sat in one of the garden chairs and drank it while Kurt and Marie watched. As he raised the glass to his mouth, Kurt noticed that Mick had both pinkies again.

Mick smiled blissfully and stretched his arms out, turning his face to the sky. "I know it's not Sol, but it's infinitely better than that giant space shuttle exhaust that passed for a light source back in... well, you know."

Kurt wanted to get down to business, but he didn't want to break into Mick's joy. Take a sunny summer morning on the streets of Manhattan and people would still be bulling along, their heads down, their eyes bleary, joylessly sipping at complicated coffee drinks. But Mick's joy in simple things like sunlight and clean water was so pure and unabashed that not letting it fade at its own pace felt almost sinful.

Kurt motioned for Marie to follow him and led her back into the house. "Let's give him a little time to acclimate," he said. She nodded her assent and preceded him back into the living room where everyone was trying to pretend they weren't interested in what was going on in the garden.

"I guess you're all wondering what just happened." Ten heads nodded in unison. Kurt quickly described how Mick saved him in the second ring, leaving out the juicier details since Junior was one of the 10 heads. Then he told them about his latest trip to Nowhere, the "break glass in case of emergency" box by God's throne, and how Mick was going to be his instructor in miracles, although he realized he hadn't yet informed Mick of that pertinent fact.

"See," Leonardo said, raising a hand and pointing a finger in the air. "I told you we needed miracles. Now we shall have them."

"So be it," Arthur said, "but how shall they manifest? Curing a leper or turning water into wine will not get us into that throne room."

"Well, hey now," Elvis said, "if there's one thing I know about, it's drawing a crowd. If Kurt did it on the steps of the Celestial Palace, it might just pull out enough angels to watch that one of us could sneak in."

"And if my mother had wheels, she would have been a trolley car," Eleanor interjected. "We cannot formulate a plan that relies on a number of unpredictable factors to go our way. If there is an angel posted at the throne room doors who does not abandon its post, or better yet, they're simply locked, what then?"

"Maybe he could 'orb,'" Barbara said.

Everyone looked at her, puzzled. "My daughter got me hooked on this TV show, Charmed, before I died. So, in the show, angels are called 'white lighters' and they basically do a sort of dematerializing in one place and then materializing in another called 'orbing.'"

Leonardo leaned forward. "So, you are saying he could teleport into the throne room, right in front of the box, and break the glass before any angels could stop him? The simplicity of it is pure genius."

"But could I do that," Kurt asked?

"If you can perform miracles, why not teleportation," George asked. "Come on. If this was a movie, wouldn't you be asking yourself 'why doesn't he just miracle himself into the throne room?' We can come up with a thousand harebrained 'I Love Lucy' schemes to get in there, but give me one good reason why he can't just miracle himself into the throne room."

The room was silent. George looked over at the two angels. "You guys know any reason?"

Nybras shook his head in the negative while Duke held up both hands. "Hey," Duke said, "I'm just an assistant angel."

"Then it's settled," George's face took on a deeply satisfied look. "Kurt has a few lessons with the professor out there, miracles himself into the throne room, breaks the glass, God comes running."

"And what do I do when He gets there," Kurt asked.

George scrunched up his face and raised a hand. "That part I haven't figured out yet."

Eleanor stood up and walked over to Kurt, putting an arm around his shoulder. "You talk to Him, dear. Tell Him why Alain deserves to be saved."

"How do I do that? Tell God he's a good guy, not bad for a vampire?"

Eleanor lifted a hand, put it on his head, and turned his gaze to see Marie sitting in a chair with Junior in her lap, George standing next to them. "You have his family right there. Between miracle lessons, maybe you could ask *them* why Alain is worth saving."

****

Albert walked away from the bucket with an eyedropper in one hand and a beer in the other. He'd filled the eye dropper from the bucket, but the beer was still sealed. "Don't worry," he told Alain, "I filtered out the smelly bits."

Over in the corner was a box with a blanket over it. Albert lifted the blanket to reveal a wire rabbit cage with an imp in it, seemingly asleep.

Alain had never seen an imp before. This one was about 5 inches tall, a miniature version of Nybras or Mammon, but with no horns and no clothes. It lay curled up, a thumb in its mouth, and it kicked a leg as the light hit it. The whole thing might have been cute if the imp itself wasn't so ugly. Albert dripped a single bead of liquid from the eyedropper onto the imp and the placid scene erupted.

The little demon leapt up into the air with a screech and ran circles around the cage, as if trying to outrun the smoking pit on its rear end where the drop of liquid had landed. Somehow it manifested two voices, one howling, the other cursing as it climbed the sides and hung from the cage's top, screaming steaming bloody murder. While the little demon screamed, Albert popped the top on the beer. He smacked the top of the cage, knocking the imp loose, and it fell to the cage floor where it lay on its stomach, whimpering loudly.

Albert poured a little bit of the beer on its smoking wound and the sizzling stopped, the imp breathing a sigh of relief and visibly relaxing. He put the beer down, picked up the blanket, and covered the cage. "Sleep now," he said, then picked up the beer, taking a sip as he walked back to the table where Alain sat.

He sat at the table. "I've got the equipment to make acid-filled paintballs. If a drop does that to an imp, we can do a milliliter per ball. I'm betting it'll only take one or two direct hits to put one of the big thugs out of commission, and I've got enough filtered urine to make up about 1,200 paintballs. So, as long as we wouldn't have to fight off more than 500 demons, we've got the ammunition. I can get us the men."

"Through Kolya," Alain said with an undisguised hint of disgust.

"You've got a problem with Kolya?"

"He beat up a kid." Alain thought of Ty falling through the door, battered and bruised. Beating up kids had a very special place on Alain's shit list.

Albert shrugged. "Who hasn't on this ring? You think Ty didn't intimidate and beat up smaller children when he was alive? This is a ring for people who hurt people, and I'm not talking about hurting their feelings. Now, we can get nine men, capable of following orders, with skill in the controlled and practical application of violence... or I can get you a lamp and you can wander the seventh ring, searching for 9 altar boys who got sent here by mistake."

"Don't you mean ten men?"

"You're looking at number 10." Albert's eyebrow raised. "You thought I'd miss *this*?"

* * * *

"I don't know how many times I can say 'thank you,'" Mick said as he and Kurt sat at the garden table. "I am forever in your debt."

"Good," Kurt said, "because I need another favor."

"Name it."

"Teach me how to perform miracles."

Mick looked puzzled. "You seem to be doing a pretty good job of it without my help."

"Yeah," Kurt said, shifting in his chair, "see, the thing is... I have no freaking clue what I'm doing. I don't perform miracles so much as stumble along and let miracles happen. I need to get a handle on it, and I was told you wrote a story where a guy learned how to perform miracles."

Mick stopped lounging and sat up in his chair. "Who told you that?"

"Jack Kerouac."

"Jack Kerouac?"

"Long story. But he said you wrote a story about a guy who got to be God for a week and had to learn how to do miracles."

Mick thought for a moment, smiled for a moment, then got a look on his face like he'd just smelled a fart. "That piece of shit? It was terrible. I wrote it while tripping on shrooms, thinking I was having amazing metaphysical insights. And then, when I read it sober, I wanted to cry. It was so hokey."

"Apparently it wasn't, or I wouldn't have been told to summon you."

"Oh, come on," Mick said, laughing derisively. "You know what I came up with for how you do a miracle? Get a vision of it happening in your mind's eye..."

"Yeah," Kurt said, leaning forward.

"Then bless the vision." Mick snorted. "'Envision it and bless it.' That was the story's mantra. See the miracle, bless the miracle, make the miracle. It's like some new age self-help seminar."

Kurt wanted to agree with Mick, but he had it on good authority that Mick knew the process, even if Mick apparently didn't believe it worked. But what was a good test miracle to try? Who was he going to heal? The whole burning bush thing was tempting, but he didn't like the idea of frying Marie's garden. Maybe manna... not manna.

Kurt looked at the table and envisioned his wish. But how did he bless it? He tried blinking and thinking "bless it" like a sort of "I Dream of Jeannie" move. Nothing happened. He got the vision again and wiggled his nose "Bewitched" style while thinking "bless it." Nothing happened.

Mick peered at him. "You're actually trying it?"

Kurt nodded. "Well," Mick said, "there's a sort of trick to blessing the vision. You have to reach down into yourself, find a little bit of love, push it into the vision, and then say 'Amen' in your head."

Kurt got his vision, reached down into himself, found a little bit of love, pushed it into the vision, and thought 'Amen.' The next moment there were two glasses of cold Bass Ale on the table. Mick jumped in his chair, then leaned forward to peer at the glasses. Kurt handed one to Mick and took one for himself. "A toast," Kurt said, smiling, "to little miracles."

Mick held up his glass of ale, looking at it. "Well, I'll be damned."

"Not anymore," Kurt said, then took a sip of the ale.

* * * *

After the experiment with the ale, Mick was a true believer and set himself to the task of helping Kurt learn how to teleport. Kurt started off with small jumps of a foot or two, seeing where he wanted to be, creating a mental snapshot of being there, and blessing it, but by the end of the afternoon, he was bouncing around the garden. He even shuffled

Mick around the garden in his chair. There was no momentum acquired by teleporting. It was sort of like one of those stop-motion movies where something just shifts from one place to another, then another.

But teleporting to places you could see was easy. The trick was teleporting somewhere you couldn't. How was he going to teleport into the celestial palace throne room, right next to the "break glass" switch if he couldn't get a vision of it in his mind.

"Envision yourself seeing that place, then bless that vision," Mick suggested. "Maybe it will allow you to see the place you need to see. Try a room in the house, then we can go to the room and see if you got it right."

"Which room?"

Mick scratched his chin. "Guest bathroom?"

Kurt stood and envisioned himself envisioning the guest bathroom, found a bit of love, pushed it into the vision, and said "Amen." The vision was replaced by a view of the guest bathroom. There was no toilet, but a nice sink and mirror provided a place for guests to freshen up. Kurt wondered what he was going to do about the lack of a toilet because he was starting to feel the need for a wicked dump. Kurt took his vision of the guest bathroom, altered it to add a toilet, and blessed it.

He must have given off some physical cue that he'd performed another miracle. "What did you do," Mick asked.

Keeping the vision in his head, Kurt added himself to it. "I'll tell you in a few minutes," Kurt said, then blessed the vision. A few minutes later, he envisioned a roll of toilet paper.

Chapter 39:
The Universe Shifted Around Him

Alain stood at the slingshot chair with the 9 men and Albert. For the sake of expediency, Albert did not recruit Kolya, but it cost another bottle of vodka and another case of assault rifles to get him to send his men while he stayed back.

Only two of them were Russian (both ex-Spetsnaz), one was a former Somali pirate, three were former mercenaries, two were from street gangs, and the last was a P.E. coach who had apparently enjoyed the dodgeball a little too much. All of them carried two assault rifles, a bandolier of magazines across his chest, another bandolier of grenades, a paintball gun stocked with 110 paintballs filled with Kurt's magic whizz, and a backpack filled with 50 pounds of sand. The backpacks were to ensure they fell when shot out of the slingshot chair. Otherwise, they'd rise and be blown back onto the 7th ring.

Alain could actually tolerate the Russians, the gang members, the mercenaries, even the pirate. They might not have been the nicest people in the world, but they were quiet and businesslike. The P.E. coach, Krist, treated this like an outing with his buddies and talked as they walked along Albert's tunnel... all 15 miles of it... all 5 hours. He was not just an asshole; he was an asshole who wouldn't shut up. He talked about women he'd slept with, asses he'd kicked, times he'd gotten so drunk he did something stupid. When he wasn't talking about himself, he was parroting Rush Limbaugh, critiquing porn movies, or going on about trucks. It had actually built up some camaraderie between Alain and the other men as they shared looks of exasperation.

Alain had initially thought Kolya had assigned him to them as a "fuck you" gesture for not being included. Now Alain had a feeling Kolya had included him in the complement of men just to be rid of him for a while. The "fuck you" gesture was an added bonus. Alain would have fragged Krist himself, but Deuce said he needed to recruit ten men.

Alain and two of the mercenaries, Peterson and Kramer, got first turn in the chair so they could secure the landing zone. While the mercenaries got themselves settled, Alain put an arm around Krist's shoulders and took him aside for a private chat.

"Look, Krist," he said, trying to sound buddy-buddy and not put the guy on the defensive. "Thanks for the entertainment during the hike, but you do understand that from this point forward, we've got to keep noise to a minimum, right?"

"Oh, yeah, sure," Krist said. "You got it."

"Good."

Alain parted from Krist, walked back to the bench, and took his seat between Peterson and Kramer. He looked over at Albert as he crossed his arms over his weapons and straps, securing them against the rapid motion about to occur. "I'll see ya when I see ya." Albert nodded.

Peterson, on the lever, counted down. "Three... two... one... engage."

The bench shot forward and then abruptly stopped, flinging the three men out into the void. Peterson and Kramer had both gone through Airborne training and had themselves angled into dives before Alain had even stopped tumbling enough to begin thinking about positioning himself. He followed their lead, slowing their forward momentum so that they cleared the lip of the 8th ring with around 200 feet to spare, then angled their dives to bring them in close to 9th ring's cliff wall, landing outside the walls of Pandaemonium.

As they landed, Kramer and Peterson jogged off to establish a perimeter as Alain waited for the other 8 men. The last mercenary and the two bangers came next, followed by the Russians and the Somali, the parties dropping in 3-minute intervals. Albert and Krist came last. Krist didn't talk as he fell, thankfully, but as he hit the ground with his knees bent, he came up from his crouch with a loud "woo-hoo" that was cut off mid-woo by Alain's hand closing around his throat and slamming him up against the cliff wall.

"What part of 'noise to a minimum' was unclear," Alain asked quietly through gritted teeth.

With whatever passed for a windpipe in the soul anatomy under so much pressure, all Krist could do was squeak.

"There a problem here?"

Alain turned his head to see Deuce approaching, trailed by Peterson. Although Deuce was a friendly, Peterson shouldn't have let him through. Alain glared at Peterson who gave a pained expression in return. None of the weapons Peterson carried or any of his fighting skills would stand up against a real, honest-to-goodness angel, so that made Alain actually feel a bit better about trusting Deuce. It also made Alain realize that, except for the holy pissballs, there wasn't a weapon or skill among his motley crew that would be of any use against demons... unless Krist could annoy them to death.

"Small disciplinary issue," Alain said, lowering Krist to the ground and releasing his throat.

"Hmm," Deuce said, looking Krist up and down. "Can't have that." He raised his hand and Krist's weapons and pack fell off.

Krist floated upward. "Hey," Krist shouted. A quick hand wave by Deuce and his jaw clamped shut, muffling his shouts as he quickly rose upward and out of earshot.

"Not that I'm ungrateful," Alain said, "but we're now a man short."

Deuce smiled a sly smile. "I'll take his place. Anyway, if you get caught again, you're definitely going to need a lawyer."

* * * *

Kurt spent the rest of the afternoon practicing bigger and bigger jumps. Elvis and Arthur both went home and he practiced teleporting to their houses, then teleporting back. In an in-between time, he sat down with Marie.

"What can you tell me about Alain?"

Marie put her elbow on the table and leaned her head into her hand, her fingers rubbing her head behind the temple and over the ear. She got a look of contentment on her face, as if she were imagining it were Alain's fingers running through her hair as she called him to mind. Kurt had noticed her French accent before, but after 64 years in the States, it was subdued. When she spoke this time, it was deeper, richer, more relaxed and less controlled. "Sweet... loving... a little shy... though you never saw any of that I would guess. Loyal and dedicated to a fault. If he called you friend, he would die for you."

"I once asked a priest if there were any sins God could not forgive. 'Only the ones you do not ask him to forgive,' he told me. 'So long as you believe in God,' he said, 'and care about your soul, it is never beyond salvation.' Alain believed, even though God had let this evil happen to him... and he cared about his soul."

"Alain always defended the people who could not defend themselves. He was not trying to — how do you say it — 'score brownie points' with God. This was who he was. It was who he was before the war and after. He has been my hero since the day we met."

Kurt was in a half-daze, watching her, listening to her talk about the man she loved. This was what God needed to hear, and he felt very inadequate as he contemplated trying to deliver it secondhand. But the bet was that *he* would convince God to save Alain, not her. So, he listened as she went on, trying to figure out how he was going to use mere words to do justice to 64 years of love.

* * * *

Deuce, Alain, and Albert sat in the Pandaemonium security office, hands cuffed behind their backs. In front of them, a team of demons and damned souls worked the monitor banks and dispatch consoles that coordinated security response not only within the 9th ring, but throughout Hell. Beside them sat the closed door of the office belonging to Andromalius, a duke of Hell and chief of security.

The door opened and one of the bouncer demons preceded Andromalius out. Alain had been expecting something on the order of Mammon, but Andromalius looked more like he could eat Mammon. He had a crocodile's head on top of a body that resembled a world champion bodybuilder wrapped in snakeskin. He wore black shorts and a blue T-shirt, both sporting Pandaemonium security badge logos.

"You're an angel, huh?" Andromalius ignored Alain and Albert, focusing in on Deuce. "Well, I know every angel created before the fall, our best intelligence says there ain't been none created since, and I don't know you."

"You don't?" Deuce smiled. "Take a closer look. Maybe you're missing something."

Andromalius stepped closer to Deuce, leaning in to peer into Deuce's eyes. Alain watched as it happened and saw a light burst from Deuce's eyes, like the pop of a flashbulb. The sequence of events that followed seemed to play out in slow motion. The crocodile's jaw dropped and its eyes glazed as Deuce's hands came up and touched the side of the beast's head.

While Andromalius was dropping, Alain and Albert were standing, their handcuffs dissolving into the ether. Deuce spread his wings, reached up under them, and pulled out Albert and Alain's paintball guns, tossing them to the two men before grabbing his own. Within thirty seconds, three damned souls and two more demons lay unconscious, two more demons lay whimpering with smoke rising off of them, and the remaining security office staff had their hands in the air.

Over the next few hours, in groups of two and three, security personnel around the 9th ring were alerted to a disturbance in the Asmodeus Arena. Upon arrival they were greeted by 8 armed souls, a small pile of smoking demon carcasses, and a cadre of wiser demons who had allowed themselves to be disarmed and take seats in section A-2 with their hands and feet tied.

* * * *

Inside the first gate of the celestial palace sat a reception desk. All visitors had to check in with the angels Sabrael and Domiel before being allowed deeper into the palace to attend to their business. It hadn't been very busy for the past few hundred years, but the two angels held their station faithfully, even if they did find ways to occupy their hours. At the moment, Domiel was deeply immersed in a Danielle Steele novel while Sabrael knitted a tea cozy.

"Domiel," Sabrael asked, his voice rising, "do you smell smoke?"

"No," Domiel answered, not looking up from his book. "Why?"

"Because the desk is on fire."

The two angels stepped back from the desk and looked at it. The desk burned with fire, and the desk was not consumed. No smoke rose. No wood blackened. Yet heat radiated as if it was engulfed.

Now things in Heaven weren't normally flammable. Flammability was one of those physical laws that Heaven seemed to get around, much like Hell got around gravity. About the only thing that burned in Heaven was Michael's flaming sword. If nothing burned, there was no need for fire alarms, and the apocalypse alarm switch was hidden under the desk. Left with no other options, the angels resorted to a tried-and-true method that had been utilized by mankind for thousands and thousands of years. They yelled "FIRE!" at the top of their lungs, and the top of an angel's lungs can pretty much be heard for miles.

Offices around the celestial palace emptied. Angels, archangels, seraphim, and cherubim flooded out into the reception lobby, but didn't evacuate the building. They gathered around the desk, reaching out hands to feel the warmth of the fire before dropping to their knees and praying.

In the throne room, a small breeze blew as air was shoved out of the way to make room for a human body. Kurt turned to find the alarm box. As he raised his hand to smash it open, he heard a voice behind him.

"Nice burning bush you did out there. Very impressive. Not distracting, but impressive. Now why don't you turn around with your hands up?"

Kurt turned to see a seven-foot-tall angel, one of the most beautiful people he'd ever seen, sporting flowing blonde hair, wings, a halo, and a huge flaming sword. "My name is Michael," the angel said.

Kurt stepped back, acting as if he were backing away in fear, then brought his elbow down and back in a fast motion, shattering the glass and triggering the alarm.

"I really wish you hadn't done that," Michael said, shouting over the alarm. "It's a pain to reset the alarm and replace the glass."

Michael raised his sword and took a step forward. "I was hoping we could have settled this peaceably!"

Kurt got a vision, loved it, blessed it, and Michael's hands were empty, the flaming sword now clasped by Kurt. He raised it, stepping toward Michael and his hands were empty again. He dove out of the way as Michael swept the sword down at him. Kurt rolled out into a wary crouch as an annoyed Michael shot angel fire out of his hand at the alarm box, turning the loud klaxon into a fizzling sputter and then silence.

"I know you're stronger than me," Michael said, approaching in an almost Samurai sword fighting stance, despite the more European style of broadsword he wielded. "But I've been training to use my holiness since God created me at the beginning of time. You've been training since when? Lunch? I don't care what your holiness rating is. I'm going to kick your ass."

The shock of hearing an angel say "ass" paused Kurt almost long enough to take a flaming sword to the neck. He ducked just in time and he could hear and smell the flames of the sword fry the ends of his hair as it passed over his head. He came out of the crouch leaping in the same direction the sword had passed, flying under it on the back swing and running to put some distance between himself and the angel.

He got a vision, loved it, blessed it, and as Michael stalked toward him, a cage formed around him. Kurt had envisioned a cage Michael couldn't teleport out of and his sword couldn't cut, but he had a gut feeling he'd missed something, and he needed a better plan before Michael figured out the cage's weakness.

* * * *

Alain and Deuce walked down an ornate hallway. Kramer and Peterson had double-timed it over from the arena to help Albert run the security office while the remaining six stood guard over hundreds of demons. Deuce offered a brilliant idea to help the six men retain control over hundreds of prisoners, telling them to have the demons sit in each other's laps. It demoralized the demons, shrunk the physical area that needed to be guarded, and made leaping into action that much more difficult.

At the end of the hallway stood a giant golden door, fifteen feet high and ten feet wide, covered in ornate scrollwork and crusted in gemstones. A giant L, composed of rubies as big as your fist and crimson as new blood, made it clear who they were going to see.

Deuce didn't have to do any hand waving to gain entrance. The door opened of its own accord and Alain followed Deuce in. The throne room was composed of stone, like a medieval castle, the only light coming from torches along the walls. The smell of burning pine pitch was thick in the air. At the end of a long red carpet, a handsome man in a Versace suit sat on a giant golden throne that threw off pings and glints of reflection in the torchlight.

"Hello, Lou," Deuce said, breaking the silence.

"I thought you'd come," Lucifer replied. He had long, brown curls, pulled back into a ponytail to match Deuce's long blonde hairdo. Now Alain knew who Vinnie had patterned his hair style after. He was clean-shaven and there was no hint of horns. He had high cheek bones, full lips, and smoldering eyes. Alain wasn't gay, but even he had to admit the man was beautiful.

"Of course I came. You worked awful hard to get my attention, Lou."

Lucifer smiled. "Haven't I always?"

Deuce frowned. "But this time you went too far. I can't allow this anymore."

"Then punish me," Lucifer laughed. "What are you going to do that's worse than this?"

Alain watched as a tear ran down from Deuce's eye. "I'm sorry, Lou."

The smile disappeared from Lucifer's face as he faded into nothingness.

Alain turned to Deuce, his mouth agape. Another tear rolled down Deuce's cheek followed by a sniffle. Deuce pinched his nose and sniffed again, shaking his head sadly from side to side.

"I prefer to think of it as 'unmaking,' not 'killing,'" Deuce said, seeming to read the question Alain was too shocked to ask.

"You're not my guardian angel, are you?"

"What makes you say that," he asked, turning to Alain and smiling a strained smile. Deuce took Alain's head in his hands and kissed him on the forehead. "Thank you for all your help, but we have one more thing to attend to. When I say 'go', I need you to tackle the guy to your right, cover his eyes, shut your eyes, and sit on him as best you can."

Deuce let go of Alain's head and stepped back. "What guy on my ri...," Alain began, and then the universe shifted around him.

Chapter 40:

I'll Miss You Most of All, Scarecrow

Kurt had thought of bars Michael could not teleport through. He'd thought of bars Michael could not cut with his flaming sword. When Michael started bending them, Kurt miracled them stronger. But Kurt had not thought to make Michael's cage soundproof. "Ariel, Gabriel... to me," he shouted at a volume so loud Kurt was afraid his ears were going to bleed. It took no more than two seconds and two angels popped into the spaces next to Michael's cage.

Kurt prepared to miracle the two into similar cages when he felt a rush of air, heard a voice shout "go," and was tackled. His tackler quickly rolled him onto his back and he found himself looking up into the face of Alain. "Hi Kurt. Long story. Stay down. Close eyes."

Kurt did as he was told, just as the man in the white sportscoat began to glow. The growing brightness of the light burned through his eyelids as he heard the angels shouting "my lord!" The angels started singing, but there was a rush of air, the singing stopped, the glare blinked out, and Kurt opened his eyes to see the man in the white sportscoat adjusting his sleeves. The angels were nowhere to be found.

"You can let him up now." Alain got up and helped Kurt to his feet. "You want to introduce us," Deuce asked.

Alain nodded. "Kurt, if my guess is at all correct, this is God."

"Call me Deuce. Pleased to meet you in person," Deuce said, offering his hand. Kurt shook it out of reflex before realizing he was holding the hand of God.

Kurt's mind went blank. He had no idea what to say. "I'm... I'm a... I'm... a... I'm a big fan," he mumbled.

Deuce used the grip to pull Kurt in and wrap an arm around his shoulder. "Alain, you don't mind if Kurt and I go off and have a private chat, do you? Anyway, I believe some people have been waiting to see you." Deuce walked off with Kurt under his arm and Alain felt a rush of air at his back. He turned just in time to have Marie leap into his arms and plant the universe's most passionate kiss on him. Westley and Buttercup's kiss paled in comparison.

* * * *

The universe shifted and Kurt found himself in Nowhere again. He half-expected Deuce to morph into Jack Kerouac, but he heard a whistle to his left and saw Jack sitting at a table with three seats in front of an empty cafe. Jack waved them over and Deuce guided Kurt to the table, gently lowered him into a chair, and took the remaining seat.

"Beers all around," Deuce asked. Jack nodded and tall frosty mugs appeared in front of them. Deuce and Jack took swigs from theirs, but Kurt just sat there and stared at them.

"He seems a bit shell-shocked," Jack said before taking another pull from his mug.

"I seem to recall someone running around here naked for three days when he found out why he was here."

"But I'm better now," Jack said, following it with an extra-long tip of glass to lip.

"Have a sip of the beer, Kurt," Deuce said. "My own special recipe. They tell me it's Heavenly."

Kurt stared at the beer. He'd been stuck in a "holy shit, holy shit, holy shit" mode, but now he frowned. God was making bad puns? What the... What in... Kurt reached forward and took the mug, raising it to his mouth. The brew inside was good. It was the best beer he'd ever tasted. He took a long draw and then put the glass down, a satisfied smile on his face.

"Okay," Deuce said, "here's the summary in a hundred words or less: This universe is part of a multiverse. Each new universe has a God who was once a mortal in another universe. Every generation the multiverse selects two souls from each universe that's ready to produce souls. The souls each go to their universe's Nowhere and get educated in all the aspects of creating and running a universe. If a universe goes two generations without delivering its souls, the multiverse assumes it to be defective and recycles it. You would have been the fourth soul Lou captured. It would have taken a few decades, but eventually... poof.'"

Kurt took another sip of his beer. "Why didn't you stop him after the first?"

"I had to give him every possible chance to turn things around on his own."

"Why?"

"Because I loved him."

"But why did he even have to exist? If you could have stopped him all along, why didn't you stop him when he rebelled? Why did you even make him?"

Deuce took a sip of his beer and smiled. "That's more than just asking about him. You're asking why evil exists."

"Yeah," Kurt said leaning forward.

Jack shook his head. "You're not going to like the answer."

Deuce raised his hand dramatically. "Evil exists because Good must be tested."

Kurt frowned. "See," Jack said, "I told you you weren't going to like it."

"No, seriously," Deuce protested. "It's easy to be good if you never have an opportunity to be bad. Evil isn't just the opposite of good. It's the conscious choice to do the wrong thing when you know it's wrong. Evil exists because for free will to exist, that choice has to exist."

Kurt was working up a full head of steam now. All the injustice he'd felt over the past couple of weeks bubbled up in a single sentence. "And if you make the wrong choice, you go to Hell," he said accusatively.

Deuce pinched the bridge of his nose. "Every single time," he said quietly, a sense of exasperation moving to resignation. "Kurt, you saw The Matrix, right? Of course you did. What happened when the machines tried to give people a virtual paradise?"

"They rejected it," Kurt said.

"You saw the planes of eternity when you beat the nothingness, but you don't remember them." Deuce pointed at Kurt. "Let me help you."

Images flooded into Kurt's mind... Hell, Purgatory, Heaven, then Nirvana, Valhalla, thousands and thousands of paradises, thousands and thousands of wastelands, and oceans, and jungles... giant waiting rooms and transfer stations, trains and buses traveling along routes that never ended. And not all the souls were human. Some were like Roswell aliens, some were like jellyfish, some were like large six-legged cats. The landscapes stretched on seemingly forever with a greater variety of lifeforms than Kurt had imagined existed.

"Souls go where they expect to go, Kurt," Deuce said. "I just need the two-per-generation and the rest I mostly try to keep content. I don't like to see them suffer, but if that's what they feel they deserve, they'll just trash and try to destroy anything better. Guilt is a powerful thing."

"You said you *mostly* try to keep them content."

Deuce frowned. "Sometimes you just get a terrible, terrible person who thinks he's entitled to paradise. Like the suicide bomber terrorists who think they should get 72 virgins."

"They go to Hell, right?"

Deuce reached out and put his hand on Kurt's, looking into Kurt's eyes. "I don't hate them. I don't want them to spend an eternity being tortured. There's no point in that. I don't want anyone to spend an eternity being tortured, even them. But I cannot, in all good conscience, let them collect a reward. They're just unmade. I revoke the immortality of their souls."

Kurt thought a moment. "What about reincarnation?"

Deuce smiled and patted Kurt's hand. "In due time, son. We've got people waiting for us to get back. You want to come along Jack?"

"Wait," Kurt asked, "doesn't he have to be here?"

"Jack moved on years ago, but his universe is mainly hot plasma now. It needs about a billion years to cool before he'll be able to do anything with it. So I asked him to hang out for a few days. Didn't want you to find the place empty." Deuce stood up from his chair. "Shall we go?"

* * * *

While Kurt and Deuce had been in Nowhere, a brigade of angels busied themselves in the throne room, setting up a banquet table and escorting in additional guests. Marie's thing in life had been playing hostess, and it took over. She wanted to hold onto Alain for another few centuries, but it would be rude to ignore the guests.

George and Alain took seats at the table, George giving Alain the story of what had happened in his absence while busy angels bustled about and Marie got everyone seated. When all was said and done, the guest list included Nybras and Duke, George, Alain, Marie, Junior, Elvis, Eleanor, Barbara, Leonardo, Mick, and Arthur. That left three seats at the table. Marie reserved the head of the table for God, seated Kurt at his right hand, and made space for the last person at the foot of the table.

A rush of air announced the arrival of Deuce, Kurt, and Jack. Everyone rose from the table and exchanged greetings with them. Jack and Alain hugged, then stepped back and looked at each other. It wasn't fair," Jack said. "You never grew old and got fat." The two of them laughed and hugged again.

As everyone sat, Deuce raised his glass. "A toast," he said, "to the salvation of our dear friend Alain. And as a gesture of apology for the injustices he has suffered, I grant him the one thing he could never have... a child. Marie, Alain, Junior is yours to raise as your son. He will grow to adulthood and be a great joy to you."

Deuce leaned to Kurt, and in a low voice said "you won your bet. Hell has no more claim on you."

Deuce sat up and raised his glass again. "Salud."

Over the course of the meal, everyone was granted a gift. Barbara got a DVD set of the final season of "Charmed" so she could see the episodes she missed. Eleanor was tasked with heading up a council of the performing arts for Heaven. Elvis was asked to give the first musical performance in Heaven in 400 years. Arthur was given a holy quest to scour the first ring of Hell and find those ready to accept paradise. Leonardo was asked to paint a mural around the outer walls of the celestial palace. Nybras got his old job back. Duke got a promotion. Jack got a keg of God's special brew, which despite an ability to perform miracles, he just couldn't quite duplicate. George was given salvation and a house next door to Marie and Alain. And Mick, once he found out that Jack was going to spend the next billion years checking out other universes, asked if he could tag along.

When the meal was over and the guests had slowly drifted away home, a core of Kurt, George, Alain, Marie, Junior, and Deuce remained.

"So," Deuce said, sitting back in his chair and looking at Kurt. "What lovely parting gift do I give you?"

"Another answer?"

"Shoot."

Kurt leaned forward, clasping his hands in front of himself on the table. "What do I do next?"

Deuce chuckled. "Live. Fall in love, maybe a few times. Figure out how to become who you wanted to be when you grew up. The purpose of Nowhere is to teach you how to be a God. The purpose of life is to teach you how to be a person. If you can figure out how to be a good person and enjoy life, everything else will fall into place."

Deuce got up from the table, and that was everyone's signal to say their goodbyes. Kurt hugged Marie, George, and Alain goodbye.

When it came Junior's turn, he wrapped his arms around the boy. "I think I'm gonna miss you most of all, Scarecrow," he said half-jokingly, half to try to keep himself from tearing up.

"Thank you," Junior whispered in his ear.

As Junior stepped back, Kurt looked up at George. "You watch out for our Lost Boy brother, George. Make sure those two take good care of him."

George shook Kurt's hand as Kurt stood up. "You got it, buddy. And you come back whenever you want to check up on him."

Kurt looked over at Deuce, but Deuce shook his head in the negative. Kurt understood. Heaven wasn't for the living, even if they would someday rule a Heaven of their own. Maybe he'd get to stop by while his universe was cooling, but he was certain this was the last time he'd see any of these people during his mortal life, and Deuce had assured him he was going to live to a ripe old age.

As Alain and his family walked out of the throne room, Kurt turned to Deuce. "Gonna send me home now?"

"Ah, but you had the power to go home all along, Dorothy," Deuce said, smiling. Kurt put out his hand for a final handshake, but Deuce pulled him into a hug and then kissed him on the forehead. "Take care of yourself, son. That's a commandment. I'll be checking up on you."

Deuce released Kurt, Kurt stepped back, envisioned himself in his bedroom, put a little love in it, said Amen, and the universe shifted around him.

Chapter 41: Epilogue

Kurt woke up to the sound of his phone playing Taylor Swift's "Shake It Off" as an alarm. The clock said it was 7:30 a.m. He had 90 minutes to get showered, get dressed, and get to work.

His bed in the shared apartment wasn't any great shakes, especially not compared to the bed in Marie's house... Did he dream all that? He was tempted to try to make a miracle, but he decided not to. It was going to be so disappointing if it didn't work. This way he could hold onto the possibility that he hadn't dreamed it all. Plus, he thought, it seemed almost wasteful to perform a miracle for such a minor reason.

As he sat up and scratched himself, his phone beeped a calendar reminder. "8:30 a.m.: Coffee with Deuce at the Starbucks on the corner. Don't worry, you can be late to work this one time."

With an hour to get himself 2 blocks, Kurt took an extra 5 minutes in the shower, just enjoying the hot water. He washed every bit of himself to make sure that no speck of supernatural dirt remained on his body. Then he scrambled an egg in the kitchenette and ate it on toast. He drank a glass of low-fat milk to wash it down. He'd have to give Henry a buck for drinking his milk, but so what? He didn't have to worry about whether it was imported or whether it might leave him stuck in the apartment.

At 8:21, he put his keys, his wallet, and his phone in their respective pockets. He decided to leave the backpack at home today. He'd been carrying it a bit too much recently. At 8:23 he was out the door and at 8:29 he was walking into the Starbucks.

For a moment he didn't see Deuce and he feared he really had dreamed it all, perhaps programming in the calendar event in some half-asleep state. He felt a tap on his shoulder and turned around to see Deuce's smiling face. The long hair had been replaced with a shorter cut. "Get a good night's sleep?"

"Yup," Kurt said. "Like the hair. Why the change?"

"Too many copycats. Coffee?"

Deuce bought Kurt a grande Mocha and got a venti Americano for himself. The place was packed, but miraculously a table opened up just as they were ready to sit down. Kurt raised an eyebrow, but Deuce just shrugged. As Kurt sat, he wondered if anyone in the coffee house knew God was in their midst. "I'm always in their midst," Deuce said.

"You know, it's kind of creepy when you do that."

Deuce hung his head, but smiled. "Sorry." He took a long draw from his coffee, finishing off with an "aahhh," and then looked at Kurt. "So, what's the plan for today?"

"Go to work, dinner with Mom and Dad, drinks with friends. Get back in touch with how human I still am before I make any big decisions."

"Wise," Deuce nodded. "No plans to rush out and save the world?"

Kurt laughed. "It's your world. I just live in it. I figure if you want me to save it, you'll arrange it so I'm pushed through a portal or roped into an adventure of some sort."

"Don't go getting a big head on me," Deuce said. Both men laughed.

Deuce stood up from the table and set down his coffee cup. "Well, I just wanted to check up and make sure you were gonna be able to adjust to being a civilian again. Looks like you've got a level head on your shoulders."

"Would the multiverse have picked me if I didn't," Kurt asked.

Deuce smiled a sly smile. "You'd be surprised." He turned and walked out, the crowd parting before him and closing behind him.

* * * *

Kurt went into work. Apparently, everything had been taken care of. There was a record of his approved vacation request and he'd had just enough time off banked to cover it. He got to his desk, loaded up Outlook, found he had a meeting in 4 minutes, grabbed a yellow pad off his desk and rushed up to the 7th floor.

He fired on all cylinders in the meeting and got some positive feedback on the way out. The rest of the day went his way as well. He just felt capable of meeting whatever challenges the day threw at him, and he did it without any miracles, big or small.

Dinner with his parents was a little more challenging. They too knew he'd been on vacation and thought it had been planned for a while, but his mother was miffed that he hadn't called the entire time he'd been away. "We thought you fell off the face of the earth."

Drinks with his friends was much the same way, but with less guilt... "How was the trip? Why didn't you text?" Everyone seemed to have something to do in the morning, and by 11 p.m., Kurt was alone at a table in the little pub they'd decided to hit. He wasn't quite ready to go home and be alone in his room yet. He still wanted to be in the presence of living people, even if he just sat back, nursed his beer, and didn't talk to a one.

A man in a grey overcoat entered the bar and Kurt watched the guy make a beeline directly for his table. "Can I help you," he asked as the man sat down.

The man put a photo of two couples on the table. As Kurt looked at it, he saw one couple was Alain and Marie, the other couple was the man across from him and a strikingly beautiful woman with jet black hair. The photo was in black and white, a bit frayed, looked like it had to be 50 years old if it was a day. The man, on the other hand, didn't look a day older than he did in the picture.

"My name's Avery Stark," the man said. "I believe you know the other man in the photo. A little under 2 weeks ago, he and George Miller entered a portal into Hell to save you. I know because I was there. Today, you showed up back in Manhattan without them. I'd like to know what happened to my friends."

Kurt leaned back in his chair and took a sip of his beer. "You might want to take off that coat," he said. "It's a long story."

Author's Note:

I hope you got to this page because you read the whole novel first. I also hope you enjoyed it.

This novel started in early 1994. Reading some beat-era literature, I thought about a "coffee klatch" and then my mind said, "what about a coffin klatch?" That brought to mind what a vampire beat poet might be like, and thus began the idea of a mortal journeying through Hell like Dante with a vampire Virgil as his guide.

I was in the last quarter at university and had finished a novel I'll never publish as my senior thesis project. I needed one more writing course to complete my degree requirement, so I took a fiction seminar. We either had to write a collection of short stories or 50 pages of a novel. I decided to run with this idea and see where it lead. Among other things, it lead to a very bad "vampirized" version of Allen Ginsberg's famed poem *Howl*, from which I have graciously spared you (you're welcome). In fact, very little of that original 50 pages made its way into this novel.

For the class, I got a C. The professor described the grade as the average of an A for the writing and an F for the vampire. Back in 1994, writers of "literary" fiction held a hatred for "genre" fiction. Some still do.

I continued working on it after graduation, reaching the point where Kurt, George, and Junior stepped through the portal into Purgatory somewhere in 1995. And then I stopped to give it some time, following Ray Bradbury's oft-quoted advice of stashing a story in a closet for 11 months before you come back to it with new eyes. I started my website, writing humorous essays, and that led to many things that kept me busy enough to only come back to the story in fits and starts for 13+ years.

I tinkered with the stuff I wrote and began a little bit of the journey through Purgatory, but the idea back then was to make three distinct books, one for each segment of the afterlife. In 2008, unemployed due to the recession and with a new baby in the house, I sat down at the kitchen table, and got to work on the story again while I was on baby watch in the early mornings, giving my wife some uninterrupted time to sleep.

I *completely* changed Alain's origin story, changed Kurt's, changed how they met, and condensed the story into one book. I finished the first full draft, ending with Kurt and Avery in a Manhattan bar, in mid-2009.

It would take 12 more years of tinkering and polishing, setting it aside for years at a time, before I was ready to ~~inflict it on the world~~ publish it.

So, what's next?

Alain and Marie's story begins and ends in this book, but I've had nearly 28 years to think about what happened to them between the war and her death.

The second book, *Sodom All Over Again*, joins Alain and Marie in 1945 as they try to stop a brewing supernatural war that will rain down Sodom & Gomorrah style destruction on Los Angeles. I'm planning to release that in mid-2026.

The third, *New York, By Midnight*, explains why Vinnie said "and this one's for sixty-two" during the fight in the ring.

In fact, there are currently 11 more books planned for this series, which I've taken to calling The New Heroes of Old™.

The New Heroes of Old™ comes from the fact that our heroes predominantly derive their power from divinity. While they are modern heroes, their lineage traces back to Moses and King David, men who wielded their divinity to be champions of their people. Our heroes will wield their powers to save humanity... and more.

Obviously, good sales and good reviews of this novel would help keep me focused on finishing them. Hint, hint.

Thank you so much for reading. Follow me on BlueSky, LinkedIn, YouTube, or visit bulmash.com to sign up for announcements. And if you want a good listen, check out my AI-assisted music on YouTube or Spotify. I love all my songs, but "Dance Badly," "Giant," and "Fill My Cup" are my favorites.

Live long and prosper,

Greg Bulmash

Bothell, WA – November 2021 and January 2026